A Rare And Dangerous Beast

A Novel

by

Lloyd Mullins

A Rare and Dangerous Beast

A Rare and Dangerous Beast

ISBN: 979-8-218-26822-0

Cover Image: B&W inversion of *American Progress* by John Gast
Original obtained from Library of Congress, Reproduction Number LC-DIG-ppmsca-09855

A Rare and Dangerous Beast

For Jess,

My own Coming Together

A Rare and Dangerous Beast

Editor's Note:

The papers that were the source for this volume came into my hands by a roundabout route: An old college friend purchased an abandoned storage unit for $50 in the tiny town of Huachuca City, Arizona and, amid the largely worthless rubbish contained inside, discovered an old trunk containing the unbound jailhouse memoir of one Anatoly Mikhailovich Lukyanov, written in the year 1892. My friend's bad investment turned out to be my good luck. Looking through the papers hoping for something of value, he realized that there was no wished-for map to buried treasure. As he put it, "I was looking at this worthless bunch of crap and thought of you." I can only assume he was referring to my love of Old West history.

At any rate, after I agreed to pay for shipping and forgive a $200 bar tab he stuck me with in college, he shipped the entire trunk to me. I was delighted to discover not only Lukyanov's diary, but various newspaper clippings and other writings that backed up his fascinating story. I had read numerous biographies and memoirs of various old west personalities, but I had never read anything like this. Lukyanov's memoir is much more than a mere recounting of his life and adventures – it also provides a philosophical look into the American pursuit of Liberty, as well as the cost of that pursuit, from the point of view of a man who spent his entire life as an outsider.

While I have tried to keep editorial changes to a minimum to preserve his unique voice, I have made a few changes in the text out of modern sensitivity about specific terms that, while extremely controversial now, would have been in common and public usage in Lukyanov's day. In those few cases, I have altered the original so as to mirror the method which Lukyanov himself used for those terms that would have been considered unprintable in those faraway days but are common and unremarkable now.

I believe his story to be true. The provenance of the papers has been beyond my abilities to trace, but my research into the events chronicled shows that his story matches those of accepted history very closely, although nowhere did I ever find any direct reference to the man himself.

I have, in some places, added footnotes where his account is verified by other historical accounts, to provide historical context or perspective, or to simply bring to light historical facts and events I felt worth noting that might not be part of the public awareness.

Please note that it is not necessary to read the footnotes in order to understand (or enjoy) the book.

Lloyd Mullins,
Richmond, IN
25 May 2022

A Rare and Dangerous Beast

A Rare and Dangerous Beast

Table of Contents

Part Three: Indian

A Rare and Dangerous Beast

Part One:

Cowboy

Chapter One

My early life and family; an ill-fated romance; a long voyage; a battle aboard ship; I make a friend; arrival in America

My name is Anatoly Mikhailovich Lukyanov, and I was born in a Mongol yurt along the eastern shore of Lake Baikal, Irkutsk Oblast, Russia, on June 27, 1838. The span of my life has transformed me from a hopeful Russian/Buriat youth to the tired, old American man who sits in this cell in Buffalo, Wyoming fifty-some years later, awaiting trial for the murder of Federal Marshal George Wellman, G-d d--n his black soul.

As I sit here now, in this tiny cell almost 40 years later, it occurs to me that I've never again been so free as I was in those days, until now. I am the opposite of the bard's melancholy Dane. Although essentially bounded in a nutshell, I may count myself a "King of infinite space" because I have a wealth of memories to draw on and remember.

Irkutsk Oblast
1853

2 – A Rare and Dangerous Beast

My father, Mikhail Alexandrovich Lukyanov, was a minor noble, scholar, and soldier who lost his left arm at the battle of Dennewitz. He was also a member of the Union of Salvation and the secret Northern Society, which led to the Decembrist[1] revolt. To his eternal embarrassment, he missed the actual uprising in Senate Square due to pneumonia. Adding insult to injury, his part in the revolt was never noticed, and he escaped being sentenced to forced labor in Siberia.

Despite this, he voluntarily followed his friend and mentor, Major General Sergei Volkonsky, into exile, determined to help his exiled comrades. His wife, Elizaveta Vasilievna, unable to cope with the harsh conditions and isolation, went mad, flinging herself into a hole in the ice of the Angara river, leaving my father alone with their daughter, Natasha Mikhailovna.

Years later, he met my mother, Namzhilma, daughter of a *Taisha* (chieftain) of the Buriat Mongols. Although she was much younger, they fell in love, and eventually persuaded her father to allow them to

---

[1] The Decembrist revolt in 1825, was a failed attempt to replace the newly-crowned Tsar Nicholas I with his brother Constantine. The Decembrists drew much of their inspiration from Enlightenment philosophers and the writings of the American founding fathers.

marry. I was born very shortly thereafter, followed a year later by my younger brother, Mikhail Mikhailovitch.

Although my father was nominally a Christian, it could be said that freedom was his religion. Deeply influenced by John Locke's[2] writings, he worked tirelessly advocating for the abolition of serfdom, mostly in the form of pamphlets published under the pseudonym "Homeless."

He taught us from the works of Locke, Voltaire, Rousseau, Paine, Jefferson, Adams, and others – often with the aid of a switch, as I was susceptible to distraction – but I was personally drawn more to the tales of high adventure in the novels of Dumas, Scott, and Fenimore Cooper. I attended an academy created by Madame Volkonsky for a time, until I was expelled. My failure to take my education – or anything that couldn't be done from horseback – seriously was a constant source of frustration for my father.

Mikhail (Mischa) was the family scholar, excelling in all areas of academics. In only one subject could I rival

---

[2] Locke was a 17th Century philosopher, often referred to as the "Father of Liberalism".

him: language. In addition to Russian and Buriat, the languages of my birth, by the time I was 15, I was fluent in French and English, and conversant in several others.

While papa was studious and thoughtful, mother was fiery and impetuous, as accomplished on horseback and with weapons as most men in her clan, and I took my affinity for action, adventure, and love of the outdoor life from her. She taught us to be independent, confident, and forthright, and to never back away from a fight.

Her religion was a mixture of Buriat White Shamanism and Buddhism, although she never allowed either to interfere with her own freedom. Following my parents' example, I never developed any strong affinity for religion. I never found Jesus until I met the Nez Perce.

Mischa and I spent our summers with my mother's people. My maternal grandfather was a jolly old rogue who taught us the Buriat ways. By the time I was 12, I was an expert rider and could fire with great accuracy a gun or bow and arrow from the back of a horse at a full gallop, the bookish Mischa achieving a much lower degree of competency. Due to our different abilities,

Mischa was clearly our father's favorite, while I was the apple of mother's eye.

My poor half-sister Tasha, 16 years older than I, was not exceptional in any way. Although much loved by all of us, she was of a shy, retiring disposition, and an appearance more handsome than beautiful which, combined with the stories of her mother's madness and death, left her a spinster and a sort of second mother to Mischa and me.

When I was 15, I fell in love with Oksana Ivanovna Volkov, daughter of an Irkutsk *Procuror* (prosecutor). My feelings for her were requited, but at the end of a delightfully surreptitious summer we were discovered in a compromising position by her father who, not for nothing, was known locally as "Ivan the Terrible". I was severely beaten but managed to escape, steal a horse, and leave town. His men pursued me very hotly, but they were town men, and soon lost my trail. After several days of hard riding, I reached my grandfather's yurt, a hundred miles east of Lake Baikal. My grandfather, a short, stout man renowned for his good humor, ferocity, and profanity, upon hearing my story spat three times upon the ground and said, "F-----g[3] G-dd--ned stupid Russian b-----d! He should be flattered that a descendant of the Great Khan deigned to notice his pig of a daughter!"

I protested that Oksana was the love of my life, and not in the least porcine, but he just snorted. "Love of your life – Hah! You're still a pup. What do you know of love, or life? Just yesterday you were sucking on your mother's teat. Wait 'til you've seen what the world has to offer before you talk about life and love! When it's time, we'll find you a nice plump Buriat girl who'll put a spark in your eye and a fire in your loins. Trust me my boy, you'll soon forget all about that Russian wench."

"Come," he said, throwing his arm around my shoulders. "I have three new horses to show you. When you see them, you'll forget all about your Russian cow. There are four things that make life worth living — a good fight, a good horse, a good meal, and a good woman, and the best of these are all

---

[3] The blanking out of letters from curse words was a common literary convention in the late 19th Century. That Nate did so in his manuscript seems to signify that he did have publishing on his mind.

Buriat!" He drank deeply from a flask of *tarasun*[4] that swung from his neck on a string, belched mightily, and offered it to me. "Have a shot of this my boy, and everything'll look better."

I took a drink of the milky alcohol, but the world still looked the same to my broken-hearted eyes.

My grandfather sent a rider to my father in Irkutsk to let him know where I was and what had happened, with a message to let us know when it was safe for me to return home. We were surprised two weeks later, when my mother, Tasha, and Mischa rode into camp. After greeting, my mother handed me a note:

> *My son,*
>
> *I am saddened that your carelessness has led you into this danger. Still, you are young, and a certain amount of foolishness is to be expected. After all, your mother and I found ourselves in a similar situation, although ours was resolved much more pleasantly. In a just society, you would be free to love who you wished.*
>
> *There is, of course, no future for you here in Russia. Prosecutor Volkov's men would find you eventually and the*

[4] Highly alcoholic Buriat liquor made from distilled and fermented mare's milk.

best you could hope for would be conscription into the army and a quick death at the front, for the talk of war in the Crimea is heating up. It is, of course, far more likely that he would simply have his men kill you.

I also fear that, if unable to find you, Volkov will take his revenge upon your brother or sister, so I have decided that the best course of action is for all three of you to emigrate to America. It is my hope that, in a land that proudly proclaims the right of everyone to life, liberty, and the pursuit of happiness, each of you will flourish and find prosperity, love, and happiness.

I know that you, perhaps more than your brother or sister, have inherited your mother's and my love of freedom. I hope you find it in that new land, but I would be remiss if I didn't warn you that true freedom is beyond value, but like all such things, a rare and dangerous beast — hard to catch and harder to keep. I believe that I have gotten as close to it as any man can in Russia. I hope you are more successful.

Go with my blessing, and my love,
Your father,
Mikhail Alexandrovich.

I wept upon reading his missive, for love of my father, regret for endangering my family, and for joy at the adventure to come. After all, what young man of spirit wouldn't see the journey ahead as the opportunity of a lifetime?

My grandfather provided us with a quantity of trade goods as well as ten riders to act as escort and, after a tearful goodbye to our mother, we made our way as traders for over 1,600 *verst*[5] across Mongolia and China, the quickest route out of Russia and a shorter route to the sea. We enjoyed many fine adventures on our journey, crossing deserts and mountains, fighting bandits and warlords, bribing our way through the Chinese wall – enough to fill another book. Upon arriving in Peking, we sold everything but our personal belongings and, after rewarding our escorts for their service, found a ship sailing for San Francisco.

The month-long voyage across the Pacific was an uncomfortable one on many counts, not the least of which was the number of Chinese — I had unwittingly inherited my grandfather's loathing of the Chinese — aboard ship. It was impossible to avoid contact with them, although I did my best. They were all male and seemed a lowly bunch; filthy, impoverished, and constantly fighting amongst themselves.

---

[5] About 1,000 miles

Early in the voyage, a huge fight broke out among them on deck, and they seemed intent on slaughtering each other, until the white crew waded into them and broke up the fight, along with several heads. Subsequently, their fighting was much more subdued, and kept out of sight. There were a few Chinese aristocrats or head men who spent much of their time smoking their pipes, and keeping themselves separated from the common Chinese.

The voyage was also disappointingly uneventful – I had hoped for a battle with pirates, or at least a terrible storm – but the biggest dangers were seasickness and boredom. Early on, I spent some time trying to learn the workings of the ship, but after being ordered — and sometimes thrown — out of the way a number of times, I abandoned it. A life at sea came to seem as boring as life in an office would be.

After a few days at sea, I discovered an American passenger, or rather, he discovered me. I was stripped to the waist and barefoot, taking the air on deck when a heavy hand fell on my shoulder, spinning me around and throwing me down. A Chinese stood shouting gibberish at me, while a large white man stood by. "Tell him to get his yellow -ss below decks where he belongs," he instructed the Chinese.

I lunged to my feet, prepared to fight. "Who are you to order me about," I demanded. "I'm not some coolie you can push around. Apologize sir, or prepare to defend yourself!"

The big man's eyes widened in surprise, both at my English and my belligerence, and he smiled broadly. "Say," he said, "whar'd a rascal like you learn to talk like that? H--l, you don't even sound Chinese!" Turning to the still-jabbering Chinese, he said, "Li Wei, you arter learn to talk like this youngun." To me he said, "I been working with this dumb sumb---h for six months, and can still barely make out what he's saying, and I don't know that he understands me any better."

I was beginning to feel foolish standing there braced for combat while he barely seemed to notice. Still, I kept my guard up, lest it be a trick. The Chinese was still yelling at me and gesticulating wildly.

The man reached out and tugged on the Chinese's queue. "Shut up, you d----d benighted heathen. Leave this boy alone, and get about your business." The Chinese' face flushed with rage, but he only turned and stomped away, muttering furiously. "Them boys don't like anybody messing with their pigtails," the man said. Finally, he seemed to register my stance. Holding up his hands he said, "Aw now, just put them mitts away. I ain't fighting no kid. Where you from, boy?"

"I am no boy!" I bellowed, "Defend yourself sir!" and struck him soundly on his lantern-like jaw. He looked surprised and touched where I had hit him.

"Say kid, what'd you do that for?"

I lashed out with a series of blows that again seemed more surprising to him than painful.

Grinning, he said, "Ain't you the little spitfire though," and grabbed me by the arms, lifting me off my feet as easily as if I were an infant. His long arms kept him out of my reach as I flailed at him. Finally, I lashed out with my boot and caught him in the — delicacy prevents me from being specific. He threw me across the deck, where I landed painfully. He was hunched over, cupping himself, and gasping for air. "You little p----rhead," he moaned, "what in h--l is wrong with you? That ain't no way to fight fair."

I resumed my feet and my pugilistic stance, "Do you admit defeat, or do you require more punishment?"

"What?" He sat down gingerly. "Alright fine, you win." Smiling ruefully, he said, "Rough little tyke, ain't you?" He held out his hand. "I'm Asa Sanford."

"Anatoly Mikhailovich Lukyanov."

"By G-d, that's a whopper of a name for a little feller," he said, throwing up his hands when I raised my fists yet again, "Calm down son, just calm down – I mean no offense. Where you from, Luckyenough?"

When I corrected him about my name, he said, "Well, you're lucky enough far's I'm concerned." It was my first American nickname.

I told him my story, and he told me his. He was an agent for an American mining company, returning from China with a cargo of laborers traveling on "credit-tickets" he had arranged. They would work off the cost of the ticket in the gold mines of California at 300% interest. "It's a d--n' smart piece of business," he laughed. "We used to do it through a Chinese agent, but the bosses weren't happy with the quality, so they sent me to do the recruiting personally," he said proudly.

Of my mixed heritage, he nodded sagely. "Oh yeah, we got half-breeds in America too," but it took some time for him to grasp the difference between a proud

Buriat and a lowly Chinese. He eventually got it, although he still insisted that I looked "about half-Chinese". "You'd best watch out when we land, or it could cause you trouble," he said.

I spent a fair amount of time with him, when he wasn't attending to his human cargo, and Tasha and Mischa enjoyed his company as well. The three of us pestered him endlessly about America, and what to expect. He also undertook to teach Mischa and I something of the science of boxing, saying, "You boys either need to get less quarrelsome or get better at defending yourselves." To Tasha, he gave a two-shot derringer.

Tasha became somewhat infatuated with him and his rough-and-tumble ways, and to his credit he took no advantage. Indeed, between her natural shyness and his general obliviousness, he barely seemed to notice her at all. As her brother, I was relieved, but I could also see how it hurt her. I hoped that in America things would be different for her.

As for myself, I put aside all thoughts of love and romance, setting my sights on a life of adventure. After hearing Asa's tales of the wealth to be found in the gold fields, I decided that I would work the mines for two or three years, until I had enough to set the three of us up for life, and then I would explore the world and all of its mysteries and wonders in style.

Between my books and spending time with Asa, the voyage passed pleasantly enough, although at the time it still seemed deadly dull, with only brief moments of diversion, but that's the way it is when you're young – any time not spent in furious activity seems an eternity. Looking back on it now though, there isn't much I wouldn't give to take another long, leisurely trip like it. In a way, I suppose that's what I'm doing now.

The morning we docked in San Francisco was just the beginning.

Chapter Two

Unexpected prejudice in the land of the Free; I try mining; A rapid succession of careers; a righteous fight; ignominious defeat; New friends; new opportunity

My grandfather was a good and wise man, and I find that at my current age I largely agree with him on the things that make life worth living (good food, horses, and women), although I am inclined to replace good fights with good friends in my own list. While I have never been a man of means, I have been fortunate to have enjoyed the very best that life has to offer in terms of food, horses, women, and friends. By my reckoning, that makes me far wealthier than those little men of wealth whose avarice and greed destroyed so many of my friends and led to my current predicament.

California
1854

The few weeks after landing in San Francisco were eventful, exciting, and disconcerting and revolved mostly around being mistaken for Chinese – Mischa and I had trouble finding work, housing, even places to eat, all because of our Asiatic features. Posing as Tasha's servants, we finally found a respectable boarding house that would let Mischa and I stay in a shed at the back of the house. I found it demeaning to be seen as a member of an inferior race. It didn't take long however, for my sympathies to begin to shift.

We were fortunate to find a position for Tasha as a governess to a freshly-widowed, newly-minted millionaire's three children – he was one of the few who struck it rich in the early days of the gold rush and managed to hang onto his money. He also took Mischa on as a groom in his stables, which left the two of them with good jobs and the remainder of our money in the bank. It left me free to make tracks to the goldfields to seek our fortune.

I made my way up the Sacramento River to the northern goldfields where, for once, my features worked in my favor – I was hired as a foreman in one of the mines. The manager was so excited to find a "Chinaman" who spoke English that it never occurred to him to ensure that I spoke Chinese well, or knew anything about mining. It only took about three days for both of us to come to some unpleasant conclusions

– I realized that I was not cut out for mining at roughly the same time that he realized that not only did I barely speak Chinese, but I also had no idea what I was doing.

We reached an agreement – I agreed to not be paid, and he agreed not to have "the living s--t" kicked out of me – and we parted ways. Those three days were enough to make me start seriously questioning my prejudice against the Chinese and my good opinion of bosses.

I drifted down to Shasta, where I spent some time working for a freight company, as a hostler in a livery stable, and a number of other menial jobs, gradually working my way down the ladder of gainful employment to work as a cook at The Angry Pig Diner, another job for which I was spectacularly unqualified, before being demoted to dishwasher. A letter from Tasha had me wondering if I had made a mistake in leaving San Francisco – she and Mischa were doing exceptionally well – when fate stepped in.

The lunch rush had ended, and I stepped outside for some air when, across the street, the doors of the Fandango Saloon burst open. A cursing fat man in a checked suit dragged the little Chinese who emptied the spittoons and swept up, into the street.

"By G-d," he roared, sending the Chinese sprawling with a boot to the rear, "I'll teach you to mind your betters!" He lifted the little man to his feet, held him upright with one hand, and struck him repeatedly with the other. A large group of men gathered, most laughing and cheering, enjoying the spectacle of this man mercilessly beating a defenseless man half his size. A few looked on uncomfortably but were unwilling to take the part of a Chinese against a white man.

My blood boiled. One thing I cannot abide is a bully. I strode across the street and grabbed his arm as he drew it back for another blow. "That's enough!" I said, "He's had enough."

The man looked at me disbelievingly. "Who the f--k are you to tell me he's had enough? I'll say when he's had enough, and d--n the man who tries to stop me!"

"D--n YOU sir! You'll not strike him again while I stand!" I stepped back and put up my "dukes" as Asa Sanford had shown me.

The lout dropped the Chinese, threw back his head and guffawed. "Look at this! This little c--ksucker thinks he can teach me my manners!" Mocking my pugilistic stance, he raised his own fists. "Come on then, you little s--t, show me what you got."

20 – A Rare and Dangerous Beast

I put Asa's training to good use, bobbing and weaving past his guard, planting a right cross that rocked his head back, and dancing back out untouched. The crowd around us cheered, some calling for me to "show him what for," and others urging him to "pound the little b-----d".

Although he was larger than I, with greater reach, he was also clumsy, slow, and fairly drunk. I more than held my own against him, landing blow after stinging blow while avoiding most of his – although those that did land hurt like the dickens. It was all going well and I was quickly wearing him down when, out of the corner of my eye, I saw an angel above me. It was just a glimpse of the sun shining through a halo of golden hair and a diaphanous robe, but it caught all of my attention. Distracted, I didn't see the haymaker that measured my length in the dust of the street where my opponent, with an appalling disdain for gentlemanly combat, began to kick the stuffing out of me.

I had a vague notion of other men pulling him away from me and the sounds of fighting, and then a splash of tepid water brought me, if not back to my senses, at least nearer to them.

"Howdy," said a young man standing above me, "reckon you can get up, or d'ya need some help?"

"I can manage," I groaned, and I finally did manage to make it to my feet under my own power, although it took three tries and I needed a little help to stay there.

"I'd buy you a drink, but I don't think that saloon's safe for you right now," he said.

"I got a full bottle in my saddlebags," said a tall black man.

"That'll do," said my saviour, a tall, stout, sandy-haired man of about 20 years, with an old scar running across his forehead. "C'mon, let's get outa the street. My name's Jack – Jack McCallister." The two of them, along with a third man escorted me away from the saloon to Johnson's Livery, where we sat in the shade of the building while the black man fetched his bottle.

I thanked them for coming to my rescue, which had come at a price. Jack's right eye was nearly swollen shut, the black man's face was cut and bruised, and the other fellow was bleeding from the nose and mouth.

"Aw h--l," said Jack, "that's alright. I ain't had a good fight in a coon's age. 'Sides, it woulda been a shame to let that feller kick you to death. What happened there, anyway? You was running circles around that bruiser, and then you just stopped and let him paste you."

"I saw an angel," I said.

"'Scuse me?"

"I saw an angel hovering over me."

All three men laughed.

"You don't believe me?"

"I ain't saying I do, and I ain't saying I don't, I'm just saying that Shasta's about the last place on earth I'd expect to see an angel. Pretty sure it's more popular with the other side."

I just muttered, "I saw what I saw," and let it go. It was clearly a vision meant for me alone, and there was nothing to be gained by arguing. I would just alienate the first new friends I'd made since landing in America, and I had no desire to lose them so soon.

Jack took the bottle, uncorked it, and handed it to me. "Have a belt o' this." I took a drink and returned the bottle. He took a long drink, winced, smacked his lips, and handed it to the other white man, a surly-looking fellow with dark, curly hair. "This here's Bill," Jack said by way of introduction. Bill nodded and passed the bottle back to Jack. Jack scowled and gave the bottle to the black fellow. "And that's Dave," he said. Dave smiled, nodded, and took a drink. Handing the bottle back to me, Dave said, "Pleased to meet you."

I took another drink and passed it on. "I am Anatoly Mikhailovich Lukyanov," I said, "and I am very pleased to meet all of you."

Jack grinned. "That's a mouthful of a name, there, Lucky," he said. He drank and passed the bottle on to Bill, who shook his head. Jack shrugged. "Yer loss," he said, tossing it to Dave.

"I am lucky indeed," I said, "especially considering where I'd be if you gentlemen hadn't intervened."

Pointing to my apron, he said, "You a cook?"

"Dishwasher."

He laughed. "That ain't no kinda job for a scrappy little feller like you. Can you ride?"

"It's the only thing I do well."

"Well, if you're interested, we might could get you on with our outfit."

I grinned widely. "If you're hiring," I said, "I'm interested."

They took me to meet their foreman, a man with a solemn, sad face, who Jack introduced as "Mournful" Joe Drummond. We talked a bit, and Mr. Drummond offered to take me along. "I can't offer you a job," he said, "but I'll take you to see the boss, Fred Borland. If he likes the look of you, he might take you on."

I explained that I had no horse, no equipment, and no money – nothing but a few books, personal items, and the clothes on my back.

"That's alright," he said, "you can ride one of our spare mounts, and I'll spot you for riding tack. You can pay me back if Borland hires you. If he don't, well, we'll work somethin' out."

"I'm very grateful, but I don't want to be beholden. All I need is a bridle, or rope."

"You sure about that?" asked Mr. Drummond. "It's nigh on 50 mile to the rancho."

"Mr. Drummond . . ."

"Call me Mournful son, everyone else does."

"Very well then, Mr. Mournful . . ."

"No need for the 'mister'."

"Mournful, I grew up riding bareback on the steppes of Siberia. Fifty miles without a saddle is nothing to a son of the Buriat," I said proudly.

He smiled and shrugged. "Suit yourself," he said, "I guess we'll find out if you really can ride. We leave at sunup. If you still want to tag along, we'll see you at the livery before then."

Mournful set a fast pace through rugged country. Jack and Dave put my boasts to the test, challenging me to races, and playing good-natured tricks trying to unseat me. Before the day was out, I'd proved at least my horsemanship. Along the way, we got to know each other more. Jack and Dave's story was of particular interest to me.

As Jack told it, they came from the Texas ranch of Jack's father, Big Jack McCallister, where Dave was a slave. Although Jack was the master's son, they were great friends, having grown up together from infancy. "We were both suckled at Dave's mammy's teat," as Jack put it. The older they grew however, the more distasteful Big Jack found their friendship. Big Jack treated Dave most cruelly, punishing him harshly for the smallest offense. "I know it ain't right to talk bad about my folks, but my daddy is a low sonuvab---h" Jack said.

One day Dave was sent to drive a few cattle back to the McCallister side of a rain-swollen river. One calf was caught in the current and drowned before Dave could get to it. For losing that calf, Big Jack whipped

Dave so badly that he would likely have died had Jack not intervened. Big Jack turned his fury on his own son, striking Jack with the lash, leaving that scar across his forehead.

Dave was laid up for days, and when he could finally stand again, he took a horse and ran. Jack was sent, along with two other men, to bring Dave back. Big Jack promised the two men a hefty reward upon their return with Dave alive. "Daddy didn't trust me to bring Dave back on my own," Jack said. "He was powerful mean, but he warn't stupid. Them two was just as hateful and lowdown as he was. They'd've sold their own mothers for a nickel, much less the hundred dollars apiece daddy offered them."

They caught up with Dave just north of Santa Fe, in New Mexico Territory. He had acquired a gun somehow and holed up in some rocks. "He said, 'I'm gonna die either way. Better to die free by my own hand than be beat to death as a slave'" Jack told me. "Well, I knew he was right, and I warn't goin' to have nothing to do with it, so I got the drop on those other two, disarmed them, and told them to go on back home and tell my daddy to go to h--l. After a couple days though, we seen them two follerin' after us again.

I don't know if they were that hot for the reward my daddy promised them, or if they was just afraid to face him, but they weren't giving up."

Knowing the chase had to end, Jack and Dave found another good spot to "fort up" and wait. "When they come up on us, I hollered out and give 'em a last chance, but they kept on, and left us no choice," Dave said, his voice low and hollow.

After that, they kept traveling west and north, eventually fetching up at the Dos Ríos Rancho, working for Mr. Borland. I was left with a profound admiration for both men, for their devotion to each other, and to freedom. It was to be a man such as these that my father had sent me here, and I was happy to have landed in such good company.

Mournful turned out to be a happy-go-lucky fellow, despite his looks. He was also very knowledgeable about his profession, and I learned much from him in the two days' ride to the Rancho.

Bill's sullenness, on the other hand, seemed to be bone deep, and he tended to keep to himself. Fearing I'd offended him in some way, I asked Jack about it. He just laughed. "Oh don't mind Bill. He just don't care for Dave much – or me either. He's okay though.

He rides for the brand, and he'll back anyone that does, whether he likes 'em or not."

We reached the rancho the next afternoon, and Mournful took me to meet Mr. Borland who took one look at me and said, "We already got a cook, Joe. You oughta know I ain't replacing Miguel with no Celestial."

"Sir," I said carefully in my best English, "I am no Chinese cook. I am Russian, and looking for work as a herdsman."

"A what?"

"A cowhand, boss," said Mournful.

"He don't look like no Russian I ever seen."

"Well, I don't know how many you've seen, but he's the only one I ever met. He even talks Russian. Show him, Lucky."

I spoke a few words in my native tongue, introducing myself properly, in case Mr. Borland spoke Russian. He didn't.

"I don't know what kinda jabber that is, but it sure ain't nothing I ever heard before. How the h--l do you know it's Russian he's speaking, you idiot? Could be anything."

"Boss, why would he say it's Russian if it was something else?"

Borland thought for a moment. "Well, these foreigners can be a tricky bunch," he grumbled. "Can he ride?"

"Better'n me," said Mournful. "I never saw anybody ride like this boy. I figured we could use him, 'specially since Badger and them others quit."

"You ever worked cattle before?" Mr. Borland addressed me for the first time.

"I have helped care for my grandfather's herds since I was a child."

"What kinda herds does a Russian have? Reindeer?" He laughed.

I was growing impatient with this rude man. "My grandfather is no Russian. He is a Buriat Mongol, descended from Temujin, the great Chinggis Khan, himself. He owns over 500 horses, a thousand cattle, and countless sheep. If it can be ridden, I can ride it. If it can be herded, I can herd it. If man can do it, I can do it."

Borland stood silent for a moment. "Think a lot of yourself, don't you boy? Well, we'll see. Stow your gear in the bunkhouse."

"Thank you sir."

"One other thing," he drew his broad frame up to his full height, thrusting his barrel chest out like a bull, "I don't stand for no back talk. You got something to say to me, you best be polite. If you want to keep a whole hide, that is." With that, he turned and went into the house, slamming the door behind him.

"Well," said Mournful, a smile on his hangdog face, "looks like you've got a job."

And that's how I came to be a cowboy.

Chapter Three

A visit from a friend; on romance; a warning to the reader; limits of the joys of a cowboy life; revelation of my "angel"; a cowboy in love

My particular friend came to see me today – I'll call her Mrs. Good – and it made for a welcome change. Not that I've been especially lonely; Sheriff Angus and my fellow deputies are all splendid fellows and excellent company, but there is something about the company of a woman that is a balm to my soul.

I have always been of a romantic nature, and it occurs to me that many of the major lessons of my life have sprung from my relationships with women. Without being unduly vulgar or salacious, I would like to say that, if this is to be a true accounting of my life and how I came to be here, there are some areas that must be covered that will be considered indelicate by many readers. It is not my intention to offend, and the less worldly reader might prefer to skip over the following.

California

32 – A Rare and Dangerous Beast

1854-56

I found my new life delightful, but there was a lack of variety, and I took advantage of any opportunity to go to town, where there were diversions of a sort not to be found on the rancho. It was on one of my earliest trips to town that I discovered – as my friends had so repeatedly and with much hilarity pointed out – that angels did not, indeed, frequent Shasta, California. The discovery that my "angel" was of a much more terrestrial nature turned out to be a welcome surprise.

She went by the name Rahab, and she was a sporting lady who worked in the disorderly house on the top floor of the Fandango saloon. When I'd seen her during the fight, she had been standing on the balcony, just as she was the second time I saw her. She recognized me and waved and smiled, and I was smitten. From that moment, I was Galahad, determined to save this fair damsel from a "fate worse than death".

She had a companion — Samson — a huge, shotgun-toting negro mute from whom she was rarely separated by more than a door. Samson was as loyal as a hound to her and as fierce as a bear with a bad tooth toward anyone who seemed a threat to her. She was probably the safest woman in Shasta, despite her profession. It took months before she was able to persuade him that she was safe with me, making for an awkward beginning to our relationship.

I spent as much time with her as I could afford. While not all our time together was on a professional basis, I always paid for her time. Big Sue, the proprietress of the establishment insisted on that: "I don't care what you do, but you're not taking money out of my pocket," was how she put it.

Even so, Rahab wasn't always "on duty" and some of my favourite times with her occurred when she'd been taken off the line, usually due to medical treatment. Tall and willowy, with long golden hair, and piercing green eyes, she also boasted very sharp and distinctive features — a proud Gallic, somewhat predatory nose, high cheekbones, a wide, thin-lipped mouth that was almost always curled in a half smile, and a long, strong jawline terminating in a slightly pointed chin. What she might have lacked in conventional beauty — for there was nothing demure or soft about her — she more than made up in character. She was the most beautiful woman I'd ever seen.

Her only physical flaw was a wandering left eye, but I loved her not for her physical charms only. She was clever and intelligent, with a bawdy sense of humour and a salty disposition masking a kind and generous nature. I came to call her my little Prickly Pear — sweet and wonderful, once you got to the heart of her, but getting past all the spines required time and careful effort.

She was always willing to help anyone fallen on hard times. I saw her assist many an unfortunate wretch, both male and female, with a meal, a room, or even a grubstake, or a stage ticket out of town. On the other hand, she had no patience with fools, never loaned money nor gave credit, and never ever bartered or discounted her services. "Christian charity is one thing," she said, "but bad business is just bad business."

My Rahab also never missed church services, which I found hilarious. She went heavily veiled and always sat by herself in the back, but everyone knew who she was. It was a sign of how well she was thought of in the town that even the strictest and most judgmental in the congregation chose to simply ignore her rather than make a fuss. "Why do you bother with all that superstitious rot, in a church full of hypocrites who wouldn't deign to acknowledge you on the street?" I once asked her.

"I don't go for *them*."

I was utterly bewitched.

Initially at least, I was little more than an amusement to her. It wasn't any one thing that got me past her defenses — it was more a gradual, almost glacial, letting down of her guard as she came to trust me and even, finally, depend on me. I had been paying court to her for months when one day we were walking in the country — followed at a distance by Samson and his ever-present shotgun — and sat down to rest in a mountain meadow, surrounded by wildflowers and she blurted out, "Rahab's not my real name."

"What is it then?"

She wouldn't meet my eyes — a trait that always accompanied any mention of her past. I don't think it was a matter of shame so much as fear of what she'd see in my eyes. "Esmeralda," she said, "but my friends used to call me Esme."

"Esme's a beautiful name," I said. "So why go by Rahab?"

She smiled her thin-lipped, lopsided smile, dragged on her pipe, and said, "I think it's funny. Besides, she was a w----e, but that's not all she was, and it reminds me that, though I may be one now, it's not all I am, or all I'll ever be."

"Why don't you let your friends call you Esme now?"

"Haven't had any until now. My line of work, it don't pay to get too close to anyone."

"May I call you Esme?"

She smiled and elbowed me. "Why the h--l d'you think I'm telling you this?" She finally looked into my eyes and smiled at what she saw there. I never knew when she would decide to reveal a little more of her real self, but it always came as a surprise.

She loved to swim and in summer we often rode to a small lake tucked away in the mountains. One such day, we'd had our fill of swimming and lay intertwined on a blanket, au naturale, letting the sun warm us — Samson had remained with the buggy. She lay pressed tight against me, her head on my chest, when she quietly said, "My daddy was a preacher. A preacher and a good man. He raised me up to love the Lord, and live right, but I was always a little bit wild. He always said I took after my mama, God rest her." I held her close until she rose on her elbow to look at me, "I wish I'd known her."

"I'll bet she was a wonderful woman," I said.

She lay her head back on my chest and squeezed me tight. "What was your mama like?"

"She was – is – unusual. She is beautiful and fierce and rides, shoots, and curses better than most men. She loves deeply, and she is generally kind and patient, although if you get on her bad side, it takes much time and effort to get back into her good books." I laughed.

"What's funny?"

"I just realized how much you have in common with her. I don't know whether to be delighted or concerned."

"Maybe both?" She laughed. "Maybe don't think about it too much."

Although she was normally sweet as could be to me, I never knew when those cactus spines might spring out. One Saint Valentine's Day, she cooked dinner for us and I surprised her with flowers and a poem — it was terrible, but I was immensely proud of it at the time — and she immediately threw both in the trash.

"Don't waste my time or yours with that nonsense," she said.

I was hurt and angry and let her know it in no uncertain terms.

She rounded on me. "I don't want flowers or poems or candy, or any of the bulls--t that passes for love from you! Not a week goes by but some dumb-ssedd dirty cowboy or drunken miner don't hand me that s--t, 'cause they loooove me. At least 'til they sober up, or their friends start givin' 'em a hard time about me being a w----e! I got a dozen or more b------ds a week telling me they love me on Saturday night that won't tip their hat to me in the street on Sunday morning! I don't want or need that from you!"

My temper got the better of me, and I stormed out, my hair full of shards of crockery from the pitcher that smashed against the doorframe over my head. Some days later, I cooled down, rode back to town and tried to apologize, but it was like talking to a block of ice.

I refused to leave town until she spoke to me and it took several more days until she thawed. My apology, which I'd been rehearsing the whole time, was heartfelt, profound, abject, and eloquent. She met it with a gaze barely room temperature, and no response at all. Finally, just as my last heartstring was about to snap, she said, "Okay. Come see me next week – I've got work to do now," and she showed me the door. It was just as well, since Jack had ridden into town that morning to tell me I was fired, and so I had time to get my job back. After a few weeks things finally returned to normal for her and me.

Chapter Four

On names; new friends; joys of a cowboy's life; new ideas, new perspectives; nicknames; unexpected trouble; a practical application of the theory of individual sovereignty; an excellent fight; Dave's new nickname

It occurs to me that names are a strange thing. They are a necessity that most strongly identifies us, and yet we have virtually no say in their choosing. Our parents name us according to whim or obligation. Others give us nicknames based on what they see in us, or what they want others to see us as. They are meant, by those who choose them for us, to represent us in our entirety but fall far short.

Looking through the bars of my window at the children playing in the street, I can already guess what their nicknames will be (if they're not already). Which ones will be "Fats", "Red", or "Shorty" just by looking at them. Although the chances are those sobriquets will follow them the rest of their lives, they are all based on superficialities.

And of course names, especially nicknames, can be dangerous, even to those who bestow them.

California
1857

Those early days as a cowhand were the happiest and most carefree of my life. The work was hot, dusty, dangerous, and I loved it. I quickly mastered the arts of roping and "brush popping" and the long days in the saddle allowed plenty of time for thinking. I especially enjoyed being assigned to the most remote parts of the rancho. I would often spend a week or more alone, high on the side of a mountain, tending the herd, no one but a book or two for company.

Not that I didn't enjoy the company of the "boys", a wild and fun-loving bunch. I was fascinated by stories about their homes, families, and backgrounds, and they listened — often with disbelief — to my tales, especially those of my time with the Buriat, and my journey to America.

They were an accepting lot — anyone who pulled his weight was welcome. They were accepting of pretty much anyone, regardless of where they were from or the color of their skin — within reason, of course. I was delighted to have fallen in with such a good lot.

Some of the best times were spent with Dave and Jack. The three of us worked well together, and we spent many happy days working cattle and camping under the stars, where we talked of many things around the fire. Dave was particularly intrigued by the philosophy I had read, particularly Locke's ideas about owning one's self[6]. For my part, I tried to reconcile the American ideals of freedom and equality with the "Peculiar Institution[7]" — the thing that had been my father's only reservation about the United States. Neither Jack nor Dave could really explain it. It was like a man trying to explain why he has nipples. It just was.

Our conversations also cast new light on my own homeland, vis-à-vis serfdom, which I was equally unable to explain. Dave found it fascinating that our serfs were actually white men, while Jack used that fact to propose that Russia was no better than America — a position I heartily agreed with. In fact, he truculently proclaimed Russia even worse than the U.S. because our slaves were white. "It ain't right to own another

---

[6] Probably from Locke's *Second Treatise on Government*, either from Chap. IV "Of Slavery" or Chap. V "Of Property"

[7] A common term for the American system of slavery.

man, but at least we don't keep our own kind as slaves," was how he put it, a comment which not only ended the discussion for the night, but cast a pall over the mood of the next day or two.

One night, I told them the story of Gogol's[8] Dead Souls, in which a man named Chichikov runs around purchasing the titles to serfs who had died since the last census. Those serfs were considered alive, officially, and since the serf's owners had to pay taxes on them until the next infrequent census, many were only too happy to sell these taxable properties that existed only on paper. Chickikov's idea is that once he has acquired enough "souls", he will mortgage them to an unsuspecting bank and pocket the money.

Jack found the story hilarious. Dave sat deep in thought for a while and then said, "You Russians sure done us one better."

"What do you mean?"

"Well here at least, a slave's free when he dies. You boys have figured out how to keep him in chains and make money off him even when he's dead."

It struck me that while men like Jack and I could appreciate Gogol's satire, only someone like Dave,

---

[8] Nikolai Gogol, 1809-1852. Ukrainian author.

who had been a slave, would be likely to realize the true tragedy of the piece.

That perspective was made even more clear to me at a later date.

***

The full moon lit up the night almost like daylight. We were enjoying the cool of the evening each in our own way – I was watching Juan plaiting a *mecate*[9], and listening to his stories of the rancho from the old days, before Borland weaseled it out from under the old Patron, Don Alvaro. Juan's brothers Balduino, and Fabricio played mumblety-peg with Dave. Charlie Murphy was torturing his harmonica and stoically ignoring Jack's and Billy Smith's jibes. Bill, Zeke Walker and Enoch Taylor were grumbling and sharing a bottle – when Borland rode up with two men in tow.

"Boys," he said, "these here are Dave Schwinghammer and Dave O'Sullivan." He told the new men to get settled in, turned on his heel and stalked to the house.

Dave took charge of Borland's horse. "You fellas 'light and set. I'll get your horses settled tonight." They handed him their reins and he led the horses away.

---

[9] Horsehair rope

Schwinghammer was a skinny little fellow, with thin arms that made his name seem a lie. O'Sullivan, on the other hand, was a huge brute of a man, big enough to make you feel sorry for the horse that has to carry him. They stowed their gear in the bunkhouse, came back out, and hunkered down with us.

Schwinghammer was from Wisconsin, with the slight Nordic accent of that region, and had come to California as a freighter and muleskinner, but "got tired of pulling splinters out of my backside. I figure I'd prefer a saddle for a seat."

O'Sullivan was fresh from "t' auld coontry" and had a thick, almost indecipherable Irish brogue. Like me, he'd quickly discovered that mining was not the sort of life he wanted. "I decided I'd rather be poor and see what's on the top of this land rather than underneath it." Of course, it sounded like "Oy disoided oy'druther be puir'n say whit's on top o' dis land rather dan oondernaith't," but after repeating himself a couple times, we began to be able to start chopping through his accent to understand him.

Jack, ever the joker, spoke up. "Well, welcome to Dos Ríos Rancho, fellers. I reckon there's just one problem we're gonna have to deal with first, to keep things working smooth around here."

"What problem would that be?" asked Schwinghammer.

"Well, it's simple," said Jack, "we just got too many Daves in this here outfit. How we gonna keep it all straight? I mean, 'sposing I need somebody in particular to help me with somethin'? If I want Nate or Joe, I could just ask for 'em by name and everyone'd know who I wanted. But what happens if I need a big man for moving something? I can't just ask for Dave, can I? The boys'd be just as likely to send the little Dave as the big. That won't do boys, it just won't do." He did allow that, since none of us knew the Daves yet, we couldn't use the time-honored tradition of basing the monikers on familiarity. "I think what we need is some temporary names to get us by 'til they earn one."

We all agreed that was an excellent solution to the problem and proceeded to toss out nicknames that we felt would prevent communication problems in the future.

The new Daves took the ribbing good-naturedly, and generally kept quiet, for of course it is a law of nicknames that the bearer cannot choose his own — although Dave Schwinghammer bristled when "Little Dave" was suggested for him. Most of the suggestions were intentionally ridiculous, but all were suggested in a spirit of bonhomie. We finally settled on "Dutch" for Schwinghammer, and "Big Dave" for O'Sullivan.

The newly christened Dutch and Big Dave shook hands all around, including Dave's, who had just returned from the corral. Dutch retrieved a bottle of whiskey from his gear, and we passed it around, toasting the newcomers.

"You forgot one," Bill said, surly as ever.

"One what?" I asked.

"One Dave. Why do these two need nicknames and he don't?"

"'Cause he was already here," said Jack. "He's the original Dave."

"It just don't seem right to me," said Bill, "treatin' him different."

Several of the boys backed Bill's position, mostly as a way of keeping the fun going. Dave himself remained silent on this subject, as he did on most things unless specifically addressed. In fact, "Quiet Dave" was one of the first names suggested. Others included "Original

Dave", "Middling Dave", "Checkers", and "Brushy Dave".

Jack took another pull at the bottle. "How 'bout 'Black Dave'? Just keep it simple, like we did with Dutch and Big Dave. That way even new men would know who we're talking about." Several of the boys concurred.

"I'll go you one better," sneered Bill. "How about 'N----r Dave'?"

Dave just got up and walked into the bunkhouse.

"Doggone it Bill," said Jack, "what's the matter with you? You just can't help tryin' to stir up trouble, can you?"

"What's the matter Jack, afraid I hurt your little pet's feelings? Can't he stand up for hisself? I reckon if he wants to be a man, he ought to learn to act like a man."

Several of the boys joined Jack in shouting Bill down. A few took Bill's side though, and the high spirits were turning ugly when Dave returned from the bunkhouse. Everyone quieted down, curious to see what he was going to do.

Dave was stripped to the waist and barefoot. He stared at us for a moment, and then held his hands above his head, as he turned in a circle. The group went dead silent when the moonlight illuminated the mass of scars covering his chest, back, and shoulders — something most had never seen. Someone let a long, slow whistle, and another muttered "D--nation" under his breath.

"I just want you all to see that I ain't armed," said Dave in a clear, steady voice, "before I get started. I ain't out to kill nobody, and I don't want nobody killing me." Then he raised his fists in a pugilistic attitude and said, "Come over here Jack."

Bill pushed forward through the boys to stand facing Dave. Bill was larger and heavier, but Dave's lean, whipcord-muscled body left no doubt in my mind that Bill was in for more of a fight than he expected. "What's the matter N----r Dave?" Bill blustered, "Can't stand up on your own hind legs like a man? You need your 'massa' to protect . . ."

"I ain't gonna fight you Bill," Dave said. "It's Jack I'm fixing to whup."

"What?" said Jack.

"I'm planning to whup your --s."

"What the h--l for? You d--nfool, I'm on your side. Why ain't you taking up against him?"

"Don't 'spect any better from him. Don't care what he has to say. He's just ignorant and mean, and ain't nothing ever gonna change that. You though, you're my friend, but I don't figure to 'low nobody to ever name me again 'thout my say so. 'Specially when you and me both know there ain't a hair's difference between 'black' and 'n----r'. You of all people ought to know better, but I guess you don't, so I'm fixin' to teach you." Looking at Bill, he said, "I'll deal with you later — if I have to."

"Now d----t Dave," Jack said, "you know I didn't mean nothing of the sort . . ."

"What you meant don't matter. It's what you said. Now put 'em up."

"No, doggone it . . .," Jack said, before Dave's punch set him back on his heels. "Alright now you're getting me mad . . ." Dave struck him again. "I'm sorry alright? I don't want to fight . . ."

I'm not sure if was Dave's third blow that changed Jack's mind, or the boys chuckling at his predicament, but Jack proceeded to enter the fight with a whole heart. He and Dave went at it hammer and tongs, punching, kicking, grappling, gouging, and biting for all they were worth, fighting like brothers while we encircled them, laughing and cheering them on. It was the best fight any of us had seen in quite a while.

The two were pretty evenly matched — one moment Dave would seem to be winning and the next Jack would have the upper hand — but Dave's wiry strength and endurance finally triumphed. Jack lay in the dust, propped up on one elbow, his other hand lifted to signal defeat. "Alright," he mumbled through split and swollen lips, "you win. I 'pologize. Your name's just Dave. That's all. And I'll whup the man that calls you otherwise — unless you'd druther do it yourself, o' course."

Dave smiled, spit out a tooth, offered his hand to Jack, and said through equally mangled lips, "I reckon that'd suit me right down to the ground." He pulled Jack to his feet. "It's been a pleasure whuppin' you."

Jack spat blood, and clapped Dave on the shoulder. "Nobody I'd druther be whupped by."

Dutch handed Dave the bottle, and held out his hand, "It's a pleasure to meet you, Just Dave." We all went dead silent, wondering how Dave would take that. Dave stood silently for a moment, staring into Dutch's smiling face, then threw back his head and laughed heartily. He shook Dutch's hand. "'Just

Dave'," he said. "I b'lieve I like that. What do you think, Jack? Not that it matters."

"Not that it matters, but if you like it, I like it."

Just Dave handed the bottle to Jack and turned back to the boys. "Bill, you got anything to say?" he asked.

"Bill done remembered some business he needed to take care of in the stable," said Charley.

***

It strikes me now that most names given us by others, including our parents, are generally a matter of affection, or at worst, convenience, and if harmful, that harm is personal and usually superficial. It is the name a man gives himself that causes genuine harm to others. A self-named man wears a mask to hide his past and his true self from others and, while his assumed name may protect him, it all too often places those around him in unexpected danger. Always beware a man who changes his own name, no matter what position he may hold. He is not to be trusted.

Chapter Five

On humility; the rocky course of true love; a show-off chastened; a feud; Ilya, my horse; professor; the snake; Dobrynya the dog; the feud intensifies; An embarrassing injury

My bones tell me it's going to rain in the morning – a real frog-strangler, by the feel of it. I once read somewhere that the road of excess leads to the palace of wisdom.[10] I don't know that I can lay any claim to being wise, but I've certainly lived excessively, and one of the results is a pretty fair ability to accurately forecast the weather. The worst thing about that "road of excess" is that so much of the tutelage is so d--ned painful. Take for instance the lesson of humility. That was a particularly painful lesson.

California
1856

My love affair with Esme was not without its difficulties. We were both hot-tempered which led to

---

[10] The quote is from William Blake's book *The Marriage of Heaven and Hell*, published in the 1790s.

frequent upheavals between us. Another factor was my *compadres* — while most of them made do with a little teasing at the beginning and then let it go, some were not so kind — Bill Morrow in particular. He was constantly dropping barbed remarks about it. I could bear his comments about me, but I had no tolerance for any disparagement of Esme, which led to several dustups. I lost most of them — after all, he had four inches and forty pounds on me — but, as they say, "He knew he'd been in a fight."

The fisticuffs with Bill frequently led to a fight with Esme: "I don't need you to defend my d---ned honor!" she'd grumble when I showed up bruised and battered. "And if I did," she'd say, "I'd pick someone a h--luva lot better at fighting than you are. Anyway, what makes you think I care what that sorry b-----d says?"

"I care, d-mmit, even if you don't. I won't allow any man to disrespect my . . . my . . ."

"Your what? Your sweetheart? Your woman? I don't belong to you — you better get that through your thick skull. I ain't your horse, that you get to say who rides it and who don't! I make my own decisions, and take care of myself, and if you don't like it, well you can just move along!" I never did, of course. You might as well ask a river to leave its banks.

Of course, it didn't always lead to a fight. Sometimes, when my pride didn't get the better of me, I'd just laugh ruefully at my lack of martial skills, and she'd hug me and call me the "Genghis Kid".

Eventually, Bill got tired of beating on me. I believe his innate cowardice got the better of him — the more I refused to back down, the more he knew his day would come. While things would never be amicable between us, we both turned to other ways to try to "get each other's goat." He liked to make a big deal of any mistake I made, and my rash nature gave him plenty to work with, such as the time when I . . . well, let's just say I gave him plenty to crow about.

For my part, I liked to show him up with horsemanship. He was a fair rider, as he had to be, but only so far as a basic ability to function from horseback and stay in the saddle. He usually rode only the tamest nags, while I chose the wildest, most spirited and intelligent mounts. I liked the kind of horse that kept me on my toes. Essentially, I was a show-off. I rarely used stirrups to mount but leapt into the saddle. I looked for any opportunity to show Bill up, like the time he lost his hat. He dismounted to retrieve it, and I dashed by at the gallop and swept it off the ground just as he was bending to pick it up. I didn't make a big deal of it, simply wheeled around and handed it to him, but his face coloured deep red.

I liked cantankerous mounts to start the day, especially on cold mornings when a good battle got the blood pumping for both horse and rider. My personal horse was like that — a fiery little mustang with an evil temperament that worked hard all day and have enough energy and spirit left over to win a few dollars in an evening race. I called him Ilya, after the legendary Rus' hero Ilya Muromets. Although small, he had a giant's spirit and his namesake's heroic strength. I loved that horse.

I also showed off my education. I was forever quoting — and probably frequently misquoting — great thinkers and authors, which led to some resentment. It wasn't intentional — I thought I was just carving out a place for myself.

One night Just Dave spoke up. "G-dallmighty Nate," he said, "we all know you're educated better'n us — you don't have to keep provin' it do ya?"

Several of the other boys seconded him, and Big Dave added, "If I'd wanted an education, I'da joined the Church like me dear ol' muther wanted. You're a good boyo, but you're no perfessor at some college, you're just anoother $30 a month cowhand like the rest of us."

I was quite chagrined at that, and made some effort to rein in my mouth thereafter. Of course, from time to time I'd forget until someone would holler out, "Alright, professor."

I did not hold back on Bill however, even when Jack and Just Dave tried to warn me off.

"You oughta back offa Bill and quit ridin' him so hard," Jack said.

I just laughed. "Aw, I'm just teasing him a bit. I'm not hurting him any."

"You tease a snake, you're bound to get bit," said Just Dave. "And Bill's more water moccasin than rattlesnake. He won't give no warning — he'll just bite you when you ain't looking."

I assured them I was capable of taking care of myself and went heedlessly on my way.

Not long after that, an old mongrel dog wandered into camp. He was a friendly, clever, polite fellow, who reminded me of the Mongolian dogs of my grandfather's people. He had long black fur, with a brown muzzle and brown spots over his eyes, and had an injured paw. I took a liking to him and doctored his injury as best I could. I named him Dobrynya, after Ilya Muromets' fellow *Bogatyr*[11], Dobrynya Nikitich. Dob, as most called him was popular around the rancho, but he and I developed a special bond. I read to him in the evenings, and I swear he listened and understood. Still, he was very much his own dog, and it was common for him to disappear for days at a time. My personal opinion was that he did it to maintain his self-respect. He held himself above the more domesticated dogs and refused to allow himself to become a pet, although he would condescend to allow me to spoil him or, as I suspect he saw it, pay tribute to him. He was also a great favorite with the children of the rancho. Although he rarely played with them, if they were out playing, he invariably accompanied them, instinctively watching over them.

One evening, Bill got after Miguelito, youngest son of Fernando — the cook at the big house — for something, snatching the boy up, cursing and shaking

[11] A sort of medieval Slavic knight errant of legend.

the terrified child like a rag doll "You little b-----d!" he roared, "I oughta tan your sorry hide!"

Before any of us could intervene, Dob took a chunk out of Bill's backside. Bill gave a howl and dropped Miguelito. Quick as a flash, Dob got between Bill and the boy, ears back, hackles up, head low, and growling. Bill grabbed for his gun, but Big Dave grabbed his arm. Miguelito ran, and I got between Bill and Dob. Bill was ranting and raving, swearing he'd "kill that d--ned dog". Finally, he calmed down and limped away. Later, when it turned out Dob hadn't done any real harm, he even managed to laugh about it — in a grudging sort of way.

Months later, Jack and I were moving cattle to fresh grazing, and found Dob dead under a bush. He hadn't been there long — no scavengers had found him yet — and his lips were drawn back in a rictus of pain. We examined him and found no sign of injury. "Poor old Dob," I said, patting his shaggy side. "At least you had a good life, didn't you, old fellow?" To Jack I said, "Think it was just his time? He was pretty old."

"Looks like he was poisoned," said Jack. "We poisoned some coyotes and wolves down in Texas, and that's what they looked like."

"But who . . .?" Then it dawned on me. "That son-of-a-b---h! I'll kill him!" I grabbed Ilya's reins, and Jack grabbed me.

"Now hold on, d--n it. We don't know it was poison — it looks like it, but Dob could have just eaten something that made him sick."

"No, it was that b-----d Morrow, and I'm going to have his hide!" I struggled to get loose, but Jack wouldn't let go.

"I wouldn't put it past him — he is a snake — but you'll just get yourself beat senseless."

"You don't fight a snake, you just shoot it."

"And you'll end up hung, and for what? An old dog that he might not have even killed? Why would he kill Dob?"

"Dob bit him!"

"Dob nipped him. Not even Bill's that low. You know what though? He mighta done it to get at you. He's low enough to do that. You and all your showin' off, and showin' him up."

"You're saying this is my fault?" I said, disbelievingly.

"I'm saying, if – if – he done this, that'd be why. To prod you into doin' something stupid. You go back like this, you'll either end up dead or fired permanent-like."

Digging Dob's grave gave me a chance to think. In the end, I decided Jack was right. I had no proof that Bill had done anything to Dob. But I resolved to have nothing further to do with the man.

As luck would have it, when supplies were needed from town, Dutch, Just Dave, Bill, and I were sent. Just Dave drove the wagon and Dutch and Bill rode. I hitched Ilya to the back of the wagon next to Just Dave's horse and rode with him. We plodded along behind them, and I grew more and more furious staring at Bill's back.

Just Dave, being the noticing type, noticed, of course. "Why don't you boys ride on ahead and have a couple drinks?" he called to Dutch and Bill. "Me and Nate'll get the wagon loaded, and then you fellas can head back with the wagon and we'll get a drink."

They liked that idea and took off.

"You need to settle yourself down," Just Dave said to me once they were gone. "You're wound as tight as ol' man Borland's watch."

"Dob never did anything to hurt anyone."

"This ain't about Dob. It's about you and Bill. You need to watch yourself."

"I don't need a babysitter."

"Nate, you're a good boy, but you ain't p'tic'larly devious. Bill is. There's nothing he'd like better than for you to get liquored up stupid and make him do something permanent."

"He's too much of a coward to take me on."

"He's yellow, but he's wily. He'd make sure he had plenty of edge, leave you no chance. The thing to do with a snake is to avoid it, not get down on the ground with it."

We got to town and loaded the wagon up with supplies, then drove over to the Fandango and hitched our mounts to the rail. The bar was crowded, and Dutch and Bill had been there about three hours. Neither looked like they were feeling any pain.

"Thought you boys had got lost," said Dutch. "That, or banditos got you."

"Lemme buy you a drink," slurred Bill. "Let bygones be bygones."

"I'll buy my own, and d--n bygones."

"Aw, that ain't no way to be. Here – let's have a drink to Dob. He was a good ol' dog, Dob. I kinda miss 'im, but I'll bet you miss 'im more, huh?" He raised his glass. "To Dob! Th' unluckiest dog in the . . ."

I slapped the glass out of his hand and punched him with a solid right that laid him out on the floor.

He was back on his feet quickly for someone so drunk. His eyes flashed murderously, and then dulled again. "Now whut'd you go 'n do that for?" he said, as much to the bar as to me, "I'se just tryna to be friendly."

I went for him but Dutch and Just Dave intervened. "C'mon Bill," Dutch said. "Let 'im soak his head a bit. I'll get us a bottle for the road."

"But I'se just tryna . . ."

Just Dave was between us, holding me back. "Let it go, Nate, just let it go." More softly he said, "You're running straight into his trap, you d--nfool! Or didn't you notice his hammer thong[12] is off?"

Dutch finally prevailed, and the two left the saloon.

The whole episode left me in a foul mood and I bought a bottle. Just Dave not being particularly welcome in the Fandango, we unsaddled the horses and carried our gear and bottle around to the shed out

---

[12] A leather loop that is placed over the hammer of a handgun to keep it holstered.

back where folks like him could drink. I threw my saddle down, and got stuck into the bottle. Esme came out, and tried to calm me, but I was in no state to be soothed: "G-d d--nit," I believe I said, "that sonuvab--h killed my dog! Just go away and lemme be mad!" She gave it up and went back into the saloon.

"That girl cares 'bout you," said Just Dave. "You oughn't take it out on her."

I groused for a while, and then turned maudlin, crying about "poor old Dob" and what a louse I was, letting Dob pay for my grudge against Bill and how badly I treated Esme. Through it all, Just Dave kept talking to me in the same low voice he used to calm a frightened horse. He finally worked me around until I was feeling better. We decided to get on the road and saddled up.

First though, I went in and apologized to Esme. She was understanding about it, and I left feeling considerably uplifted. She walked me out, and rather than simply mounting Ilya, I decided to show off for my girl.

Ilya was standing sidelong to the hitching rail, so I took a couple running steps, leapt onto the rail, and then onto the unsuspecting Ilya. I was not expecting the explosion of fury my foolishness met with, and I woke up on a pallet in the shed behind the Fandango. There was barely an inch of me that wasn't bandaged, wrapped, or splinted, and Esme told me I'd been there for three days. I felt like the entire *Grande Armée*[13] had marched over me, but apparently it had only been Ilya, who had followed throwing me with dancing a jig on top of me. "You are one lucky G-dd--ned fool," Esme said, welcoming me back to the living.

It was another week before the doc would allow me to be moved, during which time we discovered that I was a terrible patient, and Esme a terrible nurse.

When I finally returned to the rancho, I was a chastened and much more humble man.

***

I think it is good that we are foolish when we are young and resilient – I was able to walk away from lessons (at least eventually) that would kill me if I had to learn them now. Of all the harsh lessons I've had to learn, humility was certainly the most painful, physically anyway.

---

[13] The army with which Napoleon invaded Russia in 1812. Roughly 600,000 men, 180,000 horses, plus artillery and supplies.

Chapter Six

A pleasant and private evening; an argument;
A selfish heart broken

Mrs. Good came to visit me again last night, and Sheriff Angus was good enough to give the night deputy the night off – a more compassionate and understanding jailer could not be hoped for. He didn't even ask me to promise not to escape; when the streets had quieted down, he simply locked the front door and went home, leaving us blessedly alone. She had brought food for us, beefsteak and potatoes with gravy, followed by pie, along with a couple bottles of good wine. After dinner, we played cribbage – she won, two out of three games, and then we retired to my cot. Later, snuggled in against me, she asked, "Why don't we just get out of here? We'll go tonight, and by the time anyone knows, we'll be far gone. We'll go far away, change our names, start over."

"You know I can't do that to Red. He's trusting me here."

The argument lasted deep into the night and reminded me that even the truest love often has a rocky road to travel.

California
1857-58

Although my love for Esme was true and deep, it was not blind. I did not blithely accept her profession – on the contrary, I tried everything to persuade her to leave that life. Nothing, not even the most ardent and sincere proposals of marriage, had any effect. She would simply smile sadly and pat my hand. "You're a sweet kid, Tolya," she would say, "but it's no use. You're never going to make enough punching cattle to take care of two of us, and you've got no ambition to be other than you are right now. All you want out of life is a horse, a few books, and room to roam."

"And you to share it,"

"Share what?" she'd ask. "You've got nothing. You want nothing. I've already got all the nothing I'll ever want. I'm aiming higher and when I see a chance, I'm going to grab hold with both hands." Sometimes she'd add, with her crooked, cavalier smile, "But if you ever get rich, ask me again."

One day I rented a buggy for an outing to enjoy the fall colours. We were bouncing along and she asked me to stop. She stared straight ahead, shoulders braced as if for a blow. "My daddy was a good man, but weak and a fool with money. When I was fourteen, he got into debt to one of the church elders, a mean, sour old b-----d who'd outlived two wives already. He told my daddy he would forgive the debt if daddy'd let him marry me. I loved my daddy, but I wasn't going to marry that old man. I decided if I was to be a w---e, I'd be one for myself, and ran off."

"I don't . . ."

"I found a bunch of miners bound for California and I used what G-d gave me to pay my way all the way to California. If I have to, I'll keep using it 'til I get where I aim to be. I'm not changing for you or no other man. If I change, it'll be for me." She looked at me with defiance in her eyes, but – it seemed to me – longing in her voice, "You need to think about that." It was a quiet ride back to town, but toward the end, she perked up and told me it was on that that trip that she met Samson. She wouldn't tell me any more than that though. "That's all between me and him," was all she would say.

Some may wonder why I didn't just find a "respectable" girl. I think I got my disdain for respectability from my parents. Their marriage was opposed by most "respectable" people, whether Russian or Buriat, but they chose love over respectability and were happier for it. All I can say for sure is even if there were any respectable girls in Shasta, Esme was the only girl I could see. She stirred my soul. I was as helpless to resist her as a leaf on a river.

Not all of my persuasions centered on her staying with me — at one point, Tasha sent me a book, *Journal Kept During the Russian War*, by Mrs. Henry Duberly[14], containing an account of her adventures during the war in the Crimea. I read it with mixed feelings — although I'd had to flee, it was difficult to read of Russia's defeat.

I shared it with Esme, using it to show her what a woman of strong character could accomplish and, although she found it as stirring as I, she rejected this

---

[14] Frances Isabella Duberly (1829-1902). One of the great adventuresses and diarists of the 19th Century, she was an eyewitness to not only the Crimean War (including the battle of Balaklava, which included the Charge of the Light Brigade), but also the Indian Mutiny.

argument too. “She’s got guts,” Esme admitted, “but at the end of it all, she’s still beholden to her husband. I’m going to make my own way in the world, or die trying.”

When one of Esme’s colleagues was horribly beaten by a client, I begged her to find a different line of work. She simply held up a six-barreled pepperbox[15]. “There’s not a woman in this world that’s safe, and a woman who counts on a man to make her feel safe is a fool. Besides, anything I can’t handle with this, Samson’ll take care of.”

I didn’t bother to point out the irony in her statement. Because of Samson’s response to unruly clients, her door had been replaced no less than four times. I had no desire to cause the fifth.

Finally, it came to an end. I received a letter from Mischa, who had rapidly risen from stable boy to trusted lieutenant — not surprising, given his enterprise and studious ways. Gold had been discovered in Kansas Territory, near what is now

---

[15] Most likely a .32 or .34 caliber Allen and Thurber Pepperbox pistol. Wildly inaccurate at any distance, it was strictly a close-range weapon about which Mark Twain said, “It was a cheerful weapon--the "Allen." Sometimes all its six barrels would go off at once, and then there was no safe place in all the region round about, but behind it. (*Roughing It*).

Denver, Colorado[16]. His employer knew the surest way to profit from a gold rush is selling necessities to the miners. He had commissioned Mischa to establish a ranch on the rangeland east of the Rockies, intending to corner the market on beef sales. Mischa offered me a small percentage to hire a crew, and several of the boys would soon be leaving with me to cross the mighty Rocky Mountains[i].

"I won't just be a cowboy anymore," I told Esme. "I've got a percentage in the business. The way those miners work up an appetite, I'll soon be rich as Croesus, with more than enough to take care of us both. Come with me. Marry me or don't, but come with me, please."

The timing couldn't have been worse. She had left the Fandango and set herself and two other girls up in a small house on the edge of town. It was a discreet establishment, catering to a select crowd. She just laughed at me. "Honey," she said, "come ask me when you are rich. It's more likely you'll end up butchered by

---

[16] Kansas Territory reached all the way to the summit of the Rocky Mountains until 1861, at which point the current state of Kansas was admitted to the Union and what is now known as Colorado became the Colorado Territory.

wild Indians. I've got a good thing here — why don't you stay with me? I'm taking on another girl, and Samson could use a hand keeping out the rough trade."

"D-mmit woman! Do you think I'd be happy being your fancy man? How little you think of me. If you won't save yourself from this horrible life, why won't you let me save you? Or do you enjoy being nothing but a w---e?"

Her eyes blazed and she slapped me. "D--n you! Is that all you see when you look at me? If you won't let me keep you, why the f--k d'you think I'd let you keep me? You sell your -ss in a saddle and I sell mine in a bed, and for a h--l of a lot more than you! I may be a w---e, but at least I'm not a cheap one, you self-righteous hypocrite!" Her door burst open and Samson stormed in, sap at the ready. Esme threw up her hand, halting him. Although her eyes were still afire, tears began to flow. "At least now I know what you really think of me — and what I'll always be to you!" She pointed to the door. "Get out of here! Just get out!"

Stung by her rejection and anger, and ashamed of my own outburst, I left. I returned, hat in hand, to beg her forgiveness the day before I left. Samson allowed me as far as the sitting room where Patty, one of her colleagues, met me.

"She won't see you," Patty said. "You're some piece of work, you know that? She won't eat, can't work. She's been cussin' and cryin' and carryin' on for three days now . . ."

"Please," I begged, "please ask her to see me. I was angry and didn't know what I was saying."

"Oh b-llsh-t! That's what you men always say, but you lie. You're all just big spoiled children — you don't care who gets hurt as long as you get what you want. Now get out of here before I let Samson pull you apart like a rag doll." Samson had murder in his eyes — he was practically salivating at the idea of killing me.

I went to the front door and turned in the doorway. "Please," I said, "tell her she's right, and I'm sorry and ashamed of myself. Tell her I'll always love her, and if she ever needs anything, she has only to call on me." I closed the door behind me and never saw Rahab again.

***

A day or two later, a cowboy rode up to our camp with a package for me. "Miz Rahab ast me to carry this to you, as I was headed thisaway," was all he said. He handed it to me and rode away. I opened it to find a

.36 Navy Colt revolver and package of cartridges, along with a note. I've long since lost the Colt but the note is still in my room now, tucked away in one of my books. It reads,

I hate you.
But don't let the Indians kill you,
as I may not always,
E

Chapter Seven

A new venture; an argument; the nature of business; an unpleasant man for an unpleasant task; death and relief

Few things concentrate a man's mind on Liberty as much as the losing of it. Although I am the first to admit that my situation could be much worse, I do wish they'd *just get on with it!* Nathan, of course, counsels patience. "The more they complain and maneuver and manipulate, the more they make themselves look like Goliath, and you like David, and you know how that came out." Poor boy – he means well, but he'd not be so sanguine if he'd been witness to how most Davids come out against Goliaths in this part of the world as I have.

Kansas Territory
1859

Mischa filed a claim on the land in Denver, and returned with a train of wagons loaded with lumber and workmen to construct the buildings. Jack had driven a herd up from Texas, steers to be fattened up and sold, as well as breeding stock to increase the herd. Another herd came in from eastern Kansas under a fellow named Poke Carlin.

Poke was a quiet, uncanny man. One night over chow, I asked how he came to be called "Poke". He stared with his pale gray eyes for a moment, and drawled, "It started as Slowpoke, and kinda got whittled down from there."

Poke was reticent about his past, but some bits and bobs escaped him. He'd gotten on the wrong side of someone over slavery, always a dangerous thing in "Bleeding Kansas[17]". It wasn't clear which side he'd taken in Kansas but he showed no animosity to Just Dave, so it never really was an issue to me. Jack felt differently.

One night Jack was unusually deep in the oh-be-joyful, which was not working. We were alone by the fire, most of the boys had either turned in or were off about their own business. Just Dave, Poke, and Bill Morrow were out on a scout.

"I wisht you'd leave Dave alone, d--n you," he said.

---

[17] From 1854 – 1861, abolitionist and pro-slavery factions waged a murderous guerrilla war over whether Kansas would be a free or slave state. Kansas entered the Union as a free state on January 29, 1861, but the violence would continue throughout most of the Civil War.

"What do you mean?"

"All that s--t you keep fillin' his head with — Rights o' Man, and ownin' hisself, and teachin' him to read, and such. You oughta just leave the poor fella alone."

"I'd think you'd want to help him improve himself. You're the best friend he has. You've killed men on his behalf."

He took another snort. "G-dd--n you! I know what I done, an' I'd do it again. It's because I'm his friend that I'm tellin' you this — leave him alone! You're gonna get him killed."

"You need to put that bottle away," I said. "You're being ridiculous."

"Ridiculous? I'll tell you what's ridiculous. Dave's out there with that no-count sumb---h Bill and that night-riding b-----d Poke Carlin, an' I ain't out there to back him up!"

"Bill is a nasty piece of work, but Poke? I've never heard him say a word against Dave. What have you got against him?"

"You wanna know what I got against Poke? He pals around with Morrow. Only thing gets along with a rattlesnake is another rattlesnake. Them two're peas in a nasty pod, and Dave's out there with 'em. You know

Bill hates Dave. There's nothing keeping them from plugging Dave and blaming the Injuns, and too many of these other b-----ds wouldn't bother to even ask questions. Hell of it is, even if Dave killed 'em both, he'd have to tell the same bullshit story about Injuns, unless he wanted to get strung up."

"Oh that's a bit much, don't you think? Dave is much more highly regarded than either Bill or Poke."

"Highly regar – highly regarded, you say?" He swigged from the bottle, and then spat. "Yer an educated man Nate, but you don't know s--t. Lemme tell you something. Back home there was a feller had a dog. Never saw a man love a dog more'n he did. Well he also had a passel o' kids, and one of 'em was a mean little s--t. One day, that little sumb—h tied that dog to a stake, and laid into it with a stick, just beatin' the daylights out of it for no reason other'n meanness. Well, he got careless and that dog turned on him and bit him good and deep. To give that feller credit, once the boy was healed up, he beat that kid like a rented mule, but before that happened, he shot that poor dog. See, he loved that dog, but he couldn't take a chance it might bite another kid. These boys'd be the same with

Dave. They couldn't take a chance he'd kill another white man."

"What can we do? Should we go look for them?"

He gestured toward the endless prairie, sloshing whisky as he did. "The f--k we gonna look?" He took another belt.

"Alright, Jack, I take your point," I said. "But shall we keep Dave from learning, from educating himself, for fear of what someone else might think? That hardly seems fair to Dave."

"Fair? Who the hell said anything about fair?" Jack's eyes shone with tears. "Is it fair he was born black? Was it fair I had to choose between him and my own family? Was it fair that my own daddy cursed me for a n----r lover and an unnatural child? F--k yer 'fair'." The bottle slipped from his numbed fingers as his eyes closed and his voice trailed off, "Smart-ss Russian -sshole, thinks he knows everthin'. . . Don't know s--t!" I'd never heard anyone snore angrily, but Jack managed it that night.

I thought deep into the night about it, and about Just Dave's circumstances, and what I – or he – could do about it. In the distance, a coyote howled, the loneliest sound in the world. I thought that must be how Dave felt so much of the time. When the sun broke the horizon, I still had no answer.

Two days later, Just Dave, Poke, and Bill rode into camp, dusty and hungry but none the worse for wear. They had found a lot of Indian sign, and several of us decided some target practice might be in order. We all had long guns, and most had handguns of some sort, but Poke was the only one who went heavily armed. He always had two Navy Colts tucked butt-forward into his belt, and two massive Colt Dragoons in saddle holsters. When he went on a scout, he added two more revolvers in a shoulder rig[18]. Naturally, we turned to Poke for advice.

"Take your time and hit what you aim at," he said. "It ain't natural to kill a man, so while the other feller is blasting away all over the place, you'll have plenty of time to aim. The good news is it's a lot easier to kill a man when you know he's trying to kill you."

"You ever kill a man?" asked Dutch. "What's it like?"

"Killing's like everything else," Poke replied, "the more you do it, the easier it gets." He might have been

---

[18] Poke's arsenal is another clue that he may have been a Southern sympathizer. During the Civil War, many Missouri "Bushwhackers" – southern guerrilla fighters - were known to carry up to eight revolvers into battle.

talking about herding cattle or roping, or any other mundane task. He just didn't seem to have any feelings about it at all. Being young and needing to prove myself, I found his blasé attitude toward violence impressive.

***

One day Dutch and Ollie Parker reported a family setting up on a corner of our range with good water and grass. Mischa was very upset. "They get away with setting up on our range, and every other penny ante outfit will move in on us. It won't be long until we're out of business," he said, when I asked him what the problem was.

"My G-d, Mischa," I said, "there's millions of acres out here – surely there's enough room for everyone."

He waved his arms broadly. "Look out there Tolya. What do you see?"

"Just range land, Mischa, miles and miles of open country."

"Yes, and what don't you see?"

"You mean other than a whole lot of empty country?"

"Water, Tolya," he answered. "There's no d----d water out there. We've been lucky so far and had a fair amount of rain and runoff from the mountains, but when it gets dry, we're going to need every drop there is. You think that fellow is going to take lightly to our cattle drinking up water he thinks is his?"

I saw his point. "But," I said, "what gives us any more right to it than him?"

"Because we were here first, d-mm-t. We've laid out a huge investment bringing these herds in here. An outfit like ours can feed hundreds, even thousands. That little outfit'll be lucky to feed itself. And how do you think that fellow is going to enlarge his herd? We drove in entire herds of breeding stock. He's got what, a few breeding cows? We let him stick around, we're going to see those two or three cows birthing three calves a year each."

"Mischa, you can't just assume he'd steal our calves."

"Tolya, listen to me," he said. "You're a good cowhand, but you've got no head for business. In business you either take what's yours or what's yours gets taken."

He was right, I was no kind of businessman, but it rankled. I still wasn't happy about it the next day when I was told to take Poke, Dutch, Jack, and Just Dave to go warn them off. I didn't want to do it, but when you ride for a brand, you ride where and how it says, or you quit. For the first time in my life, I had money coming in and I wasn't ready to give that up. After breakfast, we rode out.

***

"What's your plan?" asked Jack. "Just ride up and tell 'em to clear off?"

"I suppose I'll try to be a little more politic than that," I replied.

"You gonna tell 'em to clear off please?" That got a chuckle from the others. "You reckon they'll just say, 'Oh certainly sir, we'll just move right on, and by the way, would you like us to kiss your ring for you?'"

"D-mm-t Jack, what would you have me do? Just ride up and burn them out? Shoot their cattle? Shoot them out of hand?"

"Well," drawled Poke, "that'd work better'n please.'"

"Well then, what do you suggest?"

"Don't give 'em a choice. Tell 'em they're trespassing and they need to clear out. Tell 'em don't stop moving 'til they're at least the other side of Denver."

"Poke's right," added Jack. "It ain't likely there's more'n three or four of 'em, so we got numbers on our side. They'd have to be some hard-barked b-----ds to buck those odds."

"You ought to let Poke or Jack do the talking when we get there," Just Dave said quietly.

"Why in h--l would I do that? Don't you think I'm man enough to do this?"

"It ain't a matter of being man enough," said Just Dave. "It's a matter of convincing them without any bloodshed. You want to kill them?"

"You know I don't."

"You really think you can reason them off this land? If you don't want to have to kill 'em, they have to know that we *will* kill 'em. Jack or Poke can do that. You're kind, and they'd see that, think they had some wiggle room, and it'd get 'em killed."

I could see his point, but it was my first time in command of men. "I'll think about it," was all I said.

He held up his hands placatingly. "All I ask," he said. He gestured back toward the rest of the boys. "Keep in mind though, them nesters are likely to kill some of ours 'f it comes down to a fight."

In the end, I swallowed my pride and told Poke to take the lead. I'd feel bad enough if we ended up having to kill the nesters. I couldn't let my pride get my friends killed, and Poke was far more intimidating and experienced than I. When we grew near, we spotted a youth of about seventeen herding a few head of cattle. He saw us at about the same time and took off like a scalded cat toward their camp.

"Well, they'll know we're comin'," said Poke. "You boys be ready. When we get there, spread out. Easier to get shot if you're bunched up."

His guidance reassured me I'd made the right decision, but I still worried. "Poke," I said, "I don't want any shooting."

"Best way to make sure of that is to make sure they see we're ready for it and know what we're doing."

The nesters were living in a rudely constructed dugout[19]. The youth was nowhere to be seen, but his mount was in a corral with several others. A bearded man of about fifty stood in front of the open door holding a shotgun. "Howdy," he said, "my boy said there was riders comin' in." He nodded at the shotgun. "Thought it best to be safe."

"Always better to be safe," said Poke. "Safe is good."

---

[19] A dugout was a common frontier shelter made by digging into the side of a hill or bank, and then adding a roof.

"My name's Whitacre — Joseph Whitacre," the man said with a smile. "You fellers 'light and set if you've a mind." Turning to the dugout, he called, "It's alright boys, come on out." To us he said, "It's good to see a white face. We ain't seen one since we got here a month ago."

"Seen injuns?" Poke asked.

"Lotta sign, but we ain't seen any in person."

"You'll want to keep a close eye out," said Poke. "Lotta fellers, their first sight of an injun is the last thing they ever see."

"Aye, you're right there," said Whitacre. "This here's my boys Joe Jr. and Sam," he said, introducing the two young men who had exited the dugout. One carried a rifled musket, the other a shotgun. Three more men with rifles stood up from the long grass atop the dugout. "That's my brother Ephraim and his boys up top. So," Whitacre continued, "is this call business or pleasure?"

"Fraid its business," said Poke. "You fellers are set up on land claimed by our outfit. You need to pack up and git."

"Friend," said Whitacre, "I appreciate your directness." He jerked a thumb over his shoulder at the dugout where two rifle barrels were now protruding from firing ports. "That's my wife and daughter. Now, I'll be direct with you. We ain't going nowhere. We're neighborly, peaceable folk — like to get along with everybody — but we won't be pushed. Not by injuns, and not by you."

"Well," said Poke, leaning forward on the horn of his saddle, "since you like directness, I'll just say this — we'll be ridin' back this way in a week or two and either you'll be gone, or you'll never leave it. Be a shame to make your wife a widow, but that's just the way it's going to be. Until then though, I'll wish you well." He gathered his reins, turned his horse and rode slowly away. We followed his lead.

After we'd been riding for half an hour or so, I couldn't hold back anymore. "Well, we sure told them," I said.

"Shut up kid," was all Poke said, but it was enough.

Over the next few days, I found myself thinking more and more about the Whitacres and the whole situation. Mischa's point made sense — our larger size meant we had a larger need, but did that mean we had more right? Was a legal claim on the land enough to justify killing? It also made me think about my position at the ranch — owning a share made me part owner. Did that make me responsible for any blood shed?

I was also forced to consider something else — what if I was a coward? I'd never really thought about it. In honesty, it was this that concerned me most — more than issues of right and wrong, or responsibility — how could I face my friends or myself if I should prove a coward? One night, I asked Jack about it.

"Lucky," he said, "you never know until you find out."

"What the h--l does that mean?" I asked.

"There's many a big talker that's turned yellow once the shooting starts, but there's a lot who worried about it that turned out to have plenty of sand. Only way to find out is to be in that sort of fix."

"Well that's reassuring," I grumped.

"Ain't something you can be reassured about," he said. "At least you've got enough brains to think about it. Just make sure you don't scare yourself too much before you find out for sure."

***

Ten days after our trip to the Whitacres' we mounted up to go back. We took fifteen men — every man we could spare.

You think they'll still be there?" I asked Jack.

"What do you think?"

"I think they'll be gone. They have to know they're overmatched."

"I hope you're right. I kinda liked that old boy. But they look to be the kind that don't run." He sighed. "I reckon we'll see."

About a half hour out from their camp, we found the two youngest Whitacre boys, stripped, scalped, and shot through with arrows. They'd been dead for days.

"J---s," said Dutch. Big Dave crossed himself, and I just stared. Even Jack and Dave, who'd fought Comanches in Texas, were visibly disturbed.

Only Poke was unmoved. "C'mon," he said, "nothing we can do for them."

"Shouldn't we bury them?" asked Big Dave.

"Need to look to the living first," Poke said. "Can't help these any. Might not be the same for the others.

We found Ephraim Whitacre and one of his boys dead and mutilated in a buffalo wallow. A blood trail led about a mile, to the remains of the last Whitacre boy and his horse. Finally, we reached their home. The corral was knocked down and the dugout was partly caved in. Whitacre was pin-cushioned with arrows.

Mrs. Whitacre lay with a crushed skull in the debris of the dugout. Her clothes had been stripped and she had been defiled. We found no sign of the Whitacre girl.

"Why?" I asked. "Why would any human being do this?"

"Oh knock it off," growled Poke. "We came here meaning to do the same d--ned thing."

I gestured at Mrs. Whitacre. "Not to do that," I said. "Never that."

Poke shrugged. "What's the difference?" he asked grimly. "Whitacre shouldn't've brought his womenfolk out here in the first place. Far as the Cheyenne go, well h--l, people get unreasonable when they think someone's takin' what's theirs."

"We're at least going to try tracking them aren't we?" I asked.

"Lucky," said Jack, "from the looks of it, this all happened over a week ago. Them Injuns could be anywhere by now."

"H--l," added Poke, "they're just as likely to have had their fill of the girl and traded her off to a different bunch. We need to get back to protect our own."

We quickly gathered the bodies and, in lieu of graves, placed them in the dugout and caved the rest of it in on them.

Big Dave recited over them: "And God shall wipe away all tears from their eyes: and death shall be no more, nor mourning, nor crying, nor sorrow shall be any more, for the former things are passed away. And he that sat on the throne, said: Behold, I make all things new."

It seemed hypocritical to be praying over the bodies of men we'd intended to kill ourselves, but in the end, I think we were all relieved as we mounted up and returned home.

***

The Whitacres seemed to be good men, no different than myself or my companions, yet they were doomed by their decision to stay. If the Cheyenne hadn't killed them, we would have, whether we wanted to or not. They were Davids, and the whole world was their Goliath. It chills me to think how close I came to being what I hate most.

Chapter Eight

Bill and Mischa; an unexpected death; an old mystery solved; Death or exile – vengeance or justice; punishment of a bad man; War!; a sorrowful parting

Kansas Territory
1861

It was no secret that I had been very sorry to see Mischa hire Bill Morrow, but Bill had a way of ingratiating himself to those in authority, and bookish Mischa, never very sure of himself among the rough-and-tumble cowhands, had proved susceptible to Bill's toadying, despite my warnings. Bill took advantage of his standing with Mischa to bully many of the younger men – at least those inexperienced enough to let him get away with it. The older men, Bill left alone. He also, just as he had at the Dos Rios Rancho, surrounded himself with men who favoured his kind of vicious fun — in any group of men, there are always those who enjoy fun at others' expense.

Within a year of arriving in Kansas Territory, Bill had used his influence with Mischa to worm his way into the position of foreman of the Circle N Ranch, for which everyone but Mischa could see he was completely unqualified. Although a competent cowhand, he was also petty, jealous, cruel, and above all, a fool. The experienced hands ignored him for the most part and simply did what needed to be done, but his overbearing ways and obvious incompetence made it hard to keep good hands. Many rode away without even asking for their wages — it was worth it to them just to get away from Bill.

Not all of the younger fellows let Bill buffalo them or drive them away. Jesus del Fuego was one such. He was a good-natured Mexican orphan of about fifteen, full of life and laughter. He worked uncomplainingly at any task, which made him a great favourite with most of us. Bill took an instant dislike to him and lost no opportunity to try to put Jesus in his place, usually unsuccessfully, which only increased his hatred of the boy.

Jesus, on the other hand, merely laughed at Bill's efforts. "Why should I take offense?" he laughed, "Every time he tries to humiliate me and fails, he harms himself more than I ever could." Jesus had a knack for philosophy that I envied. I suspected he also had a knack for good-natured vengeance. Not long after

Jesus arrived, it seemed that whenever Bill got carried away picking on any of the youngsters, his food would be spiked with unusually hot chilis, or his boots would be found full of water in the morning, or the outhouse door would be mysteriously tied shut with Bill inside on a hot day — the inventiveness of Bill's tormentor was an endless source of frustration for Bill and amusement for the rest of us. Although no one ever saw Jesus do anything, and he was often not even around when the pranks came to fruition, Jesus was the main suspect, purely because of his unflappable calm in the face of Bill's boorishness, and Bill swore revenge against the affable youth. Jesus, as always, just laughed and went about his business.

One day we had some mustangs needing to be broke in. One, an uncut stallion we called Old Scratch was extremely aggressive and wild. You took your life in your hands just getting a bridle and saddle on him – it took a special courage to try to mount him. On the day in question, Bill and two men undertook to saddle Old Scratch. Jesus had been pleading for a chance to prove himself in the breaking of horses, and once they had him saddled, Bill pointed at Jesus. "Give the kid a try," he said.

"D-mmit Bill, you can't start the kid off on that man-killer!" cried Salty Davis. "That's too much hoss for most of the full-grown men around here!"

Most of the men nodded in agreement. "I sure wouldn't want no piece of that hoss," said one. "He ain't called Old Scratch for nothing," called another, "I'd druther face the Devil hisself than throw a leg over that b-----d. Least I could run from the Devil." Several more chimed in likewise. None of these men were cowards, and all were experienced, competent horsemen, but Old Scratch was a demon wrapped in horsehide, and even the best riders on the ranch, like Salty and myself approached him with an abundance of caution.

"Bill," I said, "start the kid out on one of the others. Let Salty or me tackle this one."

"No, d-mmit," said Bill, "the kid's been begging to show what he's made of, and I aim to let him." Turning to Jesus, he said, "Well boy, you gonna climb aboard, or you gonna show yellow?"

The blood drained from Jesus' face, but he squared up and climbed through the rails of the corral. He approached Old Scratch slowly, talking in a low, encouraging voice. Salty, Jack, and I continued to argue with Bill, finally telling him that we'd hold him responsible if anything should happen to the boy.

"All right, all right," he said, "You win." He called Jesus back and told Dutch to go get the roan. "We'll see what the kid's made of," he said, eyeballing me, "and then we'll bring Old Scratch back out and see what you're made of."

Bill helped get the roan, the most docile of all the unbroken mustangs, saddled. Jesus, who'd been justifiably frightened of Old Scratch, looked positively insulted. "Alright kid," Bill called to Jesus, "she's all yours."

Dutch held the horse while Bill left the corral and turned to watch. Jesus swaggered forward and swung aboard. He'd barely landed in the saddle when the horse went insane, bucking and twisting and sunfishing like it was possessed. Jesus was flung around like a sock puppet, but hung on gamely, grabbing leather for all he was worth. There was nothing we could do but hope Jesus could hang on until the roan tired. Finally the horse leapt into the air, landed wrong, and we heard its leg snap. It toppled over and Jesus was trapped under it while it writhed in agony, it's flailing legs keeping us at bay. Just Dave got a loop over its head, and several of us grabbed hold and dragged it off the boy. Just Dave lay across its neck while Jack put a bullet in its brainpan, and the rest of us turned to Jesus. He was bloody, broken, and stove in, clearly not long for this world. We couldn't move him without his screaming in agony, and we couldn't help but notice that though his obviously broken arms flapped helplessly, his legs didn't move at all. His suffering was blessedly short — within a few minutes it was over.

We were all in shock. We had all seen death, but never like this. That roan had never acted like that before. How in G-d's name were we to know it would react like that to the saddle? Jack, Dutch, Big Dave, and I took the body to prepare it. Since he'd been wearing pretty much everything he owned, we went amongst the boys to get him outfitted. Most everyone contributed something: clothing, boots, mementos — Jesus was well-loved. We built him a coffin, and Salty lined it with his best blanket. Joe Johanson and Danny Bailey carved him a headstone. We gave Jesus the best sendoff we could, and many spoke at the funeral, Big Dave finishing it up with his usual recitation. Even Bill Morrow seemed broken up about it.

The next morning before breakfast, Salty and Just Dave drew Jack, Big Dave, and myself aside. “That horse didn’t go crazy and kill that poor boy,” said Salty. “It was drove to it.” He held out his hand, showing us four burrs. “Me and Just Dave found these under the saddle blanket. Soon’s Jesus hit that saddle, these started diggin’ in, and it just got worse with ever’ bounce.”

Jack and Big Dave looked at Just Dave. “Remind you of something?” Jack asked.

Just Dave nodded. “We’ve seen this before,” he told the rest of us. “Few years back, Nate here near got killed by a horse. We found the same thing under his saddle. At the time, we figured Nate’d just been careless ‘cause he was drunk. I’m not so sure now.”

“What are you sayin?” asked Danny. “One of us did this on purpose?”

Jack shook his head. “I’m saying Bill Morrow did this. He hated Nate, but couldn’t never get the better of him. It was the same with Jesus. We never suspected Bill ‘cause — well, it just didn’t seem the sorta stunt anybody would pull intentionally, not even him. But we all watched him saddle that roan. Who else coulda done it?”

"That sonuvab---h," breathed Salty. "What we gonna do 'bout this?"

"We oughta hang him," said Big Dave. Jack, Salty, and I agreed.

"No," said Just Dave. "I got no love for Bill Morrow neither, but we can't just hang him out of hand. Ought to at least have some kinda trial."

We decided to leave it up to the men. Salty gathered the rest of the fellows while Jack and Big Dave corralled Bill and I rousted out Mischa and explained the situation to him.

Bill tried to bluster his way out of it, but when the talk turned to hanging, he went pale and started begging. "It was an accident," he cried. "I didn't mean the kid to get hurt, just to teach him a lesson."

"Teach him a lesson!" exclaimed Salty, "You tried to make him tackle Old Scratch!"

"I wasn't gonna make him ride Scratch," protested Bill. "That was just for show! I wanted to scare him, and then see him get throwed offa that roan. You all know how cocky he was. I just wanted to take him down a peg or two! Tell 'em, Dutch!"

Dutch, who'd remained quiet throughout the proceedings, coloured as we all looked at him. He nodded. "It's true," he said, "Bill was just playing a trick on the kid. If he'd've meant to hurt Jesus, I wouldn't have gone along with it, and I wish to G-d I hadn't anyway. I swear, I didn't think he'd get hurt. That kid was a h--luva rider, and that horse was d---ned near tame as could be." Dutch's head hung low, and tears ran down his face. "I swear I thought the only thing that'd get hurt was his pride."

There was some murmuring that Dutch ought to be hung alongside Bill, but those voices were quickly shouted down. I looked to Mischa to take charge and get things under control, but he didn't seem to have any idea of what to do – he was clearly longing to be back in his San Francisco office, and far from here.

The arguing among the men was getting worse, some wanting to hang Bill, while others were for stripping him naked, taking him out and leaving him to the mercy of the Cheyenne. Some simply wanted to beat him within an inch of his life, and those few friends he had were all very quiet.

Poke was just watching it all with those watery grey eyes of his. Finally, he fired a shot in the air, getting everyone's attention. "Listen to you all. Buncha tough guys you are. There's been enough death around here.

We ain't hanging nobody, and we ain't leaving nobody out for the injuns, so just shut up about that right now." He saw Bill nodding gratefully, and said to him, "You got half an hour to pack your s--t, get outa here, and don't ever come back. I see you around here again, I'll kill you myself." He turned to the shrinking group of Bill's supporters. "Any of you want to go with him can go. Otherwise, keep your mouths shut." To Bill he said, "I ain't kidding," and drew back the hammer on his Colt for emphasis.

It only took twenty minutes for Bill to leave the ranch.

After that, Poke and Jack took over the ranching operations. Mischa established an office in Denver, an atmosphere he was much more at home in, and life went back to normal. Occasionally, someone would pass through and bring news of the world at large. In early March, we learned that the eastern part of the territory had been admitted into the Union as the state of Kansas, and we were now located in the Territory of Colorado.

It was about the middle of March that a passing whisky drummer[20] brought news of the secession of

[20] Traveling salesmen were known as "drummers".

several southern states, including Jack and Just Dave's home state of Texas, and the impending war. We had a lot of questions, and he had very few answers, but he left us a couple newspapers for us to pore over and argue about. Right away, the ranch was divided. Oddly enough, the most violent divides weren't between Northerners and Southerners, but within the ranks of each. There were states-rights Southerners, pro-slavery Southerners, pro-Union Southerners, anti-slavery Southerners, and the same among the Northerners. Several fights broke out over the next few days.

Three days later, I saw Jack, Poke, and several of the other Texans and southerners, along with a few Northerners saddling up.

"Jack," I said, "what are you doing? After what you went through . . ."

"I know Nate," he said, "but it's still my home. A man's gotta defend his home."

"But you know slavery's wrong."

"This ain't about slavery, not for me anyway. It's about home, about family. It's about honour."

The others had mounted. "Jack," Poke said, "you comin' or what?"

"Poke, what are you doing riding south? You're from Kansas and Kansas is for the Union." I said.

"I'm from Missouri," he said. "I just spent time in Kansas fightin' them Jayhawkers, 'til it got too hot an' I come out here to let it cool down a bit. I reckon it's time to go back and take another crack at Jim Lane, Charley Jennison[21] and the rest of them Yankee sumb--hes." He turned to Jack. "We're leavin'. You can catch up." To me he said, "Good luck kid," and he turned and rode away, the rest of them following.

Jack looked as lost as I've ever seen a man. He watched Poke and the others go, and then looked back to Just Dave, who was leaning against the corral, watching. He handed his reins to me. "Hold her for a minute will you?" He walked slowly over to Just Dave, and the two of them stood talking quietly for a few moments; Jack appeared to be pleading with Just Dave, who just shook his head sadly. Finally, the two shook hands, and Jack returned, wiping away tears.

He took the reins and mounted. "I guess when you can't have what you want, you just gotta keep what you

---

[21] James Lane, Charles Jennison were two leaders of Jayhawkers, anti-slavery guerrilla forces in Kansas. Essentially the northern equivalent of the South's Bushwhackers.

have, whether you want it or not. Be seein' you," he said, and rode away after the others. Just Dave stalked away in the other direction, shaking his head.

Part Two:

Soldier

Chapter Nine

War games; on war; more than just two sides; "Jining up"; Army life; new pals; a long march

Children are playing army in the streets this afternoon. The air is full of their cries of valour as they take and retake positions, attack and counterattack, accompanied by the usual "I shot you!" and "No, you missed!" arguments. Frequently, one will clutch his chest or head and fall dramatically to the ground, only to be resurrected moments later, flushed with excitement and glory. It makes me sad.

I will say that there is something special about being a soldier though – the camaraderie, the common purpose, the sense of belonging, the brotherhood. The Army is a family, albeit a sometimes harsh one, with its own customs, traditions, and discipline, and like all families, you have to take the good with the bad.

Colorado Territory
1861

After the departure of Jack, Poke, and the others, the war became an even hotter topic of conversation. Several of the men talked about going east to "jine up" back home. Others planned to stay out of it any way they could. "I ain't got a dog in this fight," was how Dutch put it. When the camp talk turned to the matter of slavery, virtually none of the fellows had a dog. The prevailing sentiments ran from the religious – "I reckon that's how God wants it" – to the scornful – "I ain't got nothin' 'gainst n----rs, but I ain't met one yet worth getting my own -ss shot off over."

While most of the remaining men were pro-Union, Big Dave and I were the only two who were outspoken about our opposition to slavery: mine was based on my own thoughts, the writings of Locke, Paine, etc., and my friendship with Just Dave.

Big Dave's feelings came from his experiences with British rule in Ireland. "The law ought to apply to every man the same, and protect every man the same," was how he put it. "Me da' was hung for defendin' me ma against two soldiers who attacked her. He killed one of 'em, and beat the other near to death, and nary a charge was pressed against the one who lived. Me uncle died in prison just for bein' suspected of fomentin' revolution. He never even had a trial."

Just Dave, of course, was against slavery but kept his opinions to himself unless explicitly asked a question, and then his answers tended to be extremely tactful.

Around July or August, we heard that Governor Gilpin was recruiting a regiment of volunteers, and there was much talk about enlisting. Mischa, worried about having enough men to operate the ranch, tried to dissuade us, especially me. "Tolya," he said, "why get involved in this ridiculous war? This is an American problem. Let them kill each other while you and I stay out of it and build something."

"This is our country, Mischa," I said. "We chose to come here, to become a part of it. Besides, it's not just the Union — it's a chance to strike a blow for the freedom of all men. It's what Father raised both of us to believe in." They were high-minded words and well-meant, but honestly, I was motivated as much by the siren song of adventure as I was by any noble sentiment.

"You'd make a terrible soldier," he said. "You hate taking orders. You'll end up flogged or in the guardhouse."

"Yes Mischa, I do hate taking orders, but d-mmit man, can't you see some things are necessary, even if they go against the grain?"

"You know what an army needs just as much as men? Supplies. Food. *Beef.* In the army, you'll be one soldier pulling a trigger. In this business, you can feed dozens, even hundreds of soldiers. You can make a bigger contribution by staying here! And the Army will be paying top dollar! You can serve and get rich at the same time!"

"There are more important things than money, Mischa."

"Tolya, the chances are they won't even let you in – you look as much Indian as you do white."

"Well then you're worried about nothing, aren't you?" I said and walked away. Mischa was a businessman through and through and always thinking of the bottom line. Regardless of his efforts, Big Dave, several others, and I rode into Denver and volunteered. I tried to convince Just Dave to join us. "How can you not want to fight to end slavery?" I asked him.

"It ain't that I don't want to fight," he said. "But you think they'll let me fight? Put a uniform on me and treat me like any other soldier? Nate, how you live here all these years and still not see how things work?"

"Well, maybe you could be a scout or something? Dammit, someone has to make the change!"

"And that someone needs to be me? I'm gonna change the army?" He gestured toward the other fellows. "Look at them boys," he said. "They're fightin' for their state, or their home, or the Union, or even for fun, but other than you and Big Dave, there ain't hardly a one that gives a d--n about slaves. They may think it's wrong, but not wrong enough to get shot over. Their friends start dyin', they're liable to take it out on the first black -ss they see, and I ain't gonna be in front of that. I'll stay right here and help Mr. Mischa sell cattle to the army. That's how I'm gonna fight."

***

Although Mischa was partly right — it took quite a bit of work, including the testimony of my comrades to convince the recruiting officers that I wasn't an Indian or a Chinese — I finally managed to enlist,[22]

---

[22] The objection to Native Americans serving in the Union must have been a local, or even a personal, decision on the part of recruitment officers. Many Native Americans served in the Union Forces, including three regiments of the Indian Home Guard, and Company M, 14th Kansas Cavalry. Lt. Col. Ely S. Parker served as General

and ended up listed as Private Luck on the regimental roster. Big Dave and I were assigned to Company A, 1st Colorado Volunteers, under the command of Capt. Edward Wynkoop, a tall, lively, dashing gentleman with drooping mustaches framing a narrow mouth, and a shock of dark hair shading close-set green eyes.

Capt. Wynkoop was determined to turn us ruffians into disciplined soldiers, and 1st Sergeant Slater and the other NCO's went to it with a will. Of course, we did not become soldiers overnight. There were many instances of poor behaviour – mostly the result of high spirits. Several of the men augmented our rations with chicken-stealing, and drunken hooliganism was an ongoing problem, but in all, they were a splendid bunch of comrades.

Besides Big Dave, David "Frenchy" Dompierre, a quick-witted, tidy little Frenchman with twinkling eyes, fierce mustachios, and a ribald sense of humour grew to be my closest friend. He had an unquenchable thirst for champagne and was notorious for stealing cases of the stuff. He had served in the Crimea and fought at the Alma, Balaklava, and Inkerman, and the siege of

---

Grant's adjutant and secretary, and the final draft of the terms of surrender signed by Lee at Appomattox is written in his hand.

Sebastopol. One of the few professional soldiers in the regiment, he was quickly promoted to sergeant. That very night, he stole a case of champagne from a saloon right in front of the owner, who apprehended and held him while waiting for the Provost Marshal.

Such was Frenchy's immense charm that he persuaded the saloon owner to enjoy the champagne with him while they waited. "I simply pointed out to him that the empty bottles and my state of drunkenness would be just as damning, and much more fun," he later said. He was reduced to private again, which was his goal.

"I will never command men again," he said. "I'll fight yes, but I'll never send my friends to their deaths again. I'll leave that to lesser men." During our time together, he was promoted at least six times, and each time he quickly acted to ensure his immediate demotion.

I asked him once about his fondness for champagne. "I've seen the worst the world has to offer," he told me one night over a bottle or three of the best he could get his hands on, "and decided to enjoy as much of its best whenever I could. The worst will always find you out, *mon ami* — you have to fight for the good."

Frenchy was not the only man in the company with prior military experience: 1st Sergeant Slater and Sgt. Tomson had served in the Mexican war. 1st Sergeant Slater was particularly ruthless when it came to matters of health and sanitation: "Your souls may be black as coal, but your persons, your equipment, and your camp will be spotless!" was his invariable refrain. "Disease and unclean habits have killed more soldiers than all the weapons ever wielded!" Although strict, he had some sympathy for the more common failings — drink, brawling, etc. — but none for any unhygienic man.

Frenchy backed him up on that. "In the Crimea," he said, "I lost far more friends to cholera, dysentery, and other diseases than to Russian bullets[23]. Keep yourselves clean, *mes amis*, and you're far more likely to survive the war."

Several other men had also served, either in the Mexican War, or one or more of the Indian wars, either as regulars or volunteers, and they helped snap us tyros into shape.

---

[23] In the Crimean War, 2/3 of French fatalities and as many as 7/8 of British losses were from disease, according to some estimates.

I was fairly typical of my company. Initially I chafed under the discipline and scorned the drill as simply "playing soldier". I longed to come to grips with the enemy, and prove my mettle – what did it matter if we could walk in a straight line or turn as a group? Would the enemy be intimidated by the shine of our boots and brass? All that mattered was that we could fight, and we certainly did enough of that in our own camp. As a result, many of us spent a fair amount of time in the guardhouse or on punishment detail until we finally became a cohesive military unit.

In October we heard a strong force of Texans was invading New Mexico Territory, driving north to capture the gold fields of Colorado Territory. That news inspired us to buckle down to our work, and by January, we were a fine, tough fighting force.

In late February, we marched for New Mexico Territory. Our march did not begin auspiciously; slogging through deep snow in freezing cold, we took five days just to make a few miles. We all grew several inches in height every day, from the snow and ice frozen to the soles of our boots, and I'm not sure we wouldn't have all frozen to death if it hadn't been for the great mounds of snow that built up on us as we marched.

Early one morning, as we were preparing to resume the march, there was a great tumult in camp, and Big Dave ran over and ordered us to "load weapons boys and form up!"

We hurriedly loaded our weapons and were formed up facing I Company who were milling about in confusion. "What's going on?" I asked Frenchy.

"How should I know? *Pour l'amour de la merde*, haven't I been here with you all morning?"

Colonel Slough, the regimental commander was on horseback, shouting and waving his pistol at the I Company commander, who was shouting back, and ordering his men to aim at the Colonel. We were ordered to take aim at I Company, and E Company was doing the same.

"*Mon Dieu*, what kind of army have I joined?" muttered Frenchy. "F--king *incompétents*!"

Major Chivington, a huge bear of a man, rode into the middle of the hubbub shouting threats. Col. Slough barked some orders to him and rode away. Chivington apparently sorted things out with Kerber[24], and I was relieved when our cold, wet, miserable march resumed — I'd joined the Army to fight the enemy, not to slaughter my own comrades.

***

On the first of March, we learned Sibley's Texans had defeated the Union forces at Valverde — the very troops we were meant to reinforce. That began a series of forced marches that pushed us to our limits through rain and snow, until we thought we'd all freeze, drown, or die of exhaustion before we ever fired a shot. Only Frenchy, that seasoned campaigner, maintained his good humour, calling us soft, and telling us of the much worse conditions he'd suffered in the Crimea. Being mad at him took our minds off our suffering and heated our blood.

"*C'est la vie, mes amis, c'est la vie*!" he laughed, "What does it matter how we die? Are we not soldiers? Stop crying and be satisfied to die like one — with your face toward the enemy!" Oh how I hated my little French friend sometimes! Although his constant clowning and

---

[24] On the morning of 28 Feb 1862, Lt. Kerber, I Company commander, refused to join the line of march over an issue with transport wagons. Chivington promised to correct the issue at the first opportunity, and the crisis passed.

teasing did help us keep marching — we all hoped to make camp someday with enough energy to give him a good thrashing!

Finally we received word that the enemy was less than a hundred miles away. We left everything behind but our weapons and two blankets per man, and marched two more days until we reached Ft. Union. Those two days were the worst of that whole long, miserable march.

We abandoned everything but our weapons and two blankets per man to make room in the wagons for those men unable to march any further, while the rest of us struggled along on shank's mare[25]. The leg I'd broken back in California ached terribly, but I refused to give in to it. To make it worse, my left shoe's sole had been flopping for days, and finally came completely off. I was able to cadge one that almost fit from one of the men in the wagons and staggered along in a daze. Even the horses began dying, forcing some of those riding to march on foot. As we marched into the teeth of a freezing gale, the line of march veered around dead horses, including Major Chivington's big gray. I would never be so exhausted

---

[25] A colloquialism meaning "to walk".

again, until years later when I was being pursued by this same army I was now marching with.

Chapter Ten

Milestones of memory; an uncertain future; first combat; a real battle; death and victory

New Mexico Territory
1862

After reaching Ft. Union, we spent about a week resting and getting re-supplied. Most of the invalids who had ridden in the wagons recovered. They received a little good-natured ribbing about riding in the wagon, but we knew it was more luck than anything that the rest of us managed to keep marching.

On the 23rd of March, we set off again, to retake Santa Fe from the Texans. "My G-dd--ned feet are gunna kill me long before we ever see a f--kin' Texan," muttered one of the men.

"Calm yourself, *mon ami*," said Frenchy. "When we finally meet your 'f--kin' Texans', you'll wish you were back here, having a lovely stroll with your friends."

We marched until we reached Kozlowski's Ranch, where we heard a large group of Texans were headed our way from Santa Fe. The next morning, we advanced into Apache Canyon. Sometime after noon, the column halted — there were hundreds of Texans in front of us, and they opened up on us with cannon. They didn't do any real damage, but hearing their blast and seeing them all drawn up in ranks ready to kill us was sobering. Officers galloped up and down their lines, shouting orders, and raising clouds of dust. NCO's were getting them formed up for battle, and the Texans themselves were shouting and cheering and daring us to come on.

For our part, Companies A and E were ordered to advance to the left, along the base of Glorieta Mesa as skirmishers.

Company E took the lead, and we followed close behind, spreading out to make sure we flushed all the Reb skirmishers who were hiding among the rocks and hills at the base of the mesa. The skirmishers fired at us, and then rapidly fell back to their main body — one ball actually struck a rock close enough to shower me with dust! — but for the most part, it was just another walk with my friends, albeit much more exhilarating than the march. Even though I never saw a single enemy's face, and never fired my rifle, just being under fire had my heart pounding like a drum.

We reached a position flanking the Texans' main body, and poured an enfilading fire in on them, firing as fast as we could, but between the smoke and the dust I could not tell if we did any damage. There was much more action with the main body under Major Chivington at the center of the canyon, but I couldn't see much of what was going on over there. The Rebel line started to buckle, and they fell back to a narrower part of the canyon where they formed up again, but we flanked them and they broke and fled. We let them go, although our cavalry captured their rear guard. Finally, the Rebs were out of sight, and we were recalled, rejoining the main column and returning to Kozlowski's Ranch.

***

The next day, we rested, and Col. Slough arrived with reinforcements. Scouts reported that over 1,000 Texans were encamped at Johnson's Ranch in Apache Canyon. On the morning of the 28th, two battalions[26], including Company A, marched out under Major Chivington, headed over Glorieta Pass. Our goal was

---

[26] 1st battalion – four companies under command of Captain Lewis. 2nd battalion – 3 companies under command of Captain Wynkoop. Roughly 400 men total.

to circle around the enemy and hit them in the flank. We hadn't quite reached the top of the pass when we heard the battle begin in the canyon. We continued our way up and over the pass, the sound of the battle fading behind us.

A few more miles and we rested while the officers advanced to the edge of the mesa for a look. The Reb supply train sat right at the base of the mesa! Captain Wynkoop selected thirty or so men, including Frenchy and I, and led us down the face of the mesa, spreading us out into firing positions that covered the entire train. It was not difficult, as the Texans' attention was toward the battle.

At a signal from Wynkoop, the remainder of the men started down the steep slope toward the enemy. They were about halfway down before a rebel sentry spotted them. Several Rebs opened fire but we sharpshooters provided covering fire for the men as they charged down the steep rock face, and most of the Rebs panicked and fled up the canyon toward their main body.

Excited, I fired at least twice, as fast as I could, then I heard Captain Wynkoop shouting, "Take your time boys! Pick your targets and put 'em down!" I took a moment to calm myself, and then sighted in on a blond Texan scrambling to reload their sole cannon. I took a deep breath, let it out about half, squeezed the trigger, and saw him throw up his hands and fall to the ground. The rest of the gun crew fled with the others. I felt myself flush with pride. I continued shooting as calmly and accurately as I could — pick a target, fire, reload, pick a target, fire, reload — until our boys had overrun the supply train. Then I fixed my bayonet and joined the rest of the sharpshooters in charging.

By the time I made it down, it was pretty much all over. We had captured the entire supply train and the Texans were hot-footing it up the canyon! The wagons were loaded with weapons, ammunition, powder, blankets, clothing, food, even forage for their cavalry. We had no way of hauling it away, so Major Chivington gave the command to burn it all, lest the Texans retake it.

As I've said, I fired as accurately as I could, but in the heat of battle, the only target I was sure I'd hit was the blond gunner. I walked over to where he lay sprawled on his back, his arms outstretched, a hole in his chest where my minié ball had struck. There was very little blood — he'd died instantly, or very nearly.

He looked so peaceful, so young — sixteen, maybe seventeen? – and so surprised. My feeling of excitement faded as pity took its place — what was a boy like this doing here? What evil had placed him in my sights the moment after I'd heard Captain Wynkoop? Many men will speak of shame over the men they've killed, but I felt none. If he'd reloaded that cannon, it might have killed my friends, might have killed me. I did what I had to do, but I no longer felt any pride in it. I'd had no choice — I was a soldier and had done a soldier's job.

My reverie was disturbed by one of the supply wagons exploding. Someone had gotten careless, and A Company incurred its only casualty of the day — Private Ritter was severely wounded in the explosion. Once we'd destroyed the Rebel supplies, we fell back to the top of the mesa, and returned to Kozlowski's ranch, where we rejoined the main force, which had been driven out of the canyon by the Rebs.

In the night, the Texans, crippled by the loss of their supplies, abandoned their position and retreated toward Santa Fe. We followed and had another scrape with them at Peralta. Once again, the Texans retreated after the fight, leaving behind those unable to march and, this time, didn't stop until they reached the safety of Texas.

On our march home, we passed a group of Confederate prisoners and who should I see among them but Jack McCallister! He and I had a brief catch-up that night. I was glad to see he wasn't wounded and was now out of the fight. At least I didn't have to worry about seeing him through my sights anymore.

We had saved the goldfields of Colorado for the Union and showed those Texas wolves what a bunch of Colorado lambs could do[27]. We returned to Colorado heroes.

---

[27] The Texans were known to refer to the First Colorado Volunteers as "Gilpin's Pet Lambs" (Gov. Gilpin was instrumental in forming the regiment). After their defeat in New Mexico Territory, the Texans apparently began referring to the First Colorado as the "Pikes Peak sons of bitches" (Bensing, 74).

Chapter Eleven

Friends and good things; Cavalry at last!; hunting Indians; unexpected emissaries; a dangerous mission; a close call; a successful rescue; hope for peace

It is surprising to me how much my time in jail here reminds me of being in the army. I find that if I concentrate on the good things, like my friends Sheriff Angus and his deputies, the frequent visits by Mrs. Good as well as many of the other friends I've made here, the correspondence from family and friends, and not least the good food, then it's really not all that bad.

Colorado Territory
1863-64

The best thing that happened after we drove the Texans out of New Mexico Territory was that Col. Chivington managed to get us changed from infantry to cavalry. What a blessed relief that was! No more stumping along footsore and miserable, for the heroes of Glorieta Pass! Although the more experienced horsemen like me were very excited, many were considerably less so.

I particularly enjoyed Frenchy's suffering. It was hilarious to see the little fellow lose his famous *sang froid* over simply mounting and riding, much less the intricacies of mounted drill. "Cheer up, *mon ami*," I called to him cheerfully as he picked himself up after falling off his mount again, covered in dust, his proud mustachios drooping like wilted flowers, "it is only a horse. Surely it cannot defeat a hero of Balaclava, the Alma, and Glorieta Pass!" Even those who were also struggling to master riding laughed heartily to see him taken down a peg – none of us had forgotten his jibes during the hardships of the New Mexico Campaign.

"*Mon Dieu*," he said, "a horse I could ride, but this is a hairy, hooved demon from hell! You see how he hates me? I think it must be my accent — he is frightened by my French voice, and thinks I am his enemy because I am not an uncouth *sauvage* like you Americans!"

"My good Pavel here has no such aversion to accents, do you *mon grand trésor*?" I cooed to my own mount, named for Pavel Pestel, a Decembrist martyr.

"Perhaps you should pick a French name for him, and persuade him that he is French also."

In the end, Frenchy and the others became, if not expert, then adequate horsemen. Incidentally, when Frenchy named his mount "Joachim" after the dashing French cavalryman Joachim Murat, the two did seem to get along better — or at least Joachim seemed less intent on killing him. Frenchy still refused to repent of his disdain of cavalry. "Did I not see Campbell's 'Thin Red Line' break a Russian cavalry charge? Did I not see with my own eyes the Light Brigade completely destroyed by Russian artillery? The only use for cavalry is against other cavalry. The only victory our cavalry had that day at Balaclava was when Scarlett's heavies charged uphill against the Russian cavalry. Now that was a fight! 800 of our heavy cavalry against 3,000 Russian light horse, and Scarlett broke their ranks and drove them back! But it would have been a different story if it had been Russian infantry[28]."

---

[28] The battle of Balaclava, 25 October 1854, had three major engagements that have been come to be known as "The Thin Red Line", "The Charge of the Light Brigade", and "The Charge of the Heavy Brigade." Somewhat ironically, the engagement of the Light Brigade – the only engagement the British lost that day – has almost totally eclipsed the two British victories of the day.

"Useless or not," I said, "I'd rather ride than march. If I'm going to fight, I'd rather not be exhausted first." Frenchy just shook his head.

After the New Mexico Campaign, Confederate forces ceased to be a concern, so we were set to guarding against Indian raids and depredations, and punishing those who transgressed. In July of '63, Major Wynkoop led us on a mission to catch and punish some Utes who had been raiding and stealing stock. We spent weeks tracking them over mountains, plains, and deserts, and never once set eyes on them. I was beginning to fear we'd be eating our horses by the time we finally limped — filthy, exhausted, and starving — back into Denver. Not everyone was as unsuccessful as us though. Lt. Eayre, of the Colorado Volunteer Artillery, seemed to have a particular knack for finding and destroying Cheyenne villages.

Depredations by Cheyenne, Arapahoe, and Sioux tribesmen continued to escalate. In June '64, Nathan Hungate, his wife Ellen, and their two infant daughters were murdered and mutilated near Box Elder Creek. The bodies were displayed in Denver, causing both panic and a thirst for vengeance. Governor Evans authorized raising more troops, specifically to kill hostile Indians. Confrontations between whites and Indians were reported almost daily, as were accounts of raids and massacres perpetrated by the bloodthirsty heathens. Most troopers' greatest fear was not being killed but captured alive by savages.

***

In early September, three Cheyenne rode into Ft. Lyon with letters from Chief Black Kettle, offering to make peace and return some white prisoners he had. Major Wynkoop spent a few days questioning them through an interpreter, John Smith, to determine the sincerity of the offer.

Chief One-Eye, his wife, and Eagle Head were held in cells where they were the object of much curiosity. One-Eye was a tall, heavy-set, stately gentleman of about fifty, with one steely eye and immense dignity. For the most part, he ignored us all completely, except for Smith, with whom he frequently conversed.

Mrs. One-Eye was short, stout, quietly good-natured, and quite a bit younger than her husband. She fussed over him, attending to his comfort, and they generally seemed quite fond of one another. Give them haircuts and civilized clothes, and they'd pass for Episcopalians.

Eagle Head, on the other hand, would never pass for anything but what he was — a warrior. He had a way about him that reminded me greatly of Poke Carlin. He was truly a killing gentleman.

On about the fourth or fifth, Major Wynkoop had the whole post formed up on the parade ground. "Men," he called, "we have been presented a rare opportunity — the chance to not only deliver white women and children out of the hands of their captors and restore them to the bosom of their families, but to also take the first steps in forging a peace with the Cheyenne! Such opportunity is not without risk, but what is that risk compared to the invaluable reward of rescuing our women and children and bringing peace to this troubled land?" He paused to sip from a cup.

"I will not order any man to undertake these risks! I ask for volunteers only. Captain Soule, Lt. Cramer, and I will be riding out, unaccompanied if necessary, but the more men we have, the more assured we are of success. I know you men are brave — you proved that at Glorieta Pass! Now I ask you brave men to ride with me to bring succour to helpless innocents and end a war!"

Then he quieted a bit. "I do not ask you to make this decision lightly or quickly," he said. "In the morning, volunteers will assemble here at 0800. We will spend the day preparing the expedition and ride out the following morning!"

Frenchy, Big Dave, and I needed no time to think. We were ready. The foremost thought in Big Dave's and my mind was, "Would the Whitacre girl be one of the hostages?" She had never been far from our thoughts, and the Hungate Massacre and other depredations provided a constant reminder.

After a day of getting outfitted, including making sure we swapped our unreliable Starr carbines for Springfields, about 130 of us rode out. Frenchy and I, along with a couple other fellows, were assigned to guard the Cheyenne prisoners. The translator, "Uncle" John Smith, a broad-shouldered, barrel-chested man of middle age with a lifetime of experience with the Cheyenne, rode with us, and I began to pick up some of the Cheyenne language, and their sign language as well.

***

On the morning of the fourth day we were nearing the village when we were confronted by what looked like about a thousand very excited Cheyenne drawn up in line of battle howling for our blood. It would have been wonderful to see — all those colorfully and grotesquely painted and feathered fighters shouting, brandishing rifles and handguns, bows and arrows, long lances, and vicious war clubs, their eagle bone whistles sounding like the shrieks of the damned while their painted ponies danced and lunged, stirring up great clouds of dust — if it hadn't been so terrifying.

"*Mon Dieu*," said an awestruck Frenchy, "we'll earn our pay today."

I doubted we'd live long enough to draw our pay. Major Wynkoop called for the prisoners to be brought to the front. The men were put in order, and we reluctantly advanced a bit further toward the screaming horde.

"Smith," said the Major, "send One-Eye out with a message for Black Kettle that we're here to make peace and receive white prisoners. Also make it clear to him that if they attack, his wife and friend will be the first to die."

The old chief rode out, holding up his hands, and shouting, and disappeared through their lines. The warriors' behaviour was unaffected — if anything, their taunts and challenges heightened, some dashed in close and then veered off, while others approached close enough to tap troopers with sticks or open hands[29].

Frenchy and a few of the more experienced men kept their cool, but even they looked very concerned. The rest of us were sheet-white and sweating, clutching our weapons with white-knuckled grips. The officers and NCOs desperately watched to ensure that no trooper did anything to escalate things.

"Keep your heads, *mes amis*," called Frenchy. "They are only trying to frighten you."

"They're doing a G-d d--ned good job of it," someone retorted.

After what felt like hours, the warriors parted and a tall, gaunt man with prominent cheekbones and braids wrapped in leather rode through the line, accompanied by One-Eye. He shouted something at us.

"That's Black Kettle, Major," said Uncle John. "He's asking what we want."

"D--n the man!" swore Wynkoop, "He's the one who asked us to come."

---

[29] Known as "counting coup", it was the greatest act of courage for a warrior, greater even than wounding or killing an enemy.

"'"Zat what you want me to tell 'im?"

"Of course not." The Major considered a moment. "Tell him we've come to talk."

More shouting between Uncle John and Black Kettle. "He wants to know why you brought so many soldiers, if you only want to talk."

"Tell him we came to talk, but we'll fight if necessary."

This went on for a while, until Black Kettle agreed to take Wynkoop to his village. Surrounded by warriors, we advanced another couple miles, and were ordered to make camp. Wynkoop, Uncle John, and a few of the officers left with Black Kettle, One-Eye, and the bulk of the warriors. The rest stayed and kept an eye on us. You can bet we kept a close eye on them.

The Major hadn't been gone long when a large group of warriors returned. The officers and NCOs, conscious that trouble here would spell doom for Major Wynkoop and the others at the council, warned us to keep calm and not start anything. Soon, painted warriors were swaggering through the camp, examining us, our equipment, helping themselves to our supplies, and trying to pick fights. Many prowled through the camp with arrows at the ready, some even cursed us in English.

They outnumbered us about five to one, and concern for the Major was replaced with concern for ourselves. A scuffle broke out near the howitzers as the crews were pushed back from the guns, and warriors began looting the supply wagon. An officer galloped off in the direction the Major had ridden.

We had no thought of fighting — our only chance was to stay cool and hope that they were only testing us. We were setting up our shelters when an angry warrior pulled out a knife and slashed a nearby trooper's shelter half. With an oath, the hotheaded young soldier reached for his revolver and the warrior pulled his knife back to strike. Several others raised their bows, ready to turn the young fool into a pincushion.

I thought we were dead, but Frenchy tackled the trooper and I leapt between them and the Indian with my hands clasped in front of me, palm-to-palm, right hand on top, praying this was the correct Cheyenne sign for peace. The warrior laughed scornfully and walked away. The other warriors laughed as well, but lowered their bows. Later, when I had time to think about what I'd done, my legs would fail and leave me shaking on the ground.

"*Nom de Dieu*, control yourself, you fool!" Frenchy hissed at the trooper. "Do you want to kill us all over a piece of canvas?"

The trooper sank to his knees shaking, "Oh G-d . . . Oh G-dd--n, I'm sorry Frenchy. I didn't . . . I don't . . . I . . ."

"Calm yourself, *mon ami*. There's no harm done — yet. But think before you act."

A short time later, Black Kettle rode into camp shouting at the warriors, who complained bitterly but mounted and rode away, firing the prairie behind them. They needn't have bothered — nothing on earth could have induced us to follow them. We hurriedly moved camp about ten miles, and it took quite a bit of effort from the officers and NCOs to get us to stop there. Only a few of the Cheyenne had followed us, and they were satisfied to watch from a distance so, although we all stayed alert, we were able to relax a bit.

When Major Wynkoop, One-Eye, and the other officers rode into camp that evening, many of the men began agitating to break camp immediately and head for the fort, but the Major would have none of it. "We came here to recover white captives, and end a war, and that is what we'll do," he said.

"We d--n' near died trying once already," said a voice from the darkness. "We can't trust these d--ned heathens. They'd like nothing better than to butcher the lot of us." There were many voices raised in agreement. None of those men were cowards — they had conducted themselves with resolute courage all day — but there is a difference between knowing there may be danger ahead and being face-to-face with an angry enemy who outnumbers you badly.

Major Wynkoop would not be swayed. "Black Kettle is a man of honor. He has personally assured our safety and promised to return their captives tomorrow." He pointed to One-Eye. "This brave man has offered himself as a hostage as a sign of Black Kettle's good faith. We would be cowards to run away now and leave those captives to their fate."

"If they're captives, they're ruint already," said another faceless voice, "They might as well be dead, and I don't want to join them." There was more angry muttering, the words "fool's errand" and "d--ned stupid glory-hunters" were bandied freely.

"Any man who leaves camp will be shot without warning," was the Major's last word on the subject. He and the other officers stood watch all night, revolvers in hand.

Uncle John bedded down near the fellows and me. "Boys," he said, "I hope to never see so many riled-up Injuns in one place again." He nodded toward the Major's silhouetted form at the edge of camp. "Him and them other officers, played it just right, no promises or bulls--t. Black Kettle's no fool — he knows Wynkoop's got no control over anything but the men under him. Lotta Cheyenne were for killing us all, but old One-Eye spoke up for us, and Black Kettle carried the day. If Wynkoop'd tried bribing them with big promises, I don't think any of us'd ever see Denver again."

We told him of our adventures, and all agreed it had been the tightest spot any of us had ever been in.

***

The next morning, every man was still in his place, but there was still much complaining and pleading to return to the fort. The Major simply ignored it — I suppose he was happy just to have not been shot by his own men — and we just waited. Around midday, a small group of Indians approached and turned over a girl of about sixteen years named Laura Roper, a round-faced girl with the wide-set, terrified eyes of a steer in a slaughterhouse. She had been a captive of the Cheyenne for over a month and did not appear to have been mistreated, although she was thin as a rail and timid as a mouse, either refusing or unable to speak or meet anyone's eyes. We made a little room for her in the supply wagon, and men stood an armed guard around her every minute, listening to her quiet sobbing. No one knew whether they were tears of joy at her rescue, or of sorrow for all she had seen and been subjected to.

The recovery of the girl cheered us all and revived our martial spirit. "We ought to send for more men and wipe these red sons-of-b---hes out," said Sgt. Carpenter, an unpleasant, truculent man who had been one of those agitating to run for the fort.

"You stupid p--kerhead," said Uncle John, "Black Kettle's been trading like crazy with the bands that took her and others so's he could give 'em to us as a sign of peace. He's trying to keep the peace, and you d--ned idiots'd do well to just shut up about things you don't know nothing about."

"P--kerhead, is it?" exclaimed Carpenter, balling his fists, "I'll show you 'p--kerhead', you d--ned Injun lover!" Carpenter was also a very large man with fists the size of hams and mine-hardened muscles to swing them, so Uncle John — no coward but much older and smaller than Carpenter — was relieved when a passing officer intervened.

The rest of the day passed in waiting, and again that night, the officers stood guard. In the morning, a brave rode into camp with a message for the Major. Black Kettle was coming! Major Wynkoop ordered Frenchy and me to mount up, and we accompanied him, Uncle John, and One-Eye to greet the chief. We met him and a large band of warriors and women about a half-mile from camp. They stopped a short distance away, and Black Kettle approached us with just a couple warriors, a squaw, and a white boy of about ten on a horse. A white boy of about six rode with one of the warriors. The older boy rode ahead of the Cheyenne, straight up to Major Wynkoop.

"What's your name, son?" the Major asked softly.

"I'm Dan," said the tyke. "Are you going to take me home?"

"We surely are Dan, we surely are. You're safe now son." He directed Frenchy to take charge of the boy, and then signaled me to accompany him to Black Kettle to accept the other child. The stone-faced warrior handed him to me, and the boy — who I would learn was named Ambrose Archer — clung to my neck with a grip like iron. My eyes filled with tears.

"My G-d," I heard the Major say, and I turned my head to see a pair of tiny white arms reaching for him from the folds of the squaw's blanket. The Major approached and she handed over a little girl, barely more than an infant.

Without a word, the Major clutched her tight to his bosom. He nodded to Black Kettle, wheeled his mount and galloped back to camp. Frenchy and I followed, while Uncle John remained behind to talk with Black Kettle.

Early the next morning, we returned to Ft. Lyon, accompanied by the Cheyenne and Arapahoe chiefs, along with a group of warriors. Shortly after we reached the fort, Left Hand and Little Raven's band of Arapaho came in and set up camp about a mile away. It was a small group of about 100 lodges, and very friendly. Black Kettle's people moved to Sand Creek, about forty miles northeast of the fort, and we were visited at the fort daily by Cheyenne and Arapaho, both individuals and families. This proved to many of us their desire for peace and afforded the Indians some protection from revenge-minded whites. Major Wynkoop, with a small complement of troops escorted the chiefs and headmen to Denver to work out a peace agreement with the Governor and other authorities.

***

Our return to Ft. Lyon with those unfortunate children remains one of the proudest moments of my life, and the only instance of my time in the Army that I am truly proud of. Sadly, fate wasn't finished with the children. Danny Marble and the three-year-old Isabella Eubanks, although healthy when rescued, both died soon after — Isabella within a couple weeks of arriving in Denver, and Danny of typhus at Camp Weld in November while waiting to be sent back east to relatives. As far as I know, Laura Roper and little Ambrose Asher are still alive and, I pray, happy[30]. I

[30] Ambrose Asher went on to have five children before dying of malaria in 1894. He left the Cheyenne with a ledger of Plains Indian Drawings that would prove to be the oldest known example of its kind. Laura Roper would go on to marry twice more and raise seven children before her death in 1930 at the age of 82.

never heard a single word about the poor Whitacre girl's fate.

Chapter Twelve

Old friends; a dangerous mission; an unexpected friend; Hostage!; a feast; I begin to learn (and think); more new friends; a horserace and a modicum of grudging acceptance

Friendship is a strange thing, it seems to me. Nothing is a greater blessing than a true friend, but even the best of friends can find themselves at odds, divided — often against their wills — by forces they cannot resist. In New Mexico, I often wondered what I would do if I were to find Jack McCallister in my sights, and what he might do if I ended up in his. I am grateful it was never put to the test.

Even my friends here, Sheriff Angus and Deputies Howard Roles and Johnny Donahue, are duty-bound, should I be found guilty, to hang me until I am dead, dead, dead, no matter how favourable their personal feelings toward me or mine toward them. I hope it doesn't come to that.

Colorado Territory
1864

When Wynkoop returned from Denver, he seemed happy. We were formed up on the parade ground and, with the chiefs and other headmen behind him, he addressed us. "Men, you have been the mechanism of momentous events," he declared loudly. "The brave volunteers who accompanied me have not only returned four innocents from unspeakable captivity, you have helped to establish peace! Colorado Territory is safer than it has ever been, thanks to you. Your conduct reflected the finest standards of the United States Army" — he remembered things much differently than I did — "and you have the people's thanks. Let us hope that this is not the pinnacle of peace efforts, but simply the first!"

I liked the Major, but sometimes I felt he liked the sound of his own voice too much. He might've been happier on a stage.

Around the end of October, Big Dave hunted me down. "Major Wynkoop wants a word." I followed him to the Major's office where he sat with his feet up, smoking a cigar. He dropped his feet to the floor and returned my salute.

"Sit down," he said. "Where are you from, Private?"

"Irkutsk, Russia, sir."

"I didn't know they had Indians in Russia."

"They don't sir. My mother is Buriat Mongol."

"Huh," he mused. "I figured Mongols'd be more yellow — like Chinese."

I held my tongue.

"Smith tells me you were picking up the Cheyenne lingo and sign language pretty quickly."

"I enjoy languages, sir."

"I've got a job in mind for you that'll give you a chance to learn more."

Here it comes, I thought. "What does the Major have in mind?"

"I want you to live with the Cheyenne."

"Sir?"

"You're already learning their language and I want to know more about them. I don't know if this peace will hold. They've got some wild young men in their villages that are hard to control and I'm not convinced that Governor Evans and Col. Chivington are fully on board. They both want Indian blood spilt, for their careers as much as anything. If you're in their camp, it will show the chiefs that I trust them. You can also get word to me if they start to act up . . ."

"Provided they don't kill me right off."

". . . don't interrupt me Private."

"Sorry Sir."

"You can also attest to their peaceful behaviour if necessary, providing a white witness to speak for them. You might just save lives, son. I've talked this over with the chiefs — they're all in favor of it and Black Kettle has personally guaranteed your safety. He'll see you billeted with a family that is as devoted to peace as he is. In addition, One Eye will keep you posted as to goings-on in the camp. If there's a threat, he'll get you out, or get word to me that you're in danger."

"He'd inform on his own people to save me?"

"He would. When I asked him why he was willing to die to bring me Black Kettle's message? He said he thought he *would* die, but the message would be found and brought to me, and so his people might be saved. It led me to see him in a different light, and to consider that if he was a man of peace and honour, so might others be. Since then I have seen that the Cheyenne are just as capable of self-sacrifice and nobility of thought and action as any white man. I'm giving you the chance to help these good men save countless lives, both white and red." He stopped to catch his breath, and drank from a tumbler. "Finally, if it all goes to h--l and you do get out alive, you may come back with information that will be useful when we fight them. You've proved your mettle, and I believe you're the only man in Fort Lyon with the skills and abilities to carry this off. So what do you say son? Can I count on you?"

It was a lot to take in. I immediately thought of at least three others at the fort, including Uncle John, who could do it, but they were all more important than I. At least he hadn't just come out and called me expendable. It all sounded very noble, but it was easy for him to ask. It wasn't his head that would be on the chopping block. "May I think about it sir?"

He seemed a little disappointed. "Very well," he huffed. "Let me know by first light. The chiefs will be leaving, and I want you with them."

I saluted, about faced, and started for the door. "One more thing, Private Luck," the Major called. "If you won't do it, any opportunity for gain will be lost. Think about that. Dismissed." He was back in his seat with his feet up and glass in hand by the time I cleared the door.

"Sweet muther of C----t," said Big Dave, once we were outside, "ain't he got a nerve on him?"

"That he does."

Back in the barracks, the fellows all wanted to know what had happened. I told them what the Major had said, and their responses were much the same as Big Dave's.

"You ain't gonna do it are you?" asked one. "Why they'll have you murdered, scalped and laying there with your p----r in your mouth the first night!"

"What do you think, Frenchy?" I asked.

"Oh, *mon ami*, it doesn't matter what I think," he said. "It only matters what *you* think. Just don't do it to prove you're brave. That is a silly reason to die, but peace — peace, *mon grand ami*, that is worth much risk."

"Dave?" I asked.

"I doon't like ta say," he said. "If ye were to go on my say-so an' get yerself kilt, I'd never get o'er it but, if ye must know, it's this — it's a h--luva risk, but if the bloody British'd made half an effort to see us as people instead o' animals, me auld one wouldnae been hanged and me mam growin' old alone. Ye might even find oot what happened to that poor Whitacre colleen."

The Whitacre girl had been on my mind as well. I liked what I'd seen of One Eye and Black Kettle and what little I'd seen of their way of life reminded me of my grandfather's stories of the Buriat old days, so I was drawn to that as well. I slept on it, but my mind was pretty much already made up. Before sunup I was outside the Major's office with Pavel saddled and ready to go.

The Major had one last word for me. He placed his hand on my shoulder, looked me in the eye and said, "Keep your eyes open, and your mouth shut. Never lie, never make a promise you can't keep. Learn everything you can, and don't forget who you are. G-d be with you son."

***

As we rode out of the fort, a light-skinned brave rode next to me. "Are you sure you know what you're getting into?" he asked, in perfect, educated English. He noted my astonishment and laughed. "Edmund Guerrier," he said, offering his hand, "at your service."

"Anatoly Mikhailovitch Lukyanov," I responded. "My friends call me Nate or Lucky."

"I'll call you Nate, at least until we see how lucky you are," he laughed. "Don't worry, you'll be fine. Probably. Come on, Black Kettle wants to talk to you."

We spurred up next to the Chief and One Eye and Guerrier translated. "I want you to help me keep peace between the whites and the *Tsitsistas*," Black Kettle said.

"*Tsitsistas*[31]?" I asked.

"Our name for ourselves. Means Human Beings." He continued, "Black Kettle says 'Wynkoop has a good heart, but there are many chiefs above him. I have seen the power of the white man. You are weak now while you fight each other, but when that fight ends, you will be strong again. I want to start peace now, so my people can prosper alongside the white man.'"

"Tell him I'll do all I can to help," I said. "I'm only a soldier, but I too desire peace."

When Guerrier had translated, the Chief grunted and spoke again, "It is good. In the end, chiefs always lead where the people want to go. It is the people who must want peace." We rode in silence for a while, Guerrier and I falling back behind the bulk of the group.

"How is it that you speak such good English?" I asked.

---

[31] *Tsitsistas* is the Cheyenne name for themselves. The Cheyenne nation is made up of two related tribes, the *Tsitsistas* and the *Suhtai*, and numerous sub-tribes.

"My father was French, and my mother Cheyenne. After my mother died, I went to school back east. I've only been home a couple of years."

"Why live with the Cheyenne instead of the whites?"

He gave no sign that he'd heard me. After riding in silence a while, he asked about my people, particularly the Buriat side. I answered his questions freely, although I was somewhat discomfited that he was learning much more about me than I was about them. Perhaps I was not cut out to be a spy. Then I realized that my situation was much more that of a hostage, in the old way that two warring groups desiring peace would each give up members to the opposing group — usually members whose death would be a great loss. In being given me as a hostage, Black Kettle had been somewhat shortchanged.

Their way of ignoring some questions was something I experienced many times — I believe it was their way of letting me know I'd asked a stupid question. They were a very polite people, and would rather say nothing than answer a question that they considered demeaning to either them or the questioner.

Shortly after arriving at the village, I was invited to Black Kettle's lodge for a feast. On the way, I asked Guerrier if there was anything I should or shouldn't do. He just led me into the crowded lodge. Following his example, I learned that upon entering a lodge, a visitor turned to the right and made his way behind those seated to his own seat. Black Kettle sat opposite the entrance at the back of the lodge, and I was given the place of honor on his left. Guerrier sat on my left.

The meal was delicious and abundant. Regarding the meat, I happily learned to love it before I found out what some of it was. Buffalo nose and lungs, blood jelly, and puppy are all things initially better enjoyed in ignorance. Of course, I didn't have all that at that first feast – it's hard to remember a single meal, even one of great personal significance, almost thirty years later — but I enjoyed them all while living with the *Tsitsistas*.

After the meal, the men split into two groups, one on each side of the fire, with Black Kettle, myself, and Guerrier staying in our places. The pipe was lit and passed around. Black Kettle smoked first, then me — following Black Kettle's example — and so on to the left, until the lodge opening was reached. Then the pipe was passed back to the right all the way around until it came to the last man sitting to the left of the door, who smoked, and passed it to his left, until it returned to Black Kettle. That is how I learned that the pipe cannot cross the entrance.

After smoking and conversation, they played some sort of game. Black Kettle would ask a question, and a stick would be passed to a brave who claimed it. That brave would then speak, and discussion ensued. The stick would return to Black Kettle, who would either stick it in the ground on the side of one of the groups or return it to the original group.

"It's a competition between the Bowstring Men and the Fox Warriors to see which society has the bravest men," Edmund explained quietly. "Black Kettle asks something like 'Who has counted first coup on a soldier with his bare hand while riding a black pony?' A warrior will raise his hand and receive the stick, and then he recites his deed. If no one can top it, his side wins the point."

There were a lot of sticks being distributed, and many disputes.

"Is this meant to frighten me?" I asked, putting on a much braver face than I felt. "Because I don't frighten easily."

"Black Kettle knew you'd ask about it. The point is to give you an idea of the kind of men you're dealing with here — these are not beggars or cowards, looking for handouts. These are warriors! Courageous men who know they're faced with an enemy they cannot defeat. They have decided to follow the Peace Road, that our people may live. Never think that just because they ask for peace, they are afraid to fight. That is what Black Kettle wants you to know."

It was a point well made.

The competition lasted for hours, occasionally interrupted by passing the pipe. Beside the fact that these were brave men, I learned one more very important lesson — the *Tsitsistas* didn't do anything in a hurry but undertook everything with a deliberate process of thought and discussion.

When the meeting broke up, I followed Edmund back to his lodge, deep in thought. In the fate of the Whitacres, Hungates, and others, I had seen the savagery of Cheyenne anger. But I had also seen One Eye's selflessness in approaching us with a request for peace. I saw first-hand how ferociously Black Kettle had driven his own warriors out of our camp, and how those howling, angry braves had obeyed him. "Do you believe peace is possible between whites and the Cheyenne?" I asked him.

"I don't know," he replied, "but I hope so. Let me ask you a question — how long ago did the Russians conquer the Buriat?"

"About 300 years."

"How do they get along now?"

This time, it was I who had no answer for him.

That first week was enlightening but frequently hair-raising. I spent much time with Edmund, and with George and Charlie Bent, half-breed sons of the famous trader William Bent and his Cheyenne wife, Owl Woman. George had fought briefly for the Confederacy but returned to his mother's people. The Bent boys were both spirited, active young men, and I learned their language quickly with such good-natured companions.

In addition I met and became, if not friends, then at least friendly with several other braves such as High-Back-Bear, Smoke, Big Head, Crow Neck, and others, who were all splendid fellows. Smoke had a cheerful, pretty young wife named Whippoorwill Woman who was enormous with child and insisted on me joining them for dinner at least twice a week. She teased me saying the Cheyenne girls didn't like their boys too skinny, after which Smoke would tell her to hush and stop meddling, that I was far too busy to be bothered with women. She would hush him back and the two would just beam at each other.

Not everyone in the camp was as welcoming, but once word spread that my mother's people were "Indians" from the other side of the Great Water, many of the black looks were replaced by curiosity. I was also surprised to learn that among the younger Cheyenne ladies I was considered quite handsome. It explained a lot of the giggling I heard when I walked through the camp.

"You're going to have to watch out for that," said George. "My advice is steer clear. You might give offense where none is intended and cause trouble you don't need."

There was little danger of that for, although my head did swell a size or two, I was still far more interested in survival than romance, despite the comeliness of the Cheyenne women. Fortunately, they were as chaste as they were attractive, and in no way impaired my instinct for self-preservation.

My friends and I spent much of our time hunting, telling stories, and in various competitions with the other young men. My reputation as half-Indian was augmented when I surprised them all with my skill at riding and shooting both guns and bow and arrow from horseback. Likewise, I was surprised at how hard I had to work just to be competitive — I hadn't seen horsemen such as these since I'd left home, and I hadn't shot a bow in years.

The Cheyenne loved games and gambling. On my sixth day with them, a brave named Yellow Bear — who made no effort to hide his antipathy toward me — began haranguing me. I only managed to catch about one out of every six words, but he was clearly issuing a challenge.

"He doesn't believe you're part Indian," said Edmund. Edmund squared off against him and the two spent some time arguing, before he turned again to me. "He's challenging you to a horserace."

"Well I'm more than happy to oblige him," I said heatedly. "I'll go saddle Pavel."

"Nope," he said, "you'll need to ride one of my ponies."

"That's ridiculous," I said. "I'm to ride an unfamiliar horse, and he thinks that's a fair race?"

"Well, that's the deal. Either race him on my pony, or eat crow."

"Fine. I'll show him what a son of Chingiz, Kublai, and a hundred generations of Buriat can do, even with someone else's horse!"

"That's good," smiled Edward. "You do that." He and Yellow Bear got the details worked out, and a boy brought me one of Edmund's horses. Edmund's eyes widened and Yellow Bear's visage went from hateful to smug.

"What's wrong?" I asked.

"Nothing," he answered. "Just don't lose."

Yellow Bear and I lined up, he on a good-looking dappled gray, and me on Edmund's bay. We were to race to the only tree in sight, about a mile away, and back. I felt confident, but Edward's reaction worried me. Still, it was a sturdy little pony and I was looking forward to making Yellow Bear eat his words. One Eye was enlisted as judge, and gave the signal to go.

We took off like a shot, riding h--l-bent-for-leather, with most of the village behind us yelling encouragement to Yellow Bear.

Southeastern Colorado looks so flat that, from the top of a tall horse, it seems like you can see Canada. It's not. It's full of gullies and washes and buffalo wallows and holes, and even the flat parts are frequently home to prairie dog towns just waiting to snap a horse's leg. Since Yellow Bear knew the ground much better, I decided to hold back a bit on the way out, and let him show me the best route, which, instead of a straight line, curved in an arc to the north. Unfortunately, I discovered it was less a matter of holding back than it was simply keeping up. Edmund's pony had a lot of heart — what it didn't have was speed.

He was ahead of me by about a length and a half as we rounded the tree. He headed back the way we'd come but, the curve he was taking added about a quarter to a half mile, so I took a straight line back. I was feeling good until a gully yawned right in front of me, but that's when my bay showed his value. He was sure-footed as a goat and had eyes like an eagle. All I had to do was stay on top of him. He barely slowed down as he skidded fifteen feet down one side, took a sharp turn to the right, and lunged up the other side without any guidance from me. By the time we were a hundred yards from the village we'd come back together, neck and neck. Yellow Bear was lashing his pony for all he was worth, but that extra distance had taken its toll, and his pony was beginning to lag. Lather was flying off both ponies, and they were straining for all they were worth, but in the end, heart won out over speed, and we crossed the line a nose ahead.

The crowd was cheering, and it appeared to me that some of those who'd been rooting for Yellow Bear were now insisting they'd been on the "Soldier Indian's" side all along. Both Yellow Bear and I walked our ponies around to cool them down, watered them, and rubbed them down with handfuls of grass. Edmund clapped me on the shoulder. "By G-d, I thought you were done for."

"I did too," I said. "But he's a fine little horse."

Yellow Bear stalked away at Edmund's approach, but returned shortly, leading the pony he'd ridden and another handsome, piebald pony. He handed the lead ropes to Edmund, muttered something, and walked away.

"What did he say?" I asked.

"He said anybody rides like that must be part Indian after all." Edmund smiled as he handed me the lead to

Yellow Bear's gray. "Here," he said, "you did the riding, you should get some of the spoils."

"You bet on me?"

He laughed. "I bet on everything. That's why I was upset when the boy brought you the wrong horse. I figured I'd lost before the race even started, but you had the good sense to trust him."

"Trusted him? I was desperate. The straight route back was the only chance we had."

"Well then, I guess *Heammawihio*[32] must favor you — at least more than he does Yellow Bear. Can't say I'm surprised, Yellow Bear's an -sshole."

We went back to Edmund's lodge, where we celebrated my victory with the Bent boys.

A couple days later, Uncle John Smith rode into camp with his half-Cheyenne son Jack, Davey Louderbeck, and Wat Clarke, with packs full of trade goods.

***

I've heard that George Bent has had some recent difficulties[33] – but I was delighted to hear that Edmund

---

[32] Principle God of the Cheyenne.

[33] George Bent found himself on the outs with both the government and the Cheyenne over his part in the breaking up of the Cheyenne

has managed to get a town in the Territories named after him although apparently, they couldn't spell his name. He at least, seems to have become very successful. I hope that he can be of some help to poor George, as I understand they live relatively close together.

---

and Arapaho Reservation in the Indian Territory (now Oklahoma) under the Dawes Act of 1997, which many Cheyenne saw as a betrayal. He spent much of his later life shunned and in poverty. Ironically, Geary, the town named for Edmund Guerrier was settled on land made available by the breakup of the reservation.

Chapter Thirteen

On mixed heritage; familiar faces; Cheyenne life; an uproar in the village; a different perspective; John Stuart Mill and the Cheyenne way of life

It's uncomfortable to look at something from someone else's perspective. I remember being very upset at the times I was mistaken for a Chinese or Indian, which would seem to be at odds with my pride in my Buriat heritage. Looking back, it seems that all too often, I was only proud of my Mongol forebears when it was convenient — something to brag about or smooth my introduction to the Cheyenne.

When it wasn't helpful, I was just white. Thanks to my primarily white upbringing and education, I never really had to look at life through Buriat eyes. That month I spent with Black Kettle's people opened my eyes to much about myself, very little of it creditable.

Colorado Territory
1864

I felt safer when Uncle John and the others rode into the village. "Good to see you boys," I said, as they stepped down and stretched their legs.

"Good to see you still got all your hair," said Davey Louderbeck, shaking my hand. He was a Private from C Company, about nineteen years old, with thin, sandy hair, and a sorry-looking excuse for a mustache that he was inordinately proud of. "Frenchy and them warn't sure you'd still be alive."

"Nope," I laughed, "They've been very kind and patient with me."

Uncle John Smith joined us while Jack and the other fellow began setting up their lodge. "Well, of course they have," he said. "They want peace. If the price of peace is not killing a scamp like you, then they'll make that sacrifice – no matter how much it pains them."

"Some do seem somewhat pained about it," I admitted.

"Davey," Uncle John said, "whyn't you give those boys a hand?" After Davey left, Uncle John turned serious. "So how have things been around here?"

"Quiet as a church," I said. "Why?"

"Wynkoop's out and Anthony's the new commander," he said. "He ain't like Wynkoop. He ain't bad, but I b'lieve he'd be happy to just peacify 'em all with lead and be done with it." He lit his pipe. "You hear anything worrisome?"

"No," I said, "but that doesn't mean much. My Cheyenne's getting better, but I'm still relying on what they choose to tell me."

He thought about that while packing and lighting his pipe. When he had it drawing to his satisfaction, he grunted and said, "Well, I reckon that's alright. If there was anything afoot that could hurt the peace, they'd tell you, or One Eye would've gotten word to us."

We strolled over to Black Kettle's lodge, John smiling and greeting old friends. Over the next few days I found myself paying more attention to the daily life of the village. I realized the amount of influence the women held. Most of us imagined they were mere chattel, existing at the mercy of their men, but we were wrong. The Cheyenne women owned a degree of power and respect that most white women would either envy or be horrified by. They worked hard, as most women do, but their knowledge, abilities, and wisdom were honored and respected by all. Their advice and opinions weighed heavily in council, often carrying the day.

The Cheyenne were also an exceptionally polite people. I had trouble reconciling those ferocious, savage warriors with the courteous, quiet, considerate people I met in Black Kettle's village. It finally occurred to me why. The Cheyenne had no walls! Everything that went on in every lodge could be heard outside. One night George and I heard a man named Broken Nose being ferociously bullyragged by his wives about his inadequate hunting and general laziness.

I felt bad for the poor fellow, but George felt differently. "If a man marries three wives and has a passel of kids, he needs to take care of 'em. A fellow wants to be lazy, he'd best keep to hisself."

In the morning, Broken Nose rose early and went out hunting. No one said anything, but there were a number of smiles, especially among the women. A community without walls has no secrets, and a village with no secrets had better be made up of people who can mind their own business.

The next afternoon, Broken Nose raced back into the village. He went straight to Black Kettle's lodge, and soon the whole village was in an uproar.

George Bent was showing me how the Cheyenne make a bow when it started.

"What's going on?" I asked.

"Dunno," he said, "but something's wrong."

The village crier was shouting for the chiefs and head men to gather at Black Kettle's lodge. People were shouting and wailing, and I could make out bits and pieces, "all dead! . . . *ve'ho'e*[34] coming! . . . even babies!"

George leapt to his feet. "Go to my lodge," he said urgently.

"What's going on?"

"I'll find out and let you know. For now, stay out of sight."

"What about Smith and the others?"

"Black Kettle'll see them safe. Right now, you're my concern."

At his lodge, Charlie was arming up. "Charlie," George said, "stay here with Nate. I'll find out what's going on."

Charlie didn't like it, but nodded assent. After George left, he said, "What have you people done now?"

I had no response.

---

[34] Cheyenne word for white men.

He just growled and went out to sit in front of the door.

A few hours later, George and Charlie escorted me to the lodge of Chief War Bonnet[35]. I had met him a few times and had always been struck by his appearance — although an important and prosperous man, he had the saddest, most haggard, exhausted-looking countenance I've ever seen. He had heavy-lidded eyes hidden between a prominent brow and high, sharp cheekbones, so that they seemed to look out from a cave. The wide slash of his mouth was perpetually downturned. Even his hair looked tired.

John and the others were there, along with Edmund, Smoke, High-Back-Bear, and Wolf Chief — one of those who had looked at me suspiciously since my arrival. He looked less happy to see me now than ever.

"What's going on, John?" I asked.

"Them b-----ds in the 3rd Colorado murdered a Cheyenne hunting party[36]," he growled. "Sorry s--

[35] Chief War Bonnet, along with Chiefs Lean Bear and Standing in Water were part of an 1863 delegation of Southern Plains Indians to Washington D.C., where they met Pres. Lincoln who spoke to them of the Government's desire to be at peace with the Indians.

[36] On November 10th, 1864, Company D, Third Colorado, under Captain David Nichols attacked two lodges of Cheyenne hunters at

theels. Broken Nose heard the fighting, but by the time he got there, they was scalpin' and cuttin' up the bodies. Says they found one live child under its ma's body and broke its head against a rock."

"That can't be," I protested. "Soldiers don't fight that way. Civilized men don't . . ."

"Shut up boy," snapped Uncle John. "You don't know s--t about what 'civilized' men do given half an excuse."

"But . . ."

"Enough!" Wolf Chief interrupted. "You call us savages! We fight yes, to protect what is ours! Who wouldn't? But you *ve'ho'e* who come here to take everything and leave us nothing — you call yourselves civilized! You bring nothing but disease and death and destruction, and all in the name of your Jesus Christ.

"I was there," he continued, "when your soldier chief Eayre[37] attacked our village at Ash Creek. Lean

---

dawn near White Butte Creek, killing and mutilating all the Cheyenne, including the children.

[37] On May 16, 1864, Company K, 1st Colorado, Lt. George Eayre commanding, attacked the Cheyenne village at Ash Creek. Eayre was operating under orders from regimental commander Col. Chivington to "kill Cheyennes whenever and wherever found." The Hungate massacre occurred in the flood of retaliatory attacks by Cheyenne.

Bear rode out to greet them with your president's paper in his hand, your president's medal[38] on his chest. 'Don't be afraid!' he told us, 'The soldiers are our friends.' The soldiers shot him down and kept shooting his body as they rode over it."

"Our warriors drove the soldiers away and would have killed them all but Black Kettle, Lean Bear's friend, stopped us! We want to live in peace! It is white men who insist on war! You kill any *Tsitsistsa* you can find, peaceful or not — yet even now, you white men are safe in our village. Would any *Tsitsistsa* ever be safe in your town?"

I didn't know what to say. Wolf Chief's version of the attack on Lean Bear's camp was very different from the official version. What if Wolf Chief was telling the truth?

"I . . . I don't know what to say . . . I just can't . . ."

"Just stop," Edmund said. "Wolf Chief speaks the truth — I was there and saw it all." Smoke and High-Back-Bear nodded agreement. "I'm glad Black Kettle talked sense into us, but a part of me wishes we'd killed every one of those b-----ds."

---

[38] This would be the Peace Medal given the chief by Pres. Lincoln.

"Davey," I said, looking for reassurance, "what do you think?"

"I don't want to believe it either," he said quietly, "but I heard some of those Company K boys laughin' about shooting some old fella was wavin' a piece of paper at 'em. Said that old injun looked awful surprised laying there on the ground, full o' holes. One of 'em was showin' off a big old silver medal he'd took."

We spent the night quietly, each of us lost in his own thoughts. Edmund, George, and Charlie came and went, keeping us informed. The two Mrs. War Bonnets treated us like honoured guests, but all night I wondered if we'd be dragged outside and torn to pieces. Eventually I slept and when I awoke, all was quiet. The lodge was empty except for one of War Bonnets' wives and a couple of children.

Outside, I found George. "What's happened?" I asked.

"Well," said George, "the people talked and argued and fussed and reasoned, and then the chiefs talked and argued and fussed and reasoned, then they smoked some, and fussed and talked and argued and reasoned some more, and decided we're going to keep the peace."

"Thank God," I said.

"I was you, I'd thank Black Kettle, One Eye, and the women. They know war's gonna bring nothing but more grief."

"So everything's alright then?"

"Alright as it can be when peaceful men, women, and children are murdered just for being Cheyenne."

"Of course. I'm sorry. I wasn't thinking . . ." I finally had enough sense to stop talking. A couple of lodges were being taken down and packed up. "Is the camp moving?" I asked.

"No," he said, "just a few families going to join the Dog Soldiers[39] at Smoky Hill."

"Why doesn't Black Kettle order them to stay?"

"Chief don't mean 'king'," George said. "They got no more authority than anybody else. They lead because they've proved their wisdom and courage and concern for the people a thousand times. Black Kettle didn't stop us from killing Eayre's men any more than he stopped us from killing you lot when you came for

---

[39] The Dog Soldiers were originally a Cheyenne warrior society. By Nate's time, they had evolved into a separate band of their own, and were adamantly opposed to peace with the whites.

the captives. We stopped ourselves because we respect his wisdom."

"But I thought . . ."

"You're looking at us through white eyes. No *Tsitsistsa* can make another do anything. We don't force anybody to go to war — every man does as he thinks right. Besides," he nodded again at those packing up to move, "better they go to the Dog Soldiers than stay here and cause trouble."

George Bent's words sounded very much like what John Stuart Mill had written in his book, *On Liberty*, which Tasha had sent me a couple of years back. I had enjoyed it immensely and it had given me a great deal to think about.

Things in the village slowly went back to normal. I redoubled my efforts to learn everything I could about the Cheyenne. Uncle John was doing a booming business trading for buffalo hides.

Toward the end of the month, we decided I would ride back to the fort to report and reassure Major Anthony about the Cheyenne. I was also planning to grab Mill's book, thinking it would lead to some interesting discussions with Edmund and George. Besides, how often would I get a chance to read it while living within a society that predated and exemplified much of its philosophy?

Despite the recent slaughter of that hunting party, I continued to hold out hope for peace.

***

Looking back now, it's hard to believe that I was ever so naïve.

Chapter Fourteen

*A feud; a night ride; back with the company;
Chivington and Anthony; a cavalry charge;
I am injured; horror; Jack Smith and Frenchy; the return of
Bill Morrow; the scales fall from my eyes*

Sheriff Angus was laughing when he brought my supper in tonight. "Tater Wallace and Big Joe Douglass were at it again tonight," he said. Tater and Big Joe had been avowed enemies for years. The fact that both were about seventy years old and neither had ever managed to inflict any lasting damage on the other caused their feud to be more a cause of entertainment than concern.

It was funny, but then I thought about "Blessed are the peacemakers." In my experience, all too often, the peacemakers pay the price for all of us. Look at Jesus. Or Black Kettle. The world would be a whole lot better off if we'd listen to men like them rather than kill them because they're inconvenient.

Colorado Territory
29 November 1864

Davey and Wat snored like an out-of-tune brass band concert, so I dressed, gathered my equipment, and stepped outside into the night. For a moment, the bitter cold made me think about returning to the warmth and comfort of the lodge, but they struck up another chorus, and I decided I was better off on the move. There was no moon, but the millions of stars in the cloudless sky provided plenty of light.

Uncle John was sitting on a log smoking his pipe near where we had our horses picketed. "Sounds like a d-m' stamp mill in there, don't it?"

I grunted in agreement and began saddling my horse. "I'll sleep better in the saddle."

"Just don't fall off."

I gave Pavel a pat. "He has a nice smooth gait, this one. Also, he knows where he's going better than I do. Best to just leave him to it." The big chestnut stamped his feet and nodded in agreement. I mounted. "Is there anything else you want me to report to Maj. Anthony?"

He stood and took hold of Pavel's bridle. "Just let him know that everything's good here, but One Eye says them Dog Soldiers are still up at Smoke Hill stirring up trouble." He shrugged off his buffalo robe and handed it up to me. "Here, you might want this," he winked, "in case you fall off."

I thanked him and he gave Pavel a smack on the rump. "Don't get lost," he called as I rode across the stream and out of the camp.

I wrapped the robe around myself and let it trail back over Pavel's rump. Before I'd ridden an hour, I dozed off until I was awakened by the rattle of harness and quiet cursing nearby. I shook my head to clear it and saw, silhouetted against the lightening sky, a column of cavalry marching north, a few hundred yards east of me. Pavel, good horse that he was, had noticed it and headed for it with no direction from me.

I took off the robe — it wouldn't do to be mistaken for an Indian — and approached. When I drew near the column, I stopped and quietly hallooed, so as not to surprise them.

"Who's there?" a picket riding flank called.

"Trooper Luck, Company A, 1st Colorado Cavalry."

The picket rode up close, rifle in hand, and looked me over, then escorted me to the column.

"What the hell are you doing out here by yourself trooper?" demanded an unshaven, filthy officer.

I saluted. "I was returning to Ft. Lyon with a message for Maj. Anthony from John Smith, in the camp of Chief Black Kettle, sir."

"The Major's up at the head of the column. Best get up there."

I spurred Pavel along the column, wondering who all these troops were and where they had come from. More importantly, where were they going? At last, I located Maj. Anthony. "Sir," I said quietly, "Trooper Luck reporting with a message from Interpreter John Smith."

"What is it?"

"Mr. Smith wishes you to know that all is quiet in the camp of Chief Black Kettle, but Chief One Eye says hostiles are camped at Smoke Hill."

"Very good trooper. Find your company and fall in."

"Yes sir," I saluted and rode back down the line, falling into place next to Frenchy.

"Good to see you're still alive, *mon ami*," he said, grinning and giving his mustaches a twirl. "*Monsieur* Parrot owes me five dollars."

"What are you all doing out here?" I asked.

"What else?" he said. "We are going to fight *Messieurs* Indian."

"Yes, but what Indians?"

"Whichever ones we can find, I suppose," he said disgustedly. "*Le Pasteur Combattant*[40] doesn't seem too particular. I had no idea Methodists were so bloodthirsty."

"Col. Chivington?"

"He rode in yesterday at the head of the Third Colorado." He spat in disgust. "Just scum and riffraff calling themselves soldiers. He threw up *picquets* all around the fort — wouldn't let anyone out. Last night we all marched out."

I felt my blood warm at the thought of meting out retribution to those hostiles who had been raiding all over the territory. If it weren't for them, that Cheyenne hunting party might have been spared. It would be good to teach the hostiles to follow Black Kettle's example.

As the sky lightened, I could see more of the countryside and realized that we were riding directly toward Black Kettle's camp. I assumed that we were going to collect Uncle John and the others on our way to Smoke Hill. When we were only a couple miles

---

[40] French for "The Fighting Parson", a term Col. Chivington was known by.

away, a battalion galloped off to the northwest, in the direction of the Indian's grazing pony herd.

The sun had not quite broken the horizon when we gained the bluffs and sighted the village below us in the distance. The column halted, and there was a flurry of activity as the troop commanders gathered around Col. Chivington. I was close enough that I could hear him giving orders for troop dispositions, and then, in a very loud and clear voice, he said, "Men, strip for action! I don't tell you to kill women and children, but look back to where your mothers, fathers, brothers, and sisters have been slain, their blood soaking the ground along the Platte[41]. You all know what needs doing!"

I was dumbstruck and galloped to the front, looking for Major Anthony. "Sir!" I called. "That's Black Kettle's village down there. The hostiles are at Smoky Hill. You have to stop this!"

"G-dd-mmit trooper, get back in line!"

"But sir . . ."

"Get back in line, or I'll have you up on charges!"

I fell back into place beside Frenchy. What else could I do? I was a soldier.

---

[41] This statement is confirmed (with minor differences) by the testimony of James P. Beckwourth.

The officers returned to their commands, and the column broke up into battalions. Lt. Wilson led one battalion parallel to ours, and we approached the village four abreast, at a gallop. Shortly after we crossed the creek, Lt. Wilson's troops veered off to the right, while we followed Maj. Anthony parallel to the creek itself. Surely, I thought, the officers would realize their mistake soon and call a halt.

I could feel Pavel strain under me as I struggled to control him, maintaining our place in formation, my heart hammering with excitement despite my trepidation. The icy air was full of sand thrown up by the flying hooves, stinging my cheeks, and I had to force my watering eyes to remain open. We were pounding along, stirrup-to-stirrup, a single, many-fanged beast of war. A cavalry charge is like being in love for the first time — exhilarating and terrifying. It was almost enough to make me forget what was coming next.

As we closed on the village, the mass of lodges separated into individual structures. People were dashing around in a panic. Black Kettle raised an American flag with a white flag below it on a pole, and still we charged.

Firing had commenced from both Lt. Wilson's command to the east, and the other battalion across the creek to the west. Several Cheyenne men were standing in a line on the edge of the camp. In the forefront was old Chief White Antelope, his empty hands held open above his head, shouting something. We were almost on top of him when he folded his arms and began to sing his death song in a strong, clear voice. I couldn't understand what he was saying, but the sound left me hollow.

We halted right on the outskirts of the camp formed up in line. The battalions on either side of the camp were pouring a very hot fire into the camp where hundreds of men, women, and children, many naked, were panicking, fleeing in every direction. A few of the men had weapons and were returning fire, but the majority were just trying to save their families.

Uncle John ran toward us waving his hands. Several shots struck near him, and he turned to run back to his lodge.

Hoping John could stop this, I rode up next to Maj. Anthony. "Major," I shouted, "let me bring him out!" Without waiting for an answer, I spurred Pavel forward, bullets ripping the air around me. I rode past

Uncle John, then swung Pavel around to sweep him up. A red-hot hammer struck me in the shoulder and almost unseated me. I was reaching down to Uncle John when poor Pavel was hit several times, going down hard and throwing me clear. I was stunned and saw High-Back-Bear pick up my carbine for me. I held out my hand to take it, but he reversed it and swung the butt at my head.

When I opened my eyes, High-Back-Bear's body was lying across my legs, with four bullet wounds in his back. I rolled him off me, and struggled to my feet. My head was buzzing, my vision fuzzy, and when I wiped my brow, my hand came away bloody. My shoulder hurt like hornets had built a nest in it. All around me, blurry troopers, both mounted and on foot, were chasing Indians. They fired indiscriminately, with no semblance of order, and the shots sounded muffled and far away, as did the ghostly, ghastly screams of the dying. Only the smells – burnt powder, blood, sweat, wood smoke, burning hides and flesh – and the coppery taste of blood on my lips seemed real.

I watched one trooper dismount and kneel to fire at a naked child of about two or three years toddling after his family. The child was about 75 yards away and he missed. Another dismounted, saying "Let me have a try at the son-of-a-b---h." This man missed also, and yet another joined them saying, "I'll bet I can hit him." He fired, and this time, the little fellow dropped and lay still as they cheered. Everywhere I looked were dead Cheyenne — men and women, old and young. Any wounded were shot by passing troopers.

I staggered on. Most of the bodies were scalped, often multiple times. My mind slowly cleared and I began to recognize the dead. White Antelope lay in front of his lodge, riddled with bullets. The poor old gentleman lay face up, his ears and nose roughly hacked off. His clothing had been torn away, and his genitals removed.

I fell to my knees and vomited, emptying my stomach, and then dry-heaving until I could crawl away. I wanted to lie down and close my eyes, to see no more of these horrors, but forced myself to keep moving.

I witnessed unimaginable, unspeakable things. Babies with crushed skulls, children chopped to pieces. I saw the bodies of two adolescent girls lying where they fell, still holding hands. Both had been scalped several times. I saw nine or ten troopers firing into a group of kneeling women and children, their hands held out, begging for mercy, until all were shot to pieces. The troopers then fell on the bodies, scalping old and young alike, cutting off fingers for their rings, all the while grinning and whooping like they'd won a prize at the fair.

The artillery had opened up, lobbing shells upstream. I stumbled out of the north end of the camp, hoping to leave the carnage behind, but everywhere I looked, Cheyenne bodies lay on the frozen ground. Here and there some Cheyenne still fled from cheering troopers. As I walked upstream, I met Jack Smith walking back down. He was clad in buckskins but, the fight having progressed away from the village, he seemed to feel safe enough.

"Nate," he said, "this is a bad place for us." I stumbled, and Jack swung my arm over his shoulders taking some of my weight. He turned me around and led me back toward the camp, where we crossed paths with Frenchy. He leveled his rifle at Jack, but I pushed the muzzle away. "He's a friend." Frenchy took my other arm.

He had tears on his cheeks, and his voice quivered. "*Mon Dieu*," he said, "we have certainly done the Devil's work this day, *mon ami*."

I was just relieved to see a friend in the midst of all that madness. In Uncle John's lodge we found Mrs. War Bonnet #1 hiding behind a bale of hides with her child and an infant that wasn't hers, along with another young lady, Buffalo Calf Woman. Most of her clothes had been torn from her, and Frenchy handed his jacket to her. She responded by thrusting a knife at him. It took some doing on Jack's part to convince them that we meant them no harm. After he got them calmed down, they got me settled a little more comfortably, and Jack and Frenchy stacked the bales around the women and children to better hide them.

We sat without speaking, the two women keening softly as they tried to comfort the terrified child. Jack began to sponge the blood from my head while Frenchy stood watch. As he worked, Jack told me what he'd seen upstream.

A large group of Cheyenne had gotten into the creek bed where the banks were very high and scooped out pits[42] to fight from. Jack had fallen behind the main part of the fight, and when he saw that there were more soldiers in front of him than there were behind him, he turned back toward the lodge, hoping his father's influence might save him. After tending to my head, he did what he could for the bullet wound in my shoulder, and then we just sat there, heads hanging, trying to make sense of what was happening.

The fighting went on into the afternoon, and the troopers began to return to the camp. We could hear them whooping it up as they continued to take their grisly trophies and looted the camp. I hoped that being in Uncle John's lodge, we'd be safe, but I held my revolver in my lap, just in case.

The door flap was thrown open, and two troopers from the Third Colorado, one a private and the other Bill Morrow with sergeant's stripes, crammed in. They grinned at each other when they saw the buffalo hides and their eyes hardened at the sight of Jack, with his long, black hair and native dress. They started to raise

---

[42] Most of the cavalry casualties occurred here. The troops had to raise up and expose themselves in order to fire down on the Cheyenne men, women, and children.

their carbines, but Frenchy and I held up our weapons. "This man is my prisoner," I said.

"We was told to kill all the b-----ds," said Morrow, who had a string of bloody ears swinging from his belt.

I stepped between them and Jack. "As God is my witness Bill, you'll not kill this one." Something in my voice — or more likely Frenchy's steady aim — convinced them, because I couldn't have looked any less threatening. Perhaps they just didn't have the stomach to shoot at someone who could shoot back.

"Alright Nate," said Bill, recognizing me, "I shoulda known you'd be a d--ned Injun lover. Well we'll see about that later. The Colonel don't want no prisoners — be careful you don't end up shot for protecting a dirty redskin."

I answered that we would indeed see, but that Jack's fate was not up to them. They each grabbed a hide and left. After that, I moved my seat to the back of the lodge, and placed Jack behind me to try to protect him better.

"You know that *connard*?" asked Frenchy.

"*Oui*," I said, "but it's not something I'm proud of. What has happened here, Frenchy?"

He shrugged sadly. "War happened here."

"This is not war," I insisted, "this is slaughter. This is murder. And it's our men doing it!"

"*Oui*," he said sadly, "our brothers have discovered their blood-lust."

"Frenchy, you've seen war," I said. "H--l, I've seen war. Glorieta Pass was nothing like this."

"The Crimea was not like this either," he said quietly, "but ask yourself, *mon ami*, what is the difference between this war and those?"

We sat there talking quietly, guns in hand, ready to kill our own fellows in defense of these Cheyenne, listening to the near-constant gunfire in the distance, and the whoops and cheers of the soldiers as they caroused.

We were lucky that the next faces to come through the door of the lodge were Davey Louderbeck, and James Beckwourth[43]. They sat with us and helped to protect Jack and the ladies. Since Davy and Frenchy were unhurt and in uniform, they stood guard outside the lodge door. Uncle John joined us around dark, and I took his advice and sought out the regimental surgeon. By that time, the other wounded had been

---

[43] James P. Beckwourth was a famous black mountain man who became a chief of the Crow Nation.

attended to, and the good doctor was put out that he had another patient. I was grateful for Jack's care for, from the stink of whiskey coming off of him, the less the surgeon had to do, the safer I would be.

After the doctor finished with me, I returned to the lodge. In my absence, three small children and a papoose had been brought to the lodge. Jack cooked some supper for all of us and when he took food to the ladies he discovered that Buffalo Calf Woman had slipped out under the lodgeskin and disappeared.

Uncle John, Mr. Beckwourth, and I took turns guarding Jack and the women and children inside the lodge, while Davy and Frenchy resumed their posts outside. I don't think any of us slept.

The next day, military discipline, which had completely broken down, was slow in returning to the command. All around us, we could hear the trophy hunters still pillaging the lodges. Several soldiers from D company came in and began collecting the hides.

"What in hell do you think you're doing?" demanded Uncle John.

"Col. Chivington's orders," said Mike Boyle, the D Company Third Sergeant.

"Orders hell, that's my property!"

Boyle's face flushed. He was a decent sort, and clearly unsettled. "I'm sorry John, but orders are orders."

"G-dd-ammit, that bloodthirsty son of a b---h can't do this! I'm a by-G-d American citizen, a white man, and an employee of the U.S. Army, not some poor Injun he can bang around any old way." With that, Uncle John stomped out of the lodge, muttering under his breath. By the time he returned, they had taken all the hides, along with everything else in the lodge. It was well that we'd already eaten breakfast, or they'd have taken that too. As it was, we were left with only the clothes on our backs.

In the afternoon, Bill Morrow and the other trooper came back with ten others looking to start trouble. They bulled past Frenchy and Davy, who followed them inside. "You sorry son-of-a-b---h," said Morrow to Jack, "You oughta been shot a long time ago, along with every other half-breed bastard."

"You want to kill me, go on ahead — I don't give a d--n one way or the other." Jack responded hotly, squaring up to Morrow.

"Hell, I think we oughta shoot him, and hang these others for protecting him," said another trooper.

"Now boys," said Uncle John, trying to calm the situation down, "Jack here is my son, and this woman and children aren't any threat."

"There's been enough killing, *mes camarades*," Frenchy chimed in.

"You shut your d--ned frog-eatin' mouth!" yelled one of Morrow's henchmen. "A Frenchman's no better'n a f--kin' Injun, far's I'm concerned!"

"Men," I said, "you can't be serious. Jack's done nothing wrong."

"You shut your damned Ruski mouth too," said Morrow to me. "We ought to shoot Uncle John too, for raising a traitor like this."

Davy turned to the door. "I'm gonna find an officer," he said as he left.

This went on for some time, the men threatening, Jack coming right back at them, and Uncle John, Mr. Beckwourth, Frenchy and myself trying to defuse the situation. Mr. Beckwourth was pointing out that Jack could be valuable to Col. Chivington when, from outside the lodge a voice called, "Uncle John! Uncle John, come out here, quick!"

Uncle John left the lodge, and things grew quiet for a moment. The troopers appeared to be having second thoughts, wary of possible repercussions. No doubt, having a man of Mr. Beckwourth's fame and reputation speak up for him weighed heavily in Jack's favor.

I had begun to think the crisis had passed when a knife slit the wall in the back of the lodge and a revolver barrel poked through. Before anyone could react, the gun fired, and Jack fell dead.

***

We were all stunned, even Bill Morrow, standing there with Jack's blood and brains on his face. He and his thugs left without another word. A little later, Sergeant Boyle returned with the same D Company men to relieve us of "the captives" — Mrs. War Bonnet and the children.

After that, there was no reason to stay in the lodge. We helped Uncle John lay Jack out, and then left him with his son.

We walked the camp, hoping to find someone capable of receiving help, but every Cheyenne still in camp, from elderly men and women down to suckling infants, was dead, the bodies even more unspeakably mutilated than before — faces smashed in, arms and legs chopped off, the ears and genitals of both men and women savagely cut out. Some I could identify by what remained of their bodies and garments, like Left Hand and One Eye, but many were unrecognizable. Some soldiers were still at their grisly work, grinning and grunting like fiends from hell as they desecrated their victims.

On the edge of camp, I found the body of Whippoorwill Woman. She had been shot in the breast and in the face and scalped. Her genitals had been cut out, and her belly cut open, her baby ripped from her womb, killed, scalped, and left lying on her breast, a macabre parody of life. These men were mad for blood and were not satisfied with mere killing. It was as if they wanted to destroy not only the bodies, but the very souls of their victims.

I fear the only souls destroyed that day wore blue.

***

Charlie Bent was saved by friends of his from a New Mexican artillery company, but would be killed later in a skirmish with soldiers. I never saw Mrs. War Bonnet or her child again, but I know the infant she'd had with her was placed in a wagon box, and then discarded on the frozen ground the next day[44]. Black Kettle and his wife escaped, although she was shot a number of times. Almost exactly four years later, both would be killed in their winter camp during another dawn attack[45] by yet another glory-hunting son of a b---h in uniform. At least Custer would pay with his life and those of his entire command at the Little Big Horn eight years later.

---

[44] Essentially all of the details of slaughter, mutilations and abuse in Lukyanov's account are borne out in the testimony of other eye-witnesses, and can be found in the official accounts of the various inquiries into the massacre.

[45] Battle of the Washita, November 1868, largely established Lt. Col. George A. Custer as the country's preeminent Indian fighter. Once again, a large number of women and children were killed, and some of the seeds of Custer's own destruction were planted.

Chapter Fifteen

Faith and friendship; self-exile; a visit from an old friend; a mysterious summoning; la belle dame sans merci; a surprise meeting; out of the grave at last

Faith can be a hard thing to hold onto in the face of adversity, no matter what it is you have faith in — a God, an organization, a friend, your fellow man, or just the existence of good. It helps to have good friends and family. I have both, and am reminded of something my grandfather said: "The winner has many friends, the loser has good friends." Though a loser I may be in the eyes of the world, in my own, I am the luckiest of men.

Colorado Territory
January - February 1865

Sand Creek took its toll on all of us and did not end when we rode away. We who were there infected those who weren't with its evil. It was a vile time, and many of us behaved vilely. Friendships fractured, and I spent much of my last month in uniform in the guardhouse for fighting with former friends whose behaviour at Sand Creek I could neither tolerate nor forgive.

After we mustered out at the end of our enlistment, I could not stand to be around people and found myself a snug little cave in the foothills to live in with my horse, where I could brood. I made enough by trapping and hunting for occasional trips into Denver for supplies, and to steal copies of the *Rocky Mountain Daily News* — I certainly wasn't going to pay for its lies — to facilitate the most unpleasant aspect of my daily ablutions. Although childish, cleaning my backside with its constant articles championing those "brave sojer boys" who "covered themselves with glory" by slaughter and mutilation, gave me at least some small amount of peace.

One freezing morning, Frenchy hallooed, and I grinned to watch the little fellow struggle up the slope through the snow. "*Mon Dieu*," he panted, "why must you live out here like an animal when equally miserable accommodations may easily be found in town?"

"I do it to find out who my true friends are."

He stopped to catch his breath and looked around at the trackless snow. "It seems to me, *mon frere*, that you should change that to the singular."

"Better one true friend than a thousand false ones," I said, holding out my hand in greeting.

"*Oui*," he said, clasping my hand, "but how much a *bon ami* are you to make your only friend suffer so to see you?"

I had no answer to that. "Coffee?"

"Merci."

I filled our cups and we sat. "What brings you out here, mon frere? And did you walk all this way?"

"Do you think me a fool? Of course I didn't walk out here — only the last mile or so. I need your help to get my carriage out of a hole."

I snorted coffee out through my nose. "Carriage? Why in G-d's name would you drive a carriage out here? Why not just ride?"

He looked insulted. "You know that I have sworn never to mount a horse again. Am I not an *homme d'honneur*?"

"I'm sorry, mon ami," I laughed. "I know you are a man of honour, I just didn't think you were to the point of foolishness."

"Honour is never foolish," he said, looking around, "What is this self-imposed exile but *un point d'honneur*?"

"So what does bring you out here, *mon honorable collègue*?"

"A lady wishes to meet you!"

"A lady? *Quel mystère*! And what sort of lady?"

"She is my new employer and *une belle dame sans merci*. If you know what's good for you, you'll help me unstick her carriage and come with me. I can't say you won't regret it, but I know you'll regret it if you don't. For one thing, I shall never forgive you for causing me to fail her. For another thing, if we don't get moving, either Indians will steal her horses or something will eat them, and you will be stuck with me, for I will never be able to return to Denver."

"If she's so frightening, why would I want to meet her?"

"Frightening? *Non*. She is *formidable*!" Even his moustaches were quivering. "She is to the average woman what the lioness is to the housecat!"

My curiosity was piqued and, since I was low on coffee, bacon, and *Rocky Mountain Daily News*, I agreed to accompany him back to town. I followed Frenchy to his carriage — he refused even to ride behind me. As it turned out, he was only nominally better behind a team of horses than he was atop one, but we finally made it to Denver late that afternoon without damaging either carriage or team too badly. We left them and my horse at the livery.

"All right," I said, "let's go see her."

He looked me up and down. "Name of a name! You cannot meet her like this! You look like you live in a cave!"

"Well, maybe that's why she wants to meet me."

He snorted Gallicly as he turned me to my reflection in a window. "If you were a beautiful woman would you want to meet this?" He waved his hand expressively.

He had a point, but I was essentially penniless[46]. Frenchy, on the other hand, protested vociferously that he would be personally affronted if I were not "suitably presentable" to meet "*une femme formidable.*" In the end, he won when the wind changed and I got a whiff of myself. A couple hours later, freshly bathed, shaved, shorn, fashionably attired, and embarrassingly indebted to him, I was ushered into The Silver Platter Opera House.

---

[46] When the soldiers of the First Colorado mustered out, their pay was indefinitely delayed due to the death of the district paymaster, Major Fillmore.

It was quite a place – no grogshop or cantina this. Onstage, a large woman with her hands clasped to her breast was valiantly struggling with an aria in apparent competition with the "orchestra," a motley accumulation of nearly in-tune violins, horns, and piano. The early evening crowd was a mix of cowboys, miners, and townsmen. In addition to the tables, there were benches set immediately before the stage. A second floor of ornate boxed seating wrapped around the sides and front of the place. "Is that for the toffs?" I asked.

"*Les patrons, mais oui*," he said. "They are very respectable persons — at least until ten o'clock." He told the bartender to send us champagne and three glasses. I noticed no money changed hands.

"What happens at ten?" I asked, as I followed him to an empty table in the corner with a clear view of the room.

"Respectable ladies are prohibited after ten, when the atmosphere becomes somewhat more . . . *risqué*?"

"So where's this beautiful, merciless lady? Don't tell me she's changed her mind after you've forced all this civilization on me."

"*Madame* Salome never comes down before eight o'clock."

"So she does have a name, eh?"

"*Mais bien sûr*. What do you suppose?"

Remembering John the Baptist, I asked, "Anything to do with the name of this place?"

Another Gallic snort. "It is nothing to be concerned about, as long as one behaves properly." He pointed to the bar. On a slanted shelf behind the bar sat a large silver platter. Setting on it was a savagely fractured human skull.

I looked at him questioningly.

He waggled his eyebrows. "A warning to those who would misbehave."

"Who is it?"

"No one knows, but the legend is that it's someone who displeased *Madame* Salome."

I was beginning to see what he meant by "*une femme formidable*."

The "music" ended — a cessation of hostilities apparently agreed upon by the singer and orchestra — to the disappointment of the audience whose applause was undeservedly enthusiastic. We drank each other's health and sat silently for a while. For both of us, the spectre of Sand Creek was always there, just out of sight but never out of mind. Everything reminded me of that day. Much as I loved Frenchy, our entire shared experience revolved around the Army — and our many good times were forever overshadowed by that day. It wasn't just Black Kettle's people who were destroyed — I lost many friends who were proud of what they'd done, and even several who weren't there, but who sided with the unrepentant butchers. Sometimes it's better to simply say nothing, even to a true and loyal friend, rather than risk forcing them to share our poison, our brokenness.

Fortunately, a pretty little thing came out onto the stage and distracted us both as she sang popular songs of the day — a venture the orchestra was much more qualified for. Soon the audience was joining in with her, and Frenchy was beaming and rapt.

"Is that her?" I asked.

"Don't be ridiculous," he said, "that is my wife!"

I congratulated him and signaled for another bottle — why not? That revelation drove the conversation until *Madame* Dompierre finished her performance, at which point she joined us. Her name was Eden and she was a vivacious and energetic whirlwind, who charmingly monopolized the remainder of the conversation, firing questions at me about myself and her "darling Davy" faster than I could answer them. Her flitting conversation was light and funny enough that it blew away the dark clouds that followed me.

I wouldn't call her enchanting, but it was impossible to be morose in the face of her cheerful, dizzying, teasing onslaught. We had a lovely time, with Frenchy and I telling stories on each other whenever she would pause for breath. It was the most — and perhaps the first — time I'd really laughed since . . .

Shortly before eight, the orchestra was replaced by a larger, more professional-looking one complete with evening clothes, tuned instruments, and talent. The room also filled up, many of the rougher customers leaving to be replaced by nicely dressed couples and individuals. Eden left us to retake the stage and, at 9 o'clock, Frenchy laid a hand on my shoulder nodding toward a stairway that led down along the left side of the stage.

"There," he said reverently. "*Madame* Salome."

She was certainly something to see. Tall, elegant, and snake-limbed in a tight jade-green gown that revealed just enough to make you want — or rather need — to see more. The allure of the gown was somewhat offset by the jewel-studded holster high and forward on her waist holding a pearl-handled revolver for a right-handed cross-draw. She had a diamond tiara in her long, flaming red hair, a heavy veil obscuring her face and she didn't walk down the stairs so much as float down them.

Coming toward us, she occasionally paused to accept obeisance from various admirers who caught her attention. She was closely followed by a slender, cold-eyed young man with a revolver on one hip and a sixteen-inch Arkansas Toothpick on the other. The flatterers were all conspicuously polite.

When she reached our table, Frenchy stood and bowed courteously and I followed suit. "*Madame* Salome," he said, "allow me to introduce my dear friend and *camarade*, *Monsieur* Anatoly Mikhailovich Lukyanov."

She extended a milky white hand, and, striving to remember what my father had taught me of courtly behaviour, I took her fingertips and raised it to my lips. "*Madame* may call me Nate, if she pleases."

She nodded, but said nothing. Frenchy held her chair while she sat, then poured champagne for her.

Through all of this, she never turned her face from mine. I don't mind saying it was more than a bit unsettling. Frenchy and the bodyguard set up a painted wood and canvas screen around us that shielded us from sight. When they stayed outside the screen, I said, "I suppose I should be honoured that you trust me so."

She nodded.

I was completely nonplussed — why had this woman wanted to meet me? Why did she refuse to speak? Why did she hide her face? "*Madame*," I said, "have I done something to offend you?"

She shook her head.

"Is there some service you require? Some favour I may do you?"

Again she just shook her head.

"Have we met before?" I asked, exasperated. "Do I owe you money or something?"

Finally, she spoke. "How've you been Nate?"

My mind whirled. That voice was once more dear to me than any other. "Esme? Is it you?" I reached for her veil, but her hands stopped me.

"Let's just talk a while."

"But . . ."

"Time enough later for that," she said. "I'm glad the Indians didn't get you."

"My G-d! How did you . . . when did . . . why haven't you . . ."

"Hush," she said in a melancholic voice. "Let me just look at you and remember the old days."

Being quiet was not difficult, as I had no idea what to say — there were so many things I wanted to ask her, to tell her, all fighting for supremacy.

"I've missed you Nate. Do you ever think of me?"

"I've thought of you constantly. I have always hoped to see you again, to say, to tell you . . ."

"What, Nate?" she asked, placing her little hand on mine. "What did you want to tell me?"

"Well . . . that I . . . ah . . . well, that we . . ."

She laughed and took a sip of champagne, lifting her veil just enough to slip the glass underneath. "Relax Nate, I'm just fooling with you. David was telling me about his brave Russian pal Nate, and I knew it had to be you. I just wanted to see you is all."

I gestured at the screen and the veil. "Why all the secrecy? Why didn't you just let him tell me you were here?"

"I wasn't sure you'd want to see me. Our parting wasn't particularly amicable."

"Yes, but the fault was mine." Again, I asked, "So why all the secrecy?"

"I have a mystique to maintain here," and her voice changed, becoming mysteriously deep and indeterminably foreign, "They don't know what to think of me, and that's the way I like it. Some of 'em think I'm a Hungarian princess who's fallen out of favour, or escaped assassination back home. Others think I'm the widow of a millionaire — or that maybe I killed one and took his money. Or I'm an actress on the run from gangsters, or a bank robber's girl who ran off with the loot after he was killed, or the Queen of the Barbary Coast, come here with my ill-gotten gains."

"Why would they think all that?"

"Because that's what I've told 'em," she laughed. "Oh, not directly, of course. I've just dropped a lot of different hints in front of a lot of little birds and let human nature do the rest. It's good for business. Half of these rubes are here because they think I'm some kind of tragic figure fallen from grace, and the other half are here because they want to be here when my past comes back to haunt me."

"So the veil's just part of it?"

"No, that's just for you."

"But why?"

She patted my hand. "Let's get out of here — go someplace quieter."

That sounded good to me, but this new Esme was far more complicated than the old one.

"Listen," she said, "let's give 'em a little more to talk about. I'll have the boys take the screen down and I'll stand up to leave. You say something, and I'll give you a good smack, and Eddie'll throw you out. Then just go around back and Frenchy'll bring you up."

"You've really gotten theatrical."

"What, you never wanted to be in show business?" she teased.

I caved in like a bad dugout in the rain. I don't know if Eddie was acting or not, but he was certainly enthusiastic. After I picked myself up out of the street, dusted myself off, and surveyed the wreckage of my new duds, I walked around the back. There was an edge, a distance to Esme, a harshness to her laughter that hadn't been there when I'd known her before. Of course, I was hardly the same feckless youth she'd known, either. Frenchy escorted me up an outer staircase and down a long hall that ran above the stage, connecting the wings of box seating. He led me through a door at the end of the hall into a small parlor where Samson was seated cleaning his nails with a penknife. He nodded amiably. I nodded back and he jerked a thumb at another door. I knocked and Esme called "Come in."

She was sitting in an easy chair, warming her hands by a stove and waved me to a matching chair. I sat and we made awkward small talk for a while. Finally, I could take it no more. "Please Esme," I pleaded, "take off the veil."

Her hands slowly approached it, then stopped. "I don't know if I can," she said. "I'm not the girl you remember. I couldn't . . ."

"Please," I said softly. "Trust me."

She turned away from me and removed the veil, then slowly turned back to face me, proud defiance in her right eye. Her left was covered with a red silk patch, with scars extending a short distance above and below the patch. While I sat back and quietly studied her face, she studied mine even more closely, gauging my reaction.

"Really something, isn't it?" she asked quietly.

She was still beautiful, but changed — neither better nor worse, just different. Always thin, she was almost gaunt now, her cheekbones even more prominent. The ironic twist of her smile was tinged with bitterness, and anger lurked in her lovely eye. She was still Esme, but it remained to be seen if she was still *my* Esme. "You're just as beautiful as I remember."

"Don't lie to me," she whispered.

It was a time for whispers. "I'm not," I replied. "You are different than you were but are no less beautiful for it. No one gets through life without scars. It is how you carry them that matters."

"Where are your scars Nate?"

"Mine are mostly inside," I said, "where they just fester. I imagine you bear your scars better than I do mine — you were always stronger than I."

She rose and walked behind a screen. "Don't believe everything you see," she called as she slung her dress atop the screen, followed by her stockings. "Everything in this place is bunkum. None of it's real — not even me."

"You're real to me."

"And you're still a sweet, romantic boy."

"No. I'm far removed from that naïve fool."

She returned to her seat, swathed in a plain flannel robe with a hint of silk showing underneath it. She'd washed off her makeup, and her hair was now yellow again, but much shorter than it used to be. "I told you not to believe anything you saw. My hair's on a stand back there. The diamonds and jewels are all paste. It's all just for show." She touched the eyepatch. "Only this is real."

"I don't believe that," I said.

She picked up a hand mirror and looked at her reflection. "I don't want to say 'I told you so,'" she said, "but we'd probably both have been a lot better off if you'd just stayed with me."

"You're likely right," I said. "May I ask what happened?"

She scowled. "Same thing that happens sooner or later to everyone in my business. I got careless and a customer who looked meek as a lamb turned out to be a scorpion. Thought he didn't get his money's worth and smashed a champagne glass into my eye."

"My G-d," I said.

"I decided it was time to get out of the horizontal entertainment business. When I'd healed, I sold out followed the gold trail to Denver and opened this place."

"It looks like you've done well for yourself."

"I could've done worse. I like it better in management. Lower risk, higher reward."

"So you're still running girls here?"

"A few, but it's a lot more discreet, and we're very careful — well, as careful as you can be in this business. Samson, Frenchy, Eddie and a couple others are very good at making sure everyone behaves."

"So what happened to the California scorpion?"

"Whose skull do you think that is on the platter downstairs?" She smiled.

I suppose I should have been horrified, but instead I found myself smiling too, pleased that at least one monster in this country had gotten his just desserts.

Chapter Sixteen

Concentration; a controversy; Esme and I; Silas Soule; a Denver romance; a tragedy; blinders

Denver, Colorado
February – April 1865

Denver was overwhelmingly supportive of Chivington and the massacre, but repercussions were beginning to be felt — Captain Soule and Lieutenant Cramer[47] had both written letters to their families and to Major Wynkoop detailing the horrors they'd witnessed. Those letters worked their way up the chain of command, as well as into the eastern newspapers, sparking an outcry. Even Major Anthony couldn't swallow his revulsion any longer and turned on Chivington. A military and two separate congressional committees were established to investigate, and Soule and Cramer, among others, testified before the military committee. Of course, Denver being what it was then, Chivington remained the darling of the town and

[47] Soule and Cramer refused to allow their troops to take part in the actions at Sand Creek.

Soule, who had taken the position of Provost Marshal, was reviled.

There were other repercussions as well. After Sand Creek, the Cheyenne had well and truly gone "on the warpath" seeking vengeance. In January, about a thousand Cheyenne had struck the town of Julesburg, sacking the town and taking the military payroll. They raided all over the territory and, people being what they are, this only served to bolster Chivington's reputation.

Esme and I resumed our habit of riding out in her carriage when the weather would allow — although Samson no longer accompanied us. She was a madwoman at the reins, laughing wildly at every close call. She laughed a lot on those rides. In the evenings, we took in the shows at all the other places in town, to ensure that the Silver Platter was providing superior entertainment and to poach any particularly good acts.

Things were different between us, however. The damage each of us had taken created a distance between us that we couldn't bridge. We spent long periods, each lost in our own thoughts but comforted by the presence of the other, glad to no longer be alone in our solitude. We didn't laugh as much as we used to, nor did we fight nearly as much. Neither of us could let our guard down enough to be that affected by the other, but we did our best to bandage each other's wounds. In our mutually damaged existence, it was as much as either of us could offer or accept.

Our days and evenings were very pleasant. Esme enjoyed being "Salome," the mysterious, dangerous queen of Denver entertainment, and I quite enjoyed watching it. We also had a small coterie of friends who provided good company. One such friend was Silas Soule. After hearing he'd told the other officers of the 1st and 3rd that any man who would attack Black Kettle's people "was a low lived cowardly son-of-a-b---h," — a statement that nearly got him hanged on the spot[48] — I made it a point to search him out and we became quite close.

Although a teetotaler, he loved a show and was a frequent visitor at the Silver Platter and spent many nights at our table. He was a charming, devil-may-care sort of chap. Solidly built, with gray eyes and auburn hair, he was also as American as it was possible to be — his family traced its roots back to the Mayflower — and proud of it.

---

[48] Soule made that announcement at Fort Lyon before the fateful march to Sand Creek.

Silas had enjoyed an even more adventurous life than I had — as a boy in Kansas Territory, he had smuggled runaway slaves to freedom, helped break another slave-smuggler out of jail, befriended John Brown, and even traveled to Virginia and gotten himself locked up in jail as part of a plan to rescue two of Brown's men. "I'll be dog-gonned, if they didn't flat out refuse to be rescued, figuring it'd be better for the cause if they was to be hung," he said, a little misty-eyed. After that, he, his brother, and his cousin sought their fortunes in the Colorado gold fields. When the war broke out, he enlisted in the 1st.

The new military commander, Colonel Thomas Moonlight declared martial law in early February, due to Indian attacks, and Silas was kept busy with his duties investigating any crime in which army personnel or property was involved. He was deeply unpopular because of his outspoken criticism of Chivington — after shots were fired at him a couple of times, Frenchy, or I, or other of our friends made it a point to accompany him as much as possible.

In early March, Silas began courting Miss Hersa Coberly and they spent many an evening in company with Esme and me. She was a lively, witty, dark-haired girl, with sparkling eyes in a happy face, and a fit match for Silas. Both loved jokes and pranks and they laughed more than any couple I've ever seen. They kept everyone around them laughing too. They accompanied Esme and I on a picnic once, and Silas grimaced horribly every time he sipped his lemonade. Hersa, on the other hand, lavished praise on Esme's recipe.

"You simply must write the recipe down for me, mustn't she Sile? I know how you love lemonade."

He blanched. "Mmh? Um, of course my dear. That would be lovely."

"Just think of it, we could have this every day! But you've hardly touched yours. Are you feeling alright, dear heart?"

"No, no," he insisted, "I'm fine, just not, um, very thirsty is all."

"Darling, don't be rude. You don't want to hurt Esme's feelings, do you?" She watched triumphantly as he drained his glass, struggling to hide his revulsion. Hersa and Esme convulsed with laughter.

"What's gotten into the two of you?" I demanded.

Hersa had prepared a separate bottle of lemonade especially for Silas, made with salt rather than sugar.

She and Esme had a wager on whether Hersa could persuade Silas to drink an entire glass. Finally in on the joke, Silas and I laughed heartily and congratulated Hersa on her victory, which she accepted most graciously. Silas, of course, vowed vengeance

Alas, one cannot be happy all the time — one evening, Silas buttonholed me. He seemed uncharacteristically worried, and I accompanied him to a nearby restaurant. We ordered coffee and, after the waitress had brought our cups, he asked, "Am I a fool?"

"No," I said. "Why would you even ask?"

He leaned over the table and said very quietly, "I've been thinking about Miss Coberly."

"If that's what you're worried about," I said, "perhaps you are a fool. She's a wonderful girl, and you're a lucky man."

He waved his hand dismissively. "Oh I know that. I may be a fool, but I'm not stupid."

"Then what's the problem?"

"It's just . . . I don't . . . I feel that perhaps I should give her up — for her own good."

"What are you talking about? You're mad for each other. Why would you break it off?"

"I can't bear the thought of ever making her cry."

"Come on," I nudged his shoulder. "Out with it. It can't be that bad."

"Sometimes I dream of her standing over my grave, and it breaks my heart. I fear my luck is running out."

I didn't know what to say. He wasn't the only one who feared he was living on borrowed time. Finally I said, "Listen my friend, Denver is not the world. Surely Major Wynkoop or another of your friends might arrange a transfer for you?"

"Maybe," he said quietly. "I don't know. The Army hates embarrassment, and I've caused them no end of that. The brass aren't exactly lining up to shake my hand."

"Well, you know Frenchy and I, and a lot of the fellows would charge Hell with a bucket of water for you. All you need do is call."

"I know that Nate, it's just — is it fair to her to risk breaking her heart like that?"

"I can't tell you what to do," I said, "but it seems a shame to break her heart over what might happen."

He just stared out the window at the rain.

I saw him a couple nights later, arm-in-arm with Hersa and her friend Margaret Burgess, all three laughing as if they hadn't a care in the world. They'd come for the show that night, *Miriam's Crime*. It really was quite good, and the performers all very convincing in their roles. Silas and Hersa enjoyed it so much they returned again for the next night's performance, sans Miss Burgess.

When the performance ended, they stopped by our table where Esme and I sat with Frenchy and Eden. Silas shocked everyone by ordering another bottle of champagne and requesting a glass for himself as well. When it arrived, he rose and, holding his glass aloft, said, "I ask you to raise a glass in honour of my fiancée, Miss Hersa Coberly." Hersa was beaming and we all fell over ourselves congratulating them, drinking their health, and wishing them long life and happiness. We agreed that April 1st was an appropriate day for them to be wed.

Frenchy and Eden left with the happy couple, and Esme and I retired to her rooms. "Does Hersa look like she's gaining weight to you?" she asked.

Fearing a trap, I said, "Has she? I've never noticed."

She smacked me on the shoulder. "Dummy," she smiled at me. "She was saying she's afraid she's gaining weight and can't understand it. Poor thing's about to starve herself to death."

"Is she pregnant?"

"She says there's absolutely no chance of that, that Silas has been a 'perfectly patient and gallant gentleman,'" she said, rolling her eyes. "As if there's such a thing."

I wrapped my arms around her. "Perhaps you're jealous?"

She snorted and said, "Not likely. I like things just fine the way they are," and kissed me.

"Well," I said, "it's probably just jitters. She'll get over it. Besides, he'll have her plump and pregnant soon enough." We later found out he was paying Hersa's laundress to take her clothes in a little at a time, every week.

Their wedding was a private affair and we were not invited. Silas had a tough row to hoe with Hersa's family — her father had been killed in a Cheyenne attack, and her brother was one of the 3rd Colorado animals. The last thing he needed was a bunch of low people like us showing up, making more trouble for him. It was one thing for him and Hersa to associate briefly and publicly with a notorious celebrity like

Esme and her ruffian attendants — everyone in Denver paid court to Esme — but to be involved with us outside our natural environs simply wasn't done. It was the difference between visiting the monkey house in the zoo and bringing the shrieking, s--t-slinging creatures home to dinner.

April 1865 was an auspicious month — in addition to the Soule wedding, Richmond fell and Lee surrendered. Colonel Moonlight held a ball for the quality of Denver. Esme and I weren't on the guest list for that either, but for the first time in years, things were looking up.

The euphoria ended on April 15th, the day we learned of President Lincoln's assassination. Denver plunged into mourning along with the rest of the nation. Most of the town, including the Silver Platter, was hung with black bunting. The scheduled performances were canceled and replaced with recitations both memorial and patriotic. The entire town was subdued — the future that had looked so promising and bright, now trapped under a pall of tragedy.

A rough-and-ready mining town like Denver won't stay down long though — after a few days, business and entertainment resumed, and life went back to normal. The country had survived the deaths of hundreds of thousands of her sons, she would survive the death of one president.

On the 23rd, Silas and Hersa joined Esme and me in dining at Frenchy and Eden's rented house. As usual, the night was filled with laughter and high spirits. We bid our goodbyes around nine o'clock. It was a lovely clear evening, so the four of us took a stroll around the town, enjoying the night air. When it started to get chilly, we decided to call it a night, the ladies only wearing light wraps. Since the Soule's home was on the way back to the Platter, we walked them home. He and Hersa were excited — he was finally being reassigned. We were nearly to their house when we heard whooping, hollering, and gunshots a few blocks away in the direction of the Platter and other entertainment palaces.

"Darn it," said Silas. "Don't those fools have anything better to do?" Turning to his bride, he said, "I'll just be a minute." He asked me to escort Hersa on to their house.

"We're almost there," I said. "Let's get them home and I'll come with you."

"You aren't even armed," he laughed. "It's just some hooligans blowing off steam. I'll make sure no soldiers are involved and be right back." With that, he kissed Hersa's cheek, and he was off.

I hurried the ladies the two short blocks to the house and then hurried after him. I heard shouting and picked up my pace. As I raced around the corner of F and Arapaho streets, Silas was confronting two men in uniform. Silas pulled out the derringer he carried when off duty, and two shots were fired. One of the men cried out and dropped his gun, grasping his wrist, but Silas crumpled to the ground. Time stood still for a moment, and then started again with a jolt. The two men ran, but one of them looked back just as they passed a lighted window, and for the second time I stopped in shock — it was Bill Morrow! I couldn't leave Silas, and they disappeared into the darkness.

I knelt beside him, but it was no use. The bullet had hit him under the right cheekbone, and the back of his head bulged where the skull was broken. Others began to gather, drawn by the noise, including another Provost Marshal. I told him what and who I'd seen.

"You're sure it was William Morrow?" he asked.

"Yes," I said. "I've known him for years. I knew he was a low dog, but I never thought he'd be this low."

I've got to hand it to the Marshal — he knew his business — he sent for a doctor, although it was clear nothing could be done, then started to form the growing crowd of soldiers and citizens into patrols to search for Morrow and the man with the gunshot wrist. He detailed a group of soldiers to carry my friend's body to the district headquarters.

I wanted to join the search for the villains, but realized my first duty was to Hersa. I went straight to the house — I couldn't take a chance that she'd find out by accident.

When I arrived, the ladies met me on the porch. They had heard the furor in the streets and were concerned when we didn't return. One look at my face told them everything they needed to know. Hersa's voice broke as she asked, "Where is my husband?" While I sought the words, she shrugged off Esme's encircling arms. Before I could speak, she whispered, "No. Don't say it. Don't say anything," and walked slowly into the house, closing the door behind her.

I swore then and there that I would see William Morrow hanged or kill him myself.

Chapter Seventeen

Bad memories; rumours; a letter from an old friend;
The vengeance trail; a reunion; success; disaster on the trail;
karma; rescue; a faint ray of light; disillusionment

There is a thin line between justice and revenge, and I'm still not sure which side of that line I was on when I rode out after Bill Morrow. It wasn't just the murder that drove me — Silas lying dead in the street mingled with memories of burrs under saddle blankets, poor old Dob lying poisoned, Jesus del Fuego broken and screaming as he died, and of course Sand Creek and Jack Smith. I intended to see him dead, and if the law wouldn't do it, I would.

Denver, Colorado Territory
1865

Silas' other assassin was a soldier named Charles Squier, and he and Bill somehow managed to escape Denver. Rumours, gossip, and speculation ran wild. Even the *Rocky Mountain News* insisted the killing was premeditated. Some said Squier shot Silas because of a grudge. Another rumour was that Squier and Morrow had done it for money. Back in February, at a rally in support of him and the 3rd, Chivington had pledged $500 "to be used in killing Indians and those who sympathize with them." To many in Denver, Silas was a "sympathizer". That soulless b-----d Chivington had the nerve to attend Silas' funeral and it was all I could do to not shoot him on the spot.

Pursuit was delayed because no one knew what direction to even look. About a week after the funeral I got a letter from Just Dave. He wrote:

Dear Mister Nate,

I hoap you ar well. Im dooing fine. As you can see, Ive bin lurning to rede and rite but Ive got aways to go. Mr. Mischas doing well and the ranch is prospering but isnt the same since you boys all left.

We herd about that Captin Soul, an how Bill Morro and anuther fella shot him. Thot you mite want to no that Bill pased thru hear a cuple days back in a big hurry. Stoal a horse and lit out north. If yure going after him Id be pleased to ride alongside you.

Yur frend,
David Lincoln

PS As you see, sins Im realy free now, I decidid I cud pik my one name, so I named myself for Mr Lincoln, G-d rest him.

Frenchy and I immediately made preparations to set out on the trail. Esme came in as I was packing my gear.

"What are you doing?"

I showed her the letter. "Frenchy and I are going after him."

"You know where he was a week ago," she said irritably. "You've got no idea where he is now."

"So I should just do nothing? D-mmit, Esme, Silas deserves better. I owe him more than that. I owe Hersa more than that. How could I ever face her again? How could I look myself in the mirror? He had the courage to do something about Sand Creek. All I did was crawl into a cave and hide."

"And look what it got him," she said. "Stirring up trouble got him killed and hasn't caused Chivington one bit of real trouble. It sure as h--l didn't bring back any dead Cheyenne. The only thing it did was make a widow out of a twenty-year-old girl."

I was shocked at her attitude, and reminded her of the skull behind the bar downstairs.

"That was different," was all she'd say.

"Not to me, it isn't."

"Still a d--nfool."

"Apparently." We had a chilly evening, but in the morning her goodbye was reassuringly ardent. Afterward, she kissed me, said "Take care of yourself, you idiot."

I smiled at her. "You know me," I said, "the very soul of caution." We kissed again, and I left to meet Frenchy at the livery. He was sitting in Esme's carriage, his gear strapped to the rear platform. I saddled my horse, a scrubby, swaybacked gelding of little spirit and disjointed gait — all I could afford after mustering out without pay. I had named him Rocinante[49]. I rode up next to Frenchy, who looked disdainfully at my mount.

"Nate, *mon frere*," he sniffed, "are you sure you can keep up?"

"Are you sure you've got enough cushions under you? I'd hate for your delicate backside to get blistered."

---

[49] Don Quixote's horse in Cervantes' novel.

"You scoff now, but we'll see who's complaining after a couple days on the trail."

We set as brisk a pace as possible, but it took us almost three full days to cover the sixty miles to the ranch. By the end of the second day my spine felt like someone had tied knots in it, and the less said about my backside the better. It was bad enough that I briefly considered riding with Frenchy, but refused to give in. Pride is a ridiculous thing, but hard to let go of.

The ranch was no longer the rough cow camp it had been. There were two large barns, a bunkhouse, and a smithy, along with a large frame house. We were surprised it hadn't all been burnt flat by the Cheyenne.

Just Dave looked the same as ever, and I was surprised at how emotional I was seeing him again. We embraced him enthusiastically. "It's so good to see you again, my friend!"

"Good to see you too Mister Nate," he said, grinning.

"Frenchy," I said, "this is Just Dave."

Just Dave smiled. "No 'Just' anymore. I'm the only Dave left." He shook Frenchy's hand. "Pleased to meetcha," said Dave.

"Likewise."

"Tolya!" called Mischa, rushing over from the house.

"Mischa!" He'd put on weight and started to go a little bald, but was expensively dressed.

"How are you?" I asked. "You look good, very prosperous." I thumbed the lapel of his coat. "A little fancy for ranching, isn't it?"

"Oh, I leave that to Dave and the boys," he laughed. "I'm more comfortable behind a desk."

"Well, somebody's got to do the dirty work. I'm glad you're willing to do it and leave the honest work to those suited to it." I introduced him to Frenchy.

After we'd caught up a bit, Mischa commented on the poor quality of my mount. "And you know if I can see it, it must be bad," he laughed.

"C'mon," said Dave, "I got somebody be glad to see you." He led us toward the corral. Before we reached it, I heard Ilya neighing from the corral. I threw my arms around his neck and buried my face in his mane. I thanked Dave for taking such good care of him.

"It helps he's calmed down a mite."

"But not too much eh, *moy staryy drug*[50]*?* We have a long hunt ahead of us." I stroked his silky muzzle as he

---

50 "My old friend" in Russian.

pushed into me, and he rested his head on my shoulder.

"He musta missed you," said Dave. "He generally tries to take a chunk out of anyone else."

All in all, it was a good homecoming, but the three of us were anxious to get on Bill's trail — we had a lot of ground to make up. Dave had followed Bill's trail far enough to decide he was headed for Nebraska, probably Omaha. It's easier to hide in a crowd, and from Omaha he could catch a train even farther east. Our main hope for catching him was hard riding and a lot of luck. We were also counting on Bill's congenital laziness. We figured the farther from Colorado he got, the more he'd relax and take it easy.

Mischa provided Dave and I with extra mounts, as well as a pack animal laden with supplies. In the morning we set off, moving quickly but cautiously — three men with seven horses and a mess of supplies would be irresistible to any hostile Cheyenne.

Our method was simple — we simply rode for the nearest settlement in the right direction, asked around, and moved on. At that time in southwestern Nebraska, there weren't much in the way of towns, so staying on the right trail wasn't difficult. It was just a matter of having the will to keep pushing.

It was good Dave was along to steady us down, or Frenchy and I might have pushed our horses too hard. Success and respect had made Dave more apt to put himself forward. The war had seriously lowered the quality of available ranch hands — most of the better men having gone to fight — and Mischa had come to rely heavily on Dave, promoting him to foreman.

"It was a little ticklish at first," Dave said. "A lot of men balked, but Mr. Mischa backed me up, and we culled the trouble-makers pretty quick. After that, things went right well." We kept each other entertained, Frenchy with his stories of the Crimea and France, Dave's ranching tales, and my own stories of Russia and my grandfather's people. If it hadn't been a manhunt, it would have been quite a lark.

We were right about Bill's travel habits. He was too lazy and complacent to stay worried, and he was relying on handouts as he went. We were well-supplied enough we could keep moving. When we left Mischa's ranch, we were a week and a half behind him. By the time we'd crossed into Nebraska, it was only a week. We met settlers that he'd stayed with, trading half-hearted work for food. There were more than a few isolated outfits who told us of missing chickens or of finding cattle shot and butchered out on the range.

We pushed hard across the vast empty plains of Nebraska, broiling during the day, and freezing at night. More than a few times we were soaked by rain and at least twice we were held up by heavy snow. Still we pressed on, mindful that anything that slowed us would likely stop him cold. Halfway to Lincoln, we were only three or four days behind him, and three weeks out from Denver, we came upon a barefoot boy driving a milk cow in with a switch, late in the fading afternoon light. A mile or so away, we could see a cabin.

"Howdy," he said.

"Hello young man," said Frenchy. "What's your name, and what are you doing out here all alone?"

"I'm Jimmy Harper an' I had to catch this doggone cow," he huffed. "Idiot drifter didn't latch the gate. Now he's sittin' down to dinner an' I'm out here 'thout even a biscuit."

At the word "drifter" all our ears perked up.

Frenchy dug out a piece of jerky and offered it to the boy.

"Thanks mister." He took a big bite. "Pa says it's a matter of Christian charity, but this fella's got me rethinking my position on religion," he said around a mouthful.

"Who is this fella?" Dave asked.

"Name's Bill. Big feller, dark-haired, scraggly beard, wearin' about half of a soldier suit. Looks like he ain't et too reg'lar lately. Ridin' a horse in even worse shape than he is." He looked at us suspiciously. "Why?"

"Son," I said, "if it's who we think it is, that's a bad man there. He got a last name?"

"Martin. Said his name is Bill Martin."

"Who's with him now?"

"Ma and pa, granny, and my two little sisters."

The last thing we wanted was to get anyone else hurt. We needed a plan, and I certainly wasn't any sort of strategist. "Does he sleep in the house?" asked Dave.

"Naw, he sleeps in a lean-to out back of the house."

"Can you keep quiet about seeing us?"

"Reckon I could."

"Alright then," Dave said. "I think the best thing would be for us to just stay out of sight and take 'im while he's sleepin'."

Frenchy and I agreed, and that's just what we did.

***

We watched the house until he came out. It was him! We waited impatiently until he was snoring, then crept up to his lean-to. Dave reached in and pulled out his revolver and rifle. Bill was still snoring away when I yelled, "Give it up Bill!"

He sat up grabbing his empty holster, then saw we had him covered. He slumped back and raised his hands. "Don't shoot d-mmit! I surrender."

"Sure you want to do that Bill?" Dave asked. "A bullet's quicker and surer than a rope."

"A rope? What the h--l for? I didn't do nothin'!"

"I was there, Bill." I said. "I saw you and you saw me."

"You saw me runnin' away. Was Charlie shot that fellow."

"You'd say anything to save your hide," Dave said.

"You shut up N----r Dave," Bill snarled. "This ain't nothin' to do with you."

Dave started forward, but Frenchy stopped him. "Do not lower yourself, *mon ami*!"

I was all for sitting back and watching Dave take him apart, but Frenchy's cooler head prevailed. We trussed Bill like a Christmas turkey and tied him on the back of the carriage while Dave retrieved the horses. We explained everything to the Harpers who'd come out to watch — after Bill had gone out, the boy had filled them in.

"Knew he warn't no good," said the old woman, spitting tobacco through her teeth, while Mrs. Harper shushed her. "Don't you shush me, girl. If you'd listened to me, none o' this woulda happened." Mrs. Harper put her arm around the old woman's shoulders and steered her back into the cabin, calling the little girls in after them.

Once they were inside, Mr. Harper said, "He really the one killed that Captain Soule in Denver?"

"One of them, anyway."

"What're you gonna do with him?"

"Take him back to Denver to hang," I said.

"Why not take him to Fort Kearney?" he asked. "It's a h--luva lot closer."

"No," I said. "Silas Soule was a friend of ours. It's a long way back to Denver, and if this sorry devil tries to escape, I want to be the one to shoot him dead."

He looked at Frenchy and Dave. They nodded in agreement.

"Well," said Mr. Harper, "I guess I understand. I'd let you stay the night here, but all things considered, I figure it's probably best you head on down the road."

We thanked him, mounted and rode into the night. We rode a couple hours, and then made a cold camp, planning to get back on the road early. Dave made sure Bill was trussed securely at night although chances are, Bill wouldn't have dared try to escape. He liked his chances with a Denver jury better than his chances with Frenchy and me.

After the first night, we took our time — the longer it took, the more chance Bill would give me a reason to not take him any further, but Bill always did have a strong instinct for self-preservation and was very well-behaved and polite. After a few days, it even got to the point where we got tired of hog-tying him and let him ride one of the horses. We'd left his horse and tack with the Harpers as payment for their trouble, but Dave rigged a hackamore[51] for him and we let him ride one of our spare mounts bareback.

The weather calmed and became a bit more pleasant but the closer we got to Denver, the more Indian sign

---

[51] A type of bitless bridle made from rope or rawhide. Used by many Native Americans of the time.

we saw. The Cheyenne were still raiding all over the territory, and we kept a weather eye out. We stopped at Mischa's ranch for a day or two for a rest and a visit, and Bill still refused to run. It was disappointing to say the least. Despite Mischa's protests, Dave decided to accompany us to Denver. "I'm lookin' forward to seeing him behind bars," he said. "I've been gone this long. I reckon the boys can keep it going a few more days."

When we left Mischa told us to keep the horses. "You fellows have about ridden the hooves off of them anyway," he said. "Maybe you can sell them for glue." It wasn't a bit true — Mischa was just saying it to justify the extravagance to the accounting side of his brain.

The day after we left the ranch, we were discussing something — women probably — when we rode over a low ridge and found ourselves face-to-face with about a dozen Cheyenne warriors cooking their lunch. It's hard to say who was more surprised, them or us, but we all got over it quickly — they grabbed for weapons, and we put the spurs to our mounts, running h--ll-for-leather out of there. We snapped a couple shots at them hoping to discourage them, but we were too great a prize to pass up, and they were after us like a flash.

I've heard people talk about "running fights" but in my experience, there's very little fight when running—at least if you're in front. Shooting accurately from a galloping horse while ducking bullets is hard enough when firing forward. Shooting behind you is pretty much a waste of lead unless you're d--ned lucky. We relied on the speed of our horses and tried to make ourselves as small as possible. I was counting on our big, long-legged American horses outdistancing the smaller Cheyenne ponies. Frenchy was cracking the whip on his team with a will, and Bill was hanging on for dear life to his mount's neck trying to stay aboard. We dropped the leads for the spare horses, hoping some of the Cheyenne would go after them. Dave and I brought up the rear, firing the occasional shot just to show willing.

The Cheyenne thundered along after us, shouting their war cries, their bullets and arrows filling the air around us. Dave grabbed at the side of his head and weaved in the saddle for a moment, then looked at me and smiled, holding his hand up covered in blood. The back of Frenchy's carriage was starting to look like a porcupine. Something stabbed me most painfully in the right buttock. It was looking like Bill might be the only one to make it out unscathed, and I took a moment to resent the irony.

Thankfully, the arrows were beginning to fall short and the bullets passing more widely as we put distance between us. I'd begun to think we'd be alright when Bill, riding alongside Frenchy's team, pulled a derringer from somewhere, stuck it in the near horse's ear and pulled the trigger. It went down and brought the other horse with it in a tangle of legs. The shafts dug in and the carriage flipped. Frenchy hit the ground and lay still. Dave and I dismounted, grabbing our rifles. I felt a shock of ripping pain in my backside as I leapt from Ilya's back — an arrow had penetrated the saddle's cantle and pinned me to the saddle. The pain made me forget the Cheyenne for a moment. Dave dragged Frenchy to the dubious cover of the wrecked carriage, and I hobbled after them. We prepared to sell our lives as dearly as we could.

The war party had thinned as some chased after our horses, but there were still a half-dozen after us. Dave and I both fired, but the Cheyenne slid to the sides of their ponies as they passed us, so all we could see was a foot above the croup and an arm over the withers. I managed to hit one of the ponies and it crashed to earth, flinging its rider into the dust. I heard Dave grunt and then a hammer hit me in the right hip and I went down. The warrior whose horse I'd shot emerged from the dust a shrieking, painted demon, and landed athwart my chest, a foot on my gun hand and a heavy war club raised to dash my brains from my skull. There was nothing I could do but close my eyes and wait for a blow that never landed.

I opened my eyes and saw that the warrior looked familiar, but it wasn't until she spoke that I recognized Buffalo Calf Woman[52] under the war paint, her eyes cold and merciless as a snake's. Several braves counted coup on us and one leveled his pistol at Dave's head. Buffalo Calf Woman threw up a hand and barked at him, "Stop. Do not kill these *ve'ho'e*!" There was a brief

---

[52] Buffalo Calf Woman, also known as Mochi, had survived Sand Creek to become a renowned warrior. Side by side with her 2nd husband, Medicine Water (who had also survived Sand Creek), she fought the white men implacably until their surrender in March 1875. Mochi, infamous for her fierceness and mercilessness, was deemed too dangerous to remain with the tribe, and was the only woman out of thirty-five Cheyenne prisoners to be imprisoned for four years as prisoners of war in St. Augustine, Florida.

argument but none seemed inclined to buck her will. Instead, they just took everything we had — weapons, food, equipment, clothes — they even took our boots.

She stared me in the eye the entire time. Finally, when they had everything there was to take, she leaned in so close I could feel her breath on my face. "Good trade. Life for life." She whipped a knife painfully across the top of my head, taking a piece of scalp about an inch across. Shaking the bloody thing in my face, she said, "See you again, I take the rest." She mounted Ilya and they rode away without a look back.

I slumped back in pain, shock, and relief. The wound in my hip concerned me the most, but it appeared to have glanced off the hipbone and while painful, wasn't life-threatening.

"What just happened?" asked Dave. "We get killed and just ain't noticed yet?"

"Dave, my friend," I said, "we are the luckiest men in the Colorado Territory today."

"I b'lieve you may be right Mister Nate," he said weakly. He'd been hit in the shoulder, and a bullet had taken his left earlobe off. "We make it to Denver, I'll be spendin' some time in church. Why you figure they let us live?"

Frenchy was unconscious, and his right arm was broken. While we tended to him, I explained how we had tried to protect her at Sand Creek. Dave and I patched each other up using strips torn from our long flannel underwear. We set Frenchy's arm using the same and wood from the wreckage. "I guess it's a good thing he brought this stupid thing along," I said, "but I don't envy him when Esme hears what happened to her rig."

Setting and splinting Frenchy's arm revived him long enough to curse us and faint again. We just let him be while we assessed our situation. We had no way to defend ourselves, no food or water, and nothing to offer but our scalps. Frenchy wasn't out long this time, and when he came to, he had a lot of questions — the first of which was, "Where did *ce fils de pute* get that gun from?" and the second, "Did the Indians at least get him?"

We had no way of knowing either answer. It was possible that they'd run him down, but more likely they'd forgotten all about him. Bill was showing an astonishing ability to avoid the consequences of his actions.

"We should have kept him tied to the back of the carriage," said Frenchy. "I wouldn't mind this so much if he'd been crushed when it flipped."

"I don't know," Dave said, "seems it was mercy saved our bacon today. You boys showed her mercy, and she repaid it. I reckon mercy don't ever go unrewarded – just maybe not in the way you expect. Mebbe treatin' Bill better'n he deserved will pay off in the end."

"*Tres philosophique*," said Frenchy. "You are *tres sage*, my friend. I hope you are right."

Dave's words reminded of my mother's and grandfather's belief in karma, which they'd passed along to me. I hoped that they, and Dave, were right — but I had my doubts.

***

It was several hours before Frenchy's head cleared enough that he could walk unassisted, and I wasn't any better, what with my hip wound and an inch-deep, three-inch-long rip in my backside.

"How far forward was you leaning?" Dave asked, laughing.

"You are a lucky man, *mon frere*," Frenchy said.

"How do you figure that?"

"*Mon Dieu*!" He laughed. "Imagine if it had struck a couple of inches to the left!"

I fashioned a crutch out of the wreckage, and we set out toward the ranch. We made it about three hours before we had to stop for the night. In the morning, we'd limped another couple of hours when we heard the rattle of equipment behind us. We turned to see the most beautiful sight we'd ever seen — a cavalry trooper and, behind him, an entire company!

The trooper rode right up to us and said, "I can't leave you boys alone for a minute, can I?" It was Jack McCallister in a Union uniform! He dismounted and embraced Dave fiercely enough to make him gasp in pain from his wound.

Once our initial relief dissipated, we had a lot of questions for Jack. The last time I'd seen him was on the march back from Glorieta Pass where he'd been a prisoner. "How did you end up here, in that uniform?"

"I figured I was gonna die there in that prison camp at Rock Island[53]," he said, "what with the smallpox, an'

---

[53] Located on Arsenal Island in the Mississippi River between Moline, IL, and Davenport, IA, it became known as the "Andersonville of the North". It is estimated that almost 20% of prisoners there died of disease, exposure, and lack of sanitation.

everything. They come along recruiting for fighting Indians, an' I figured I'd druther be shot, so I took the oath. 'Galvanized Yankees' they call us. Lucky for you boys we patrol this area regular — Nate's brother's got the Cap'n in his pocket."

We told him what had happened to us and he said, "Well I swan. That d--ned Bill's turned out to be a real no-account ain't he? I can't hardly credit it."

Dave assured him it was true. "I never seen a man so bent on earning h--l as Bill."

The cavalry took us to the ranch where they bivouacked for the night, and we all had a good catch-up. A few days later, some of the hands were taking a bunch of horses to Denver, so Frenchy and I rode along with them in the supply wagon. Dave had elected to stay put. I was not in a hurry to get back on a horse and spent most of the trip lying on my stomach in the back of the wagon.

We learned that a Lt. Cannon from the New Mexico infantry had captured Squier and was returning him to Denver. Squier was swearing it was Bill who'd shot Soule. It made no difference to Frenchy and me — we'd be happy to see both of them hanged, but Bill had disappeared off the face of the earth. Maybe the Cheyenne had gotten him after all.

In early July, Lt. Cannon and Squier finally arrived in Denver. He was locked up, and Frenchy and I went over to take a look at him. He was a sorry-looking specimen, bearded, filthy, fitted with manacles on his wrists, and his feet shackled together. A heavy iron bar connected the restraints and he was chained to the wall. We had no sympathy for him.

Lt. Cannon enjoyed his new-found celebrity. We warned him to be careful about the company he kept, but along about the end of the month, Cannon was found dead in his room, poisoned.

Things went back to what passed for normal for Esme and me, but I was increasingly surly and difficult. I just couldn't get over my failure to deliver Bill Morrow to justice. Finally, in October, Squier was broken out of jail by supporters and disappeared.

It was the final straw, and something inside of me broke. I packed my few belongings and left without a word.

***

Is there any endeavor more self-destructive, foolish, or futile than the pursuit of vengeance? I think not.

The Lord has claimed vengeance as his prerogative, and we mortals would be well-advised to leave it to him. But it's hard — so hard.

Part Three:

Indian

Chapter Eighteen

A haunted solitude; madness; oblivion; rebirth;
a new home, a new people, a new beginning

It may be that only in absolute solitude is absolute freedom to be found — but it is a lonely freedom. While a certain amount of solitude certainly holds a restorative balm for a disturbed soul, too much of it plays tricks on the mind, particularly one as prone to brooding as mine is. If one is not careful, freedom can turn into its own kind of prison, one as damaging as the more traditional incarceration I am currently experiencing. I was lucky and came through those bad times and ended up with a second chance — something most people never get.

Montana Territory
1865-67

When I left Denver I had no plan — I could not understand a society that would fight a war to free millions yet celebrate the murder of peaceful men, women, and children who were following the directions of the authorities. A society that could lionize a butcher like Chivington, vilify a decent man like Silas Soule, and barely be bothered to notice, much less take action, when Soule's murderers escaped justice.

Or maybe it was that I didn't want to understand it. Everywhere I went, everywhere I looked, everything I heard were constant reminders of what an intolerable cesspool I was living in.

I wandered north along the eastern foothills, ever north. I had some idea about trying my luck in Canada, having seen beneath the façade of American freedom. I soon lost all concept of time. If I found a place I liked, I might stay a couple of days or a month. Sometimes I traveled for days without stopping. I believe I went a bit mad.

For company I had ghosts — Silas, Jack Smith, Whippoorwill Woman and her baby, my own Texas gunner, and so many more. They watched me constantly, their eyes peering from a deadfall of trees, or just beyond the light of my campfire, or reflected in water when I'd kneel to drink. It was at night that they tormented me most often — none of them ever dead, only dying — sometimes begging for help, sometimes accusing me. The only memories I have of that time are the nightmares, the constant fear, and the hiding. I thought I was hiding from my ghosts, but I now believe I was hiding from myself. I became a sort of living ghost, haunting myself. It was a long, bad time for me — how long or how bad, I didn't know until it was over.

***

I was burning in hell and Jesus came to me. He restored the souls of those who cried out to me in torment and they were at peace. They raised me up out of my anguish, and Jesus looked upon me with the kindest, softest brown eyes and the gentlest, loveliest smile. He laid his hand on me, and I burned no more. Then his hair darkened and lengthened, his robe became buckskin, his face became beautifully and beatifically feminine and I was awake and looking at an Indian woman with the eyes and smile of our Saviour. That smile widened and she turned away from me to speak in a language I didn't understand, and then back to spoon hot broth into me. A tall, handsome Indian man with serious eyes approached and studied me, also speaking in that language.

My eyes closed, and I slept — blessedly dreamless for once. When I woke, she was doing beadwork on a pair of moccasins. "Hello," I said. Startled, she jumped, then smiled that wonderful smile and left the lodge, returning moments later with a small man.

"Feel better?" he asked in broken English with a booming voice that belonged in a much larger man.

"I don't know," I said, "I don't remember how I felt before."

He smiled. "How feeling now?"

"Weak. What happened to me?"

The girl brought a bowl with more broth, and the man propped me up on a back rest. "Feed yourself?"

I tried, but my arms felt encased in lead. The girl started spooning it into me slowly while he talked. "Dunno what happened," he said. "Flatheads found you all crazy, leg all bust up. Then, hunting improved, so figured you good medicine — touched by *Hanyawat*[54] — so took care of you. I buy you."

"So why did they sell me? Why did you buy me?"

"Screams keeping them awake. Decided had enough meat, selfish to keep you." He laughed at that. "I bought you to see how turn out."

---

[54] "Creator" in *nimipuutimt*, the Nez Perce language.

"So now I'm your slave?"

He laughed again and shook his head. "Don't need slave. Got enough people take care of. Owe me gun with cracked stock."

That was a relief. "Thank you. I'm grateful." I looked at the girl. "Very grateful." She smiled demurely.

The man said something harsh to her, and she came right back at him just as vehemently, handed him the bowl and spoon and left. "Be careful that one," he said, nodding after her. "Unlucky."

"What? No, I'm just very grateful for the — what happened to my leg?" My right leg was crooked just below the knee, and looked shorter than the left.

"Dunno. Flatheads find you like that. I think you fix yourself." He shook his head. "Bad job, that."

"Can anything be done?"

He shook his head, "Too much time gone by. Healed as well as going to."

I leaned against the backrest and closed my eyes. What had happened to me out there? Where was I? I didn't even know what month it was.

"What tribe you from?" he asked.

"Hmm?"

"What tribe your people from?"

"No tribe," I said despondently. "I'm from Russia. My mother's people are Buriat Mongols."

"Look Indian to me." He placed a hand on his chest, "Lean Elk. Most whites call Poker Joe."

"I'm Nate."

"Girl name *Ta Mai Ke Yon Mai* — mean 'Coming Together'. Granddaughter of Chief White Bird."

"What do you mean she's unlucky?"

"Not mine to tell." He would say no more about it, and I was too weak to talk more, so he ladled the remainder of the broth into me and helped me lay back down to sleep. "Sleep now," he said, rising to his feet, "talk tomorrow." I was asleep before he left the lodge.

The next day, I was a little bit stronger, and a few days after that, I was able to hobble outside and sit in the sun, with Lean Elk's help. My G-d, how good that felt. I discovered several new scars on my torso, one large scar across the back of my head, the last joint of my left little finger was missing, and I still had no idea what had happened to me. I learned that it was late June 1867 — two full years since I had left Denver!

Coming Together continued to be very kind, and my recovery sped along, as did my knowledge of the Nez

Perce — or *Nimiipuu*[55] as they called themselves — language and ways. They were a handsome and decorous people — the men tall, strong, and well-formed, and the women plump and beautiful. All behaved with a propriety that would be the envy of any polite society. Like the Cheyenne, they were as particular about their personal cleanliness and appearance as they were about their behaviour, taking great pride in even their day-to-day appearance — more than most whites — and the pains they took to dress for "formal" functions, dances, feasts, and the like, were absolutely wonderful. I saw them as nature's aristocrats.

In many ways, meeting the *Nimiipuu* was like a rebirth. I was helpless as a baby, and they cared for me. As I gained in strength and knowledge, I began to feel as if I belonged — as if I'd come home — and they were very welcoming and hospitable. They were a new family, a new beginning, a new life for me.

I learned their homeland was west, across the Bitterroot Mountains, but Lean Elk's small band of six or seven lodges lived mostly in Montana. The rest had crossed the mountains to hunt buffalo. Now they were

---

[55] *Nimipuutimt* for "The People".

just waiting for another group or two to arrive before returning home.

As I spent more time outside, I became quite a sensation with the children, who were very curious about me, especially when they learned that I was an "Indian" from across the sea. I was completely at their mercy, and loved it. They were a jolly bunch, full of exuberant life, with a thousand questions about my people. They were particularly adept at teaching the *Nimiipuu* language — possibly because they felt no compunction about laughing at my mistakes. You have truly learned a language when you can communicate with a six-year-old child in it without them laughing. I became particularly attached to two of the children, a scamp of about ten years named Yellow Wolf, and a sweet little girl of about two, named Walks Through, the daughter of Coming Together. She loved to sit on my lap and play with my scraggly beard. It was Yellow Wolf who teasingly gave me my first *Nimiipuu* name — Walks in Circles — because my right leg was now about an inch shorter than my left.

I noticed similarities between the *Nimiipuu* and my grandfather's people far beyond simply being horse cultures. For example, the length of weddings — often months would pass between the first and final events of a wedding in both cultures — and religion — the Buriats with their *Ongons*[56] and the Nez Perce *wyakin*[57]. The killing of a deceased's favorite horse at his funeral was another similarity. All this, of course, also got me thinking about the similarities between the beliefs of the Buriats, Nez Perce, and my own Christian heritage, which were surprisingly many. Instead of shamans, Christians have priests and ministers, instead of *Ongons* or *wyakin*, many Christians believe in personal saints, or guardian angels.

The Nez Perce believe that everything — people, trees, animals, even rocks — has a spirit which can communicate, and didn't Jesus himself say the rocks would cry out to acknowledge him[58]? Of course, I am no theologian — suffice to say that these similarities and others have influenced my own beliefs.

I was soon walking and even riding again and spent much time with Lean Elk and Ollokot, a young chief from the *Kamooenem* band. He was an easy-going chap, with a handsome, open face, and a tall, strong frame.

---

[56] Personal Gods

[57] *Nimiipuu* guardian spirits.

[58] Luke 19:40

We enjoyed many fine times together, and I surprised them with my skill with the bow — once I was strong enough to draw one! I enjoyed not only the hunting, but the opportunity to contribute. After all they had done for me, providing fresh meat seemed the least I could do.

In the evening, the talk around the fires often turned serious. Uppermost in their minds was their ancestral homeland, which was being overrun by whites seeking gold and free land. A new treaty had been signed in 1863 by Chief Lawyer, ceding all but a small portion of the Nez Perce lands to the government, and all Nez Perce bands were subject to that treaty, whether their own chiefs had signed or not.

"Who are the *soyapo*[59] to tell us we have a head chief[60] to speak for all of us and give our land away?" asked Ollokot one night. "What use are treaties, when it is clear that the *soyapo* will just take, until there is no place left for the *Nimiipuu*?"

---

[59] *Nimipuutimt* for "white man"

[60] Territorial Governor Isaac Stevens had appointed Chief Lawyer as head Chief of all the Nez Perce bands, a position that had never before existed, due to Lawyer's embrace of Christianity, friendliness toward whites, and recognition of the government's supremacy. The 1863 Treaty reduced the Nez Perce reservation by 90%.

Many of the men asserted their agreement. "The *soyapo* are like a bad man after a good girl," said White Bird, "they speak sweetly and make great promises until they get what they want, and then leave it ruined. They are men of no honor."

A man named Kicking Horse spoke up, "What choice is there? The *soyapo* are like the blades of grass. There is no end to them! How are we to fight them?"

"We must not fight!" said Eagle Robe "None are braver than the *Nimiipuu*, but we are few and they are many. We must think of the old ones, the women, the children. What will happen to them when all the warriors are dead? We must find a different way — a way to survive through peace."

There was a great deal of agreement. "Eagle Robe is right," said Ollokot. "My father Tuekakas, my brother, and I are one on this. We must bargain, learn to make weapons of words, as they do." He gestured at the group. "We all have many friends among the *soyapo*. We have traded and lived with them for years[61]. We must win them to our cause, use their influence to protect ourselves."

---

[61] The Nez Perce had lived peacefully with the white men since saving Lewis and Clark's expedition from starvation in 1806.

There were a few hotheads pushing for a fight, but a strong majority were in agreement — war must be avoided. However, it would remain a constant subject for debate over the ensuing years.

Finally, the last group came in, led by Toohoolhoolzote, a fierce old giant of a man. A feast was held, and what a time it was! There was food in abundance, not only buffalo and other game, but dried fish, camas roots, bitterroots, and berries of every variety. The dancing went on until late in the night. Everyone was happy and grateful for a good hunt.

I was becoming enraptured by Coming Together. Over the past weeks, I had seen her first as saviour, then a nurse, a translator, and finally, a friend, but when I saw her that night, laughing and dancing in her best finery, I saw her only as a woman. Her long, black hair glistened in the firelight, which gave a lovely, coppery tint to her soft, brown skin. When she smiled, her face lit up and drove the shadows from my heart. I hadn't seen nearly as much of her since I became ambulatory — it wasn't seemly for an unmarried man and woman to be alone — and I was caught off guard by these feelings. For the first time since waking in the camp, I felt whole again. I felt like a man.

Lean Elk noticed me noticing her. Nudging me with his elbow, he said, "Be careful Nate. I told you, that one's bad luck."

"Why do you keep saying that?"

"Ask yourself, why is a woman unmarried at her age? It isn't her looks. She is a very beautiful, very good woman. The young men should be fighting over her, but they're not. Even she knows she's bad luck." Then he walked away.

His dismissal of her as "unlucky" offended me on her behalf. I knew she had been married and had a daughter, but other than that, I knew little about her. Still, her kind and solicitous care of me, a stranger, told me all I needed to know, unlucky or not.

Chapter Nineteen

On love; new friends; across the Lolo Trail; the Wallowa Valley; I am adopted; an awkward courtship; a winter mission; a merciless boy; a delightful surprise

Washington Territory
1867 – 1868

When the hunting camp broke up, I decided to go with Ollokot to the *Nimiipuu* homeland west of the mountains. Much of my decision was based on my attachment to Coming Together. Chief White Bird's band, the *Lamtama*, lived near the lands of Ollokot's band and, because she had many close relations among the *Kammooenem*, she spent a great deal of time visiting there. I had considered staying with her people, but was afraid that my burgeoning affection for her would be unrequited — she was a beautiful woman and I was a scarred cripple. She treated me with a sort of detachment which could have been coyness or disinterest, and I thought a little distance might clarify her feelings toward me. At any rate, Ollokot and I had become fast friends, and I was also very attached to little Yellow Wolf. I decided it was better to love her from a distance than face rejection.

Ollokot had given me one of the beautiful and spirited spotted horses of the Nez Perce, and as we rode out of camp Lean Elk shouted at me good-naturedly, "You still owe me a broken rifle, but I'd take that broken-down nag you're riding!"

I laughed and waved. "Don't worry, I'll bring it to you next year!"

We took the Lolo Trail over the mountains, some of the roughest, most beautiful country I've ever seen. The tortuous trail led up and down the mountains, from high passes nearly as high as the snow-covered peaks to valleys so deep and narrow they never saw the sun. It was wonderful to see, these men, women, and children — and their herd of four- or five-hundred horses — traversing this perilously narrow trail without a care in the world. I, on the other hand, was terrified that first crossing. I spent most of the time concentrating on keeping the rump of the horse in front of me between my mount's ears, as to look anywhere else prompted a vertigo that threatened to pull me from my saddle. To look up was dizzying, down was terrifying, and horizontally disorienting —

as if we were flying rather than riding — there was as much sky below us as above us. The mountains were heavily forested with towering pine trees that swayed hypnotically, and we were occasionally halted by trees fallen across the trail.

The *Nimiipuu*, from the oldest to the youngest took all this in stride and were greatly amused at my reaction. Little Yellow Wolf especially liked to tease me, insisting that "You need to stay on your horse! No room here to walk in circles!" Then he would laugh and laugh.

I was heartened by the fact that Coming Together always seemed to ride just ahead of me in the narrowest parts, and near me when the trail was wider. I thought I saw her watching me sometimes, usually accompanied by giggling friends. It seemed odd for someone considered so unlucky to be so popular. I had made some subtle inquiries about her to Ollokot and others but got no answers. Like the Cheyenne, the *Nimiipuu* knew how to mind their own business. All I learned was that she was much loved, highly regarded, and no one would marry her. At least there was no competition for her hand. It also gave me something more pleasant to think about than falling to my death.

At last, we emerged from the mountains onto the Weippe Prairie, where we camped for a couple of days before each party returned to their own bands. The land around the prairie was still quite rugged and mountainous, but with large plateaus and prairies too — nothing like the Bitterroots. Happily, the White Bird party traveled with us for several more days across the Clearwater River, the Camas Prairie, and the Salmon River. There was a big get-together once we crossed the Salmon — the bands of both Toohoolhoolzote and White Bird joined us to welcome their hunters back home and we camped with them a couple days. I was happy to spend a little more time near Coming Together. We had both managed to put ourselves in the other's way quite a bit on the trail. We spoke very little to each other but exchanged many looks that seemed to grow more meaningful as time passed.

When the celebration wound down, I rode with Ollokot's party through mountains and canyons until we crossed the Snake River and climbed up to the Wallowa valley. It was beautiful country, rich in everything a man could want — big and small game, towering timber, clear, fast-running water, broad meadows with rich grazing for the horses and cattle — my Buriat grandfather would have wept with envy. In the late summer and fall, the rivers were full of salmon, which the *Nimiipuu* harvested by the hundreds.

Hunting buffalo was only part of the reason for crossing the mountains every year — they also went to trade dried fish, salmon oil and other foodstuffs, shells and ornaments, and weapons, especially their horn bows, made from the straightened horns of Bighorn sheep. Those powerful bows were highly prized and much sought after by the Flatheads, Crows, and other friendly Plains tribes.

Upon arriving at the *Kammooenem* camp, little Yellow Wolf insisted that I stay with his family, "You will like it with us," the little fellow announced. "My father is very wealthy, very generous. My mother is a very good cook. She'll fatten you up good."

His parents, Horse Blanket and Swan Woman, lived up to his claims — their hospitality was impeccable. In fact, all my efforts to contribute through hunting to the family's welfare was refused, and I was directed to other families, particularly the elderly, whose need was greater. This established my reputation for generosity, a highly respected virtue among The People. Despite their wealth, Horse Blanket and his family lived no differently than any other family in the band. It was considered shameful to hoard possessions when others were in need.

One night, Horse Blanket gave two horses to a young man needing to travel to relatives up north, and I commented on his generosity.

"Why not help when others are in need?" he asked. "I have many horses, but I can only ride one. Young Hawk Looking's only horse broke its leg. His father is dying far away, so I help him. *Nimiipuu* are all one family. We all need each other to survive. Maybe sometime Young Hawk Looking will help someone else, maybe even my son." He looked over at the sleeping Yellow Wolf with affection. "Why is it so different among the *soyapo*? Why don't they all help each other? A few rich, many poor, all fighting for more of everything? Foolish way to live."

"I don't know," I said. "If I figure it out, I'll let you know." I would spend many hours pondering that. I still do. If I ever do get it figured out I'll have to tell Yellow Wolf — Horse Blanket is long dead.

After a month or so, Coming Together and her little girl came to visit her cousins, and I paid as much attention to her as I could without being forward. I thought I was awfully subtle, until one day I was out hunting with Ollokot and he said, apropos of nothing, "If a man wants a woman for his wife, that man could have a friend speak to her family." He grinned knowingly.

"What are you talking about?" I bluffed.

"Nothing," he said. "I know how strong you are to learn our ways. Thought you might not know how we do it." He shrugged. "Just in case."

"Well . . . thanks?"

He just nodded, and we continued our hunt. Later, I asked him, "What would make a woman be considered unlucky?"

"You talk a lot for a hunter." A little later, he said, "One woman, or any woman?"

"Oh, you know, just any woman."

"Could be many things. Maybe she's just clumsy or careless. Just something that makes all men avoid her. Something like that maybe."

"Clumsy, huh?"

"No man wants a clumsy wife — they ruin food, break arrows, drop babies."

"Still, nothing wrong with marrying an unlucky woman is there?"

"Nothing wrong," he said, "but such a man better have good medicine."

Coming Together stayed for a month or so before returning home, and I started finding excuses to visit the *Lamtama* band. Once, I took little Yellow Wolf to visit his *Lamtama* cousins. We had a splendid time, and I always managed to steal some time with Coming Together. I began to believe my feelings were requited. As we spent more time together, our relationship became the worst-kept secret in Washington Territory. We were always careful to observe the proprieties, were never completely alone, especially after dark, and always kept a respectable distance from each other, but gentle teasing and knowing looks followed us everywhere.

One evening, under the guise of learning more of the *Nimiipuu* ways, I asked her, "What do *Nimiipuu* women look for in a husband?"

"Why," she asked archly, "have you found one you liked?"

"Hmm? Oh. No, nothing like that. Just curious is all. I want to learn as much about The People as I can."

"I see," she said solemnly, but with a sparkle in her eyes. "It depends on the woman. All women want a good man, a good hunter, a brave and kind man. Outside of that, who knows? Some want a wealthy man, others a generous one, or a handsome one. Some look for one who is patient, who would be a good father. It is hard to say about women in general."

"Well how about you?" I asked. "Just as an example, of course."

"It doesn't matter," she said, her face suddenly gone sad. "No man will marry me. I am unlucky."

"Why would you say that?"

"Not just me. Everyone knows."

"Well I think you shouldn't give up. Maybe you just haven't met the right man yet?" It was the closest I had ever seen her to being in tears.

"I met the right man – three times. All brothers[62]. All died within two winters of marrying me. The fourth brother refused to marry me. No one blamed him, including me." She was quiet a moment. "At least my last husband gave me my daughter, so I am grateful. I won't die alone."

---

[62] In Nez Perce culture, if a woman was widowed, she would/could marry his brother after a year of mourning.

My heart broke for her, but I was still too unsure of myself. "Maybe it's not you who is unlucky, but them," I said feebly.

"That's what we all thought after my first two husbands, but no denying it after the third. It would take a very brave man to marry me now. Maybe no such man lives anymore," she said sadly. Then she squared her shoulders and raised her head. "I have had three good husbands and still have my daughter. It is enough." She paused, and then looked into my eyes and shattered my heart, "None of The People will marry me, but I will only ever marry a man of The People." Then she retired for the night.

Soon, I was too busy for visiting, as the *Kamooenem* prepared for winter. We left the Wallowa valley to camp in a sheltered place hidden deep in the canyons below, where we waited out the brutal cold and fierce wind, huddled around our fires and thankful for the bounty of the spring, summer, and fall that enabled us to survive the starving time. I only saw her once, late that winter.

***

A messenger arrived from Chief White Bird asking for help — rot had gotten into much of their food stores and a fierce blizzard had driven away what little game there had been — they were starving.

Although our own stores were dwindling, the headmen of the band went through and collected whatever people could spare which, given the *Nimiipuu* veneration of generosity, amounted to a great deal of food. Everyone gave what they could, except for one man — White Bull, a man of bad reputation — who gave next to nothing.

"Not my fault they do not know how to prepare food to last," he said. "Some of them starve, maybe the rest will learn." The headmen just shook their heads and moved on. Like the Cheyenne, no one had the power to compel any man. I wondered if John Stuart Mill had studied any Indian societies during his work. I also wondered what White Bull would do if his food went bad. From what I knew of the man, I very much doubted he'd insist on going it alone.

The foodstuffs were packed onto horses and several of us volunteered to make the hazardous journey to the *Lamtama* winter camp. Before we left, Horse Blanket asked me to take Yellow Wolf with me. I was hesitant to take a boy of eleven with me on a trip across such treacherous, icy terrain.

"He is old enough to learn to sacrifice for The People," said Horse Blanket. "A boy needs to learn that doing what is good, what is right, is not always easy. He is a good boy and will do as you say."

"I just . . . I'm not sure that I'm the . . ."

"You are uncle to Yellow Wolf. Who else would I trust with my son?"

When we rode out, Yellow Wolf was right beside me. The little fellow was very excited but doing his best to appear grave — he'd been entrusted with a man's responsibility — I had no doubt he understood the gravity of the mission.

Ollokot led Two Moons, Bow and Arrow Case, Five Wounds, and Rainbow — all brave men and proven warriors — myself, Yellow Wolf, another young boy named Wahlitits, and the *Lamtama* messenger out at first light, pushing as hard as we dared. The horses had lost much fat and strength, so we were very careful with them. The trail was tough — sometimes the ground was bare and icy, and sometimes deep drifts blocked our way. Creeks and streams were frozen over and made for unsure footing — we spent much time leading our horses to spare their strength. The route wound through canyon mazes and up over highlands that would make a mountain sheep nervous. Through it all, Yellow Wolf worked as hard as any man. I was proud of him.

It took us about eight exhausting days to reach Chief White Bird's camp, and they were plenty glad to see us. Although groups had also arrived from the other bands, ours was by far the biggest and so had more to give. The *Lamtama* headmen took charge of distributing the food, Yellow Wolf went to see his cousins, and I sought out Coming Together. Despite what she had said about marrying only a *Nimiipuu* man, I still hoped.

I found her in her father's lodge, weak and exhausted. She gave me a wan smile. "Don't you know it's dangerous to travel in this weather?" she scolded.

"Well, I was passing by, and tired of carrying so much food, so I thought I'd stop and see if you could use some," I answered.

"Oh no, we're fine," she said in a wavering voice. "But, if it will help you, we'll be happy to take some." She smiled again.

I sat down next to her, pulled food — Kouse biscuits, dried berry cakes, camas, meat, and fish — from my bag and handed it to her father to distribute.

They accepted it graciously, and after ensuring everyone had a share, washed, gave thanks, and ate. It felt good to see the relief on their faces.

In order to not strain the food supply, we stayed only long enough to rest the horses, and I spent as much of it as possible with Coming Together. With a steady supply of food, she quickly regained her strength. We didn't speak too much, and there was no talk of love or attachment — just everyday things — and mostly of food, which was still foremost in everyone's mind.

"I hope the hunting is good soon," she said one day.

"I do too," I said. "I'm plenty tired of dried meat. I'm glad we've got it, but fresh would be wonderful."

"Maybe you will kill an elk?"

"It's possible. At this point, I'd settle for a rabbit."

"Rabbit is good, but elk is better."

"Yes."

"If you get an elk, maybe you will bring me its hide?"

"I don't know," I teased, "It's an awfully long way to go just to bring it here. Maybe you'll cook the meat for me?"

"Could be," she said, and scooted a little closer to me.

The morning we left, she tugged on my pitifully thin beard, which I had allowed to grow in hopes it would keep my face warm. She didn't say anything, just made a dismissive noise, giggled, and let it go. "Be safe on the trail," she said.

"I will," I promised. "I'll come back in the spring."

"Bring me that elk hide."

"I will."

She touched my beard again, shook her head and then, quick as a striking snake, her hand shot out and plucked a hair from my face. Then she walked away.

I thought about that all the way home. The return trip was easier — a strong southerly wind had arrived in the *Lamtama* camp with us and warmed things up. The snow was melting, the streams cleared of ice and, with no need to rush, we even managed to hunt up some game. All agreed that the signs were of an early spring.

I was too busy thinking about my beard. What was she trying to tell me? Was she trying to tell me something? Or was I reading too much into it? Was she changing her mind about me? Was she sad that I wasn't one of The People? Why would she say she couldn't marry me if that's what she wanted? There were many *Nimiipuu* women who married white men — why couldn't she? And if she couldn't, why would she allow me to grow so close to her? Was it some *Nimiipuu* thing that I hadn't learned about yet? Did it even have anything to do with my beard? Had I completely misread her feelings toward me? It was all very frustrating.

About the fourth day, Ollokot approached me. "Is your stomach alright?"

"Yes, it's fine. Why?"

"You've had a sour face ever since we left White Bird's camp."

"I just have some things on my mind."

Yellow Wolf spoke up, "His something is a somebody." I gestured threateningly at him and he and Wahlitits galloped away laughing.

"That boy needs the whipper[63] after him," I griped. "Teach him to mind his own business."

"Maybe — but I think he speaks truth," said Ollokot, laughing.

"That's ridiculous!"

---

[63] Nez Perce parents rarely disciplined their children, but had a community whipper whose job it was to whip older children who needed it.

"I think you should never play cards with Poker Joe. You have a face for horse racing."

"What's that mean?"

"No need to bluff in racing."

I gave in and told him what she'd said, and how she'd acted about my beard. "What do you think she means by all of that?"

"I think only a fool tries to figure out what a woman is trying to say before she just comes out and says it," he said. "My wives say many things I don't understand. I just do as I think I should. Sooner or later they tell me plain — if they have to. If they never do, then they got what they wanted or decided they didn't want it after all."

"Why can't women just say what they mean?"

He laughed. "I think if they did, we wouldn't want them so much." He rode on ahead, then turned back. "One thing — being a man of The People is more than just blood." Then he rode away.

Maybe he was right — was she hoping for a husband committed to her, and to The People as well? Most of the *Nimiipuu* women married to soyapo men were Christians living much like the *soyapo* did. She wasn't willing to give up the ways of The People, and I didn't blame her. I'd had enough of the *soyapo* way and had no desire to go back. But how to make that clear to her?

In the spring, I asked Ollokot to arrange the marriage between Coming Together and myself, if she was willing. I sent an elk hide with him, plus another package — a piece of folded doeskin containing the plucked hairs of my beard and mustache.

When he returned, Coming Together and Walks Through were riding with him. I'd gotten it right after all.

Chapter Twenty

On happiness; brother and uncle; Nimiipuu wedding; wedded bliss; two surprises; soul mates; family; vagaries of time

True happiness is in direct proportion to gratitude. To be truly happy, we must be grateful for what we have, rather than endlessly scrabbling for what we do not. I learned that from Coming Together, and it has stood me in good stead to this very day. It's not that I haven't had bad times, but that she taught me to focus on the good times and, in my life, I have had very, very good times.

Washington Territory
1868-76

In the way of The People, we lived together for a while — a sort of trial period — and each day we grew happier together. Soon, a date was set for the first ceremonial exchange of gifts — the beginning of the actual wedding.

Coming Together's quiet cheerfulness and charm quickly endeared her to Horse Blanket, Swan Woman and their children. We set up housekeeping in a small lodge of our own but took many of our meals with Horse Blanket's family. Coming Together, Swan Woman, and Ollokot's wives Fair Land and Cloudburst, grew thick as thieves, and soon all three ladies developed the troubling habit of giggling whenever I was around, while Coming Together blushed happily. I wasn't sure whether to feel affronted or complimented.

I was at a bit of a loss throughout this time — somehow, I'd completely neglected to pay attention to the wedding traditions of The People. I was panicking, trying to come up with enough gifts of the appropriate quantity and quality to adequately express my feelings about Coming Together. After all, I was quite poor — I'd accumulated a few horses through gambling and trading, and a good reputation, but of worldly goods, I had virtually nothing.

"Your family provides the gifts," said Horse Blanket. "We are your family."

"I can't ask you to do that," I protested, "you've already done so much for me. It is not your responsibility."

"Do not insult me!" answered Horse Blanket. "Are we not brothers? Are you not Yellow Wolf's uncle? Did I not trust you to help show my son how a man sacrifices for The People? You are my brother. I am saying this three times[64]! Would you deny me this honour?"

"But I can never repay you . . ."

"That is the *soyapo* way — to worry about who owes who! If you would marry Coming Together, you need to decide — are you *soyapo*, or are you *Nimiipuu*? If you are *Nimiipuu*, live in our way. If *soyapo*, then go back to them and spare yourselves much pain."

All I could do was apologize. Later it would occur to me that gracious acceptance was as much a part of The People's veneration of generosity as the giving itself. On the givers' side, it was about quietly acknowledging a blessing and passing it along as a sign of gratitude to the Creator. For the recipients, it wasn't admitting a deficiency in themselves, but a way of honouring both the giver and the Creator, who provided the gift in the

[64] A Nez Perce way of emphatically declaring something said is true. A man could lie about something twice without harming his reputation, but a third time would be a source of shame, and result in a loss of respect from his tribesmen

first place. No one was looked down upon because of need. The People, like Rousseau, understood that when we work for others, we also work for ourselves, that cooperation is a necessary and mutual requirement for a free society[65]. It was a beautiful way to live.

The first exchange was in early May. Horse Blanket hosted Coming Together's family and provided a feast for all — since the ceremony represented my family, the masculine side of the match, the feast was heavy on meat and fish — and many speeches were made. Coming Together's father, Strong Eagle, a tall, dignified man made a very touching speech during which he, as well as her entire family, had trouble restraining their emotions. Chief White Bird also spoke many good words, as did Horse Blanket and Ollokot. At the exchange, the families sat across from each other and exchanged gifts. As with the feast, the gifts given by my side reflected the masculine aspects of *Nimiipuu* life — horses, meat, fish, hides, hunting and fishing gear, etc., while the gifts given by Coming Together's side reflected the feminine — root vegetables, bags, baskets, clothing, tools, beads, etc.

---

[65] Appears to be from Jean-Jacques Rousseau's *The Social Contract*, Book II, Chapter IV.

There was much laughter and merriment throughout the event. When her family went home, a close bond had been forged between the families.

That spring and summer were wonderful. During the day, the women would dig kouse and camas and other root crops while we fellows would fish streams and rivers that were full to bursting, or hunted for deer, elk, and other game. After each first successful hunt or digging, thanksgiving ceremonies would be observed to thank the Creator and also to thank the root, fish, or game for returning and giving itself to The People.

Especially joyous was the gathering of many bands on the Weippe and Camas prairies to gather camas roots. Days were spent harvesting, hunting, and visiting friends and relatives not seen in many months. In the evenings there were games, dances, races, singing, trading, and other amusements.

Coming Together and I often went off by ourselves. We would find a good place far from any villages and camp along a stream or lake, and spend long, glorious days enjoying one another. We played many little jokes on one another and made little gifts to surprise each other with. Once again, I thought I was as happy as any man could ever be until one morning in early August, when I received two shocks.

I awoke late and stretched luxuriously, in no hurry to rise. I could smell food cooking and hear Coming Together singing quietly as she prepared breakfast. I took her singing as a good sign. She'd been a bit moody for a few days — not argumentative or unhappy, but pensive, quiet, keeping her thoughts to herself.

When I asked if I'd done something wrong, she just smiled and shook her head. The day before, she'd spent the day sitting alone atop a nearby hill, singing and praying. I hoped that whatever was worrying her had worked itself out. Before long, the smell of the food conquered my sloth. I rose and walked outside undressed to wash in the lake. When I returned, she smiled.

"That water must be cold this morning," she said.

"Woman," I growled, looking as manly and fierce as a naked man can with a woman laughing at him, "that's no way to talk! Didn't your mother teach you to respect your husband?"

"She taught me to speak the truth." She leapt up giggling and ran.

She wasn't trying too hard to get away, so even with my game leg, I quickly swept her up in my arms. "Maybe you need a cold bath to teach you about consequences!" She shrieked and laughed as I threw her into the stream and then plunged in after her. We splashed about a bit and then set about warming each other up. By the time we were finished, breakfast was burnt. We didn't mind.

Coming Together raised up on her elbow. "That is no way to treat the mother of your son."

"What?" I'm not sure what surprised me most — what she'd said, or that she'd said it in English.

"We're going to have a baby."

I sat up — some things can't be properly considered lying down. "That's wonderful! When are you due?" And then, "When did you learn to speak English?"

She sat up facing me. "The baby will come this winter. I learned English as a girl. My father sent me to learn *soyapo* language and Jesus at mission school."

"Why didn't you tell me sooner?"

She reverted to *Nimipuutimt.* "About the baby, or the English?"

"Well . . . both, I suppose."

"Maybe we should talk about one at a time?"

"Erm . . . the baby? How long have you known?"

"Just a few days."

"Why didn't you say something?"

Her face grew very serious. "I needed a few days with it, just for me. I thought I would never marry again, never have more children. I was content with what I had — Walks Through, my family, my memories. And I was happy. But I am happier now."

"I'm glad to hear it. I too am happy. But how do you know it's a son?"

"A mother knows," was all she'd say.

I found the thought of fatherhood exhilarating and terrifying — I was excited by the idea of having a child, but at the same time I was assailed by self-doubt. My life up to this point had been one of abject self-interest and failure. What if I failed this child? What if it grew up to recognize what a pitiful specimen I'd been? Conflicting thoughts and emotions ricocheted off the inside of my skull and heart like hailstones.

Coming Together saw it in my face. "What is wrong, husband?"

I told her.

She took my hand. "You talk nonsense. You will be a good father — I would not have chosen you otherwise."

"I thought I chose you."

She smiled indulgently. "Of course you do. But you were chosen for me before you ever woke up. My *wyakin* told me my husband had fallen into camp, and I needed to make you one of The People. And that, I have done."

"How do you figure that?"

"Would you have learned our language so quickly or so well if you knew that I spoke yours? Would you have sacrificed your silly beard? Would you have learned to put the needs of The People ahead of your own safety and undertaken the journey to bring food to my people if not for me? Those are the things that make you one of The People."

I wasn't offended, but felt I needed to make some defense. "Wait just a minute, woman. It was Horse Blanket and Ollokot who taught me about how a *Nimiipuu* man should concern himself with the well-being of all the people!"

"Yes," she smiled demurely, "but would you have become part of Horse Blanket's family if I had made my feelings plain to you?"

Finally, I conceded defeat. I was getting used to being married.

We ended up moving the second gift exchange up a couple of months — normally six months elapsed between the ceremonies — due to the ill-health of one of her grandmothers. Horse Blanket's and Ollokot's families rode with us to White Bird's camp, where the celebration was made even more joyous by the news of the baby. The feast and exchange followed tradition, the food being primarily roots, berries, etc. That celebration finalized our marriage and was also when I became known as Lucky Man, a sobriquet bestowed upon me by the good-humoured Ollokot.

In time, our son was born, red-faced and squalling. He was a happy, bouncing little fellow with a broad, devil-may-care grin. We called him *Wallommottinin* — Twisted Hair — in honour of an ancestor of Coming Together.

Being a husband and father filled my heart with joy. I remember my sister Tasha had embroidered on a pillow a line from Coleridge[66] about having a soul mate as well as a work mate, and Coming Together proved to be mine. Where I was mercurial, she was steady and calm. She balanced my dark thoughts with dogged optimism — and was right far more often than I was. I was prone to occasional grand gestures of affection, which she matched with a thousand daily kindnesses. We managed to complement each other's good qualities and counter the bad.

We also prospered materially — I managed to amass modest but respectable herds, both through trade and raiding our enemies, the Snake, Bannack, Gros Ventres, and Blackfeet tribes. Ollokot and Horse Blanket taught me the finer points of horse breeding and I was soon raising horses known for their speed and stamina. I was also helped by No Feet, a fellow who — despite having lost both feet and one hand a long time ago — was a great horseman and breaker of wild horses. He was a cheerful, roguish fellow with a treasure trove of jokes and stories of his adventures, some of which were probably true.

---

[66] From an 1822 letter to "a Young Lady" from poet Samuel Taylor Coleridge: "To be happy in Marriage Life, nay in order not to be miserable, you must have a Soul-mate . . ."

The children only added to our happiness — after a couple of years, we gave Twisted Hair a brother, Many Wounds, and four years after that, a daughter named Five Times Over. Walks Through doted on her younger siblings, and I was the only father she'd ever known. For my part, I loved her just as fiercely as if she were my own.

It wasn't all good times, of course, no one is that lucky. We lost two babies between Many Wounds and Five Times Over, but we clung together and carried each other through the bad times. But enough of that.

I loved telling the children stories, both those of the *Nimiipuu* and the Buriat people. I gradually worked in the stories and legends of the Bible — particularly those of Jesus, who was loved and held in high esteem by many of The People — and of the Russian people, along with all of the *soyapo* stories I had picked up through years of listening to tall tales around campfires. Throughout all of this, I taught them to look for the connections and similarities in the beliefs of the *Nimiipuu*, the Buriats, and the *soyapo*.

It is amazing to me how fast those times went — one day we were welcoming Twisted Hair into the world and overnight, Walks Through was pouting because I hadn't made her a bow and arrows like I had for her brothers. "I'm a better shot than Twisted Hair and Many Wounds is so clumsy it's a wonder he hasn't shot himself yet!"

Twisted Hair pulled her braids, "You are not! Besides, what would be the point? Women can't be warriors! Go dig some roots with the women!"

She tackled him and I let her beat on him for a bit, then pulled her off. I started to tell him that clearly women could fight when I was interrupted by a howl of pain from Many Wounds who had tripped and burnt his hand in the fire. After his initial shriek of pain, the little fellow was trying manfully not to cry, and I put Walks Through down with a stern warning, "Either leave your brother alone or go outside to thrash him!" While I examined Many Wounds' hand, I found myself wondering if perhaps we should have named him after a different ancestor. Thank the Creator, Five Times Over was cooing to her doll and contentedly ignoring all the hubbub.

Meanwhile, Coming Together was calmly beading a new pair of moccasins for Many Wounds, whose feet were already larger than his brother's, and laughing at my attempts to rein in our turbulent offspring.

"Husband," she said, "let them fight. They will learn respect for one another regardless of who wins. They will also learn that fighting always carries a cost, whether they win or lose."

My Lord, what I wouldn't give to have those days back!

Chapter Twenty-One

Civilization and natural philosophy; invasion; injustice; trespassers and neighbors; two murders; the last council

Rousseau wrote something along the lines of, "The first fellow who marked off a piece of ground, claimed it as his alone, and found people stupid enough to believe him, was the founder of civilization. Think about how much misery and crime, wars, and other horrors would have been avoided if someone had knocked his markers down and told the people, 'Don't listen to this fool! The things of the earth belong to everyone, and the earth to no one[67]!'"

The People had never heard of Rousseau, but he had nothing to teach them that they didn't already know. Unfortunately, the *soyapo* weren't ever going to read Rousseau or listen to The People.

Washington Territory

[67] This appears to paraphrase a passage from Jean-Jacques Rousseau's *A Dissertation on the Origin and Foundation of the Inequality of Mankind*, "The Second Part."

1872 – 77

The previous pages may have given the reader the idea that everything was sunshine and happiness for both myself and The People. In large part it was, for me, because I made it a point to avoid *soyapo* as much as I could. For the leaders of The People, that was not an option. Ever since gold was discovered, *soyapo* had encroached deeper and deeper into *Nimiipuu* lands, leading to the murder of numerous *Nimiipuu* men and women by *soyapo* acting with impunity. When the 1863 Treaty took away ninety percent of the Nez Perce lands including the Wallowa Valley, Ollokot's father, Old Joseph — an early convert to Christianity, signer of the 1855 Treaty, and outspoken advocate of peace with the *soyapo* — refused to sign and shredded his American Flag and Bible. He renounced his Christian name in favour of his *Nimiipuu* name, Tuekakas, swore his peoples' land was not for sale, and that they would never leave.

Even the Christian chiefs like Lawyer, who already lived on the reduced reservation lands and had signed the 1863 Treaty, protested that the government had not fulfilled any of its promises, and four of them traveled to Washington in 1867 to speak directly to the president about it. Chief Utsinmalihkin refused to sign the proposed amendments and was thrown from a high window and killed. They say his body lay in the street until a group of women took responsibility for burying him[68]. The government, of course, claimed his fall was simply an accident.

When Tuekakas died, around 1871, his eldest son, Young Joseph, assumed chieftainship of the *Kammooenem* band. In the spring of '72, Ollokot asked me to ride with him. We rode in silence, far out to the very edge of the valley and stopped near a cairn of rocks. In the distance we could see two wagons, a couple of horsemen and a small herd of cattle trundling along the toll road that a fellow named Smith had built over the mountains to our valley.

Ollokot nodded toward them. "More come every day. Smith's road is a snake pumping poison into our lands." He gestured toward the cairn, "My father put these markers all around the boundaries of our land to warn these settlers off, but they ignore them. One has

---

[68] This was the story as told by Wottolen, who was part of the *Nimiipuu* delegation, and what the non-treaty Nez Perce believed. Ultimately, the official cause of death was reported as Typhoid fever.

been taken down, its rocks used for a chimney. Others have just been knocked over, the stones scattered. I don't think they will ever stop."

"I think you're right. What will The People do?" I asked.

"What would you advise?"

I considered for a moment. "I don't know, but fighting is not the answer. If *soyapo* are killed, soldiers will come to kill us or drive us away. They won't care whether those they kill have fought or been peaceful. Men, women, children, old ones, won't matter. To be *Nimiipuu* will be to be guilty. I have seen it before. It is their way."

Ollokot said, "That is what I think as well. But we must do something. We will not give up the land where our fathers' bones lay."

We sat in silence for a while. One of the horsemen saw us, and they scurried away as fast as they could.

"If we can't fight, and we won't leave, what is left?"

He considered for a moment. "We must talk with them. Not all *soyapo* are bad men. Maybe we can find a way to live with them, in peace."

I couldn't share his hope, but I had no other solution, so I said nothing.

"Joseph wants you to come with us," he said. "He wants you to translate."

That set me back. I barely even knew Joseph. I doubt we'd exchanged more than a dozen words the whole time I'd been with The People. "Why me?" I asked. "There are others among The People who speak English. Why would he choose me?"

"Because you are half-*soyapo*! Because he knows you are a good man with a good heart. They will trust you more than they would one of us. He also hopes that if they see a *soyapo* living with us, even a half-*soyapo*, but one who is educated like you, it will help them see that we are not their enemies — that we want to live in peace."

It hurt a little bit to be reminded that no matter how I tried, I would never really be one of The People. I think Ollokot saw it in my face. "Maybe," he continued, "that is why you were sent to us — this is how you help The People."

I thought for a moment about Coming Together and our children, about Horse Blanket, Swan Woman, Yellow Wolf, and all of the friends and family I'd made among The People. I also thought about Colorado, about all the slaughtered innocents, Indian and white, and all of the mindless, pointless violence. I couldn't bear to think of the same thing happening here, not if there was anything I could do to prevent it. "I will do as you ask. Although I am not of The People, they are my people."

Joseph, Ollokot, and I set out early the next morning to meet and talk with as many settlers as we could. Our first visit set the pattern for all the others. We stopped some distance away from the cabin and waited for them to notice us. A woman was the first to see us, and she stood there a moment, unsure what to do. We all waved as peaceably as we could. She made a sort of half-hearted wave, and then called her husband who came out of a lean-to next to the cabin with an axe in his hand. They talked a moment, and she went into the house while we slowly approached. He was a short fellow, but burly, his face was almost completely hidden behind an enormous red beard, mustaches, and remarkably bushy eyebrows. The only visible features he had that were not fur-bearing were a pair of piercing blue eyes, and a set of buck teeth giving the impression that he was an enormous groundhog in pants.

We were unarmed, other than Ollokot's hunting bow, which was stored in a case unstrung, and kept our hands visibly empty. I was wearing soyapo clothing and took the lead. "Hello sir," I said as cheerily as I could manage with a rifle barrel protruding from a window of the cabin.

"Howdy," he said, eyeing Joseph and Ollokot warily. "Help you fellows with something?"

"These gentlemen are chiefs of the local band of Nez Perce, and they'd like to talk with you."

"Chiefs, huh?" He looked Joseph and Ollokot over closely. "I ain't never met a chief before."

"Well, Mr. . . .?"

"Wood. Jeremiah Wood."

"Mr. Jeremiah Wood, I have the honor of presenting Chiefs Joseph and Ollokot of the *Kammooenem* band of the Nez Perce." To Joseph and Ollokot, I said, "This gentleman is named Jeremiah Wood." They smiled and nodded.

Then Wood surprised me. Shifting his axe to his left hand, he stepped forward, smiled, and extended his hand to Joseph. "You tell 'em I'm pleased to meet 'em," he said to me without taking his eyes from Joseph's.

"No need, Mr. Wood," I said. "Your behaviour speaks for itself."

After shaking Joseph's hand, he shook Ollokot's, and then mine, with a firm grip that hinted of great strength.

"Never been accused of bein' a gentleman afore, but I do aim to be hospitable." He stepped back and gestured toward the cabin. "Why don't you fellers 'light and set?"

We hesitated, an eye on that unwavering rifle barrel.

Seeing that, he called, "Des, honey, you can put that down now! These fellers just come by to say 'hello.' Come on out here and say howdy!" The rifle disappeared, and a moment later, a tall, raw-boned, flaxen-haired woman in a gingham dress with a little red-haired girl clinging to her skirts stepped out, followed by a boy of about twelve. "This is my wife Desdemona and my boy Jack. The little 'un is Rosie." At the mention of her name, Rosie shyly buried her face in her mother's skirts.

We all dismounted and I made the introductions again. Mrs. Wood said, "I'm pleased to meet you," and my companions shook both her hand and Jack's. Then Joseph, that tall, dignified, somber man squatted next to Rosie and waited patiently until she gathered the nerve to look at him. He smiled and produced a small beaded doll from behind his back and offered it to her. She looked up at her mother for approval, and then reached for it slowly and cautiously, keeping her eyes on Joseph as if afraid he'd bite. Once she had it in her hands though, she ran away giggling, clutching the doll to her breast.

"Well, you've made a friend there, right enough," said Wood.

Ollokot took a small bow and arrows from a *parfleche* on his horse and offered them to Jack, holding them out with both hands.

The boy looked at Wood. "Can I Pa?"

Wood looked at me questioningly.

"They are gifts, freely given in a spirit of friendship," I said.

"Well, alright then," he said, nodding at his son.

The boy accepted them with due solemnity. "Can he show me how to shoot?" he asked me while pointing to Ollokot, then himself, and finally mimed shooting the bow. I didn't even have to translate — Ollokot nodded, and the two walked a short distance and began practicing shooting at a piece of firewood set on a stump. I noticed that Ollokot kept them close to the cabin. Wood also noticed and nodded at me approvingly.

"Well, you all come in and sit a spell" he said.

We followed him and Mrs. Wood into the cabin, Joseph stooping to get through the low door. Wood offered us seats at the table, but I noted that he sat facing the open door so he could see his son. He noticed me noticing, and I nodded approval. A man should not let friendliness and hospitality make him foolish, especially a man with a family to protect. He offered us coffee, and Mrs. Wood put the pot on to boil.

While we waited, he got down to brass tacks. "I'm glad to meet you fellers, and the young'uns like the toys, but you all didn't ride out here just to play Santy Clause in the middle of summer. So what's this really all about?"

I translated, and Joseph said, "It is good for people to be on good terms, to be at peace."

"You'll get no argument here," Wood said.

Joseph continued. "This land belongs to my people, and you should not be here. Your government promised this land would always be ours. Your government should have kept you out. But I want to tell you face to face that my people are not your enemies. You have nothing to fear from us. We desire only to live in peace."

Wood took a moment to contemplate what Joseph had said. "Well," he said finally, "I been told this land is up for grabs. We've put ever'thing we got into this place, and I got a family to feed. So there's that. On the other hand, I'm a peaceable man, and I got no wish for anything but peace with your people. Your folk will always be welcome in my house, and at my table, long's we can treat each other honest and direct, like men should."

I translated and Joseph spent some time in thought, carefully studying Wood's face and the tone of his voice, as well as his words. Finally, he spoke. "It is good that we can speak as men, with good feeling for each other. I tell you three times, we will have peace between us." As the two men shook hands in agreement, we heard Jack whoop with excitement as he finally hit the target. I took it as a good sign.

We spent a few hours getting to know the Woods. At one point, Joseph sat down on the floor with little Rosie and listened intently as she introduced him to her other dolls. Mr. Wood tried his hand at the bow and failed spectacularly, much to Jack's delight. "Reckon I'll stick to my rifle," he said. "I'm a lot better with it."

Men being men, that led to a shooting contest between Wood and Joseph, at the end of which they declared themselves pretty evenly matched. I busied myself chopping wood on the other side of the cabin — I had not fired a gun since awakening in Poker Joe's village, and still found the sound of gunfire unsettling. I tried to time the fall of the axe with their firing.

We ate dinner with them and contributed some of our food, which they enjoyed greatly. As the shadows lengthened, we said our goodbyes, and rode away, Joseph wisely deciding that a friendship begun in the full light of day might not be so firm in the dark of night.

Our reception at the other camps and cabins in the valley varied of course, but most of the settlers took a friendly view of us — although there were a few who were outright hostile, including one sorry, surly b-----d who set his dogs on us — and all of them at least had the good sense to realize that most of them would never make it out of the valley if The People went to war.

Our success was largely due to Joseph's diplomacy. I grew to greatly admire him on that trip. His care and concern for keeping the peace was for the well-being of both The People and the *soyapo* families. He was firm in his insistence that they were trespassers, but also made it clear that neither he nor The People bore them any ill will.

He didn't just stop with the settlers in the Wallowa, either. He and Ollokot accepted an invitation from the town of La Grande in the Grande Ronde Valley to take part in their Fourth of July celebration, where they had an audience with a congressman. They both asserted their loyalty to the country, but insisted that the Wallowa Valley still belonged to The People. Joseph also spoke to anyone he could find about the killings of *Nimiipuu* by *soyapo*, insisting that the white men who killed our people must be arrested and tried. He attended meetings, councils, and conferences with any number of government officials, political appointees, and military officers, almost all of whom professed sympathy for our plight and were very sorry, but they had no power to change policy, and promised to forward Joseph's petitions up the chain to someone who might be able to help. In the meantime, The

People would just have to abide by the 1863 Treaty, give up their lands and move onto the reservation.

If that weren't enough, Joseph and the other chiefs had to work tirelessly to keep our hotheads from starting trouble.

In '74, the murders struck closer to home. The People left their winter camps and returned to the Wallowa Valley in the spring. I rode out with Yellow Wolf and Wahlitits, to help Wahlitits' father, Chief Eagle Robe prepare his garden. Both had grown into splendid young men, quiet and well-mannered. Despite his rambunctious youth, Yellow Wolf was inclined toward solitude and contemplation, while Wahlitits was well known for his derring-do and had become a popular leader among the young men. When we arrived, we saw that someone had fenced in the ground for cattle. A moment later, we found the old chief struggling with Larry Ott, who lived nearby.

Eagle Robe saw us and called out "My son, help me!" We were already moving forward when Ott pressed his belt gun against the unarmed Eagle Robe's breast and fired. The old man fell to the ground groaning. Ott fired twice at us, then leapt on his horse and fled. We let him go and attended to Eagle Robe.

He was fading fast. Wahlitits wept and clutched his father to his chest. "I will kill that man!" he vowed.

The Chief raised a trembling hand to his son's face. "No, my son," he said. "Do nothing to that *soyapo*. Let him live his life! Vengeance destroys those who seek it. Do not waste your life on it."

Wahlitit's tears fell onto his father's face. "I will do as you say father," he said, as if the words were tearing at his soul.

"You were a good boy," Eagle Robe said, his words scarcely a whisper, "Be a good man." And then he was gone.

The tension just kept ratcheting up — the more *soyapo* that got away with murdering *Nimiipuu*, the more emboldened and belligerent others became. The newspapers, those vile manipulators of public feeling, began agitating for settlers to "rise up and wipe those Indians from the earth!"

In the spring of '76, a group of hunters galloped into camp, calling out, "Wilhautyah is dead!" They had been accosted by two *soyapo*, named McNall and Findley, and accused of horse thievery. A struggle had ensued, and Findley had shot Wilhautyah. Then they ran away.

Joseph was devastated — Wilhautyah was one of his closest friends and Findley had been friends with both Joseph and Wilhautyah. A few days later, the missing horses were found. They had only wandered off and not been stolen at all. That killing led to another round of councils, at which Joseph and Ollokot insisted that justice be done. Ollokot went so far as to say that he didn't want the men punished, just driven from the valley. None of it made any difference. Nothing could have — in June of '76, Custer, that bloody-minded slaughterer of women and children, and his entire command were wiped out by Sitting Bull's Sioux. Nothing creates hatred in a people like a disaster.

We made it through another winter, and the following May, there was a council with the one-armed General Oliver Otis Howard, Commander of the Department of the Columbia. Howard was a professional soldier, a decorated and courageous veteran of the Civil War, a devout Christian, and had been head of the Freedmen's Bureau following the Civil War, protecting and defending the rights of former slaves. Maybe he would give us a chance.

Instead, he proved a petty martinet — impatient, arrogant, and disrespectful. Over the course of a few days, he had Toohoolhoolzote chained in the guardhouse for speaking like a man, "showed the rifle" by threatening to use the army to force The People onto the reservation, and finally issued an ultimatum — we had thirty days to move onto the reservation or face war. When Joseph asked for a few extra months to allow the rivers to drop and to gather our herds, Howard said, "I will not give you one extra day! If you aren't on the reservation within thirty days, we will drive you onto it, and you will lose everything!"

After the council, all the bands scrambled to gather their herds, and recover food caches, but the efforts were hampered by the racing rivers, flooded by the spring melt. Some *soyapo* took advantage of the situation and helped themselves to The People's herds. We lost hundreds of head of cattle to thieves, and hundreds of packs of cured food were destroyed by the army. Nearing the deadline, the five bands of non-treaty *Nimiipuu*, those of Joseph, White Bird, Looking Glass, Toohoolhoolzote, and Husishusis Kute's small band of *Paloos* gathered at *Tepahlewan*, an ancient gathering place just west of Tolo Lake to make their final preparations to move onto the reservation.

***

In the sixteen years between the discovery of gold and the outbreak of war, thirty-two *Nimiipuu* men and women, were killed by whites. Only one white man was ever even tried for his crimes. He was sentenced to hang for murdering a *Nimiipuu* woman, but I never heard that the sentence was carried out. In all that time, not a single one of The People shed white blood. It was a good thing for the settlers that The People weren't "civilized".

Chapter Twenty-Two

On war; preparing for the move; bad news; confusion and indecision; a lesson in hunting and humility; a warning; soldiers!; White Bird Canyon

Of all man's follies, war is the most stupid, and the most evil. Of the legion of stupid misconceptions about war, perhaps the worst is that it is glorious. It isn't. It is only pain and terror and hunger and disease and tears. And money of course. There is always profit in the suffering of others.

Last evening, I watched the children playing at war. They were all having a splendid time, including quite a number of dramatic "glorious" deaths, made all the more so by the fact that the deceased always rose to fight again. All was well until one of the boys, Jimmy Newcomb I believe it was, misstepped and broke his ankle. In that moment, the pain and suffering of war became terribly real, and when they'd fetched his parents, the other combatants faded away to their homes. I doubt it occurred to them to be grateful they still had homes to go to.

Washington Territory
June 1877

While the women were hurriedly harvesting the camas roots, Chief Joseph, his daughter, Sound of Running Feet, Ollokot and his wife, Cloudburst, Welweyas — a half-man-and-half-woman who dressed as a woman — and I undertook a hazardous crossing of the Salmon River to slaughter beef. In the evenings, Ollokot and Welweyas would compete to keep us entertained. They were evenly matched in jokes, but Welweyas had a way with a song or story that Ollokot, for all his jocular charm, could not match.

In just a few days, we managed to load twelve or so pack horses with beef and headed home. We had just recrossed the still-flooded river — without losing a single horse or pack! — when we saw Two Moons skidding down into the canyon toward us. "Something must be wrong for him to ride so hard to find us," Joseph said.

"Maybe not," Ollokot said. "Maybe Springtime has given you a son while we were gone," — Joseph's younger wife, Springtime, was due, and he was anxious to get home — and we men rode ahead to meet him.

Two Moons' horse was lathered with sweat, and he didn't bother with any formalities. "War has started!" he called. "Come quick! Big trouble! War is here!"

"What has happened?" asked Joseph when we reached him.

"Three *soyapo* killed on the Salmon!"

"*Soyapo* killed? Who has done this?"

"It was Wahlitits," said Two Moons, "He, Sarpsis Ilppilp, and Swan Necklace went seeking vengeance for Eagle Robe. They couldn't find Ott, but killed three other *soyapo* in his place."

"Oh, I find that hard to believe! Wahlitits is a good lad! It's been three years." I scoffed. "If Wahlitits wanted revenge, he wouldn't have waited this long surely."

Two Moons stared at me. "Walks in Circles," he said, mockingly, "I tell you this three times! Those boys have brought war on The People!"

"Why would they do this?" demanded Joseph.

"We held a *tel-lik-leen*[69] to boost The People's spirits," Two Moons explained. "Wahlitits and Sarpsis Ilppilp

---

[69] A *tel-lik-leen* was a sort of war parade in which warriors would boast of their exploits, and old victories and feats of courage would be remembered and celebrated.

were given the place of honor at the rear of the march. Yellow Grizzly Bear started taunting Wahlitits, asking why, if he was so brave, was his father unavenged. The next morning, the young men were gone, raiding and killing settlers[70]." He paused for a moment, "We didn't know about it until last night, when Swan Necklace returned. He said Wahlitits and Sarpsis Ilppilp had stayed away from camp hoping The People wouldn't be blamed for their actions. This morning, more young men rode out to join them."

"What are The People doing?" Joseph asked.

"Looking Glass's people have already left for their home on the reservation. The rest are packing up to flee."

We left the women, including Welweyas, to bring the pack horses along and rode as quickly as we could to the village where we found the other bands ready to leave. Only the *Kammooenem* had hesitated, unsure of what to do with their two main chiefs gone. All the

---

[70] Although several settlers were killed during the Salmon River raids, including a man known for setting his dogs on passing Indians, the Wood family were not attacked or harmed in any way. In fact, Sarpsis Ilppilp asked Mrs. Wood to fix them some lunch. After eating, they bid the Woods goodbye, and continued with their raids.

chiefs held a hurried council, where Joseph and Ollokot argued for staying put.

"If we run, the *soyapo* will think we are all guilty of these killings," said Joseph. "If we stay, we may be able to convince One-Arm Howard we had nothing to do with those raids. Perhaps we can still avoid war."

"I think you are wrong," said Toohoolhoolzote. "General Howard is a man of no honour! I believe he wants war. We must leave while we can." There was more debate, but everyone's minds were set. The only thing accomplished was casting Joseph and Ollokot in a suspicious light. Many feared they would make a deal for themselves and leave the other bands to go hang. Their dogged resistance to war worried the others, especially since Joseph's band was the largest, boasting almost sixty men, including those too old or young to fight.

Only after the council broke up did Joseph go to see his new-born daughter — he always put the needs of The People ahead of every personal consideration.

Joseph kept us in place, promising the others that we would act as a rear guard while they headed for *Lahmotta*. A number of warriors from the other bands stayed with us, although it was not clear whether they were staying to stand guard against soldiers or to keep an eye on Joseph and Ollokot. Trust is hard in wartime.

All night long, riders came close in to camp and fired a few shots. When we returned fire, they'd run back into the night. I don't believe they were soldiers, but civilian volunteers who wanted a fight until they got one. When morning broke, Joseph had decided to follow the other bands. We hurried after them, catching them at *Sapachesap*, a cave on Cottonwood Creek.

We were headed to *Lahmotta* — White Bird Canyon — where we could rest and the chiefs deliberate. The chiefs sent out scouts, and we reached *Lahmotta* without incident. I prepared to take the boys hunting while Coming Together and Walks Through put up the lodge and arranged things. Walks Through was now twelve, and unhappy about the arrangement. "Why do the boys get to go hunting and I have to stay here and do women's work?" she demanded.

This was a common theme whenever we moved camp. "Daughter," I heard Coming Together say, "we all have our part to play. It does no good for the men to bring back game if there is no home to come to. It does no good to have a home if there is nothing to eat."

"But why do the women have to do this part? Why can't the boys do it?"

"Because it is not just hunting! War has come to The People. The boys must hunt to practice shooting. If they can hit a rabbit or a deer running, they can hit a soldier standing still! Enough talk — work now!"

Twisted Hair snickered as we left camp. "Stupid Walks Through. Why can't she just be a normal girl?"

"What makes a normal girl?" I asked him.

"Setting up the lodge, cooking, mending things, digging roots, taking care of children, so the men can do the important things like hunting and fighting."

"Boys, hear me. Among almost all peoples, the women keep the home, and the men go out to hunt or work. But that does not mean that women cannot hunt or fight. Some are even better at it than most men."

Twisted Hair laughed at this, while Many Wounds, being more contemplative, listened as I told them of Joan of Arc, Queen Boadicea, Alyona Arzamasskaya, and many others. "Who are we to say women can't fight?"

"Those are all *soyapo*. They are not real women!" said Twisted Hair.

So I told them about Khutulun, — an ancestor of ours — and Lakshmibai of Jhansi. I told them about their grandmother Namzilma, who would have knocked them senseless for saying such things. Then, the *pièce de resistance* — I showed them the scar on top of my head. "Do you see that? What would you say if I told you that your father was defeated and scalped — by a woman?"

They were aghast as I told them about Buffalo Calf Woman and how she and her comrades had run us to ground. "The only reason you boys are here is because a woman showed me mercy. Never tell me that women can't be warriors!" We'd been so busy talking that we returned to camp empty-handed. Coming Together was cooking up some plump rabbits that Walks Through had killed while we were blathering away. The point was not lost on the boys.

No one slept well that night. Some of the raiders had returned with whisky, and many got drunk, carousing all night long. "Fools," I growled when a particularly loud whoop woke me yet again. "When the soldiers come, we'll need clear-eyed, alert men, not a bunch of swollen-headed sots."

Coming Together laid her head on my breast. "Nate, my love, when the soldiers come, you must not fight."

"What foolishness is this, wife? How can I not fight? What sort of man do you think I am?"

"I know what kind of man I have, but I have been warned that you must not fight tomorrow."

"Warned? By whom?" When she didn't answer, I knew it had been her *wyakin.* I had never seen her afraid, and tried to jolly her out of it. "Don't worry, my pet," I cooed while rubbing her back. "The only fighting today will be with aching heads and sour stomachs." We held each other close and finally drifted to sleep.

I was proved no prophet just after dawn. No Feet galloped into the village from the mountain summit where he'd been keeping a drunken watch with others. "Soldiers coming! Soldiers coming!" he shouted as he weaved in his saddle. Immediately, the whole village was astir. Many of the men were either still drunk or hungover, but all hurried to prepare for battle. I ducked back inside to grab my weapons and Coming Together laid her hand on mine. She said nothing, but her eyes said everything. I handed her my bow. "I won't fight," I said, "but I won't just stand by either." Then I rushed from the tent.

Joseph, Ollokot, Toohoolhoolzote, and the other head men were gathered outside White Bird's lodge. I joined them as the rest of the sentry party rode in. Only Hand in Hand appeared to be sober. "Soldiers are right behind us!" he called.

The head men were divided as to what to do. "We must not fight!" exclaimed Joseph. "If we fight, we are lost! The *soyapo* will hunt us all down and punish all for what a few have done."

"They leave us no choice," said Toohoolhoolzote. "I wish it were not so, but war is here and we must fight."

They decided to send a small group to parley — one last effort to avoid war. Vicious Weasel would lead the group, and Joseph asked me to go along as interpreter, "To make sure their interpreter speaks truth." I agreed, and six of us rode out under a white flag to meet the soldiers descending into the canyon.

Before we left camp, Coming Together caught me and handed me her "Book of Heaven[71]". "Take this," she said, "Jesus may be your *wyakin*." I tucked it into my belt, squeezed her hand, and hurried to catch up with the others. Ollokot led a group of young men on a loop to the west, where they would be screened from the soldiers' sight by hills, and another group, including Yellow Wolf, was doing the same to the east. The two groups comprised about 60 warriors total, most of whom were with Ollokot, and the head men had admonished everyone to not fire a shot unless the soldiers shot first.

A war is a terrible thing — even more terrible is having a hand, however inadvertently, in starting one. As the six of us rode toward the lead troops, our responsibility weighed heavy on us. We were unarmed, and approached the soldiers' vanguard slowly — there were about eight of them, all holding weapons at the ready, including a civilian with bushy mustaches under a wide-brimmed white hat.

[71] No doubt this is a copy of the Christian bible, received from a missionary, possibly Henry H. Spalding, who was protected by the Nez Perce in the aftermath of the Whitman massacre.

Something familiar about the way the civilian sat his mount made the hairs on the back of my neck stand up. Soon we were close enough that we saw each other clearly and his eyes opened wide in surprise at the very same moment I recognized him. It was Bill Morrow! He threw his rifle to his shoulder and fired at me[72]. Fortunately for me, he was as rotten a shot as he was a human being, but his bullet killed my horse.

All hell broke loose. My horse fell heavily, pinning my leg to the ground. Morrow fled toward the soldier's main body, which was deploying along a ridge line. Vicious Weasel and the others wheeled their mounts and galloped back toward the village. As I struggled to free my leg, two thoughts were uppermost in my mind — what in h--l was Bill Morrow doing here, and I really needed to learn to listen to my wife. Bullets striking my horse and the ground around me brought me back to more pressing issues, and I finally freed myself and took cover behind my dead horse. The warriors to the east and west broke cover to attack, while the

---

[72] Nate may have just solved one of the great mysteries of the Indian Wars. To this day, while it is universally accepted that "Chapman" fired the first shot, no one has ever been able to provide a reason *why* he fired.

lieutenant in charge tried to form his men into a skirmish line.

It all fell apart for the soldiers when their sole trumpeter was killed[73]. The lead soldiers fell back, while the main body advanced, deploying along the ridge to the east, a group of civilians at the farthest point.

It was over quickly. Some of Ollokot's men charged the troops at the right end of the line, Sarpsis Ilppilp, Wahlitits, and Strong Eagle leading the charge. They were three of the bravest men I've ever seen — all three wore bright red blanket coats, and charged through the cavalry's heavy fire with no more concern than if it had been a light rain. The soldiers on the west end of the line began to panic and fall back. On the eastern end, the civilians had fled and Yellow Wolf and the others were rolling up the soldiers' line like a rug. More and more of the troopers were breaking

---

[73] On the battlefield, trumpets were a primary form of communication. This one was killed by an impressive long-range shot from a warrior named Otstotpoo.

formation to flee. Several were unable to mount or were flung to the ground when their saddles turned[74].

The whole thing, from Morrow's shot to the last survivor's scramble out of the canyon, couldn't have taken more than half an hour. It was a great victory — over 100 soldiers and civilians had ridden into the canyon, opposed by just over half their number of warriors. We killed almost a third of them, and only three of our warriors were even wounded — including me. The weapons we gathered from the dead greatly increased our firepower.

I was lucky — my knee was badly sprained and I'd been grazed by a bullet, but relief battled anger on Coming Together's face when I rode back into camp on a cavalry horse. She and Walks Through got me into the lodge and settled before she took me to task. "I thought you were dead!" she said, alternating loving caresses with disciplinary smacks. "What would we have done without you?"

---

[74] It was common for cavalry to travel with their saddles loosely cinched. Apparently some neglected to tighten them before descending the canyon.

I held her tight and she squeezed me fiercely. "I promise, I will never leave you," I said. "Nothing will ever take me from you."

She sat back and eyed me sternly, wiping tears from her face, then from mine — seeing her so frightened for me broke my heart. Finally, she was satisfied. She gave me one last smack on the back of the head before examining my knee. "Don't you know to kick clear of a falling horse?"

"It took me by surprise."

"Pay more attention next time."

A little later, Vicious Weasel and Ollokot entered. We discussed the battle briefly and Ollokot asked, "Why did Chapman fire at you?"

"Who?"

"Ad Chapman — the man in the white hat."

"That wasn't anybody called Ad Chapman," I said. "His name is Bill Morrow. Did anyone find his body on the field?"

"No," said Ollokot. "He got away while the soldiers were dying."

"That sounds about right for him." It turned out they'd known Morrow for years as Arthur "Ad" Chapman. Apparently he'd changed his name, married a Nez Perce woman, and settled down near Mount Idaho, where he had a bad reputation. A leopard may change his name, but never his spots.

Chapter Twenty-Three

Mischa; No deal; across the Salmon; holding the ford; on soldiers; across the Salmon again; Camas Prairie; Looking Glass joins us; fight at the Clearwater; breaking camp on the run; to the Lolo Trail; Red Heart's people

Mischa came to visit. My happiness at seeing him quickly turned to anger when he told me that his employers just wanted this whole thing to go away, and casually mentioned that a jailbreak could be arranged. I looked at my paunchy little brother, with his balding head and the pallor of a prisoner. "Mischa," I said to him, "you are a fool." He promised that he was working in good faith and was only trying to save my life. I laughed in his face. "I wouldn't make it half a block before I'd be gunned down trying to escape by some 'innocent bystander' on the same payroll as you." I almost felt bad for him when he slunk out the door.

Washington Territory
June-July 1877

The chiefs decided to put the Salmon River between us and the soldiers. The river was at full flood and about 200 yards wide, so we built bull boats — a willow framework with a buffalo hide stretched over it — and towed everything across in them. Our scouts reported that General Howard was advancing toward us with about 500 men — in contrast, we had less than 200 men total. Our hope lay in speed and outmaneuvering our enemies.

The People headed into the mountains while several of us stayed at the crossing as a rear-guard. When the army did show up, we taunted them, trying to goad them into something foolish. We fired a few shots, simply because it was funny to watch them scrambling for cover at a single shot or two.

About the second day, after we had fired a few shots to scatter the soldiers, some of our warriors ran down to the banks to taunt them. Yellow Wolf asked me, "Why do the soldiers run and hide at a few shots? Are they all cowards?"

"No," I said, "they are not cowards, but they do not fight as we do. When we fight, each man does as he thinks best — a soldier must do as commanded. We were lucky at White Bird Canyon. The officers in command were foolish and contemptuous. We taught them to respect us. But time is on their side, and they know it. They have no families to protect and feed as we do. They are many and we are few. We cannot afford to ever let our guard down."

He nodded agreement. "I think it will be a hard war, with much suffering for the people."

***

It took Howard four days to begin the crossing, and all our rear guard, save a few young men, hurried downriver to catch up with The People. We recrossed the river about 25 miles from where Howard had crossed, and within hours had the river between us and the soldiers again. While they struggled slowly through the mountains on our trail, we made our way across the broad Camas Prairie toward the Clearwater River and the foot of the Lolo Trail.

We fought only when forced, for the chiefs still hoped to find some pathway to a peaceful outcome. If any soldiers or civilians approached, our warriors tried to just drive them away. In one of the skirmishes, we almost lost Ollokot — his horse was killed leaving him afoot — but Cloudburst rode to his aid and both escaped whole. During that fight, a warrior named

Wounded Mouth became the first of The People to die in the war.

We reached the Clearwater and set up camp while the chiefs and headmen gathered to decide what to do — "Perhaps there is still some way to make peace," Joseph said. "We have beaten the army and out-marched them. They might be more open to negotiation now. Maybe they will be satisfied with the surrender of the young men who raided along the Salmon, starting all this mess, and leave the rest of us alone."

"I too wish we could make peace with the *soyapo*," said White Bird, "but it is not possible. They want war, it is war we must give them."

"What of the women, the children, the old ones?" asked Joseph. "They cannot live on the march like warriors! Where will we find food for them? Where will they lay their heads to rest? Who will protect them while we fight?" He shook his head sadly. "If it were only us warriors, I would happily fight and die here, on the land of our fathers, but it is not just us."

White Bird nodded. "You speak the truth, my friend, but I have no hope for peace. Perhaps we should try for the Old Woman Country like Sitting Bull? The women and old ones could make it that far, surely."

The discussion was interrupted by a furor at the edge of camp. The men all grabbed weapons and rushed toward the noise, but there were no soldiers attacking.

It was Looking Glass' people straggling into camp, hungry and exhausted, with little more than the clothes on their backs. The army had attacked their village on the reservation, destroying anything they didn't want or couldn't carry away. No one could understand it — Looking Glass had always spoken strongly against war, and they had been in their village during the White Bird Canyon fight that started the war.

"What is wrong with those soldiers?" Coming Together asked me. "You were a soldier. Do you think they'll ever leave us alone?"

"Not as long as the men in command aren't the ones getting their hands dirty. The farther away a man is, the less clearly he sees. To a powerful man in Washington, or even Olympia, we are just an inconvenience to be eliminated."

"Have you talked about this with Joseph or White Bird or the others?"

"There's nothing I can tell them that they don't already know. We must trust them."

***

The attack on Looking Glass' village made it clear there would be no peace, but Looking Glass suggested a third option. "What do we know of the Old Woman Country? What welcome would we have there? We don't know that land, or the people who live there. We should take the Lolo Trail to the buffalo country. We can easily outdistance the army, and once over the mountains, I have many friends among the Crow who would happily give us shelter."

"Looking Glass is right," said Rainbow. He and Five Wounds had just returned from the buffalo country and joined us after the White Bird Canyon fight. "The Crow are thinking of making war on the whites. They would be happy for us to join them. The Crow are many and powerful — our women and children would be safe with theirs while we help the Crow warriors whip the army."

The lure of powerful allies and familiar country was powerful, and though nothing was decided that day, the voices of three of our most famous and respected warriors carried the day, even to the point of Looking

Glass, as the chief most familiar with the buffalo country and the Crow, being chosen to be leader[75].

***

Since the fight at White Bird Canyon, my nightmares had returned, and neither I nor Coming Together had had a full night's sleep. Several times I had awakened on my feet, shouting and looking for the enemy. The children were frightened by the change in me and spent several nights in the lodges of Coming Together's parents or Horse Blanket.

I was better in the daytime, when there was hunting to be done — there were many mouths to feed and game grew short when we camped for more than a couple of days. The chiefs felt confident that Howard was far behind, and The People relaxed. There was some minor skirmishing with civilian volunteers, but no sign of any major troop movements.

We were looking in the wrong direction. We expected them to come from the northeast, along our trail, but Howard had gotten lost in the mountains and stumbled upon us from the south. "Soldiers coming!"

---

[75] Nate's memory may be incorrect here. Some accounts state that Looking Glass wasn't selected as leader until some days after the *Nimiipuu* left the camp on the Clearwater River.

rang through camp and a long line of soldiers could be seen descending the mountain toward us.

Toohoolhoolzote quickly gathered twenty or twenty-five good shots, and rushed up the mountain to meet them. Many of us began piling rocks for fortifications as the sounds of gunfire began on the mountainside.

I was trying to help pile rocks when Joseph tapped me on the shoulder. "What are you doing?" he asked.

"What does it look like? I'm helping!"

He smiled. "My friend, your heart is strong, but your leg is injured. I think you might be more useful helping me get the camp moving."

"D-mmit, I want to fight!" The sound of firing was lessening up the mountainside, and Toohoolhoolzote's men were beginning to fall back.

"There will be plenty more fighting to do when you can walk. It is better to do what you can, than to try to do what you can't."

I knew he was right, but I still swore a blue streak as I hobbled back to the camp.

About sixty or seventy warriors had taken defensive positions by the time Toohoolhoolzote and his men were forced back. They put up a good fight from the rock forts and stopped the army advance. The soldiers dug in, and the fight continued through the night and well into the next day.

Coming Together had left the children to pack our belongings — necessities only — while she helped her parents. They had things well in hand, so I left them to it and hobbled around helping out where I could.

Most of the camp was moving by the time the soldiers forced our warriors back, but much was left behind in the rush. After my family were on the trail, I stayed behind to try to help those who needed it. I was helping an old couple load a pack horse when our men fell back. Some of the warriors maintained a harassing fire at the advancing troops while the rest aided the few remaining people to get moving. I got the old couple on the trail, and heard a woman crying out for help. Through the dust and smoke, I saw a young woman with a baby struggling to mount a panicking horse. Before I could help her, Yellow Wolf stepped in and soon had the horse under control. As she galloped past, I recognized her as Joseph's younger wife Springtime, with the baby born just before the White Bird Canyon fight. I don't know how she was left behind, but there was much confusion, and Joseph was busy getting all of the camp on the move. He must have thought she was up ahead with the others of his family.

Our narrow escape cost us the lives of four warriors. Five more were wounded, including Yellow Wolf. We killed and wounded many more soldiers than we lost, but our losses were irreplaceable. Our escape was aided by the avarice of the soldiers, who stopped to plunder the stores and possessions we left behind.

At the foot of the Lolo Trail, we encountered Chief Red Heart and his small band returning from a long sojourn in the buffalo country. They were shocked to learn that we were at war. They wanted nothing to do with it and continued on their way, although a few of their young men, including Red Heart's two oldest sons joined us. We learned later from our scouts that Chief Red Heart and all his people were arrested as hostiles the next day by One Arm's soldiers[76]. For our part, we started up the winding, perilous trail to what we hoped was freedom.

---

[76] Red Heart's people were arrested as hostiles and marched in chains – men and women, young and old alike – sixty miles on foot through scorching heat to Fort Lapwai and then shipped to Fort Vancouver where they were imprisoned for almost a year.

Chapter Twenty-Four

Across the Lolo Trail; suffering and privation; pitching in; a soldier corral; beliefs; scouting the enemy; bloodless detour; rest in the Bitterroot Valley; a shopping trip; a little flirting; harsh words among friends; a parade

Washington and Montana Territories
July – August 1877

Even after the Clearwater, The Peoples' spirits were high, and many believed that we stood a real chance of finding safety with the Crow. As we climbed the Lolo Trail however, the hardships increased. It was one thing to cross those mountains at a leisurely pace in the company of small groups of well-supplied, capable warriors and their families, and quite another to scramble over them with everyone we loved — many of whom could not take care of themselves — to stay ahead of a pursuing army. Almost no one had adequate shelter and even in July, the nights were bitter cold among those high, jagged peaks. As always, it was the very old and the very young who suffered the most.

The trail was very rugged, and wound along and over jagged ridgelines, with rock falls and downed trees often blocking the path. The men worked endlessly to keep the trail clear. Many of the old ones couldn't walk the trail and had little strength to ride, and often the older children rode double with an old one, just to keep them in the saddle. Every day was a brutal struggle. Even the hardiest were worn down — the weakest were pushed almost beyond their limits.

Welweyas, the half-man-and-half-woman, took charge of an old couple who had no family left. They were both ill, but because of Welweyas' care, their health improved, even under those grueling conditions. Because of the number of people, we broke into smaller traveling groups and those in the rear frequently slogged through ankle-deep mud stirred up by those in the front when it rained, or choked on dust when it was dry.

As we made our final camp on the Lolo Trail, our scouts reported a manned fortification ahead. Looking Glass, White Bird, and Joseph rode forward to parley with the soldiers while all of the warriors gathered at the lead camp. It was growing dark when they returned.

"Warriors!" Looking Glass said, "There are soldiers in front of us. Even worse is that there are Flatheads, who we thought our friends, with them, and also many volunteers. The chief, Captain Rawn says that we must lay down our guns and surrender or be killed, or captured and hanged!"

There was much angry murmuring at this, as he continued. "I think he is wrong. Their fort is more a corral than fort, and his men look frightened." White Bird and Joseph nodded their agreement. "But I know you are tired. Our families are hungry and cold. We want to know what you think. I told Captain Rawn that we don't want to fight. I want no bloodshed on this side of the mountains. These white men have done us no harm. What do The People say?"

"I will not give up the fight!" Sarpsis Ilppilp shouted, holding his rifle above his head. "They have shed our blood, and I will shed more of theirs before I die!"

"One-Arm Howard started this war, not us!" called Rainbow. "I will never lay down my rifle!"

Almost to a man, the warriors made it known they would not surrender. The chiefs sat down to discuss the situation, and Joseph asked me to join them. "I want to know what you think."

"First," I said, "I'd like to see the situation for myself."

He smiled. "I hoped you would say that. Ollokot, Five Wounds and Rainbow will go with you." When we rode out. Rainbow was still angry.

"Relax, brother," said Five Wounds, "We are going to look, not to fight. It is a long time before the dawn." Rainbow just grunted disgustedly. Five Wounds rode on ahead.

"What was that about?" I asked Rainbow.

"Oh, he's just being an old woman."

"How so?"

"I must not fight at night," he said. "I was promised that my enemies cannot hit me after sunrise but could not miss me before it." He laughed. "He worries I'll lose my temper and do something rash."

I had seen enough to know these beliefs were no mere superstition. Before the battle at White Bird Canyon, the three Red Coats had been told by their *wyakins* they could not be harmed by the soldiers' bullets. After the battle, I saw their coats had been pierced many times, and when Wahlitits, Sarpsis Ilppilp and Strong Eagle unbelted them, the flattened bullets fell out. I have no explanation but, I tell you three times, I saw it with my own eyes.

When we neared the fort, Rainbow stayed back with the horses, grumbling, and Ollokot, Five Wounds, and I reconnoitered. We had just come in sight of it when a low voice spoke from the darkness. "Be careful," it said. "Those soldiers are jumpy."

It was Yellow Wolf. A spirit had told him that in war, he should be alone, so he spent a great deal of time out scouting and fighting by himself. This night, he had taken it upon himself to keep watch on the "fort".

When I saw it, I had to hold back laughter — Looking Glass was right, it was more a corral than a fort. All it would be good for in a fight would be keeping the few soldiers it held contained while we killed them. "Where'd they all go?" I asked Yellow Wolf. "I thought sure there'd be more here than this."

"I don't know where they went. There was a lot of arguing, and then men started leaving in groups. The soldier chief scolded them, and then begged, but they just rode away." He'd followed a large group, in case they were preparing an attack, but once he was sure they were leaving for good, he'd returned to the fort.

"All they've been doing is arguing and shooting at shadows."

We verified his story for ourselves, and returned to camp. Rainbow and a few others were all in favor of wiping them out, but the chiefs insisted there be no fighting. "It is one thing to fight when it is forced upon us," said White Bird, "but another thing to kill *soyapo* unnecessarily. We must show them that we are not their enemies."

"We could just go around them," said Five Wounds.

"You are crazy," said Rainbow. "That trail is hard enough for fit men."

Five Wounds explained. "There is a trail up the ridges to the north. It is rough, but we could pass without a fight. A few warriors could stay behind to keep the soldiers in their fort."

"Can our old ones and herds make it?" White Bird asked.

"I think they must," said Looking Glass. "I know that trail too, and I think we must try it. Once over the Lolo pass, we'll be into softer country where the traveling won't be so hard."

We decided it was worth the risk, to bypass the soldiers. Most of us wanted no more bloodshed — or at least none that could be avoided.

In the end, we made it around the soldiers without firing a shot[77], and were laughing and joking as we descended into the Bitterroot Valley. We had seen no soldiers other than Rawn's in days. We had covered over 200 miles of the roughest country on earth in eleven days, with almost 800 people and about 5,000 horses. Now, in the broad, gently rolling Bitterroot Valley, we began again to feel real hope.

***

Looking Glass slowed the pace of the march to allow the herd and people to recover from the hardships of the trail. We started our daily marches late and stopped early, allowing much time for rest, hunting and foraging, and letting the horse herd graze and fatten back up. Almost all of the food had been used up in the mountain crossing, and the women insisted that

---

[77] Captain Rawn's failed attempt to stop the Nez Perce was met with ridicule and contempt by the army and settlers. The "soldier corral" went down in history as "Fort Fizzle". It is currently commemorated (perhaps appropriately) as the Fort Fizzle Historic Site Picnic Area and includes a partial replica of the fortification.

something be done to resupply — especially staples that we could not forage for along the trail.

When we entered the valley, the chiefs and older warriors kept a close eye on the hotheads, insisting that no blood be shed, but in a few cases, it was a very near thing. Looking Glass decided to go into the town of Stevensville to resupply. We had always been on good terms with the Bitterroot Valley settlers, and believed that those friendships would see us right. The one thing everyone had made sure to grab in our hurry to escape the Clearwater fight was money. We had much gold, both coin and dust, and silver from years of trading, and many women carried greenbacks braided into their hair.

Looking Glass and a few older men rode in first, to reassure them we were there for trade, not trouble. Afterward many of us — including most of the women — rode in. We wanted to make a good impression, so everyone was rigged out in their finest clothing and ornaments. Coming Together was beautiful in her long, fringed doeskin dress with its beadwork and elk's teeth, wide, beaded belt, long bead, bone, and shell necklace, and stone disc pendants hanging from her ears, all topped off with her best, intricately beaded, woven grass hat. She saw me smiling at her and blushed. "What?" she asked.

"You are beautiful."

She puffed and fluttered her hand at me, "And you are foolish," she said, with a coy smile.

I leaned close and whispered in her ear, "What do you say we let your mother and Walks Through do the shopping and you and me slip away for a bit?"

"What do you say you act like a sensible man of your age, and not like a randy boy?"

"My love, no matter how old I may be, I'll always feel like a randy boy when I see you."

We were coming into town, so she just said, "Hush now. Maybe when we know where our next meal is coming from, I'll be ready to rethink this."

I hushed.

***

Most places were shuttered and locked but Buck Brothers' was open and ready for business. I knew them from my trips to the buffalo ground, and I visited with Amos while Henry and Fred scrambled to fill the ladies' orders.

"How's life Amos?" I said. I could see they were nervous, and that Amos was within reach of his rifle at all times.

"Oh, fair to middlin' I s'pose."

"Been doing a good business?"

"Passable, passable." He nodded toward the gaggle of women crowding the store. "It's lookin' up."

"Well, we appreciate you boys opening up. We were getting pretty desperate."

"Well, you folks always done right by us. 'Sides, Looking Glass gave his word you all'd keep them young bucks under control."

"And we will."

"'Course he also made it pretty clear that you all needed this stuff and meant to have it, one way or t'other."

"Well," I said, "he is an honest man."

Amos nodded. "That he is. Aw h--l Nate, me 'n the boys'd much rather sell you this stuff than get shot by friends and lose it all anyway." He held out his hand to shake.

I took it gladly. "I'm happy to hear it," I said. "I wish more folks had your good sense."

"Yup," he said. "It'd be a quieter, more peaceful ol' world, wouldn't it?"

Figuring he'd be happier if I was to move on and not take up so much of his attention or field of view, I signaled to Coming Together that I'd be outside, and left.

I mounted and rode up next to Yellow Wolf and Wahlitits. "How are things out here?"

Yellow Wolf shrugged. "Quiet so far."

Wahlitits was on edge. His beautiful and very pregnant wife was in the store, and he was anxious to get her away from town. He jerked his head toward the store. "What's taking so long in there?"

"My friend," I said, "there are many women with long lists in there, and only two men to help them. Be patient. You know the Bucks. They're friends of The People."

He spat. "It is fine for you to trust the *soyapo*. All you need is a haircut and some white man's clothes, and you can walk away from all this."

I shouldn't have been offended — he was just worried for his wife and unborn child — but his words still stung. "My friend," I said hotly, "you have known me most of your life. When have I ever turned my back on The People? What have I ever done, that you would speak so to me?"

He just grunted and rode away. Yellow Wolf started after him. "I'll talk to him," he said.

"No," I said, "leave him be. For weeks he's been either killing whites, or running from them. Now we're sitting here while our wives shop. That's enough to unsettle anyone. I shouldn't have let myself get angry." I looked down the street to where Wahlitits sat alone. He saw me and looked away, unwilling to meet my gaze. "I'll see what I can do to get his wife sorted out and on her way." I was glad to see Walks Through helping Mrs. Wahlitits finish her purchases. By the time they'd loaded everything, Coming Together and her mother had come out.

Coming Together nodded toward Mrs. Wahlitits as I helped load our goods. "Her back is hurting bad. That baby's going to come soon. Mother and Walks Through will go with her back to camp. The Bucks don't have any flour, so we'll go to the mill by Fort Owen to get some."

Wahlitits and Yellow Wolf escorted Walks Through, her grandmother, and Mrs. Wahlitits out of town, Wahlitits looking like a huge weight had been lifted from his shoulders. He was smiling as his wife and Walks Through chattered like magpies. Yellow Wolf looked back at me and waved. Wahlitits did the same with a rueful smile. Smiling, I returned the wave.

Rainbow, Five Wounds and a couple other men went with us to the mill so the ladies could purchase many bags of flour, then we all rode back to town. Joseph and Ollokot were about to ride back to camp with their wives, and Coming Together and the flour buyers went with them.

"I'll stick around here a while," I said. "Just in case."

She nodded. "Well don't wear yourself out so much you can't live up to your earlier threats," she said archly, and rode away, her friends all giggling with her.

Late in the day, things got more dicey. Some jackass was selling whiskey to our young men, and it was taking effect. One of the townsmen put a stop to it, but the damage was done. A group of Flatheads had entered town, presumably to help keep the peace, and I saw one grab a rifle away from one of our men who was aiming at the store. The drunk man protested, but stopped when White Bird began lashing him with a riding whip. A couple of men grabbed the drunk and hustled him out of town. White Bird took the rifle back from the Flathead and returned to his horse. There were a few more incidents of that sort that were handled just as swiftly and decisively.

We spent two days in Stevensville without incident. When we broke camp and rode south past the town, we again all dressed up and created quite a pageant for the townspeople to watch. Thus ended perhaps the most surreal and pleasant event of the war.

Chapter Twenty-Five

A lucky sneeze; Lean Elk joins us; worry and disagreement; dire prophecies; a fractious council; resignation; a good hunt; a talk with my father-in-law; sleep

Someone took a shot at me through the window today. Sheriff Angus said the Lord must have been looking out for me, as I sneezed at just the right moment and ended up with a wide part in my hair rather than a bullet between the eyes. God bless this dusty cell. It felt like I'd been stung by a hornet, but the crack of the rifle had me diving for cover, so whoever it was never got a second chance. Sheriff Angus and the fellows looked, but could find no sign of the dry-gulching s.o.b. It never pays to let your guard down.

Montana Territory
August 1877

Not long after leaving Stevensville, we were joined by Lean Elk and a small band of buffalo hunters. He was limping from a nasty gash in his leg. "Just a run of d--ned bad luck," he said, his voice booming. "Bad luck, bad timing, bad everything. I was missing the old home country, so I packed up and headed west. Was almost to Kamiah when the war started up. I didn't want any part of that, so I headed back here. Shot a doe up in the mountains, went to dress her out, slipped, and fell on my knife."

"You ought to be more careful."

"Lotta things I oughta be," he laughed, "but it'd take all the fun out of life." Then he sobered, "how have you all been?"

I filled him in on our exploits and trials. "I wasn't sure we were going to make it over the mountains," I said. "Things have gotten better since we got down into the valley though. We've had a few easy marches and resupplied, so things are looking up."

"Who's in charge? White Bird?"

"Looking Glass."

He grunted. "That figures."

"He thinks the Crow'll take us in.

"Uh huh."

***

We stopped early to set up camp. Yellow Wolf and I rode out for a short scout and to see if we could find some game for the pots. He was uneasy and I asked him what was wrong.

"Bad feeling. We should be moving faster. No good will come from taking it so easy."

"I know what you mean," I said, "but the old ones, the children, they can't stand the same pace that you and I can." Still, I was worried too. It seemed like the chiefs thought the army here was a different one from Howard's.

Lean Elk joined us. "What are you two pulling such long faces about?" I told him, and he considered a few moments and then said, "Looking Glass is a great warrior and a brave man and he loves The People, but he likes being the big man a little too much maybe. Wants everybody to like him."

I was not surprised by his comments — he was no admirer of Looking Glass — but it seemed a little presumptuous, considering he'd only recently joined us. "The People have gone through much," I said. "Almost more than many could take."

"I know, my friend, I know," he said. "I worry about them too. But sometimes it's better to suffer some in order to stay ahead of trouble than to risk more by waiting for it."

"What choice do we have?"

"I don't reckon there is any choice," he said. "The die's been cast. Maybe it'll be alright. I hope so. But I'm not unpacking any more than I need to at night."

I agreed that was wise, and advised Coming Together to do the same.

***

Looking Glass led us south toward the Big Hole, a good place to camp and rest. We would cut new lodge poles and have proper shelters for the first time in weeks. Everyone was looking forward to it, but others worried about the slow pace too. In the week it took us to get to the Big Hole, they were letting their concern show.

One morning, Wahlitits mounted his horse and rode around camp prophesying: "My People, hear me!" he shouted. "I saw myself killed last night! I will die soon, but it is alright! I will kill more soldiers before they kill me! I am not afraid! I will not turn from death! We will all die anyway!"

Another morning, Lone Bird spoke up. "My heart tells me we must hurry to the buffalo country! Trouble and death will take us if we do not hurry! I must speak of what I have seen!" Another day, he rode through camp shouting, "Why do these chiefs not hurry? Soldiers are coming! We must be ready! Death is upon us!"

They were far from the only warriors predicting doom, but Looking Glass ignored their pleas for speed. When we reached the Big Hole unmolested, I dared to hope that the chiefs were right. Perhaps the government had decided — now that they had our land — that our small group wasn't worth the effort and expense.

The morning after we arrived, the women got busy cutting and stripping lodge poles to replace those we'd lost at the Clearwater, and several of the warriors met with thc chiefs.

The warriors elected Rainbow and Five Wounds, to speak for the group. "Scouts should be sent far out to watch our back trail," Rainbow told the chiefs, "so the soldiers can't surprise us." The other warriors nodded in agreement.

Looking Glass seemed more annoyed than angry. "Are you turning into an old woman, my friend? Why do you see enemies where none exist?"

"Even an old woman is wise enough to make sure there are none before she sleeps," retorted Rainbow.

"The People might be better off with a worried old woman in charge than a chief that refuses to even look."

"You have seen how slowly One-Arm moves — he fears catching up with us more than he fears letting us get away. Have any of our scouts seen any soldiers? No. Because there are none to be seen."

Five Wounds spoke up: "You may be right, but it is better to be safe."

"Safe?" Looking Glass asked. "I am thinking of safety. The *soyapo* in the valley are afraid of us. If they see our warriors riding around on their own, they might think it a war party and call to the soldiers for help. A scouting party is more likely to bring soldiers down on us than prove we are peaceful."

"It wouldn't have to be a strong party, just a few trusted men on good horses. They can stay away from any settlers and towns."

"And where would these 'good horses' come from? I've seen your horses. They are worn out from your endless scouting already."

"Coals of Fire could lend us horses," interjected Sarpsis Ilppilp, impatient with all the palaver. "His horses are famous for speed and are still fat and strong."

"You ride your own horses near to death and expect me to let you do the same to mine?" asked Coals of Fire, clearly insulted, "No. I trust Looking Glass. You young men started all this trouble in the first place. If it weren't for you two," he said, looking directly at Sarpsis Ilppilp and Wahlitits, "we would still be on the right side of the mountains. We would still have our herds and possessions. The old ones would not be worn out and in pain. The children would not be crying from hunger and cold. I tell you three times it is your fault, and I will not help you find a way to make things worse!"

Stung by the old man's words, Sarpsis Ilppilp, Wahlitits, and the other young men started to argue, but Rainbow, Five Wounds, and Two Moons intervened, and the young men turned and stalked away.

Rainbow bit back his anger. "What good is it to place blame now? Those young men know what they've done, but the *soyapo* have been killing and robbing us for years. They may be young, but they are still men. They, at least, have fought and bled for The People. You are not even willing to risk a few horses!"

"Coals of Fire should not have spoken so," said Looking Glass. "But as you said, our young men are men. All it would take is for one hot-headed *soyapo* to meet them and the fighting will start all over again. More dead *soyapo*, more dead *Nimiipuu*. It is a war we cannot hope to win, only to avoid."

"But how can we avoid the soldiers if we don't know where they are?" Rainbow asked.

"One-Arm is lost in the mountains, or has stopped now that we've given up our homes. Why would they want to fight more, when they have everything they wanted?"

"Looking Glass is a great warrior," I said, "but he doesn't understand how the soldiers make war, nor why. They will never let us go, never stop until we are beaten, our belongings and herds taken or destroyed. They are like wolves. They will follow until we are weak, and then they will pounce." Rainbow and the others nodded in agreement.

"But we are not weak," said Looking Glass. "Every day we grow stronger. We will stay here a few days to make new lodge poles, fatten the horses up, let everyone regain their strength, and then we'll join the Crows, where we'll be safe. There will be no scouting. Keep your warriors near camp and keep a firm hand on the young men. All will be well, so long as we remain peaceful."

I gave up. I had made no secret about what had happened at Sand Creek and now, even after years of persecution, the chiefs were incapable of recognizing what they faced.

The council came to nothing. Looking Glass was adamant, and the other chiefs supported him. We had no choice — dissension would only weaken us further.

Five Wounds had the last word on the subject. "Looking Glass," he said, "the decision is yours but if you are wrong, every death will fall on your head."

As we walked away, my boys ran up, full of questions. "Why won't they listen to you?" asked Many Wounds. "Are the soldiers really coming here?"

"I wish they would," said Twisted Hair, aiming an imaginary rifle, "we'd show them just like before. They'd be sorry they hadn't given up"

I hushed him and tried to reassure Many Wounds as we gathered mounts and rode out a short distance in search of game. My head was full of bad memories and the boys sensed it and tried to keep quiet. Fortunately, silence was not their strong suit, and they were soon singing and joking and teasing and jollied me out of my sourness. Things improved even more when we spotted some pheasant. I stayed with the horses while the boys stalked. I didn't expect them to have any luck, but I felt they should give it a try on their own. When Twisted Hair appeared on top of a hill waving excitedly, I rode up and was surprised to see that both had managed to bring one down.

On the ride back to camp, listening to them crow about their prowess and argue over who made the best shot and boast about how impressed their friends would be and so on, I hoped they would never forget that day, that it would always mean as much to them as it still does to me.

***

Walks Through set to work on the birds, and I sent the boys to return the horses to the herd and bring three fresh mounts in, to be tied near the lodge — I hoped Looking Glass was right, but I wanted my family to be able to escape in case he wasn't. I went to see my in-laws. Her father, Strong Eagle, had been feeling poorly.

"How are you feeling?" I asked.

"Oh, some better," he said. "A few more days' rest and I'll be good again."

"I'm glad to hear that."

His eyes were troubled. "Do you think we'll have a few days to rest?"

"I don't know," I said. "Looking Glass thinks so. I just hope he knows what he's doing. The other chiefs think he does, so that's something."

He nodded. ""I wish I had not lived to see this time. I miss my home. I wish I had died there." We stood in silence a while, and then he shook off his black thoughts. "Don't listen to me," he said. "I'm just a foolish old man."

We walked on and spoke of many things, speculating whether we would be able to find peace with the Crow, or if we should instead try to join Sitting Bull's Sioux in Canada. Neither of us really knew what would be best. We would both be relieved when we were on the move again.

Later that night after the children had fallen asleep, I lay awake listening to the night when Coming Together's hand rose from my chest to stroke my cheek. “Husband,” she said quietly, “why do you not sleep?”

“I’m fine,” I whispered. “Go back to sleep.”

“You are a terrible liar. I can see the black thoughts whirling through your head. Put all that behind you. All is well. We are safe.” She rolled onto her back, pulling me with her to pillow my head on her breast. “Go to sleep now,” she said, stroking my temple. “You worry too much. Worry cannot change the future. It just makes the present miserable. Let us make each other happy instead.” Later, we both finally fell into a blessedly peaceful sleep, the sound of our children’s breathing providing a sweet lullaby.

Chapter Twenty-Six

A harsh awakening; panic; a brutal fight; we counterattack; a horrible discovery; vengeance; so many lost; on the trail again; Lean Elk takes command; nights the worst

Nathan is angry with me. I had to go to court for some motion or other, and I was so distracted by the painting in the hall that I paid no attention during the proceedings. "D-mmit, Nate, how am I supposed to defend you if you can't even bother to help?" was how he put it. I brushed it off of course. He is young and thinks all this is important.

The painting that took up all of my thoughts is called *American Progress*, by John Gast, and represents the idea of Manifest Destiny. I spend a lot of time thinking about that idea, and can only say that if this country's Destiny is Manifest, then it is a festering sort of Destiny, and no God worthy of the name would ever ordain such a manifestly corrupt and evil scheme.

Montana Territory
August 1877

We all awoke at the same time, sitting up in our blankets and looking at each other. Was that a gunshot? A moment later, someone called "Fire!" in English, and bullets ripped through the lodge. Screams erupted all over the camp. "Stay down!" I yelled as I scrabbled for my weapons. A second volley ripped through the lodge as I rushed for the door. "Take the horses and run!" I called to Coming Together. Outside was chaos — The sun was not up yet, but there was light enough to see screaming women and children fleeing, while others lay dead or bleeding on the ground. Here, some wounded tried to crawl to safety, there, mothers and grandmothers shielded children with their bodies. A woman shot in the back fell, still clutching her infant. Most men tried to get their families away, while others returned fire. Horses screamed in pain and terror. Of the three we'd tied close to the lodge, two were dead, and the third broke free and ran before I could reach it. Coming Together and the children were right behind me and I pushed them south, away from the firing and the soldiers who were charging the camp on foot.

I put an arrow through a soldier's throat and yelled exultantly as he fell. I fired again and again, moving behind my family to cover their escape. I saw a *Paloos* man named Five Frogs standing stock still in front of his lodge, firing arrow after arrow, as calmly and deliberately as if he were practicing. A soldier tried to bayonet a woman who twisted the rifle out of his hand and struck him down with the stock before she was shot. I hit another soldier in the hip, and a boy of about twelve flung himself on the soldier, slashing at the man with a skinning knife.

The air reeked of burnt powder, burning hides and flesh, blood, p--s and s--t. A man's head exploded showering me in blood and brains and I vomited, but the coppery taste of his blood stayed in my mouth. I ran out of arrows and grappled with a soldier for his rifle, but he was a big fellow and knocked me to the ground. He reared back to plunge his bayonet into my chest, and then crumpled to the ground. Behind him stood Walks Through, my war club bloody in her hand.

"What are you doing here?" I demanded.

"I came to find Many Wounds!"

"What?"

"He wasn't with us!"

"Go back and help your mother! I'll find him!" I pushed her away, and grabbed the soldier's rifle and ammunition. "Wait!" I called to Walks Through. She paused, and I tossed her his revolver. "Now go!" I yelled. She tossed me my war club. I tucked it into my belt and ran back to our lodge.

The panic was dying down, and more people were fighting back. White Bird was on the edge of camp haranguing the warriors to fight, and many were seizing what weapons they could find and attacking with the ferocity of men who had only everything to lose.

I scanned the bodies as I ran and was relieved that Many Wounds wasn't among them. I shot another soldier, wounding him, reloaded and put another round through his head. When I finally reached our lodge, it was still standing — many had collapsed or been set aflame. I rushed inside and began digging through the blankets and robes, hoping he was hiding there. When I found him, he wasn't hiding. He lay as if asleep, his beautiful, clever little head shattered by a bullet.

I wanted to scream, to curse God, and damn every white man on earth to hell and torment everlasting, but all I could do was clutch my son to my breast and rock him, moaning like a wounded animal. I don't know how long I sat like that before arms encircled us. It was Walks Through. "Father," she said through tears, "we must fight now. The time for mourning is not yet here." She gently pried my son from my arms, laid him down, smoothed his hair and covered him with a robe. Then I felt her fold my hands around my rifle.

The blackness of despair was replaced by a blood-red rage. I took one last look at my beautiful boy, and rejoined the fight. Looking around me in the dawn light, I saw Five Frogs dead on the ground, shot to pieces. As I moved toward the soldiers, who were falling back toward a small, timber-covered hill, I saw a charred child's arm sticking out of the burning wreckage of a lodge. I saw the bayoneted body of a woman lying beneath the body of her husband, and a small child, its skull crushed, next to them. Wahlitits was dead, shot through the neck. His pregnant wife lay across him, his rifle in her dead hands. There was a cluster of empty shells around them, and at least three dead soldiers.

I fired and missed one soldier, fired and wounded another, and was out of ammunition. I handed the rifle to another warrior who had ammunition but no gun, and drew my war club. Shooting soldiers was not enough. I wanted their blood on my hands, wanted to bathe in it. Their retreat turned into a rout as they began to panic. I knocked one to the ground, planted my foot on his arm, and rejoiced in the terror in his face as I swung my club. He flung up his free hand to ward off the blow, and I shattered his arm first, and then his skull in a spray of blood, bone, and brains. His blood was sweet on my tongue.

Along with the other warriors, I chased the soldiers toward that hill. I tackled another, grabbed his head, and twisted until his neck snapped. Still kneeling, I swung my club low, breaking a trooper's leg as he ran past. Before I could fling myself on him, another warrior shot him in the head. I think I struck down at least one more before I was overcome by exhaustion. My rage faded to a dull gray numbness, and I crawled to the river. I drank too fast and had to turn away to vomit again. I drank again and then lay there on the riverbank. Part of me wanted to continue killing. Another part needed to find my family — if I had any left. Love won out over hate, and I returned to camp.

The sun was well up now, the full horror of what had happened exposed under its uncaring light. The fighting slackened behind me, as the soldiers improved their fortifications. Our warriors' tempers cooled and the need for vengeance subsided beneath the realizations that dead men couldn't protect The People.

Numb and bloody, I returned to our lodge. Walks Through ran to me, bloody knife in one hand, revolver in the other, and flung her arms around me. "Mother said you were still alive!"

"She's alright? What of your brother and sister?" I steeled myself for the worst as she fussed over the wounds I hadn't even noticed. They were of no consequence — and there was no bandaging the wound that hurt most.

"Mother and Five Times Over are fine," she said. "Twisted Hair is shot through the arm, but mother says he'll be fine. It took everything we had to keep him out of the fight."

My trembling legs gave out and I sat down hard. "Where . . .?"

"With grandmother. I gave Twisted Hair my revolver, told him to protect them, and came searching for you."

"Where did you get this gun?"

"Where do you think?"

I held her close. "No man ever had a braver daughter than I," I said. "But you take too many chances. What would your mother have done if something had happened to you?" I didn't even try to hold back my tears. "What would *I* have done?" I wept with grief for my little boy and with gratitude that my wife and remaining children had been spared.

When I could stand, she led me to them. Danger still hung over us like a black cloud. Coming Together couldn't even look at me. I wrapped my arms around her.

"Why?" she asked. "Why him and not me? My poor boy . . ."

"It's not your fault," I said softly.

Her grief turned to rage. "I know that, d--n you! White devils shooting into homes where children sleep! Stupid men leading us to misery and death! It is *their* fault that my son is dead!"

"I'm, I'm sorry . . . I've avenged him many times over this day."

"Revenge? What does that matter? Will more blood bring him back or take away this pain? Even if you kill all the soldiers, all the *soyapo* everywhere, my little boy will still be dead!" She curled up into a ball and struck the ground furiously as she wailed.

Strong Eagle laid a hand on my shoulder. "Come away from there my son. She doesn't know what she is saying."

I followed him outside. All over the camp was heard the keening of grief, the shrieks of terrified and injured children. "We must salvage what we can," said Strong Eagle. "We need to move."

The enormity of our losses was began to sink in. Alongside Many Wounds and Mrs. Wahlitits, far too many innocents were killed and so many more wounded, including Ollokot's pregnant senior wife Fair Land. The soldiers were pinned down and helpless, but reinforcements might be near. He was right — grief would have to wait. We needed to care for the wounded and get the camp moving before things got worse.

Most of our greatest warriors had been killed — in addition to Wahlitits, both Rainbow and Five Wounds had fallen, as had Sarpsis Ilppilp and others. Two Moons and many more were wounded and unable to fight. Almost a hundred of The People were either killed outright or died later from their wounds. About twelve warriors and ten or twelve women were killed there on that ground. All the rest were children or old ones.

Thirty or so warriors and boys kept the soldiers contained, while we men buried our dead and the women prepared to move, striking what lodges were left, and searching for salvageable items. *Travois* were built to carry the wounded. Coming Together managed to put her grief aside, and help her mother and Walks Through. Twisted Hair, once his arm was bandaged, helped bring the herd in. In that one thing we were fortunate — the soldiers missed our horse herd. If they had taken, or even scattered it, we would have been doomed.

The sun had just reached its zenith when White Bird led us out, with Joseph in his usual role as caretaker of the women, children, and old ones. A small body of warriors, led by Toohoolhoolzote and Looking Glass stayed behind as a rear guard.

We made about fifteen miles before we camped. Fair Land gave birth that night and then died from her wounds. At least the baby survived. A few others died that night too. In the morning, the rear-guard joined us, we buried our dead and moved on. For the first few days, our back trail was marked with graves like milestones.

***

Lean Elk was chosen as our new leader and pushed us hard. He was up early every morning, exhorting everyone in that giant voice to get moving. We traveled until midday and stopped for a few hours to cook, care for the wounded, and rest the horses, and then continued on until dark. Every day, we pulled a little bit farther away from the pursuing soldiers.

Coming Together and I didn't speak much for the first couple of days. Neither of us could find a way to help the other, we were so filled with our own pain. We each grieved in our own way, or rather she grieved, and I kept myself too busy to think. I didn't trust myself — I could feel the old blackness following me, trying to draw me back in. I was afraid if I gave in, it would never let me go. The nights were the worst. I held her while she cried, my own tears soaking her hair. My nightmares returned with a vengeance, and I would lash out wildly, but she would pull me back down, wrap me in her arms and hold me until I slept again — even when we weren't really speaking.

Chapter Twenty-Seven

Disillusionment; war, bloody war; self-sacrifice; a desperate pace; a raid; a cooperative captive; more captives; disappointment; a long, hard road; stealing army supplies; forty miles to Canada

No one who wants power should be allowed to have it, but time and again, I've seen sensible people drawn to evil, corrupt, or at best, well-meaning incompetents too in love with themselves to truly serve the people. Good leaders are hard to find and harder to keep. There's always someone worse willing to tell the people what they want to hear.

Montana, Idaho, and Wyoming Territories
August-September 1877

After the Big Hole, we lost any illusions we'd had about peace. We had lost too much, and none of us older men had the energy to restrain the younger warriors, even if we'd been inclined to. We had tried peace — now we made war, raiding homesteads and a freight-wagon train[78], killing *soyapo* and stealing horses. While our young men were out raiding and scouting, Lean Elk pushed The People hard to stay ahead of the soldiers.

Some couldn't take it. We buried people at almost every camp we made and that wasn't even the worst of it. One morning, Walks Through realized she'd forgotten something. She immediately turned her horse around and galloped back toward our previous campsite. I rode with her and as we grew near, we heard a terrible wailing. We found Welweyas weeping and embracing the elderly couple she'd been caring for.

"Lucky Man," she called, "help me! They won't go!"

"We're tired," said the old man. "We miss our old home. We will rest here a bit, and then walk home."

"If you won't go," insisted Welweyas, "I won't either."

"Don't be ridiculous," the old man said. "You've been like our own child, but you have done all you can for us. There are others who need you now. You must help them."

We all knew what was happening here.

---

[78] Interestingly, two Chinese men with the freighters were released unharmed by the Nez Perce (McWhorter. Hear Me My Chiefs 410).

"They are right, Welweyas," I said. "They'll be fine. Two old ones on their own are no threat to anyone. We'll leave food and water, and a horse to speed them on their way."

"That's right," said the old woman, "Anyone would be ashamed to harm us. But keep your horse. Our backsides are rubbed raw, and we're likely to break a hip trying to get on it. Besides, we like a nice stroll, don't we old man?"

The old man put his arm around her. "Of course we do." To me, he said, "Keep your food as well. I've still got my bow and where we're going, there'll be game aplenty. Just leave us a little water, and a blanket if you've got an extra, and we'll be fine."

Walks Through and I wished them well and rode away to complete our errand while Welweyas said goodbye privately. We found two blankets and offered them to the old couple when we went to collect Welweyas.

"Thank you son," said the old woman, handing one of the blankets back. "One is enough. We'll build ourselves a nice fire here and rest. If the soldiers come, we'll tell 'em you went back north." She cackled toothlessly. "Send those d--ned stupid soldiers the wrong way."

"Many thanks," was all I could say.

Welweyas embraced the old couple one last time, and we rode away. They weren't the first old ones to stay behind so as not to be a burden, and were nowhere near the last. We were still close enough to hear the shots when the Bannock scouts arrived.

At Camas Meadows, one of the injured warriors had a vision — in it, warriors raided One-Arm's camp and stole many horses. Several of us decided to put it to the test that night. Wottolen and Two Moons wanted us all to enter the camp, locate and kill Howard and his staff, then attack the camp from the inside and escape with the horses. Looking Glass insisted that only a few men should go after the horses, and then the rest of us would charge the camp. Wottolen and Two Moons were overruled and they, along with a couple of others, crept into the camp and began freeing the horses. They hadn't been at their work long, when Yellow Wolf's cousin Otskai, a nervous young man, accidentally fired his gun. There was nothing to be done but attack the camp and drive off what animals we could. We were in and out of the camp before the soldiers knew what hit them, driving their herd away as they fired fruitlessly into the dark behind us.

When daylight came, we found that we had stolen the soldiers' mule train, not their saddle horses. Otskai came in for a lot of mocking — if he weren't so twitchy, we'd likely have gotten the horses too — but to his credit, he took it like a man and didn't make up excuses to let himself off the hook.

Less than two weeks after the Big Hole, we entered Yellowstone Park[79] through the Targhee Pass, looking for the quickest route through the mountains to the land of the Crow. Not long after entering the park, Otskai, who'd been out scouting with Yellow Wolf, returned to camp with an armed, elderly white man.

He led the man to Lean Elk, and I rode along — both Otskai and Lean Elk spoke a little English but not much. "Ho, Lean Elk," said Otskai, "look what Yellow Wolf and I have found! He says he knows these mountains!"

With me translating, Lean Elk and the other chiefs questioned the man, a prospector named Shively.

---

[79] Yellowstone was the U.S.' first national park, established in 1872. It immediately became a popular destination for tourists.

"First," I said to him, "they want to know if you are friendly."

"Mister," he said with a wide smile, "I'm the friendliest feller you're ever gonna meet, I'll guarantee that," and he nodded to the chiefs. He watched The People as they trudged past us. "Looks like you folks've had a rough time of it."

"You know who we are?"

"I reckon you're them Nez Perces everyone's so het up about. But you've always done right by me. Shared many a campfire with yer folks over the years."

"You're not scared?"

"Would it do any good? In my 'sperience, most folks ain't looking for trouble an' as long's I don't give you none — which I don't plan to — I don't figger you'll give me any. You all got enough worries already.

No," he continued, "John Shively — that's me — is a Christian man who does unto others as he wants to be done to — leastways as long as that's practical. I figger if you'uns wanted me dead I'd be dead. Since I'm still breathin', I figger you'uns are friendlier than them newspapers make out — or you reckon I'm more use to you alive than dead." He rubbed his balding head.

"'Sides, I don't reckon anybody'd bother with a hair-deficient scalp like mine."

"You know these mountains?"

"Like the back of my hand friend, like the back of my own hand . . ." He went on for some time, including a tangent regarding his position on marriage — it was fine for some, but didn't appeal to him personally. I'll give him this, if he was afraid, it didn't show.

"Yes," was what I told the chiefs.

"He said a lot just to say yes," said Looking Glass.

"He's talkative," I said. "If I translate everything he says, we'll be here all winter." At the chiefs' request, I asked Shively, "Do you know the Crow country around Elk Water?"

"Well sure I know that country . . ."

"He says yes," I told the chiefs when he wound down.

They wanted to know if he'd be willing to see us through the mountains.

It took him several minutes to say he'd be happy to — especially if it embarrassed that "Yankee army" but he didn't have a horse.

"How about if we give you a horse?"

Another rambling oration revealed that he'd be delighted to accept one of our "fine spotted ponies I've heard so much about."

The chiefs agreed to give him the horse as a gift if he'd act as a guide, and the deal was struck.

The next day, scouts rode in with ten tourists — eight men and two very pretty women — their wagons, and equipment. They were treated well, although several of the warriors wanted to kill them. That afternoon, seven of the men escaped, two of whom were shot. About noon the next day, the chiefs released the women and the last man. Lean Elk told them to follow the river to Bozeman, but to hurry so no ill-meaning warriors could catch them. He asked that they tell the people in Bozeman that we did not want to fight, then gave the ladies horses and sent them on their way.

The way through Yellowstone was almost as tough as the Lolo Trail, because everyone, including the horses, were so worn down. There were several other run-ins with tourists as we traveled, but we didn't bother taking any more captives. Shively stayed with us almost two weeks longer than needed, mostly helping with the packs, and then slipped away one night with his horse. I don't know why he left us when he did — maybe some of the wilder young men spooked him — nor do I know why he stayed with us so long, but he was one of the few Christians we met who behaved honourably toward us and never tried to do us harm.

***

Leaving the mountains, we learned that the Crow were scouting against us for the Army, and turned toward Canada as our last hope. The day after we crossed the Yellowstone River on our way north, some soldiers caught up with us at Canyon Creek. Instead of charging us, they dismounted to fight on foot. We warriors interposed ourselves between them and The People, the women and boys took charge of the horse herd, and we just kept moving. Within a couple of days, we had left those soldiers far behind.

If traversing the plains was easier, it was also dispiriting. In the mountains, you would set your sights on the next pass as you trudged along, and feel you'd gotten somewhere when you reached it. Every day held different vistas, different challenges. The plains had a dreary sameness to them. You could see for miles and miles, but it all looked largely the same, just an endless, rolling prairie, with a horizon that never got any closer.

The only way to judge our progress was how our position changed in relation to the western mountains. For weeks, we just struggled to put one foot in front of the other, trying to get across an imaginary line into what we hoped would be safety.

At least, we had very few clashes with *soyapo*, civilian or soldier. Near the end of September, we reached the Missouri River at Cow Island, where the army had a supply depot. The depot was lightly manned and the river was low, and we crossed in full sight of the soldiers who did nothing but watch from behind their improvised barricade. After The People had moved on, several of us stayed behind to keep an eye on the soldiers. Somebody even talked them into giving us some bacon and hardtack.

We passed the night exchanging shots with the soldiers to little effect on either side. While we kept the soldiers busy, many of the women returned, snuck in behind the soldiers, and resupplied themselves with flour, sugar, coffee, bacon, beans, and other necessities compliments of the U.S. Army. After the women returned to camp, warriors set fire to the remaining supplies. At dawn, the chiefs recalled us and we continued on the trail.

With our bellies full, the soldiers so easily beaten, and Canada slowly growing nearer, we began to regain our confidence, and the drudgery and pain of daily forced marches weighed even more heavily on us. Within a couple of days of crossing the Missouri, Looking Glass began to agitate again.

"Look at these old ones," he exclaimed in council, "they are worn out. Too many have stayed behind because they couldn't keep up. I saw a man yesterday walking off alone toward the mountains. 'Brother,' I said to him, 'where are you going?' He told me he wanted to die in mountains, not these flatlands. I could not stop him. He is gone. The soldiers are far behind us. Why force our old ones to sacrifice themselves?"

There were many who nodded agreement.

"How long will this food last?" continued Looking Glass who, like all politicians, loved nothing more than the sound of his own voice, "What will we eat when it runs out? It will not last through the winter, but buffalo are plentiful here. Why not hunt, store up meat enough to last us? Are we to greet Sitting Bull as paupers with our hands already out? What kind of welcome will that get us? We must look to the future, not just down our back trail! Lean Elk is no chief, yet we have chosen him as leader because we were frightened and we've paid the price for being afraid — our people are worn down, our horses are worn down. It is time to stop running and act like men."

He was a persuasive son of a gun. Bringing up the winter and Sitting Bull's opinion of us, and our pride as men and warriors brought even more to his side. It was clear how most of The People felt.

"Looking Glass," said Lean Elk, "if you want to lead and The People want you to lead, then go ahead. I did my best to get us to the Old Woman Country, to save The People. Now, I think the soldiers will catch us and we will all be killed, but you go ahead and take over."

And that was that. Looking Glass was reinstated as leader. The next day, a week after Cow Island, we reached *Tsanim Alikos Pah* — Place of Manure Fire — on Snake Creek. We made camp early that day so that we could butcher several buffalo that our scouts had killed while other hunting parties went out to look for more. We were only forty or so miles from Canada. Two more days should see us there and out of danger. For the first time since the Big Hole, I began to have hope.

Chapter Twenty-Eight

Morning; a vision; reassurance; we are attacked; a hard fight; terrible losses; death of my heart; the longest night; a truce; betrayal; a captive; An exchange; more tragedy; no surrender for me

I have no prelude to the following — philosophy is inadequate. Even so, never give up hope.

Montana Territory
30 September - 5 October 1877

That morning, we were up early. Coming Together built up the fire and began cooking breakfast while Walks Through began packing. Twisted Hair was playing a game with the other boys. Strong Eagle, Yellow Wolf, and I were speculating about what would happen when we reached Canada, when Wottolen emerged from his lodge shouting about a vision: "Soldiers are coming! We must leave now! Pack your things and go before it's too late! No time to waste! They will be here soon!"

This caused an uproar — Wottolen had strong medicine — but Looking Glass mounted his horse and rode through the camp reassuring people. "Take your time," he called. "Let your children fill their bellies! Plenty of time!"

Reactions were mixed. Some of us were packing even before Wottolen's warning and were almost ready to move. More began packing, while others just carried on with their morning. Not long after all that, scouts came in telling of buffalo stampeding and claiming it must be because of soldiers. It wasn't until another scout started signaling from a bluff that soldiers were right on us did everyone act, but by then it was too late.

Joseph and Sound of Running Feet ran past shouting, "Get the horses! Save the horses!" I ran back to grab my weapons, and met Coming Together and Walks Through coming with my rifle and ammunition. Both of them were armed with knives and revolvers. "Here," Coming Together said, thrusting my rifle at me, "We'll get the horses, you fight!" Over her shoulder I could see cavalry beginning to charge along the bluffs above camp, and Ollokot and our men climbing up to oppose them.

"Be careful," I said to her.

"Be brave."

I scrambled to the top of the bluff, arriving just as the cavalry closed in. The bluff narrowed considerably at our end, forcing the cavalry to compress, losing formation and most of their momentum as we opened a furious fire. Several officers went down immediately and I heard Husishusis Kute calling out "I got one" several times as he fired. I know that I killed at least one and wounded two more soldiers. The soldier's bullets fell around us like hail. With their officers down, they began to mill, some dismounting to fight, while others fled. It was a hot fight, but soon all the soldiers who could withdrew.

I looked around me and my heart broke. Lying dead just a few feet away was Ollokot. It was unreal to me that that great, good-natured warrior and chief, could be dead. Not far away from Ollokot lay the body of Looking Glass[80]. He was a brave man, but a fool, and too many others paid the price with their lives, both here and at the Big Hole.

He wasn't the only one to make mistakes though. At least three of those shot by Husishusis Kute were

---

[80] Nate seems to be mistaken here. According to various sources, Looking Glass wasn't killed until the second or third day of the battle. He did fall, however, close to where Ollokot was killed.

Nimiipuu warriors who took positions too close to the soldiers. Lean Elk was also dead, killed by one of our men who mistook him for a Cheyenne. Toohoolhoolzote, and many other warriors had been caught in the open and killed.

After the army withdrew, we dug rifle pits to protect ourselves while our noncombatants took shelter in a narrow gully right below us. I watched fruitlessly for any sign of Coming Together or the children, telling myself that surely they were alright. They had to be alright.

That afternoon we heard a cheer, and saw about twenty-five soldiers charge straight into the middle of camp. We killed about half of them, and sent the rest running for their lives. I spent the rest of the afternoon scouring the camp for my family. I found Twisted Hair and Five Times Over with Coming Together's mother, but no one who had seen Coming Together or Walks Through until I found Yellow Wolf.

"Your daughter is fine," he said. "By the time we got to the herd, there were soldiers everywhere. Joseph and your wife put the girls on horses and sent them north. Last time I saw them, they were going over a ridge with no one chasing them."

"And Coming Together?" I asked. "Where is she?"

A look of pain flashed across his face, and my heart stopped, as he shook his head and lay a trembling hand on my shoulder. "Come with me, Uncle."

He led me a short distance to the west and pointed to where she lay, shot through the chest, her dress scorched by powder. I sank to my knees next to her. She could not be dead. She was my heart, my life. I was numb — how can a man without a heart feel anything? I couldn't touch her. If I touched her it would all be real.

I don't know how long I knelt beside her like that before Yellow Wolf grasped my shoulder. "Uncle, we must go, or die here with her."

He didn't understand that I was already dead. I was hollow, I was nothing. I heard bullets buzzing past me, felt them parting the air like the sweep of a scythe, but I couldn't move.

He swept her up in his arms. Her hand hung before my face and as I clasped it, life flooded back into me, all that she had been returned to me, and my mind went to my children. "Wait," I said, "I thank you, nephew, but I will carry her." He gently handed her to me, ignoring the bullets as though they were mere flies.

We returned to the ravine where many had taken cover and lay her down. "Stay with her a moment, nephew," I said to Yellow Wolf. He nodded, and I went to what remained of my family. My mother-in-law looked at me, my shirt stained with her daughter's blood.

"Are you hurt son?" she asked, as I embraced Twisted Hair and Five Times Over. I shook my head, unable to speak. "Where is Walks Through?" she asked. "Where is Coming Together?"

I finally forced the words out. "Your daughter is dead. I don't know where Walks Through is." As I said it, the wails of my mother-in-law and my children joined the chorus of others' mourning.

Yellow Wolf helped me dig the grave while her mother and the children prepared her as best they could. When it was done, I handed a horse's lead to Twisted Hair and instructed him to lead it over and around the grave to obscure it. There would be no enemies despoiling her grave or her body as they had done to others. Yellow Wolf and I returned to the bluffs.

The temperature continued to drop and that night, rain turned to a heavy snow. No one slept, most just dozed in their rifle pits as the women wailed in mourning down below and wounded, freezing soldiers groaned where they'd fallen. Some of our people snaked out beyond our defenses to gather guns and ammunition from the fallen soldiers. Welweyas and some of the women took water along with them for the suffering soldiers.

Yellow Wolf was in a pit a few feet away. "Did you see it happen?" I asked softly.

"I did."

"Tell me?"

He sighed. "I couldn't catch a horse so I took shelter with some of the other warriors. Grizzly Bear Lying Down was talking in sign language with a Cheyenne chief. He asked why they were fighting us. The Cheyenne signed back that they would not fight us, that they would fire over our heads. Then he rode just a few paces and met Coming Together riding back into camp. He took hold of her bridle, shot her, and rode away with her horse. We all shot at him, but he had strong medicine and we couldn't hit him. I am sorry uncle."

On that longest, darkest night of my life, I was torn between grief, concern for my children, and a desire to die. I sat in the cold and the dark, alternating between despair and seething fury. Never again would I hear her singing over the supper pot, or feel her tender touch. Her laughter, the smell of her hair, of her flesh, were gone forever. The light in her eyes, in her smile, that smile that had welcomed me back to life years ago was snuffed out, and I was alone in the dark. My face was crusted with frozen tears as the dawn came.

Along with the dawn, I had a vision — I saw her standing beside that lake back in the Wallowa Valley, dressed in a white deerskin dress, with all her best finery. She was sitting on a rock, smiling, as if waiting for something. I hoped it was me.

The army greeted the sun with artillery fire. The soldiers respected our marksmanship and remained in their lines, letting the big guns do the fighting. Early that morning something snapped in Yellow Wolf and he sprang from his rifle pit, standing fully exposed to the enemy. He fired rapidly at the soldiers, shouting "I am ready to die here! I will die for my people!" I don't know why he didn't. The soldiers were firing so fast that the air was as full of lead as oxygen, and yet he was unscathed. Eventually, either bored or frustrated by their poor aim, he returned to his pit. About midday, we saw a white flag go up over the soldiers' lines.

"What do you suppose that means?" someone asked.

"Maybe they're surrendering," answered Yellow Wolf with a grim laugh.

General Miles[81] wanted a parley with Chief Joseph. Joseph, Tom Hill, and a few warriors met General Miles and some soldiers halfway between the lines. We watched anxiously to see what would come of it. Suddenly, the soldiers took Joseph and Hill back to the army lines. The warriors hurried back to our lines, and we got ready to fight again.

About that time, Twisted Hair crept up to me. "Father," he said, "come quick! Our men have captured a soldier!"

Yellow Wolf and I hurried down the bluff. A powerfully-built young lieutenant in a yellow slicker was sitting nonchalantly on a white horse, puffing on a cigar and gazing placidly around him — he may have been a little drunk — while warriors argued about what to do with him.

White Bull, who had not fired a single shot in the war, suddenly came over all warlike and tried to drag

---

[81] General Nelson A. Miles had marched northwest from Fort Keogh, attempting to cut the Nez Perce off. He located and attacked the camp on September 30th. General Howard and his force did not arrive until the eve of the surrender, October 4th.

the officer from his horse, shouting that he was going to kill the man. Yellow Wolf and I pulled him off the soldier while Espowyes shouted at him, "What is wrong with you? We can trade him for Joseph! You want to shoot someone?" He gestured toward the soldier's lines. "Go shoot at them for once!"

Many warriors joined in jeering at White Bull and he walked away muttering under his breath. Yellow Bull and Wottolen took charge of the prisoner, bringing him food and a buffalo robe and placing him in a shelter pit with some of our women and children. Yellow Bull asked me to speak to him.

"What's your name, Lieutenant?"

If he was surprised to be so well treated and hear an educated voice speaking English, he hid it well. "I am Lieutenant Lovell Hall Jerome," he said calmly. "Who do I have the pleasure of addressing?"

I gestured at the others, "This is Chief Yellow Bull and Wottolen."

He nodded to them. "Tell them I'm grateful, both for my life, and for their treatment of me."

"You know your General Miles has betrayed a flag of truce and taken our chief prisoner?"

"I did not," he replied, "and I am sorry to hear it. General Miles is normally an honourable man. I hope he is treating your man as kindly and generously as you are treating his."

"I hope so too," I said.

"By the way," he said surreptitiously, "I don't know if anyone realizes this, but they've left me my revolver."

"Are you planning to use it?"

"Not at all," he said, "I just don't want one of you fellows shooting me over it later."

"Well, leave it where it is and you'll be fine."

He looked around, taking in his surroundings.

"Makes you proud, I bet, chasing a handful of women and children and old people to death," I said, bitterly.

"It's not just women and children and old people my friend," he said. "And you fellows have done your share of killing the helpless too."

"I'm not your friend. I'd love to cut your throat, but you are valuable right now. We get you traded for Joseph and I'll happily scatter your brains for the birds to peck should you cross my sights."

"The feeling is mutual," he replied coolly. "But I am sorry about your noncombatants. I wish it weren't so, but that is the nature of war." He eyed me carefully. "If I'm not mistaken, I think you know exactly what I mean."

"I've seen war from your side," I said. "It made me sick, to see what 'civilized' men can justify as war."

He nodded. "It is a nasty, brutish business."

"But it's only short for the wrong people," I said.

We left him to sleep — under guard, of course — and I returned to the bluffs.

In the morning, Yellow Bull sent for me again. "The soldier wants to speak to you."

"What do you want?" I asked Jerome.

"First," he said, "I'd like you to express my gratitude again to the chief and Mr. Wottolen for their generous treatment."

I did so, and Wottolen replied, "What did he expect? We are not animals. There is no honour in humiliating or mistreating a helpless man. What is wrong with these *soyapo*? Are they all crazy?"

I told Jerome, "They said you're welcome. What else do you want?"

He held up a paper. "I'd like someone to take this to General Miles."

I took the letter and read it aloud for Yellow Bull and Wottolen. It explained his situation, that he was being well treated, and that we wanted to exchange him for Joseph.

After an exchange of correspondence, the exchange was made. In contrast to our treatment of Jerome, Joseph had been chained hand and foot, rolled in a blanket, and left outside on the ground with the mules, like a discarded cigar. We returned to our rifle pits, and the artillery barrage began again. We spent the rest of the day trading shots with the soldiers, and the night watching for any movement by the soldiers, and listening to our women keen and our children cry.

The barrage continued the next day, focused largely on the ravine where our noncombatants huddled for shelter. We were very angry about that — surely Jerome had told Miles there were no warriors down there — but our people were well dug in and as safe as we could make them. About noon, I saw Twisted Hair climbing the bluff with no attempt at concealment. As he drew near, I saw the stricken look on his face and my heart fell. I left my pit, sweeping him up and hurrying him to cover. "What is it?" I asked. "What is wrong?"

"It . . . a shell . . ." He said in a hollow voice. His eyes were dry — after his brother and his mother, he had no tears left to cry.

I held him close for a moment, then said, "Show me." He led me down to where a shell had directly struck one of the shelter pits dug into the wall of the ravine. People were digging furiously, pulling women and children out. Miraculously, they pulled three women and a small boy out shaken and injured, but alive. The only dead were my mother-in-law and my little girl.

We left them there, their shelter becoming their grave — we were all too spent, physically and emotionally, to do otherwise. I sat with Twisted Hair for a time, and then left him with Welweyas while I searched for Strong Eagle to give him the news. When I found him, he had already heard and was sitting in his pit in shock. We sat without speaking — what was there to say? We had both lost almost everyone we loved. Other than Twisted Hair, the only thing either of us had left to lose was our lives, and those we counted as worthless.

When I left him, I gave Twisted Hair a rifle, and took him to my rifle pit. We would live or die together. That night, I had another vision — Coming Together, Many Wounds, and Five Times Over were standing together, holding hands in bright sunlight. They smiled as they turned and walked away. Now I knew what she had been waiting for, and I knew that Twisted Hair and I would survive, and that Walks Through still lived as well.

I spent the day pondering my vision, and realized that none of them were lost. Nothing lasts forever, but nothing ever ends either. Everything just becomes something else. Our bodies are born to die, but our spirit cannot be destroyed by any act of man. All those I loved were still there, just out of sight. Even in death, Coming Together was able to stitch the edges of my tattered spirit back together and give me new life.

Joseph spent the day negotiating our surrender. With most of the other chiefs dead and too few warriors to protect them, the lives of the women and children were dependent on him making the best peace he could. White Bird refused to surrender and his people slipped through the army lines that night, headed for Sitting Bull and Canada.

Strong Eagle, Twisted Hair, and I resolved also to escape and search for Walks Through. Yellow Wolf joined us to search for his mother and Sound of Running Feet. Even with the vision I'd had of Coming Together and the children, it was hard to be optimistic as we planned our escape, shivering in the dark.

Chapter Twenty-Nine

Escape; reunion; one last tragedy; safety; we go home; years pass; education, heartbreak, and worry; a homecoming and the return of an old enemy; one last heartbreak; exile again

The future never turns out the way you expect. I certainly didn't think mine was going to end on a gallows. To be honest, I'm still not completely convinced it will. My luck may have faltered here and there, but it's generally come through. Nathan, Mrs. Good, Sheriff Angus, and most of my friends are not so sanguine about my prospects and they may be right, but I'm not ready to give up yet. I believe in a higher justice than I'm likely to find in a Wyoming courtroom.

Montana Territory, Canada, Idaho Territory, and Washington Territory
1877 – 1885

We slipped through the army lines in the wee hours of the morning, and walked north until we found horses, and then rode north, all the while looking for some sign of our people. At the Milk River, we found some mixed-bloods who gave us food and coffee and pointed us in the direction they had seen some of our people traveling.

We rode on and, about nightfall, found a small *Nimiipuu* camp, our missing people among them! Twisted Hair and I tearfully embraced Walks Through. We didn't even have to tell her about her mother and sister — their absence was enough. As was our custom, she began to wail and cut her hair. We joined her in mourning — it was our first chance to do so properly. We never spoke their names again, nor the names of any of the dead. These pages mark the first time I've ever even written my wife or children's names, much less spoken them.

Yellow Wolf's reunion with his mother was happier — she had been told he was killed and fainted, thinking him a ghost. "I will never die from being shot," he told her once she revived. "Someday, I'll get old or sick and die, but no gun will ever kill me. I tell you three times, I will not die of the gun[82]."

---

[82] This very closely mirrors Yellow Wolf's account of his escape from Bear's Paw and finding his mother. Interestingly enough, Yellow Wolf never mentions Nate or Nate's family in his account. Perhaps he considered it not his place to tell their story. Readers interested in learning more about this great man should read *Yellow Wolf: His Own Story* by Lucullus V. McWhorter.

Joseph's daughter, Sound of Running Feet, was there also. Joseph had asked Yellow Wolf to bring her back, but he decided it would be better to take her to Canada.

We moved on cautiously toward Canada, for there were many enemies besides the army between us and that magic line — Strong Eagle went out scouting and was killed by Walk-Around Sioux[83]. He was the last of our group to die in that war.

We finally crossed the border and found our way to Sitting Bull's village. White Bird's people arrived nearly the same time. We got along well with the Sioux, but it was a hard winter. The addition of our people put added pressure on the already scarce game, and some of the Sioux resented it. The U.S. constantly pressured the Canadians to send us back but the Canadian government refused — although it was clear they'd like us to leave.

That next summer, Joseph sent word for all his people to join him in the Indian Territories, and a small group decided to go. We slipped across the border and made our way back to the Nez Perce Reservation. It was a harrowing journey, filled with trouble from both Indians and whites, but we made it.

---

[83] What the *Nimiipuu* called the Assiniboine tribe.

Once there, most went to the agency at Lapwai and surrendered, but I learned that Morrow/Chapman was now living in the Territories as Joseph's interpreter, so the children and I remained with the reservation *Nimiipuu*. I sold a horse, purchased white clothes, cut my hair, and became Nate Luck again. I left Walks Through and Twisted Hair with relatives near Kamiah, and found work at a nearby ranch to support them.

I spent as much time as I could with them, continuing their education. They could already read and speak English, but I knew that in order to survive, they would need the white man's knowledge. I had lost all my books during the war, so I reached out to my sister Natasha, now a widow, in San Francisco for replacements. I taught the children from Mill and Locke, Paine, Jefferson, and Adams, as well as the Declaration of Independence and U.S. Constitution, and Blackstone's law commentaries.

Walks Through had a quick, incisive mind, and before long, she was explaining much of what we read to me. One day, when it was clear she'd gone as far as I could take her, she said, "Father, if I'm going to be educated properly, I need to attend a real school."

"You're not going to one of those d--ned mission schools," I growled, "and the agency school's no better. They'll teach you what they want you to know instead of what you need to know."

"What about a boarding school?" There were Indian boarding schools at Carlisle, Pennsylvania and other places.

"No," I said. "Absolutely not. It would be the same thing, only worse, and I wouldn't be there to protect you. Besides, we're doing alright, aren't we?"

"Not in science and mathematics. You're hopeless at those — how are you going to teach me what you don't understand?"

"You're only fifteen years old," I protested. "Too young to be living away from your family."

"Only fifteen?" she asked, frustrated. "Only fifteen? Sound of Running feet is 'only fifteen' and she's married already! Mother was 'only fourteen' when she was first married! I killed two soldiers when I was twelve! I can take care of myself." With that, she crossed her arms, lowered her head, and stared at me through her eyebrows with her bottom lip sticking out. She looked exactly as her mother always did when her mind was made up.

I refused to give in, barked, "That's the end of it," and stomped out before I saw the triumphant look in her eyes telling me that she knew she was going to get exactly what she wanted somehow.

After a correspondence with my sister, I sent her to San Francisco, where she could attend a private school under her aunt's protection. Natasha was a vital supporter of the school, influential in society, and had important political connections. If anyone could keep her safe in white society, it was Tasha. Walks Through chose a "white" name — Joan Olga Luck — for Joan of Arc, and Princess Olga of Kiev. It was a fitting name for my brave girl.

She and Natasha wrote frequently to inform me of her progress, and within a few years were bullying me into allowing her to attend Toland Medical College. Naturally, they got their way. I know when I'm whipped.

Twisted Hair refused to leave the reservation, and I was glad — the white world would have eaten him alive. He was a deeply troubled boy, eaten up by guilt that he hadn't fought the whites, that he'd been unable to protect his siblings, that he'd survived, and I am sure burying his mother and camouflaging her grave left deep scars. As a result, my happy, enthusiastic little boy became a surly, bitter young man. I tried to help him, but he often was unable to see past my whiteness — and I know he tried.

As he grew older, he came to hate schooling, and love alcohol and bad company, leading to minor but escalating scrapes with the law. Finally, there was good news — The People were coming home from the Indian Territory. Twisted Hair worked hard to straighten himself up — he wanted to make a good impression on the chief and his old heroes like Yellow Wolf and Wottolen.

Joseph was not allowed to return to the Nez Perce reservation — the authorities wouldn't guarantee his safety, so he was taken to Colville reservation in Washington Territory, hundreds of miles away from his beloved Wallowa Valley. About half of those who survived the Indian Territories — what they called "The Hot Place" — followed him to Colville and the rest came to Lapwai, on the Nez Perce reservation.

Twisted Hair and I journeyed north to see our old friends. Morrow/Chapman was still with them, but he stayed at the agency, so there was little risk of running into him. We visited Yellow Wolf first, and learned how unspeakably hellish life had been in The Hot Place. Of the roughly 420 *Nimiipuu* who had surrendered with Joseph, only 268 survived. Almost as many had died in captivity as in the war, and that doesn't include stillborn infants or those who were born and died in captivity. It was so bad that even Morrow/Chapman stood up for The People.

"Chapman tried to help the best he could," Yellow Wolf said. "He fought the agent for better food, told him to stop cheating us. Lived with us all the time. Even got sick and almost died. He was a friend to us down there."

That caught me flat-footed. I knew how much good living with The People had done me. Perhaps they had changed Morrow as well.

I asked why he'd chosen Colville over Lapwai.

"Joseph is my uncle," he said, "and my chief. Also, when we got to Wallula, the agent said we could either go to Lapwai and be Christians, or come to Colville and be ourselves. To become a Christian would be like an eagle choosing to be a dog."

We spent a few weeks at Colville, but came close to running into Morrow/Chapman a couple of times, and decided our people would be safer without me around.

Despite the good he'd tried to do in The Hot Place, I couldn't bring myself to trust him. The morning we left, Twisted Hair stopped at the reservation boundary.

"You go on," he said. "I'm staying here with my people."

I could see the tears in his eyes through those in my own. We were both lost. "You're my son," I said. "If you don't belong with me, where do you belong? If I don't belong with you, where am I to go?"

"I don't know," he said. "I don't know much of anything except all this hate is eating me up."

"Son, let me help you. I want to help you."

"I know — but how can you help me when you're part of what I hate?"

"I can't help what I am, where I am from . . ."

"And I can't help that I hate the white blood I got from you! Every time I look at you, I see the father I love, but I also see a white man, like those who killed my mother, my brother, and sister. I know it's not your fault. It's the same thing I see when I look in a mirror."

"Walks Through doesn't feel that way."

"She knows who she is! She is fully *Nimiipuu*, even if she was raised by you. She has no white blood corrupting her soul!"

"That's not fair son . . ."

"D-mmit, you think I don't know that? I hate this. But I have to let this hate go, have to find where I fit in this world. Maybe here with Joseph and Yellow Wolf I'll find harmony again."

We sat there quietly until he offered his hand and I shook it. "I'll write you," he said.

"I don't know where I'll be. Without you and your sister, I don't know where I belong."

"Well, you can write me at the agency."

"Yes," I said, "I'll do that."

"I am sorry, you know," he said.

"I know you are son. I'm sorry too. But I understand — maybe more than you know." At least he would have friends to guide him. Maybe letting him go was the best thing I could do for him, but my G-d it hurt!

We sat there a little longer, until finally I said, "Well, I'd best be going."

"I suppose so. Take care."

"You too." I said, and we turned our horses in opposite directions and rode into our separate futures.

Part Four:

Lawman

Chapter Thirty

San Francisco; Snotty; a joyous reunion; a new friend; Tasha the matchmaker; a long-lost letter; on to Buffalo

It is always a surprise when what feels like the end of a story turns out to simply be the beginning of another chapter. It shouldn't be, but it always is. I suppose the lesson here is that too many of us give up on life way too early.

California
1886 – 1887

Being at loose ends after parting ways with Twisted Hair, I returned to Kamiah for a time, but could find no rest there. Being slapped in the face — so to speak — with my whiteness by my own son stung, and with no family there I felt like an outsider in my own home. I decided to go out to San Francisco to visit Walks Through — or Jeanne Olga, to use the white name she'd chosen — and Tasha. I gave away everything I owned, with the exception of two horses, my weapons, and some equipment, and set out for California.

For the first time in years, every day was not a struggle to support and guide two sad, frightened, angry youngsters. I had only myself to take care of and plenty of time to think about, well, everything really. It was a long ride but it was good, for I felt that Coming Together rode with me. I spoke to her about all that had happened since her death, and I felt her smiling on me. I reminisced about those good years we had and once again felt the warm glow of her love. She visited me often in my sleep. She still does. I don't know if they are actual visitations or mere dreams, but they comfort me and help to keep my demons at bay.

I spent the whole trip largely lost in thought, and I found myself pondering more and more about why this country had fallen so short of its potential, of its own self-stated principles and goals, and what the solutions might be. Sadly, the reasons why all boiled down to two things, at least in my mind, greed and lust for power — the same things that man has been tripping himself over since the dawn of time. Even more sadly, I could come up with only two solutions: that democracy must be based on equality, and that the rule of law must be applied equally to all. If only those principles were as easy to implement as they are to write! My thoughts on this were guided by Mill's *Considerations on Representative Government*, which I recommend to anyone interested in proper governance, but enough of that for now.

I reached San Francisco in time for Christmas, having been in no particular hurry and, after selling both horses, along with what little I still possessed of any value, spent the proceeds on a largely unsuccessful effort to improve my appearance — a new coat of paint won't hide the fact that a house is half burnt down.

I finally washed up at Tasha's Nob Hill door on a cold, wind-blown Saturday, a battered, shabby, worn-down shade of the cocky boy who'd gone to seek his fortune years before. The man who answered my knock was tall, bald, and thin, elegantly dressed, and unwilling to let me in the door. He stared down his long nose at me. "Workmen need to go to the servants' entrance," he said haughtily.

Now, I knew I looked a little rough, but his supercilious attitude got my back up. "Well if I see one,

I'll let him know," I said. "I'm here to see the lady of the house."

"Mrs. Carmichael cannot be disturbed at the moment. What is the nature of your business here?"

I could have taken an easier approach but, as I've said, he got my back up. "My business is with Mrs. Carmichael, not with you, buster," I said. "Now run along and fetch her before I do something you'll regret."

He immediately stepped back and with a mocking sneer slammed the door in my face. I heard the bolt shoot home, and through the door he called, "If you do not leave immediately, I shall have no choice but to call the police."

I looked around. Although there were plenty of people out and about, there wasn't a single constable to be seen. On the other hand, there were quite a few folks who were watching all this with interest. I decided that perhaps making a scene on her front step was not the best way to be reintroduced to my sister[84]. Much as

---

[84] Nate almost certainly made the right decision here. Although apparently unaware of it, San Francisco's first major telephone exchange was established in 1878. As a member of the city's elite, Natasha would almost certainly have had a telephone line with which the police could have been called out.

I would have liked to smack that fellow around a bit, embarrassing Tasha was the last thing I wanted. "All right," I called, "you win. I'll go around back." I walked around until I saw a "Deliveries" sign above a door and knocked. Curtains fluttered in a window off to the side, and a wide-eyed girl peeked out.

I waved, and she jerked the curtains shut. There was a bench next to the door, so I sat down to wait. Sooner or later, that door was bound to open. I was right. It opened and the snotty fellow stuck his head out. "What is it you want?"

"I want to see the lady of the house."

"Mrs. Carmichael is not available at . . ."

"Who is it, Fairbanks?" a young lady's voice interrupted him. I saw a pair of dark eyes peek around him. "Father?"

"Walks Through?"

"Father!"

It was my own dear girl! She launched herself from the door and embraced me, alternating between fussing over me and excoriating the snotty fellow. It was clear that "civilization" had not dulled her combative proclivities. She sent Snotty to fetch Tasha, and ushered me inside. "Why didn't you write to tell us you were coming? Why aren't you taking better care of yourself? How is Twisted Hair? You've gotten too skinny. What have you been eating? How are Yellow Wolf, Sound of Running Feet, and . . ." I couldn't get a word in edgewise. Moments later, Tasha flew into the room, as excited to see me as I was her. It couldn't have been a more pleasant reunion.

They took me to task about my condition, and immediately set about rehabilitating me, almost killing me with kindness. Tasha's French cook saw me as a challenge, and they shoveled his rich food into me like locomotive firemen going up a steep grade. It took months for my bowels to recover. Tasha had a barber in to cut my shaggy hair, and a tailor to measure me, and I spent an embarrassing three or four days in a dressing gown while new clothes were made for me, Walks Through having burned all my old ones. I, of course, protested manfully, and then settled in to enjoy being spoiled for a while.

Wealth and widowhood had been good to Tasha. Tall and regal, with her silver hair elegantly coiffured, attended by a battalion of servants, and commanding an army of friends, admirers, and sycophants with benevolence and charm, she was as close to a queen as

I'm ever likely to meet, and her velvet gloves concealed fists of iron as ruthless as those of any despot when crossed. She was, and is, a formidable woman. The tongue-lashing she gave Snotty the day I arrived was a work of art. He spent the next two weeks waiting on me hand and foot — a task thoroughly unpleasant to both of us, but it made Tasha happy.

Walks Through was the image of her mother. She had grown into the promise of her youth — strong, whip-smart, determined, and capable, with no tolerance for "nonsense" which translated as anything that didn't suit her — but was also kind, generous, and affectionate. She adored her Aunt Tasha, and Tasha treated her as a daughter rather than a hard-luck charity case.

It took me a couple of weeks to convince Tasha to make her cook take it easy and give me smaller quantities of simpler fare, and that only succeeded because I was finally able to enlist Walks Through in my cause — Tasha always deferred to her in medical matters. She was doing well at Toland and was determined to become a doctor. She had found a mentor in a female doctor named Lucy Maria Field Wanzer.

"We will have her to dinner so you can meet her," Walks Through told me excitedly.

"That is an excellent idea," exclaimed Tasha. There was a glint in Tasha's eye that I didn't much care for. There may be nothing in the world so dangerous as a wealthy woman with good intentions.

I found Lucy to be artlessly charming and refreshingly direct. Over after-dinner drinks, I asked her what it had been like to be the first female to attend Toland Medical College, and she said only, "Well it wasn't easy," and sipped her sherry.

"You're being far too modest," said Walks Through. "Tell him about your ovaries!"

When I'd finished blowing whisky out my nose and caught my breath, I managed a weak, "What?"

Lucy laughed. "It's really not all that exciting or scandalous. In one of my earliest classes, the professor was angry that a woman would dare to invade the *sanctum sanctorum* of his classroom, and told me that a woman should have her ovaries removed before being allowed to study medicine. I simply responded that I would happily submit to such a procedure — under the condition that all male medical students' testicles be removed as well[85]. That was the last I heard of that line of nonsense."

I was pleased that Walks Through had found such a strong-willed and determined mentor. Things had settled down somewhat in regard to female medical students, thanks to ladies like Lucy, and I was grateful, for I'm pretty sure that in the same situation, Walks Through would have pulled a knife and offered to start gelding students on the spot.

We had a splendid evening, despite Tasha's attempts at match-making. Lucy seemed to have no more interest in being matched than I did, and together we enjoyed thwarting Tasha's decreasingly subtle tactics.

After Lucy left, Tasha came right out with it: "Why don't you like her?"

"I like her just fine. She's a lovely woman."

"Well, I think you two would be a good match."

"Tasha," I said as patiently as I could, "Why is this so important to you? After all, you seem quite content with your life."

---

[85] This really happened. Dr. Wanzer was a remarkable woman, about whom very little is known today. Readers interested in learning more about her and what she went through and accomplished should seek out Dr. Emma L. Merritt's tribute to Dr. Wanzer on her 83rd birthday. It can be found in *California and Western Medicine*, May 1925.

"I am content," she said, "but I'm not alone. I am settled and comfortable and surrounded by family and friends. You are just drifting aimlessly."

"I like drifting. I don't know how to explain it any better than that."

Tasha let it go, and though she spent the next few months trying to pair Lucy and me up, she never pushed so hard again. Sometimes though, I would catch her looking at me with eyes full of sadness and pity. I had no way to ever make her understand.

Mischa wrote to me in March, suggesting that if I found life in the city unsatisfying, there was plenty of work for a man of my talents in Wyoming. I found his offer intriguing and, in truth, as delightful as Tasha, Walks Through, and Lucy Wanzer were, I was finding the constant noise and frantic pace of the city very wearing.

The next day, Tasha found me moping in the library. "I have something for you." She held out a very dusty letter.

It was from my old friend Dave, and was years old. "Why didn't you send this on to me?" I asked, tearing it open. "Why did you wait until now to give it to me?"

"Where should I have forwarded it too? It's only the last few years that I've had any idea where you were, you numbskull. To be honest, I had completely forgotten about it, until Mischa's letter came for you."

I mumbled my thanks as I eagerly read. It began:

Dear Mister Nate,

I hope this letter finds you doing well. I am doing well, running a small spread near Buffalo, in Wyoming Territory . . .

Dave went on to inform me that Frenchy had also landed in Buffalo, and that if I should ever find myself over that way, I should stop and see them.

I felt my heart quicken at the thought of a new adventure. It was time to move on.

Chapter Thirty-One

Prophets, desert, and solitude; the frustrating love of womenfolk; a long ride; Charlie and Tom; the Cheyenne Club; a distasteful offer

I used to wonder why the prophets of old were always going off into the desert by themselves. I think they were seeking clarity. It is so hard to find any amid the hubbub and perpetual business that accompanies society — there are just too many distractions and necessities clamouring for attention. Only in solitude can a man find the peace needed to sort out his own thoughts — to examine himself, his life, and the world, and find some sense in it all, some consistency, some truth. That is what I found — or at least started to find — on my long solitary rides. I believe the difference between the clarity I found in those times and the madness I fell into following Sand Creek and its aftermath is that back then, I wasn't seeking clarity. I was hiding from it. I'm tempted to say that nothing good ever comes from that, but if I hadn't gone through that, I wouldn't have ever met Coming Together. Of course, for that clarity and truth to matter, you've got to come back in from the desert and put it to the test.

California and Wyoming Territory
1888

Naturally, my departure from San Francisco was made more difficult by Tasha and Walks Through's concerns, especially when I announced that I was planning to go on horseback. They both tried to persuade me to go to Cheyenne via the Transcontinental railroad — Tasha's argument was based on her opinion that, at fifty years of age, I was "too d—ned old and battered to try riding that far!" and Walks Through's was more focused on persuading me to see the advances and benefits of modern technology and all its wonders. Neither argument won me over, although they certainly gave it their best efforts. Tasha scorned my own argument that I'd ridden a horse to get here.

"Yes," she said, "but just look at the condition you were in when you arrived. Why you were nothing but skin and bones wrapped in rags!"

I admit I was a little hot at her insinuations, but what man ever likes being told he's too old and infirm to do exactly as he pleases? "Nonsense," I snapped. "I've always tended to be on the lean side."

"You've always tended to be on the stubborn side!"

There really wasn't much I could say to counter that.

She took my lack of response as an opportunity to begin an attack from another vector. "Besides, you don't even have a horse, nor money to buy one!"

"I don't have money for a ticket either."

"Oh, you know I'd be happy to purchase your ticket for you, and a first-class ticket at that!"

Walks Through took the opportunity to join the assault. "Father, think how glorious it would be! To ride in comfort, with good meals, as you watch the country speeding by! I think it would be magical!"

"I think a saddle is the most comfortable seat in the world, and I can cook my own beans and bacon. There is no food on any train anywhere that can rival fresh-killed venison. Why would I want food prepared by some lackey when I can eat like a king on food I've provided myself? As far as 'watching the country speed by' who in his right mind would want that? I want to see the country! I want to feel the wind on my face and smell the good, clean scent of the air, the trees, even the soil, not the smoke belched from some infernal machine! I want to be able to sit and watch the sun set over the mountains if I choose, to listen to the squirrels chattering in the trees, to enjoy this country like a man should, and not scurry through it like . . . like . . . like some creature obsessed with reaching a destination rather than enjoying the road. It is the road that matters most. You should know that."

"Yes, but Father, you've ridden that road before. Perhaps a new way of seeing it will be a treat. Perhaps it would give you a new appreciation . . ."

"My darling girl, whether I see it through a rail car window or from horseback, I will be seeing it with these same old eyes, interpreting it with this same old heart. It is inconceivable that a quick glimpse will satisfy, any more than a nibble will assuage a starving man. Besides, I'm not even sure I want to stop in Cheyenne."

"Don't be ridiculous," interrupted Tasha. "Why wouldn't you go to Cheyenne? Didn't Mischa promise you work? A chance to finally make your fortune?"

"I don't know that I want the kind of work he's promising, and I don't care a penny for the kind of fortune he's got in mind for me."

"You are a stubborn, stubborn, ridiculous man, Tolya," grumbled Tasha.

"You'll get no argument from me on that," I said.

They let it go for a time, but continued to argue and politic to get their way. When they gave up on a train, they tried to get me to go for a coach, and when that failed, tried to get me to join a party of teamsters. They let their opinions be known on every aspect regarding the manner of my going, down to the quality of the horses I took. Tasha insisted that I take a pair of her riding horses. It was all I could do not to laugh when I thought of those pampered, beautiful, city-bound, pure-bred beauties facing deserts, mountains, rivers, and canyons with little to eat other than what grazing was available. Chances were that I'd end up eating them or just leaving them where they fell, long before Buffalo. I thanked her, and politely declined her offer. When she saw the three little mustangs I purchased with some gambling winnings, she was near apoplectic. Fortunately for me, Walks Through reassured her that those sturdy little mustangs were much more suitable for the mountains, and she calmed somewhat, but insisted on outfitting me with what few needs I had. "If I leave it to you, you'll head out without a reliable firearm or even a blanket," was how she put it.

It was mid-April by the time I finally headed out, as well-equipped as I'd ever been in my life. I took my time and enjoyed the ride, which consequently took longer than it should have. Perhaps I should have hurried, but I decided that whatever it was that awaited me in Buffalo, a little more wait wouldn't hurt it. I felt myself once again slowly falling back in love with this country, its beautiful, unforgiving deserts, rich ranchland, rugged mountains, and, eventually, even its people. I spent much time just sitting and admiring the view, and meditating on everything that had brought me to this moment, the good and the bad. I even began to rediscover G-d, whom I had found with the *Nimiipuu* and abandoned with the deaths of my wife and children. I could once again see his hand in the creation all around me, even in the Americans I met along the way, who were generally as kind and generous, and decent as any I've ever met, even among the *Nimiipuu*. I was reminded that it is not man who is bad, greedy, or evil — or at least his capacity for such things is extremely limited — it is men, or rather mobs and those who incite and direct them who are the problem.

***

In the end, I decided to stop in Cheyenne after all.

Mischa teased me about how long the trip took me. "Well," he proclaimed dramatically when I arrived at his office in the Wyoming Stock Growers Association, "look who finally turned up. I was starting to think you'd gotten a better offer, maybe found another tribe to hobnob around with, or maybe just decided to stay with Tasha and enjoy the good life." He always did enjoy playing the big man.

I refused to take the bait. "Well," I said, "it's a long ride, and us old men like to take our time."

He just laughed and we embraced, pounding each other's backs in that way brothers do — just a little harder than necessary in a childish attempt to assert dominance. "It's good to see you Tolya. We can use a good man like you. These G-dd--ned rustlers are robbing us blind."

"Mischa," I said, "I just got here. At least let me get my boots off." He apologized and we went inside.

We intended to spend my first evening in, visiting with his wife, Julia, and son, Michael, but Julia seemed to smell something foul all through dinner, excused herself early, and retired in a huff. Michael also found better things to do, once he realized no stories of blood-thirsty savages were forthcoming. Mischa and I decided to go out for a drink and found ourselves at John and Henry Dillman's saloon in Eddy Street.

"I'm sorry about Julia," he said. "I don't . . ." He sat back and sighed. "I don't think life in a cow town is what she had in mind when we got married. She'd like things a little more genteel."

"Don't worry about it, little brother," I laughed. "My rough ways would put any society woman off her feed."

"Tasha didn't think so," he said.

"Well, she's prejudiced in my favour." We laughed. "Now," I said, "tell me about this stock detective business."

"'Scuse me gentlemen," said a fellow at the next table, "but did I hear you say something about stock detecting?"

"That's right," said Mischa.

"Well," the fellow said in a Texas drawl, "that's a field in which I have some experience, and one that my associate," he gestured toward a tall gentleman with a receding hairline, a long, strait nose over a bushy mustache, and pointed chin, "is developing an interest in." He extended a hand. "Name's Charlie Siringo. Pleased to meet you." He was of average height, with dark, lank hair, a deeply groomed mustache, and an open smile.

We introduced ourselves, and invited them to join us. "This here's Tom Horn," he said by way of introduction. We shook hands all around and settled in. They were quite a pair — Charlie was easy-going and garrulous, full of laughter and charm, and laughed at himself as often as at anything else. Tom was taciturn and distant, with cold, grey eyes that took in everything and gave nothing away. He was another who reminded me of Poke Carlin, from my old cowpunching days. I suspected that Horn too, was a real killing gentleman.

"Are you gentlemen looking for work?" asked Mischa.

"I'm not," said Charlie. "I'm just up here taking a break from work."

"What line are you in?" I asked.

He looked around at the other tables, and then leaned in. "Well, you fellas look like upstanding citizens, so I reckon I can tell you. I'm a detective with the Pinkerton Agency. I'll ask you to keep that under your hats though." He gestured around the saloon. "Never know when I'm going to have to get on the trail of somebody. It's easier when I'm not recognized as a detective. That's part of why I'm up here — I'm not too well known in these parts, so I can relax a bit. An' lemme tell you, I could use it. Trust me fellas, don't ever get locked up in Gunnison, Colorado. Worst jail I've ever been in."

Neither Mischa nor I had ever been in jail, and Charlie's eyes sparkled like a man who told a good yarn, so I prompted him a bit. "I thought you were a detective. What were you doing in jail?"

He took another drink to wet his whistle. "Why detecting, of course. See, there was some desperados — the Smith brothers and a fella name o' Rhodes — I'd been tracking in connection with a coupla train robberies. They got theirselves arrested in Utah, and was shipped back to Gunnison. Well, ever'one knew they'd done it, but there was a shortage of actual evidence, so the sheriff, Doc Shores, and me met their train at Montrose. Ol' Doc put me in cuffs and leg-irons and we got on the train with 'em, pretending I was a desperado too, see if I couldn't wangle a confession out of 'em." He laughed and took another drink. "You shoulda seen the show I put on for those boys, vowing to escape and take my revenge on Doc. 'Course it was kinda wasted on one of the Smith boys who'd got shot through the head in a dispute over divvying up the loot. Never saw a wound that stunk like that one. But anyway, ol' Doc locked us up together in the worst cell I ever seen — turns out that another prisoner had slit his own throat in there and died just a couple days before, and whoever was in charge of cleaning the jail just wasn't up to the task. Dried blood all over the place. To make things worse, we come to find out that Alfred Packer the maneater had been locked up in that same cell before going to the penitentiary."

"You're kidding," said Mischa, who only got that in edgewise while Charlie took a drink. That fellow was a born storyteller.

"I do not," Charlie replied. "I don't mind telling you, it didn't half make my skin crawl thinkin' about it.

Them other boys was so shook up they spent most of their time praying, well the ones that wasn't shot in the head, that is. The one that was talked a lot, but didn't make much sense. Anyway, it took me two weeks to get a confession out of 'em. Anyway, I signaled Doc the next day, and he came and took me out of the cell, talking about how I was being extrydited to Wyoming to be hung. I'd got along so well with them boys that Rhodes and the unshot Smith had tears in their eyes when I shook their hands on my way out the door. Turned out I didn't even have to testify. They was so shook, they just broke down and pled guilty. They're on their way to the penitentiary now." Pleased with his tale, he sat back and finished his drink.

The girl waiting tables wasn't coming around often enough, so I went to the bar to get another round in.

"So what is your experience with stock detecting?" I asked when I returned.

He pulled a sour face. "Well, I've done my share of chasin' cattle rustlers and horse thieves. Shoot, I chased Billy Bonney all over New Mexico territory. But what they're calling stock detective work around here sure don't sound like my kind of work."

"But surely, as a detective," said Mischa, "you don't approve of outlaws getting away with their crimes scot-free?"

"No, of course not," Charlie said. "But I'm interested in bringing criminals to real justice, not takin' the law into my own hands. I was in Chicago during that Haymarket affair. I got into this business to stop anarchists and the like — the sorts who'd throw a bomb into a crowd just to start trouble — and to help bring them to justice. A fella slapping a brand on a maverick just ain't in that league."

Horn spoke up. "Far's I'm concerned, a fellow claiming cattle that ain't his ain't no better than an anarchist or a robber, and a bullet's justice enough."

"Don't you believe in the courts?" I asked. "Aren't they entitled to their day in court? Innocent until proven guilty and all that?"

"A couple o' years back, I had me a nice little ranch. One night I was away and a bunch came in and ran off all my stock. I lost everything, and the law couldn't do anything about it. I'd shoot a rustler as quick as I would a rattlesnake."

We drank and talked — well mostly, Charlie talked — late into the night. He had a trove of stories that seemed endless. Full of adventure and misadventure, if half of them were true, he'd led quite the exciting life. I won't recite any more of them here, for I fear I wouldn't nearly do them justice. Anyone interested can just read his book[86].

He was not a heavy drinker, and seemed to only imbibe enough to fuel his endless supply of stories.

Horn, on the other hand, took his drinking much more seriously, and became both darker and more outgoing as he drank. At Charlie's prompting, and perhaps to put Charlie in his place, Horn, now deep in his cups, began telling stories of his own — dark and bloody tales boasting of fighting Apaches and Mexicans, gunning down rustlers, and that sort of thing. I was glad I hadn't been drinking heavily, for I was in no mood for self-aggrandizing tales of fighting Indians, but one thing he said stuck with me. "I was paid to find 'em, and to translate. Those inclined to

---

[86] Charlie Siringo published several books about his life. Nate is referring to his first, *A Texas Cowboy; or Fifteen Years on the Hurricane Deck of a Spanish Pony*, published in 1886. He also published two books on his experience as a Pinkerton Detective, *A Cowboy Detective* and *Two Evil Isms: Pinkertonism and Anarchism.* He also wrote *History of Billy the Kid*, a biography of the famous outlaw. Incidentally, the Gunnison Jail story appears in A Cowboy Detective.

talk, I brought in to talk — hell, I brought that crafty rascal Geronimo in three or four times to talk — but those who only wanted to speak in gunpowder and lead, well, I was happy to oblige, and made sure I always got the last word in." He seemed determined to convince everyone that he was the most dangerous man in the place[87]

Charlie and I were clearly discomfited by Horn's gloating arrogance, and the party drew to a close. As we shook hands in parting, Mischa invited them both to lunch at the Cheyenne Club the next day to ". . . meet some of the fellows and at least hear what they were proposing."

Charlie appeared dubious, but Horn was definitely interested. "Can't hurt to hear 'em out, I reckon," was how he put it.

***

We walked to the Cheyenne Club late the next morning. "Now Nate," Mischa said nervously on the

---

[87] Tom Horn's tendency for drunken boasting eventually led to a confession to the murder of 14-year-old Willie Nickell. He was convicted and hung on November 20, 1903. His confession, and guilt are still the subject of controversy to this day. His own autobiography, *Life of Tom Horn, Government Scout and Interpreter, Written by Himself*, was written in his jail cell.

way there, “these are important men you’re going to meet.”

“Important to whom?” I asked.

“Important to the country,” he said crossly, “important to Wyoming. Important to me, d-mmit!”

“Oh calm down Mischa. Do you think I don’t know how to behave myself in public?”

“Well, you’ve gotten prickly in your old age, and you haven’t been around important men like these. You’ve been gallivanting around . . .”

“Be careful Mischa,” I growled.

He wilted a bit. “I’m just saying, try to behave with a little decorum. How you’re received here might not matter to you, but it will reflect on me.”

“Don’t worry, I’ll be decorous as h--l. I’ll even try to keep the war whoops to a minimum.”

“D-mmit Tolya, I’m serious.”

“I’m not. From what I’ve seen of ‘important’ white men, they tend to be arrogant b-----ds when dealing with those they think are below them, and pathetic, groveling toadies to those above them. So I’ll go in there, and I’ll be polite, and try not to do or say anything to embarrass you, but what I won’t do is put on some obsequious act. I don’t give that,” I snapped my fingers, "for any man whose warrant for respect comes from a bag of money, I don't care how big it is."

"That's all I'm asking," he said.

We were silent for the rest of the walk. I even felt a little bit guilty. After all, Mischa was just trying to help me, according to his perception of how the world works. I just wasn't sure I wanted to live in that world. I sensed he felt the same about the barrier between us, and was just as lost about how to bridge it as I.

That Cheyenne Club was something to see though. Even past its prime, it was still impressive. The chairs and couches were lavishly upholstered and sitting on them was like sinking into a cloud. All the furniture and fixtures were ornate and tasteful, and beautiful carpets covered the floors. The dark-paneled walls were covered with expensive paintings, and numerous sculptures stood about the place. Everything that would take a shine gleamed like the sun, and an army of staff ensured that everything was spotless. I know my poor description doesn't half do it justice, but it was the kind of place where any civilized man would feel right at home. I hated every inch of it.

On the other hand, the food was good, and the wine excellent. Horn and Siringo both joined us for lunch. "Charlie," I said, "I didn't expect to see you today."

"Well," he said, "I haven't changed my mind but I heard this place's got the best cook west of the Mississippi, and I figured it would be a shame not to put it to the test."

And put it to the test he did. For a skinny fellow, he could really put it away (after he made sure Mischa was picking up the tab). He was so busy eating that it blunted his natural loquacity and gave Mischa a chance to make his pitch:

"Gentlemen, things have never been so dire in the cattle industry. Many major ranchers were ruined by the blizzards of '86 and '87. Those who managed to hang on are having their recovery restricted by rustling. The '84 Maverick law gave the WSGA clear ownership of all mavericks and unbranded calves, but the law is unable to enforce it, and our cattle are stolen with impunity. We need good, seasoned men to protect our interests." He paused for a drink. "The interests of the WSGA mirror the interests of the country. These are the sort of men who build libraries and hospitals and universities for the benefit of all, who stand behind the rule of law, who bring prosperity to the nation! These rustlers are nothing more than parasites, but the strongest bull can be laid low by enough parasitical attacks."

He went on in that vein for the rest of the meal — I tried to concentrate on the food.

After lunch, which was frequently interrupted by glad-handing acquaintances of Mischa, he led Horn and I — Charlie had downed one last piece of pie, excused himself, and left — up one of the two grand staircases to a meeting room full of the sort of self-important, wealthy men I had expected.

"I am confounded, gentlemen," declaimed a tall fellow with deepset eyes and a Van Dyke beard, "The Europeans have subdued most of Africa, Asia, and South America. We have ourselves conquered this great continent. How then is our progress to be stymied by lesser men of our own race? Inferior men clinging to our business like ticks on a calf, sucking away our life's blood? Do we not owe it to ourselves and . . ."

I was heading for the door when the pompous filibuster was shouted down. I decided to stay a bit longer. Maybe that fellow was an aberration.

"Oh for G-d's sake, Albert[88]," said a portly gent with thick black hair, small, piggish eyes, and a moustache that matched his military air. "Pipe down, won't you? This is the third time this month you've given this speech." That got quite a laugh. "We can argue philosophy all day long, but what we need is action. The law . . ."

"Now hold on a minute, Major," another man spoke up, this one a tall, balding fellow with a determined-looking set to his jaw. "It's not fair to blame the law. Frank Canton's done all a sheriff can do, and H. S. Elliott is the best county prosecutor money can buy." There was some laughter at that. "But it doesn't matter how many of these rustlers Frank arrests or Elliott prosecutes, if we can't get a jury to convict . . ."

"They won't convict because the d--ned juries are made up of scum no better than those on trial," someone interrupted, inspiring many hearty "hear hears!" Someone called out, "hang a few and the rest'll leave or fall into line!" That got an even bigger ovation.

---

[88] "Albert" may be Albert John Bothwell, a member of the WSGA and outspoken proponent of Herbert Spencer's theories concerning social Darwinism.

I left. Horn stayed, clearly liking what he heard. I did pause to fill my pockets with very expensive cigars from a humidor on my way to the front door — I considered it a bulls--t tax. I was sitting in a rocking chair on the broad, wrap-around veranda enjoying the breeze and the very fine smoke when Mischa came out with two gentlemen, the portly one and the bald one, from upstairs.

"There you are, Tolya," he said good-naturedly. He turned to the others, "Didn't I tell you he wasn't ever comfortable under a roof?" Turning back to me, he said, "Tolya, I'd like you to meet Major Frank E. Wolcott . . ."

The chubby one stuck out his hand, "Pleased to meet you."

As I shook his hand, Mischa continued, ". . . And William Irvine.'

The bald one stuck out his hand. "I'm Billy to my friends."

I shook his hand. "Are we friends?"

He smiled ingratiatingly. "Well I certainly hope we will be. Michael here tells us you're quite the outdoorsman, adventurer, and tracker."

I eyed Mischa, "I don't know if you gentlemen know this, but 'Michael' is prone to exaggeration."

"I don't doubt it a bit," said Wolcott, "but if you've survived half the things Michael's credited to you, then I believe you'd do."

"Do for what?" I was going to make them work for it.

"As you have heard," said Irvine, "we're increasing our detective bureau, and need men like you who can track, and are familiar with the harsher facts of life."

"Well I don't know what he's told you, but I will admit to some familiarity with the 'harsher facts of life' as you put it." I was trying to mind what I said. I didn't want to do anything that would reflect badly on Mischa — whether we agreed or not, he was still my brother. "But I don't know as how I'm especially looking to increase that familiarity right now. Besides, I'm thinking I might be a little long in the tooth to be tackling any desperadoes, no matter how 'inferior' they may be."

Mischa colored at my reply, and Wolcott and Irvine were visibly annoyed. They were clearly not men who were accustomed to hearing 'no'. "I see," said Irvine.

"Disappointing," said Wolcott — I refuse to think of him as "Major". I generally despise men who insist on being called by their former military rank — it smacks of misplaced pride mixed with an undoubtedly well-deserved insecurity.

"I'll tell you fellows what," I said, "I'm heading up Buffalo-way. While I'm there, I'll take a look around and see if maybe your proposal sounds any better to me. It may be that I'll change my mind. If I do, I'll let you know. At any rate, I want you to know I appreciate the offer, and the hospitality." I saluted them with my cigar and left the veranda. I waited a few yards away to give them some privacy while they appeared to quietly tear strips off Mischa — presumably for wasting their time with me.

After a few minutes Mischa joined me. We walked in silence until we were out of sight of the Club. """D-mmit Tolya," he said suddenly, "is that your idea of behaving yourself in civilized company? Those were important men you just turned your nose up at!"

I'd had enough. "Listen little brother," I said, stopping to face him, "they aren't 'important', just rich and greedy. Under all their expensive clothes and affected sophistication they're no more civilized than dogs fighting over a dead steer. If they ever do get rid of all those 'rustlers', they'll tear each other apart trying to get the whole rotting carcass for themselves. Nothing is ever enough for creatures like them — they are more like *Mangathais* than men."

Mischa looked at me in disbelief. "Have you lost your mind? *Mangathais*? I suppose next you'll be telling me you're *Gesir Bogdo*[89] reborn."

"I'll say nothing of the sort," I said hotly, "but you're delusional if you can't see those men for the ravening wolves they are."

"They are neither wolves nor monsters," Mischa retorted. "They are simply men trying to build something greater than themselves . . ."

"To men like that, there is nothing greater than themselves! The only thing they're interested in is their own wealth and power. Be careful you don't get eaten up too." I turned on my heel and stalked away. Mischa went home by a different route. When we met again at his home, things were still strained between us. I told him I had decided to cut my visit short and leave in the

---

[89] The hero *Gesir Bogdo* and the monstrous *Mangathais* are an important part of Buriat creation legend. Those interested can find the story in Jeremiah Curtin's *A Journey in Southern Siberia.*

morning. He said nothing, but only nodded as I headed to bed.

***

I rose early, grabbed my gear and headed downstairs. Mischa was sitting in the kitchen. "Coffee?" he asked.

"Sure."

He poured me a cup and sat back down. We sat in silence for a few moments, neither of us quite sure what to say. Finally, I bit the bullet and spoke up. "Mischa, I . . ."

He held up a hand to stop me. "No need for an apology."

I swallowed my exasperation as best I could and said calmly, "I wasn't going to apologize. I meant every word I said about those men . . ."

"But Tolya, don't you see . . ."

I held up my hand to stop him. "Let me finish. Please. I was talking about them, not you. I know you are a decent man. That I disagree with you does not lessen the love I feel for you. You are, and always will be, my brother above all else. I hope you know you can always count on me."

His eyes were as teary as mine as he nodded in agreement. "I feel the same," he said. "Who knows —

perhaps a time will come when we'll find common ground beyond blood on which to stand."

"I hope so. But if we don't, our shared blood is enough for me."

"And me," he said.

I finished my coffee and stood. "Well, I should be going. Give Julia and Michael my love — I know how much it'll mean to them."

He laughed. "I will. Tell Dave I said hello." We shook hands and he walked me to the stable. When I rode away, neither of us said anything, we both just nodded.

Chapter Thirty-Two

Justice vs. Mob; a new friend; a tense meeting; the Buffalo sheriff; I surprise old friends

I have spent a great time pondering the disparity between men as individuals, and men as a group — in truth, I still do — and my thoughts always lead me back to justice.

Take any man, no matter his race, and he is generally kind and contented with even a modicum of prosperity. Take that same man, group him together with similar men and convince them that they don't have enough and have a G-d-given right to take something from someone else, and they become beasts. The problem isn't the individuals, it is the ones who are doing the convincing. In my experience, it is those who are convincing the mob that they don't have enough and to take it from someone else, are the very people who have worked so hard to keep the mob from having enough in the first place, and using the mob to do the dirty work for them. The individuals comprising the mob end up little or no better off than they were, and do all the killing and bleeding and dying.

The only creatures who truly benefit are the carrion-eating *provocateurs.*

Only justice, evenly applied and administered by disinterested officials (if any can be found) can protect the individual from the vultures winging through the corridors of power.

Wyoming Territory
1888

Hurrying to see my friends, I covered the 300 miles to Buffalo in about a week, but it was still plenty of time to look the country over. I could see what everyone was so het up over — it is d--ned fine cattle country.

One night, I had just shot a deer and was looking for a good place to camp when I spied a light and saw a cabin near a bridge over a creek. I watered the horses and then approached, stopping a couple hundred feet away. When I halloed the cabin, a man opened the door wide and was briefly silhouetted by the lantern light before he stepped outside and sideways into the shadows.

I heard him lever a shell into the Winchester rifle he was holding. "Who's there?" he called out calmly.

"Name's Nate Luck. Saw the light and thought I might try sleeping indoors for a change — provided you have no objection. If you've not eaten yet, I've got some venison I'll gladly share."

"C'mon up," he said, stepping out of the shadows, rifle at the ready.

I kept my hands in the open as I rode slowly up. We took a minute to size each other up — he was small, about my size, a handsome young man with an open, honest face, dark-hair, deep, wide-set eyes, and a wide mouth hidden beneath a drooping mustache — and he offered his right hand.

"Nate Champion," he said.

I shook his hand and dismounted. "Nate Luck."

"Welcome," he said. Pointing to a ramshackle barn about a hundred yards away, he said, "You can put your horses in there. There's not much feed, but take what you need."

I thanked him and assured him no feed was needed. "You said something about venison?"

We got the deer hung under the eaves of the cabin and he proceeded to work on it while I got my animals bedded down.

By the time I got to the cabin, he had steaks frying and was heating up a pot of beans. "Make yourself comfortable," he said.

"What kind of name is Luck, anyway?"

I told him how the army shortened my name.

He studied my features closely. Finally he said, "Any relation to Michael Lukyanov from Cheyenne?"

"We're brothers."

"Thought you favoured him."

"Is that a problem?"

"I don't think so, but you tell me."

I assured him it wasn't, but I noticed he kept his Colt revolver close at hand. He noticed me noticing, but made no apology.

Champion had come to Wyoming a few years ago, working on other men's ranches but had recently registered a brand and struck out on his own. "Don't like those big outfits," he said. "I've got a start on a nice little herd of my own, and I plan to keep it."

"Seems reasonable."

"So what brings you up thisaway?"

"I've got friends around Buffalo," I said, "or at least I used to. I'm hoping they're still here."

"They got names?" he asked.

"A black fellow named David Lincoln, and a little Frenchman named David Dompierre."

He smiled. "Sure, I know those fellows. Dave runs some cattle, and Frenchy tends bar at the Occidental." He gave me directions to get to Dave's little spread, just a few miles north of Buffalo.

As we talked, I found myself liking him more and more. He was a serious-minded young man, but as friendly and open-handed as anyone I'd ever met. He reminded me a great deal of Yellow Wolf and Wahlitits. That night, I dreamed I was with The People again, before the war. I woke up to the smell of hot coffee and frying venison, feeling like I belonged. It had been a long time since I'd felt that way.

"They're a couple days old," Nate said, handing me a biscuit, "Haven't got 'round to fixing a new batch."

I split the biscuit open, slapped some venison into it, and took a bite. The grease from the meat softened up the biscuit nicely. "Tastes good to me," I said around a mouthful. After breakfast, I carved some more meat off the deer carcass, wrapped it in paper, and left the rest for him.

"Many thanks," he said. "Mind how you go now. This is gettin' to be a dangerous part of the world."

"Aren't they all?" I thanked him and rode away.

***

The next evening, I was camped in a small hollow, cooking the last of the venison over a buffalo chip fire when a voice called out, "Halloo the fire." I pulled my revolver and held it in my lap. I wasn't too worried, but I'd hate to die surprised. "Come on in," I called back. You could have knocked me over with a feather when my nemesis came walking out of the night, bold as brass.

I recognized him a second before he did me, but it was enough. My gun was cocked and aimed between his surprised eyes before he even thought to reach for his. We froze like that for a long moment before either of us could speak, much less move.

Bill Morrow was the first to recover. Slowly raising his hands to shoulder height, he said quietly, "I ain't lookin' for trouble." His voice was steady enough.

"Looking or not," I said, "you've by G-d found it."

"Any chance you'll just let me back out of this and go on my way?"

"None."

We stayed like that for a while longer, then his left hand lowered itself to unbuckle his gunbelt, hold it at arm's length, and drop it to the ground. Speaking softly as his hand worked, he said, "What say we just put this hardware away and talk a bit. You ain't no murderer, and I know you don't believe me, but I ain't either."

He would never know how close he came to being proved wrong. I wanted to pull that trigger like I hadn't wanted anything in years, but I couldn't do it. Killing him wouldn't undo all the evil he'd done. It wouldn't bring back all that I had lost. Reluctantly, I lowered the hammer and laid the gun in my lap.

"Mind if I sit?"

I nodded.

He gestured at the coffeepot. "Mind?"

"Go ahead."

"Cup's in my saddlebags."

I tossed him mine.

He filled the cup and took a swig. "Thanks," he said. Then we just sat in silence a while. I found myself wondering what kept bringing the two of us together

— was it circumstance, or dumb luck, or fate? If the latter, the Fates must have been laughing themselves sick.

"You know," he said, "you're making me a little nervous keepin' that gun so close to hand."

"Good," I said. "You don't want to get too confident and make me rush to judgment on what to do about you. What are you doing here anyway? Last I heard, you were still up north with Joseph's people."

"You mean your people, don't you? Shocked the h--l out of me to see you there at White Bird Canyon."

"Not so shocked you didn't start shooting. Killed a d--ned fine horse and started a war. I ought to shoot you just for that."

"Just hold on there Nate. I didn't start that war and you know it."

"I know I don't want to talk about that. What I want to talk about is why you're here now."

"I'm working for the Hoe Ranch. What about you? You ain't still huntin' me, are you?"

"You stopped being important enough to chase a long time ago," I scoffed.

"Just passing through?"

"Maybe. I might decide to stay. Don't know yet."

"Say you do stick around? I don't want to be lookin' over my shoulder all the time."

"Don't worry," I said. "If I come at you you'll see it coming. Not like Silas Soule."

"Oh G-d d--mit," he said, "I didn't shoot Soule. I was just in the wrong place at the wrong time."

"You ran."

"H--l yes I ran. You'd have shot me stone dead if I hadn't."

"You knew what Squier was going to do."

"I never did," he protested nervously.

"Bulls--t," I said. "Finish your coffee and ride out of here."

"You're one hard-barked b-----d Nate," he said. "Ain't you ever heard of letting bygones be bygones?"

"Heard of it. I even try to do it, but in your case I'm making an exception. Get on your horse and ride while I'm still feeling generous and peaceful." I holstered my Colt and picked up my Winchester. I looked up at the full moon and cloudless sky. "Night like this, I'll bet I could drop you at a half-mile, so clear out and don't tempt me." I kept him covered while he picked up his gun, mounted, and rode away. As soon as he was out of sight, I packed up, moved camp about five miles in the opposite direction, set up a cold camp, and slept lightly.

In the morning, I rode back to my original camp and had a scout. I was curious if he'd doubled back in the night. I couldn't find any indications that he had, but I noticed that his horse left distinctive tracks — it drug its left front hoof. I thought a moment about tracking him and decided against it. I'd let the law do its job. I rode into Buffalo and went in search of the sheriff, Frank Canton. He was in the WSGA's pocket, but I hoped that he was at least honest enough to track down a murderer. I found him in his office, a hard, lean-looking fellow with cold brown eyes, a sharp nose, broad mouth, and mustache to match. I didn't much like the look of him. He was drinking coffee and playing checkers with Bill Morrow.

"What can I do for you?" he asked distractedly, while Morrow's face went dead white.

"Thought you'd want to know there's a murderer hereabouts."

That got his attention. "A murderer you say?"

"I do," I said. "His name is William Morrow, and you're playing checkers with him."

"Now hold on a minute . . ." Morrow started.

Canton held up a hand for silence as he looked at Morrow who, if possible, turned even paler. Canton moved a piece and then asked, “And who’s he supposed to’ve killed?”

“A U.S. Army Captain named Silas Soule, in Denver, Colorado.”

“D-mmit Frank,” Bill burst out, “this is that crazy man I met last night! I told you about him — accusing me of all manner of crimes — I was lucky to get away from him with a whole hide!”

Canton nodded and smiled. “Oh calm down George,” he said to Morrow. “What kind of sheriff would I be if I didn’t listen to allegations as serious as this?” Turning back, he told me to continue.

I told him about Morrow and the killing, of our pursuit and capture of him, and of his escape. I didn’t mention his part in the Nez Perce War, not wanting to muddy the waters.

Bill brought it up himself. “S--t Frank, he doesn’t even know who he thinks I am. He accused me of starting the whole Nez Perce mess as well. Couldn’t make up his mind whether I was this Bill Morrow fellow or that Ad Chapman that was interpreter for the Army.”

"Is that true?" Canton stood up and faced me.

"I wasn't mixed up."

"Well then, which one is he? A murderer or an interpreter?"

"He's both!"

"D-mmit Frank," Bill broke in, "can't you see this fellow's spent too much time in the sun without a hat? It's cooked his brains — if he ever had any to begin with."

That was too much. "Bill, you son-of-a- . . ." I said as I reached for my Colt. I stopped speaking and reaching when Canton's pistol appeared in his hand and between my eyes like he'd conjured it out of the air. I hadn't even cleared leather.

"Anybody does any shooting in my town," Canton said quietly, "it's going to be me." He pressed his gun to my chest, and his eyes never left mine as he reached down and undid my gunbelt, letting it drop to the floor. He stepped back and pointed to a cell. "Walk," he said. Once he'd locked me in, he holstered his gun. "What's your name, mister?"

"Nate Luck."

"Well Nate, you're lucky enough today. If you'd touched that shooting iron, you'd be dead." He paused to lock up my gun. "Now then," he said, turning back to me, "you say this fellow is a murderer named Morrow, but I know him as George Wellman. I'll tell you what I'll do though — I'll see if I can find any paper on him. I'll even cable Denver about it. If there's anything to what you say, I'll arrest him and send him down there, but you need to leave this to me."

"But . . ." I began to protest.

"But nothing," Canton said. "If I can't find anything to support your claims, then that's the end of it. Anything happens to him, I'll hang you. This is the only warning you're going to get."

There was nothing left for me to say. All I could do was hope Morrow was remembered in Denver, and that Canton would do his duty. If that all worked out, I needed to take up gambling for a living.

Canton kept me overnight to cool down. He released me the next morning with a warning to remember what he'd said, and I left town, wanting to put some distance between Bill Morrow and me.

I'd had low expectations when I'd walked in and Canton had not disappointed.

***

I found Dave's cabin in a broad, shallow valley, exactly where Champion had said it was. I stopped about a hundred yards from the cabin and halloed. A moment later the door opened and a white man with a rifle hobbled out on crutches, sat down on a straight-backed chair, and jacked a round into his rifle's chamber. "Come ahead on," he called, "but mind yourself."

It wasn't until I was within about five yards that I recognized his face under the beard and scars. "Jack?" I asked. "Jack McCallister?"

He set aside his rifle and took up his crutches. As he stood I saw his left leg was missing from the knee down. "Howdy Nate," he said, smiling around the cigarette dangling from his lips. "It's good ta see you. We been wonderin' when you was going to show up."

"How'd you know I was coming?" I asked.

"Your daughter wrote Dave. Said we should let her know if you didn't show up in the next coupla years."

I laughed. "She may know me too well." I dismounted and climbed the steps to embrace him.

He returned it warmly, pounding my back while grumbling, "You d--ned Europers and your hugging. That d--ned French feller's hugged me more since I come here than my ma ever did in my life." We both laughed and took a step back.

"G-dd--n Nate, you look like you been through the wringer."

"A couple of times," I said. "Looks like you've been no stranger to trouble, yourself."

He nodded. "You could say that," he said. "C'mon in and siddown."

I followed him inside.

"Gimme a minute," he said, sitting down to strap on a peg leg. "I'm thinkin' 'bout takin' up piracy," he said with a grin.

"So where's Dave?" I asked while he put the coffee on.

"He's out huntin' a coupla wandering steers. I 'spect he'll be along 'fore dark."

"How's he doing?"

"Aw, Dave's Dave. He don't change much. A little grayer, a little stiff in the morning, but that's about all." He smiled ruefully. "I reckon he's maybe made better choices in his life than you 'n me."

I laughed. "Of that, I have no doubt. Dave always did have more sense than either of us."

While waiting for the coffee we took a closer survey of each other. Jack's thinning hair was long, lank, and greasy, and he was thin as a politician's excuse. The old scar across his forehead now had company — a jagged scar snaked from his forehead, between his eyes, and down to his jaw and another from his nose to his left ear. A scar from an old bullet wound showed on his bare left forearm, and the haunted look behind his green eyes spoke of deeper, hidden scars. I probably looked equally beat up to him, just with more hair.

I didn't ask him what had happened. If, and when, he wanted me to know, he'd tell me. He did me that same courtesy. Instead, we spoke of the distant past and the present day, laughing about our old adventures and misadventures before the war changed our worlds, and discussing our current situations.

"I do the cooking for Dave and me, and keep an eye on things 'round here. I ain't much use on a horse any more, but I can still be useful," he said somewhat bitterly. He sat silently for a moment. "I can still shoot too. You was smart to sit off a ways and holler before you rode in."

"Had trouble?"

"Not yet," he said, "but I can smell it coming. Just a couple days ago a couple fellers stopped on top of the ridge and just sat there. Didn't come down to say howdy, didn't wave, just sat there and watched. Then they just rode off. Been a lot of that sort of thing going on at homesteads all over. Got a lot of folks worried."

I told him about meeting Nate Champion, and that Champion had been on his guard as well.

"Champion's no fool. He's a top hand and one tough individual. Ain't scared of nothin'. Good man though. Do 'bout anything to help a feller out, but you don't want to get on his bad side."

"I got that impression as well," I said. "I liked him a lot."

"He's a well-respected man in these parts, but them WSGA'ers don't like him one bit, nor anybody runnin' their own herd."

I asked him how he'd come to be here.

"Oh, it was 'bout three - four years ago," he said. "After the war, I just kinda drifted hither and yon. I ended up breakin' horses over in Nebraska . . ."

"Weren't you a little long in the tooth for that kind of work?"

"I didn't think so at the time, but one day a bronc rolled over on me and I couldn't get clear quick enough. Busted me up somethin' fierce." He gestured at his missing leg. "When I lost this. After that, I weren't good for much an' ended up livin' rough, swampin' out bars, an' eatin' s--t from anybody that might be good for a drink sometime. One day, Dave just rode in, poured me into the back of a wagon an' brought me here. Never did say how he heard about it. I been here ever since."

The coffee was ready and he poured us each a cup. "So what've you been up to?"

I gave him a brief account of my life with The People and Coming Together.

When I finished, he said, "G-d d--n Nate, I'm sorry to hear about that. We heard about that mess, but I never dreamed you'd got caught in it."

"Bad times," I said. "Still, I've got a son and a daughter left in this world. That's more than a lot can say." We sat again in silence, each of us lost in what the years had taken.

The shadows were growing long when we heard hoofbeats. "That'll be Dave, I imagine," said Jack. He stood and picked up his rifle. "Just in case," he said.

Sure enough, it was Dave. His smile beamed when he saw me. "Nate!" he called, "I'll be dog-gonned. I didn't think I'd ever see you again!"

"There's been no shortage of people trying to make sure you didn't."

"Well I'm glad they failed," he said.

I walked to the barn with him to bed our animals down while Jack went to work on supper. "You're looking good Dave," I said.

"Thank you kindly," he said. "You're lookin' better than I expected from your daughter's letter."

"She worries too much." I gestured around us. "Nice little spread you've got here."

"Well, it's only part mine. The cattle're half mine, but the spread is in the name of a widow woman from town named Missus Good," he said. "I b'lieve you'd like her." His eyes sparkled a bit.

I don't know what it is about me that made people want to play matchmaker. We finished with the horses, and returned to the cabin where Jack was frying some beefsteaks.

They were raw in the middle and burnt on the outside, the beans were undercooked and hard, and the biscuits could have been used for cobblestones, but the coffee was strong and the whisky smooth, and we had a grand time.

After dinner, we enjoyed some of the fine cigars I'd filched from the Cheyenne Club.

Jack puffed his and declared, "'S'much's I hate to give those fellers credit for anything, they have d--ned fine taste in smoking materials." Dave nodded agreement.

"Unfortunately," I said, "they aren't as discriminating about their employees. You fellows should know that Bill Morrow's on the loose hereabouts." I told them what I'd seen and heard in Cheyenne, and how I'd met Bill the previous night.

Jack considered for a moment. "I ain't surprised at all he's workin' for one o' them big outfits. He always was prone to runnin' with the disreputable, 'specially if there might be money in it."

"You especially ought to watch out," I told Dave. "I doubt he's forgotten about you helping bring him in the first time."

Dave nodded. "He wasn't never one to forget a slight nor an injury. I reckon he'd figure that for both."

"You boys shoulda just shot him dead on the spot," Jack said. "Would've saved a mess o' trouble."

"Well," I said, "maybe the sheriff'll do his job."

"Canton?" Jack scoffed. "That sorry son-of-a-b---h ain't likely to arrest nobody with the WSGA behind 'em, is he Dave?"

"Not likely," Dave admitted. "I'm hopin' Mister Red'll beat him in the election and that sort of thing'll change 'round here."

"I know I'd feel a lot safer with a whoremaster as sheriff than a whore," Jack said.

"Now hold on there, Jack," Dave said. "Mister Red's a businessman." He looked at me, "He runs a bar."

"An' his wife runs a whorehouse," Jack interjected. "H--l, she used to be one herself."

"Jack," Dave said, "Mister and Missus Red've never been anything but decent to us."

"I wasn't saying nothin' bad about 'em," Jack said defensively. "Red pours an honest drink, an' they say Miz Deborah's got the nicest bordello and sweetest, cleanest girls this side of Denver. If I could play piano, I'd quit this place an' go to work for one o' them. The company might be more congenial."

Dave laughed. "I imagine they smell better anyways."

***

I spent the next few days helping Dave with his herd. It was a nice little herd of seventy or eighty head, and he had to keep a close eye on them, for there were often strange tracks in and around his herd. "Somebody's been surveyin' my herd awful close," he said. We were vigilant, but never laid eyes on anyone near the herd, just tracks and signs.

At night, we'd drive the herd into a fenced pasture behind the cabin, and have a high old time swapping stories, some of which were even true. The only drawback was Jack's cooking.

Finally, after a typical dinner, I said, "Jack, I wish you would learn to play the piano."

"Why's that"

"So you could go work in a whorehouse and Dave could hire somebody who knows their way around a stove."

"Well, I'll tell you something," Jack said. "I'm secretly a h-lluva cook. I'm just cookin' like this in hopes that Dave'll get tired of it an' marry that girl he's been sparkin' in town. That girl can cook."

"I'm workin' on it," Dave laughed, "but Miz Claudette's a beautiful woman, and I'm an old dog. That sort of fish, I got to work the line careful, or she'll throw the hook and I'll be stuck eating your cooking forever."

"Uh huh. Way you work that line, she's likely to die of boredom. Whyn't you come into town with me tomorrow? Can't hurt to look in on her an' say howdy."

Dave shook his head. "I need to keep an eye on the herd," he said. "Nate, you ought to ride along though, see the town. I reckon you'd find it awful interesting."

"I'd rather be out here with you and the cattle."

He shrugged. "Suit yourself," he said. "But Frenchy gonna get his feelings hurt you don't go see him soon."

"That's true enough," Jack said. "Plus, I've got a lot of stuff to pick up. I could use some help."

He kept at me until I agreed to go with him, and noticed the sly looks they sent each other. "What are you two up to?" I asked.

They looked at me like butter wouldn't melt in their mouths. "Why Nate," said Jack, "we ain't up to nothing, are we Dave?"

"Nope," Dave said. "Just thought after all the complainin' you've done about Jack's cooking, you'd appreciate a chance to get some good vittles in you. And Jack could use a hand with the freight."

Well, I didn't believe either of them, but the twin ideas of seeing Frenchy and getting properly cooked food carried the day, and I agreed to go.

Chapter Thirty-Three

Jack's pride; an old joke; Buffalo; Frenchy; champagne and rotgut; an epiphany; Odile's; another old friend; reconciliation; a surprising revelation; an unsurprising development

I've never been big on surprises, although I've certainly had my fair share since coming to Wyoming. Many have even been very pleasant. I'm hoping my trial will start soon – even though I don't like surprises, I've got a nasty one waiting for those b-----ds at the WSGA. I've even been urging Nathan to try to get as much press for the trial as possible. I want everyone to know what they've done.

Wyoming Territory
1888

In the morning I watched Jack harness a pair of good-looking mules to the wagon. It was something to see, how he got around on that peg, and something he was rightly proud of — maybe a little too proud. "I don' need no G-dd--n help," he growled. "You tend to your business and I'll tend to mine."

We didn't say another word until we'd traveled a mile or two and I said, "I didn't mean to offend you back there."

He spat tobacco to the far side of the wagon. "Aw h--l Nate," he said sheepishly, "I know that. I knew it then, but pride's a hard thing to swallow. I don't like people thinkin' I can't do things."

"Getting sensitive in your old age?"

He laughed. "Maybe so." A few moments later he said, "It shore is somethin' ain't it?"

"What's that?"

"Life. Ever wonder why the older we get, the more life feels just like one kick in the b--ls after the next?"

"I know I don't get surprised when things go sideways anymore. I guess I've grown to expect it."

He nodded. "Yeah," he said, "but expectin' don't make the blows fall any lighter."

"You're right enough there," I said. "Sometimes just the memory of old blows is enough to knock me down." We continued in that vein until we were both thoroughly depressed, but on a day as glorious as that one — especially for a Wyoming October — neither of us had the willpower to remain in low spirits.

Before long we were back to trying to out-lie one another. Jack was spinning a yarn about being trapped in a box canyon by the Cheyenne. "I'll tell you what Nate," he said, "I've been in some tight spots, but never one as tight as that. There I was, horse dead, nowhere to run, out of water, out of ammunition, an' I could hear them devils creepin' up on me. Finally, I decided I warn't gonna wait. I had my Bowie in one hand and a good-sized rock in the other hand, an' I just reared up and went amongst 'em swinging and slashing like Billy-be-d--ned . . ." His voice trailed off.

I waited.

He waited.

I wasn't giving in that easily.

Neither was he.

Finally I gave up. "All right, so what happened then?"

"Why, they killed me dead as Jesse James." He threw back his head and laughed like that old joke hadn't been circulating around the frontier since before either of us were born. I laughed too. I couldn't help it.

A little later, we came in sight of Buffalo. I'd been in a hurry my first time through there and hadn't paid attention, but it was a pleasant enough little town. On the north edge, a large, good-looking house sat on the west side of Main Street. Jack kept a close eye on it as we passed.

"Something wrong with that place?" I asked.

"Hmm? Naw. Pretty little widder-woman lives there, name of Ruth Good."

"Thinking of settling down?" I asked.

"Me? You know me Nate — I ain't never had much use for women. I guess I just ain't romantic."

"I thought maybe you'd changed."

He looked at me closely, trying to judge if I was mocking him, and then relaxed. "Nope," he said wistfully, "I'm a dyed-in-the-wool bachelor. Tried to change my ways a coupla times an' it just didn't take. I done give up tryin'."

"'To thine own self be true," I quoted, "and it must follow, as the night the day, thou canst not be false to any man.' By that standard, I reckon you're about the most honest man I've ever known."

He nodded. "'Preciate that, Nate," he said. "Anyway, that widder's a mite salty, but a feller'd do well to get his feet under her table. You might want to give it some thought."

I laughed. “No wealthy widow worth her salt would give a tramp like me the time of day, much less an invitation to dinner.”

We passed residences and offices and stores of every kind, a log church, and about anything else a town could want. A lot of people were on the street, and one fashionably-dressed young man caught my attention. “That young fellow looks familiar,” I said.

“That good-looking kid in the frock coat and bowler? That’s the Widder Good’s son, Nathan. Far’s I know he grew up here, ‘til she sent him back east fer schoolin’. He come back here when he finished an’ hung up his shingle. You spend any time back east in yer travels?”

“No.”

“Maybe he just favors somebody you know’d.”

I let it go as best I could, but I couldn’t get it out of my head. “How many Nates and Nathans have you got around here anyway?” I asked.

“I b’lieve there’s three now. You, Nate Champion, and young Nathan Good there. Any more Nates come in, we may have to start assignin’ nicknames again.”

We both laughed at that.

Jack pulled up outside the H.H. Helphamatine General Store and Meat Market and pointed across the street at a large log structure with a sign reading "Occidental Hotel." "Go on in there an' have a drink," he said. "I'll meet you there 'n we'll get us a bite to eat."

"Sounds good," I said, "and I'm buying."

"D--n right, after all the whining you done 'bout my cookin'. By the way," he called after me, "Don't ask about his wife. He's kindly sensitive about it."

"Did something happen to Eden?"

"Eden?" He laughed. "She left him years ago. Naw, he's gutted about Alice. She's the second wife he's gone through since Eden. I figure some fellers just ain't meant for marriage, but he don't seem to ever learn. He'll be sparking another'n soon enough. Just can't get enough of champagne or showgirls." He clucked at the mules and drove down a narrow alleyway between the store and Rounds' Livery Stable.

Inside the Occidental was a large saloon, empty but for a drummer passed out with his feet up on his trunk and a couple men at the billiard tables. Frenchy stood behind the bar polishing glasses. What hair he had left was gone gray, he wore thick-lensed, wire-rimmed spectacles, and his belly protruded over his belt, but his mustache still bristled with the same old panache. He didn't even look up when I bellied up to the bar.

"What can I get for you?" he asked uninterestedly.

"Champagne," I said. "That is, if you'll join me *mon frere*."

He looked up with confusion at first, then recognition. "Nate!" he cried. "My friend!" He rushed around the bar and we embraced like long-lost brothers.

"It's good to see you," I said, "You're looking fat and happy."

He laughed delightedly, "And you *mon ami*, look like you've been dropped and broken a few times."

I laughed too. "You're not too far off there."

He went back behind the bar to pour the champagne.

"Better pour a third glass," I said, "Jack McCallister's with me."

"Hmph. Jack has no taste for the finer things of life. He turns up his nose at this — what does he call it? Ah yes, this 'fizzy woman's drink.' I keep a bottle of the vilest whisky I can find just for him. *Le sauvage* neither wants nor deserves any better. But enough of that — tell me everything!"

I told him enough to satisfy him. While I talked, Jack hobbled in and we sat down to drink. Jack's rotgut must have been bad, judging by his face, but he just licked his lips and poured another.

After a couple of drinks and the end of my story, Jack said, "Say Nate, what about that meal you promised to buy me?"

I looked at Frenchy. "Join us? I presume they serve food here."

"But of course! We have one of the very best . . ."

"No, no, no," interrupted Jack. "I want some real cookin'." Over Frenchy's sputtered protests he said, "The food here's alright, but the best in Buffalo's up at Ma Odile's." He looked pointedly at Frenchy, "I reckon we owe it to Nate to feed him the best eatin' available."

I looked at Frenchy. "Is he right?"

He looked pained, but said, "*Oui*, *Madame* Odile is the superior chef. Unfortunately, I cannot leave. I must stand my post."

Jack looked around us. "Stand your post? For what? Ain't nobody in here."

Frenchy looked grave. "Even so, I know my duty. *Mes amis*, I beg you, stay here and dine with me."

"What're we going to do if you're called away on some bartendin' emergency?" Jack asked. "Stare at each other while we eat inferior vittles?" He stood. "Come on Nate. We'll go get some real food an' then come back and visit with Monsewer Responsibility."

"*Mon frere*," I said, "after my own cooking and a few days of Jack's swill, the best food in town sounds mighty good. Sure you can't sneak away?"

He sighed. "Very well, you win. *Un moment s'il vous plaît.*" He walked to a door beside the bar and roared, "Shambo! Watch the bar, you laggard!" He grabbed three bottles of champagne from behind the bar, explaining, "*Madame* Odile doesn't serve liquor." Once again he bellowed, "Shambo!"

"I heard ya, ya d--ned snail-snapper!" A tall, extremely pale, sleepy-looking, but nattily dressed young fellow shambled out of the back room and behind the bar as we left.

"I swear," said Jack, "that fellow don't half give me the creeps."

"Oh, Shambo's a good boy," said Frenchy, "just a trifle unmotivated."

"I don't care how good he is," said Jack, "he looks like he orter be layin' in a coffin rather'n up walkin' around."

As we walked slowly up the street — Jack was nimble, but not speedy — they tormented each other, and I fell into a sort of reverie. Recently, I had been feeling different, lighter somehow. I felt alive. I felt free. I felt happy. I realized that I'd been sleepwalking for years, but now I was beginning to feel again like life might be worth the trouble.

Odile's looked unlikely to house the pinnacle of epicurean delights. A sloppily-lettered sign hung above a door that was half off its hinges, the roof resembled a Swiss cheese, and the whole place leaned to the east — log braces kept it from collapsing — but the scent of cooking wafting through gaps in the wall was intoxicating. There were several crowded trestle tables and benches outside, patrons apparently preferring to dine al fresco rather than risk being trapped inside the building during its inevitable collapse. Judging by the gusto with which everyone was eating, the food was worth it.

Frenchy and I set up a table, while Jack hollered through the door, "Ma! Got some hungry men out here!" Frenchy produced two champagne flutes and poured. Soon, a pretty, smiling black woman in her thirties, with arms like a longshoreman appeared with plates piled high with steaks, potatoes drowned in gravy, and beans.

Jack patted her backside and said, "Miz Claudie, when you gonna marry me?"

She swatted his hand away as casually as if it were a moderately annoying fly. "You be careful Mister Jack. You keep takin' liberties, you'll have an arm to match that leg of yours." She winked at me.

"It'd be worth it, long's you married me," Jack said. "Least it would be if you can cook like your ma."

"You be glad she's cooking today. If I was cooking and knew you was out here, I'd be making your gravy with lye powder instead of flour." She winked at me.

"Why would a lovely young woman like *Mademoiselle* Claudette burden herself with a broken-down old relic like you?" Frenchy chimed in.

"You need to stop fooling around and eat before that food gets cold or mama'll be barring you for not appreciating her food proper," Claudette said.

Jack held up his hands. "All right, you win. I ain't giving up though. I'll win you over sooner or later."

"Old as you are, you don't have much 'later' left to you," she said. Smiling at me and Frenchy she said, "You gentlemen enjoy your meal."

"Merci, ma chère amie."

She gave Frenchy a smile that would break a dentist's heart. "Oooo, you know I love it when you talk that French, Mister David." She kissed the beaming Frenchy's cheek, nonchalantly swatted the back of Jack's head, and walked away with a little extra swish in her step.

"Is that the girl Dave's fishing for?" I asked.

"I'm hopin' a little jealousy might motivate him," Jack said. "He needs a good woman to look after him."

We dug in, and the food lived up to its promise. I've never tasted anything so good in my life. We finished our meals and Claudette was back again, this time with enormous, steaming slices of apple pie.

I struggled to get it down. I ate the last bite with a groan of ecstatic suffering and washed it down with champagne. Frenchy had just poured me a fresh glass when a voice spoke behind me. "Good afternoon gentlemen. Life treating you all right?"

I would have known that sarcastic, playful voice, no matter how many years had passed. I stood up and turned around, and it was Esme standing there with that dapper young lawyer. She looked as surprised as me, although she dealt with it better. She smiled. I threw up on my boots.

Esme and her son both leapt back. Jack almost fell off his bench laughing.

Frenchy patted my back. "*Mon Dieu*," he said, struggling to maintain his composure. "Perhaps we should have prepared you for this." Disgusted patrons were already moving away, taking their tables with them.

Mortified, I rinsed my mouth with champagne and wiped it with my sleeve. "I beg your pardon." I said. "It's good to see you."

"Is it?" asked Esme. "You used to respond better to seeing me. What are you doing here?" She looked bemused. Her son looked angry and offended.

"I came to see Dave and these fellows," I said. "What are you doing here?"

"I live here," she said, shooting Jack and Frenchy the evil eye. "Funny how nobody mentioned this to either of us."

"In my defense," Frenchy piped up, "I thought this was a bad idea."

"With a defense like that, you should just be quiet," she said. To me, she said, "Let's walk."

I followed her onto the prairie. I didn't know what to say, and I don't think she did either.

"You look good," I ventured. She'd changed — put on a little weight, her glorious golden hair had gone largely gray, and she wore it in a matronly bun. A pair of tinted glasses disguised the glass eye she wore. She looked healthy, relaxed, and happy. She looked beautiful.

"You look like hammered buffalo s--t," she said. "What happened to you?" However much her appearance may have softened, that edge was still there. It was strangely reassuring.

"That would take years to explain."

"You going to be here that long?"

"I honestly don't know."

"Sounds about right." She rolled a cigarette as we walked and lit it, saying nothing more.

She won the awkward silence when I finally spoke. "I guess I owe you an explanation . . ."

"Don't bother," she said. "What's done is done."

"You say that, but you sound angry."

"Do I?" she asked innocently.

She always could get my goat. “Listen,” I said. “I didn’t even know you were here . . .”

“Are you saying you wouldn’t have come if you’d known I was here?”

“That’s not what I’m saying, and you d--n well know it.”

Her eyes softened a bit. “Have you thought about me then?”

I was moving slowly from flustered, through angry, to exasperated. “Of course I’ve thought about you.”

“Then why didn’t you ever come find me?”

“I – well, I guess I thought it better to let sleeping dogs lie. I didn’t want to cause either of us any more pain. I don’t know what else to say. I’m glad you’ve done well for yourself. You look prosperous and Nathan sounds like a promising young man.”

“He is.”

“Why’d you name him Nathan anyway?” I asked. As soon as the words left my mouth I realized who he reminded me of.

She looked at me scornfully. “J---s C----t, are you really that dumb? I named him after his father.”

“Oh my G-d.” I felt like I’d been poleaxed.

"You're not going to puke again are you?" she asked, sounding very pleased with herself as she took a couple steps back. "Maybe you ought to sit down. My G-d she was aggravating.

"D-mmit woman," I said, "will you just let me catch my breath?" She was right though, and I sat on the ground, my head in my hands. "Does he know he's mine? Does he even know about me?"

"Of course he knows about you. You aren't some secret I'm ashamed of. As far as knowing he's yours, I imagine he does now, back there with those two busy-bodying old gossips. Even without that, he's seen you and he's looked in a mirror. He's smart enough to put those two things together." Her voice softened. "He loves books as much as you, although he's smarter."

All that confidence and life I'd felt earlier drained out of me like dish water. "Oh Lord," I groaned, "now I've got two sons who hate me."

"Oh calm down," she said, "he doesn't know you well enough to hate you."

That made me laugh in spite of myself, "Maybe I should get out of here before he gets to know me."

"You know what some people would say . . ."

"What?"

“You’re an idiot.” We both laughed and I stood up and we began to walk again.

“So what did you mean by ‘two sons’?”

“I had a family. I lost my wife, a daughter, and a son in the Nez Perce war. All I have left are a step-daughter and a son who hates me because of his white blood.”

“I’m so sorry, Nate,” she said softly. After that, we walked in silence a while.

“So you don’t hate me?” I asked eventually.

“Well not anymore,” she said. “To tell the truth, I don’t think I ever really did. It was just easier to think I did. I realized I was pregnant about two weeks after you left.”

“I’m sorry. If I’d known . . .”

She waved me off. “It’s okay. Neither of us was in any shape to deal with each other’s s--t and a baby. G-d only knows how badly we’d have messed him up if we’d stayed together. As it was, having him saved me.”

“Thank you.” A little later, “So how’d you end up here?”

“I decided to get out of the pleasure business before Nathan was old enough to start asking questions. I sold the Silver Platter, moved to Omaha, and made a fresh start as the Widow Good. Around ‘78 or so, I met

McCray and Buell when they were trying to finance the Occidental. I liked them and they liked me, so I moved here and became a silent partner. Been here ever since."

"You always had a good head for business."

She shook her head. "I'm done with all that."

"That's hard to believe."

"I like the quiet life now. Frenchy looks after my interest in the Occidental, and Dave takes care of the cattle business."

"Whatever happened to Samson?"

"Oh he's here too. He's married to Odile. He was as tired of busting heads as I was of — well, you know. Odile was cooking at the Germania House. She liked a strong, silent man and they don't get any stronger or silenter than Samson. Anyway, I fronted them the money for Odile's . . . ."

"I think maybe you should have fronted them a little more."

She laughed. "So did I, but that was all they'd take, just enough to get 'em set up. They paid me back years ago and been working on building a better place ever since."

"I hope the next one's better at keeping the weather out."

"I do to, but I'm not sure it will. Samson works d--ned hard, but he sure ain't no carpenter."

As we talked, we walked in a big loop that eventually led us back to Odile's, where Nathan, Frenchy, and Jack were waiting.

Nathan stepped forward to meet us, anger coming off him in waves.

"Nathan," said Esme/Ruth, "meet your father, Anatoly Lukyanov."

I stuck out my hand. "I'm pleased to meet you Nathan. Call me Nate."

He ignored my hand. "I wouldn't call you if I was on fire and you had a bucket of water," he said, and stalked away.

I looked at Esme. "Guess I should have expected that."

"He's a little hard-headed," she said. "Probably gets that from you."

"Yes," I said, "I have no idea whom else he could have gotten that from."

She patted my arm. "He'll come around. I always did, didn't I? Maybe stick around, give him time?" A moment later she quietly added, “I think I’d like that too.”

And that’s what I decided to do.

Chapter Thirty-Four

Red Angus; A strange and bloody coincidence; I become a lawman; a posse; James Averell and Ella Watson; a ghastly discovery; ice and heat, fear and rage; urging caution; an argument; good cooking

They've set a date for my trial. Two more men have been murdered by stock detectives. I feel like I'm running out of time.

Buffalo, Wyoming Territory
1889

'88 faded into '89, and I found my footing in the world again. I was more settled than I had been since living with The People before the war. I enjoyed helping Dave, and was happy with my friends. Esme and I became closer even than we had been in those early days in California — emotionally anyway. This time around, we had no expectations of each other and were pleased just to enjoy each other as the people we had become. That good feeling I had just kept getting stronger.

Late in the spring, I found work that felt even more meaningful — or rather, it found me. William "Red" Angus won the sheriff's office from Frank Canton in the '88 election, something I was happy to see. Canton was bitter over the loss and left town, and I hoped we'd never see him again. Red was stocky and balding, with a fringe of fiery red hair, a good-natured fellow with a live-and-let-live attitude and a tolerance for human weakness — as long as it didn't disturb the peace — but he was conscientious in the performance of his duties. He seemed likely to serve the law and the people of Johnson County, diligently and even-handedly.

I had never really spoken with him at length until late May at an engagement party for Nathan and Eleanor Griggs, a young lady from New Haven, Connecticut. He and I were still not on friendly terms, and I was sitting out of the way on the edge of the crowd when Red approached me.

"Mind if I sit?" he gestured to an empty chair next to me.

"Help yourself."

He sat. "Nice party," he said.

"It is."

He cleared his throat. "I'm told you lived with the Nez Perce for a while."

"What of it?"

"Nothing. I'm only asking because I could use a deputy who's a tracker. The deputies I've got couldn't track a cat across a sand box, and I'm no better. If you lived amongst Indians you're likely better than any of us." He paused to drink from a flask and offered it to me. I looked in his eyes and saw no insult there, so I took it.

"I can track." I took a slug and handed it back.

"Ruth also mentioned you had some experience with the Cheyenne, that you was at Sand Creek and was still angry about what happened there."

"She talks too much sometimes."

"I was at the Washita when Custer and his boys attacked Black Kettle's camp."

"Trooper?"

"Muleskinner," he said. "But I heard what happened from the troopers, and saw how they treated their prisoners. I thought it was a d--ned shame then and now, but I just wanted you to know up front."

"Just being there doesn't make you guilty," I said. "Some of us soldiers at Sand Creek did what we could to stop it. Still not sure why you think you need me though."

He leaned in closer so as to not be overheard. "Things are going to be heating up around here, I'm afraid. The WSGA is offering big rewards and swearing out warrants for rustling on every man who crosses 'em. I'm afraid people are going to start getting killed, guilty or not. I figure a good tracker has a good chance of bringing in accused rustlers alive before reward hunters gun 'em down." He handed me his flask again and I took a deep drink and handed it back.

"I'll think about it."

"That's all I ask," he said, standing up to rejoin the festivities. "You know where to find me."

It didn't take too much thought, just enough to remember what I'd heard at the Cheyenne Club. I was sworn in as a deputy sheriff, and shortly thereafter was kept busy bringing in "rustlers" accused of stealing anywhere from one to five head of cattle — hardly the sort of large-scale rustling operations that Cheyenne was making so much noise about and totally unworthy of the enormous rewards the WSGA was offering. Every trial ended — rightly — in acquittal. But things were about to get much worse.

***

In July, I was a few days south of Buffalo, near the Sweetwater River. I'd apprehended another alleged rustler, Archie Harrell, and was taking him back when we encountered six or seven men riding hard, with a couple more men on a buckboard bringing up the rear. They drew up and demanded to know who we were. I showed them my badge, and they relented considerably.

"Have you come across any fresh wagon tracks?" asked the lead man, who I recognized as Carbon County sheriff George Ferris.

I told them I had and he asked me to show them. Little Jimmy Averell and Ella Watson had been kidnapped and lynched by a band of cattlemen and Sheriff Ferris and his posse were on their trail.

I was shocked. I knew Jimmy and Ella and liked them both very much, had spent almost a week very pleasantly snowed in with them during the winter. They both had small spreads, far out from any town, with good grass and water. Jimmy was good-natured and generous, a postmaster, notary, and merchant. Ella was a sweet but strong-willed woman known for generosity and kindness. Both were openly defiant in the face of pressure from the big ranchers. Jimmy had written letters to several newspapers protesting their actions. Ella ran a small herd she'd purchased from a fellow traveling to California. They were no more cattle rustlers than I was the Tsar of Russia. The only "crime" they'd committed was staking claims on land a bigger rancher wanted.

I told Archie, "You can ride with us, or I'll trust you to turn yourself in to Sheriff Angus in Buffalo."

"Nate, I b'lieve I'm safer sticking with you." We led the posse to where I'd seen the tracks.

The sheriff looked at one of the men. "Frank," he said, "this look familiar?"

"Yeah," said a burly young man in a torn checked shirt, "this is them." He pointed across the river. "They're up there amongst those rocks."

We crossed the river and rode up into the hills. We hadn't gone far when Sheriff Ferris stopped in his tracks. "Oh my Lord," he said, taking off his hat, "oh my sweet Lord."

Jimmy and Ella hung swinging in the breeze. They had been there for two days, the ropes cutting deep into their necks, eyes bulging out and black tongues protruding from their blood-engorged faces. Their hands and feet were loose, and their hands were scraped raw from trying to lift themselves on the rough ropes. Ella's feet were bare and black with blood. She had several broken toes. Looking at them, my chest grew tight, my vision darkened around the edges, and my blood pounded in my ears. I felt as if I were trapped under ice. In my breast a fiery rage seethed, but not hot enough to free me.

Then I saw the pair of brand-new beaded moccasins[90] lying on the ground beneath her, kicked off in her thrashing, desperate struggle for life, and the ice cracked.

Archie nudged me. "You okay Nate?"

"I'm fine," I barked.

We all stood hat in hand for a moment while Frank told us how it had happened. "I follered them up here and got up in them rocks. It was Al Bothwell, Jack Durbin, Ernie Maclean and three other fellers I didn't get a good look at. They drug Jimmy and Ella up on top of that there big rock. They was both fighting and pleading for mercy, but they didn't stand a chance. I

---

[90] Ella Watson had been returning from a nearby Shoshone camp where she'd purchased these moccasins when she was taken by the lynching party.

started shooting, but all I had was my revolver. I managed to hit Durbin." He spat on a patch of dried blood on the ground. "Didn't do any good. They pushed Jimmy and Ella offa that rock an' started firing at me with rifles. Ella was still struggling when I had to skedaddle or join her and Jimmy. It was the G-dawfullest thing I ever saw." He dried his eyes on his sleeve. "I just keep thinkin' if I'd grabbed a rifle instead of my Colt, they might still be alive."

Archie and I climbed up the rock, cut the ropes and lowered them gently into the waiting arms below. From the rock, I could see .45-70 cartridges littering the ground below, and the top of the rock. There was blood smeared on the face of the rock where Ella's bare feet had kicked and scraped against it as she swung. I walked up to where Frank said he'd taken cover and sure enough, there were at least a dozen .45 cartridges on the ground, and the rocks all around were scarred and pitted from bullet strikes. He'd been lucky to escape with a whole hide.

I offered to help track the murderers down.

Sheriff Ferris shook his head. "No," he said sadly, "our horses are worn out, and we need to get Jimmy and Ella laid to rest. We know who they are and where they live. We'll get warrants and more men and bring them in later."

I wasn't surprised — George Ferris was a decent enough man, but he was also wealthy and ambitious. He'd do his duty, but he'd definitely tread lightly in the face of power. In Wyoming, like everywhere else, there's no greater power than money, and the men Frank had named had plenty.

As Archie and I continued to Buffalo, I found myself wondering why, after all I had seen in my life, seeing Ella and Jimmy hanging there was so shocking to me.

Archie was equally shaken. We rode quite a way before he broke the silence. "My Lord," he said, "I ain't never seen nothing like that in all my born days, and hope to never see its like again."

I just nodded.

"Why'd they do it? To Ella and Jim, I mean. They warn't no rustlers."

"That was just an excuse."

"Probably that G-dd--ned Bothwell," he muttered, as if afraid Bothwell was listening. "He thinks he's the Lord G-d Almighty in the flesh." We fell silent again and rode for an hour or more before Archie spoke up again. "Nate?"

"Yes?"

"You ever kill anybody?"

"Yes. But only to protect me or mine."

He nodded in agreement. "I ain't never kilt nobody, an' there ain't a thing in this world I'd kill anybody else over." He laughed. "Fer that matter, I ain't got nothing worth getting kilt over. I get clear of this rustling bulls--t, I'm clearing out. This ain't a healthy place for a man to try to make a life no more."

"You're a sensible man, Archie."

As we rode, I thought about Dave and Jack, alone with the herd. Their situation was too similar to Jimmy and Ella's. They were both fighters, but that doesn't count for much when outnumbered and outgunned.

The pace I set almost killed the horses, and didn't do Archie and I any good either, but Archie never complained — he didn't want to end up swinging from a tree.

When we reached Buffalo, I turned Archie over to Red, borrowed a fresh mount, and high-tailed it out to Dave's spread. I stopped at the cabin and filled Jack in, then hurried to where Dave had the herd pastured. He was fine, and holding his rifle at the ready when I rode up.

"You look like you been put through the wringer," he said.

"I'm just glad to see you haven't been." I told him about Jimmy and Ella.

"My Lord," he said, "what call did they have to do that?"

"No reason or authority," I said. "Just power and greed."

"You reckon the law'll get after 'em?"

"What do you think?"

He considered for a moment, then said, "I 'spose it'll put on a show, but that's all it'll be." He shook his head. "It's too bad. They was good people. Always treated me fine and fair." When I asked if he'd seen anything suspicious, he said, "Not much. The usual tracks here 'n there, but that's about it. Jack said a fella came by one day askin' questions. Jack didn't much like the look of him. Said he had scary eyes an' made a big show of his rifle. Made Jack middlin' nervous, and he ain't the nervous type. Ain't the type to admit it either, so that was worrisome."

I helped Dave drive the herd back to the fenced pasture near the cabin and we went in to supper. "I hope you fellers are hungry," Jack called out. "Nate, I've burnt the beans extra, just for you."

***

Newspaper coverage of the lynching was as lurid as you'd expect, and the farther from Buffalo, the wilder and more inaccurate the stories got. Jimmy and Ella were pilloried in the press, Ella especially. She became known far and wide as "Cattle Kate" and branded as a prostitute and perpetrator of every other iniquity imaginable. The Cheyenne papers portrayed Bothwell, Durbin, and the others as the real victims, forced to take the law into their own hands because of ineffective lawmen. In Buffalo, there were a few drunken suggestions made that some of us should ride down to Cheyenne and "lynch us some newspapermen", but in the mornings sorer but clearer heads prevailed.

Within weeks, Frank Buchanan and another witness disappeared without a trace, and a third witness died suspiciously. The grand jury refused to indict, and the killers walked away scot-free.

I spent most of my time helping Dave with the herd and keeping an eye out for trouble. Despite Dave's and my objections, Esme made a habit of driving out to the ranch alone.

"Miz Esme," Dave said, one such day, "everything out here is fine. Me and Nate have got our eyes peeled for trouble, and Jack's forted up at the cabin real good. Ain't nothin' going on the three of us can't handle. I wish you'd keep yourself back in town where you're safe an' I ain't got to worry 'bout you."

"Now you listen to me, David Lincoln," she bristled, "This herd is as much my responsibility as it is yours, and I'll do as I d--ned well please."

"I understand that, but . . ."

"But me no buts Mister Lincoln. I can take care of myself. I'm a better shot than either of you, and I've got enough hardware with me to fight off an army."

She wasn't far off there — in addition to the Colt in the gunbelt she wore out on the range, she had a Winchester rifle in a scabbard attached to the seat, a shotgun tucked under the seat, two more revolvers in saddle holsters mounted to the sides, and a derringer tucked into a hidden pocket in her skirt.

"Esme," I said as placatingly as I could, "it's not a question of whether you're capable of defending yourself . . ."

"You just be still. This is none of your business. It's between . . ."

"None of my business! D-mmit woman, you know I care about you — we both do — and I know you catch h--l from Nathan too, every time you do this!"

"Well all three of you can go straight to h--l if you think I'll hide at home for fear of bushwackers or love of the three of you!"

"Miz Esme, you made our point right there," Dave interjected. "They may not try kidnapping you like they did Miz Ella. All the shooting ability and hardware in the world won't be any help 'gainst some backshooting snake laid up behind a rock with a rifle. You'd be dead 'fore you knowed you was shot."

She made a visible effort to calm herself. "Mister Lincoln. I am grateful for your concern, and I have no wish to cause you any pain or worry. Either of you," she added grudgingly. "But your concern for me is certainly no greater than mine for you. I wouldn't trade your life or Jack's for all the cattle in the world. I would stay out here with you, but that is not practical. But I will not be intimidated, and I will continue to visit as I please."

"I notice you left me out of that cattle deal," I said.

"In your case, I suppose it would depend on how many cattle were on offer." She patted Dave's arm, "Mister Lincoln here has never left me in the lurch even once, much less twice."

"That's a fair point," I conceded, "but please, at least let Samson or someone accompany you. If not for your own sake, for Dave's and Jack's."

"Not yours?" she asked coquettishly.

"I seem to have forfeited any claim to concern for you." I coquetted back.

She smiled and kissed us both on the cheek. "You boys are sweet." She jerked a thumb at the herd. "Let's get them home? I've got food from Odile's — you boys are wasting away eating Jack's cooking."

"He ain't that bad," said Dave.

We both looked at him incredulously.

"Well, he tries hard anyway."

Esme insisted on driving ahead, alone. "I made it this far on my own," she said, "I think I can make it to the cabin by myself," and then cracked the whip and took off like she was on a Sunday drive.

Chapter Thirty-Five

Sitting Bull and Wounded Knee; calm before the storm; Nathan; another lynching; an ambush; Champion, Tisdale, and Jones; on the hunt; A rainy night in Buffalo; more tragedy; a burial; more bad news

Buffalo Wyoming
1891

The two full years from July 1889 to June 1891, were quiet, at least as far as Johnson County was concerned. I was saddened to learn, in December of '90 of Sitting Bull's murder, and of the massacre of Sioux men, women, and children at Wounded Knee two weeks later. I wondered how many of those victims I had known in Canada, and mourned Sitting Bull and the others in private. Even my closest friends had a hard time understanding my grief.

In Wyoming, all of the hullabaloo surrounding Jimmy's and Ella's lynching had put a black mark on the territory, and with the push for statehood reaching its peak, the WSGA chose to conduct its war on the small ranchers and settlers in the newspapers, rather than with bullets and rope. The small ranchers dared to hope that the bad times were over. I didn't say anything, just kept my eyes open and my weapons clean, loaded, and close to hand. When Wyoming achieved statehood in July of '90, Buffalo had the biggest celebration it had ever seen.

The biggest thing on my mind over that two year period was my children. I had written to both Walks Through and Twisted Hair several times. Walks Through and I had a healthy correspondence, but between Twisted Hair and I, it was sporadic and reserved. Things between Nathan and me were as strained as ever. I was surprised when one day, he drove out to the ranch. Even from a distance, I could tell he had a bee in his bonnet.

After some small talk regarding business, he looked me dead in the eye and asked, "When are you going to do the right thing and marry my mother?" It was so out of the blue I had to laugh, which he resented fiercely. "What is so funny about it?" he asked. "Don't you care what people are saying about her?"

"What makes you think she cares?" I asked. "What your mother and I . . ."

"What you are doing is creating a scandal that only hurts her! Eleanor is embarrassed to be seen with her because of all the wagging tongues."

Now it was my turn to be angry. "Don't blame your mother and me that you've married a woman more concerned with gossiping neighbors than family."

"That's hardly . . ."

"Have you talked to your mother about this?" I asked.

He flushed with embarrassment. "Yes," he muttered bitterly.

"And?"

"She laughed in my face."

"I'm not surprised." I laughed. "You know, I did ask her to marry me once, years ago, to try to save her. She threw a vase at me. We're as married now as we're ever likely to be. Besides, I don't think we're up to nearly as much scandalous behaviour as those prattling old biddies at church like to think."

He let it drop and everything continued as before. Just as in the old days, I still accompanied her to church every Sunday, where we sang and worshiped our Lord — the G-d who lived, and died, and rose again, to save fallen women, saddle tramps, thieves, and sinners of all stripes — regardless of the sneering looks and whispers of some of the congregants. Nathan wasn't as openly rude to me, but honestly, I couldn't blame him. There's just about no way learning I was his father wasn't a disappointment.

Dave and I finally browbeat Esme into bringing Samson, Frenchy, or Nathan with her when she'd come out. The deputy sheriffing business was slow, so I continued to help Dave with the herd. It was a nice, quiet time. It was too good to last.

***

In June '91, three men claiming to be deputies from Newcastle, over in Weston County "arrested" a horse trader named Tom Waggoner. Almost two weeks after he was taken, his body was found hanging in an out-of-the-way gully. There were numerous similarities to Jimmy and Ella's deaths — the manner of taking, the out-of-the-way place to do the deed, the arms and legs left loose to flail, the slow suffocation rather than a sharp drop and mercifully broken neck.

In the last couple days of October, Sheriff Angus asked me to ride out to Hole-in-the-Wall and have a word with Nate Champion. In May, Nate had been elected President of the new Northern Wyoming

Farmers and Stock Growers Association, formed to help the small ranchers and settlers present a united front against the WSGA. Since then, he'd had a couple run-ins with big ranchers that had come within a whisker's breadth of gunplay. Red didn't want to find Nate swinging from a tree too.

On Halloween night, I found Nate and Ross Gilbertson at a tiny cabin tucked back in the canyon.

As usual I hallooed from a distance and then rode in. "Howdy Nate, Ross. How are you boys doing tonight?"

Nate stood to greet me. "Good to see you pardner. What brings you out thisaway?"

"Sheriff Angus asked me to come see you. He's worried about you, Nate. He'd like you to back off of the WSGA some."

"What's he worried about me for?" Nate asked. "I'm just out here minding my own business."

"Nate, you know d--ned well why he's worried about you. He doesn't want you to end up like Jimmy, Ella, and Tom Waggoner."

"Seems like he ought to be sending you to Cheyenne to talk to the WSGA then. Everybody knows it's their boys doin' all this lynching."

"He knows that too. If he thought it would do any good, I believe he'd ride down to Cheyenne himself to have a word."

"Well I don't know what he wants me to do. They're already calling me King of the Rustlers, but I keep having to get my cattle back from them. Am I supposed to just let them walk away with my herd?"

I simply restated Red's request and let it go. I sympathized with Nate, and was impressed that he'd kept his cool thus far. G-d knows the WSGA was pushing him as hard as they could, trying to prod Nate into giving them an excuse.

He invited me to bunk in with them. "It'll be a might crowded, but we'll make do."

I took a closer look at the cabin. It was maybe the smallest I'd ever seen. Nothing but a stove and bunk bed that blocked the door from opening all the way. A tall fellow like Ross couldn't stand upright in it, and even Nate and I would have to remove our hats to stand up. It was less a small cabin than it was a large box. "Appreciate the offer, but I think I'll find a nice spot out of the wind back in the canyon," I said.

He shrugged. "Suit yourself," and went inside. I found a little nook a few yards behind the cabin, broke up some deadwood for a fire, and sacked out. About dawn, I was awake and pondering whether to stick around another couple days or head straight back. I'd banked the fire against a big rock, and between the coals and my blankets I was warm and reluctant to get moving too quickly, when I heard the cabin door kicked open and bang against the bed inside.

A voice called out "Give it up boys."

As I scrambled out of my blankets and grabbed my rifle, I heard Nate sleepily ask what they wanted, and then shots rang out inside the cabin, one bullet penetrating the wall and buzzing past my nose as I ran to the front. I got there in time to see four cursing men fleeing, supporting a fourth who was bleeding heavily. Nate stepped outside in his long underwear, firing his Colt and I threw some lead at them too. My firing startled Nate, who snapped a shot at me as he jumped back inside to cover.

"It's me, Nate," I called out, lest he start shooting through the wall.

The door opened and he stepped out. "Didn't hit you did I?"

"No, but it was a close thing."

The fleeing men were mounting up about seventy-five yards away and clearing out like scalded cats, the wounded man held in his saddle by one of the others.

"Who was that?" he asked. "I didn't get a good look before the fireworks started. The one holding the horses looked like Mike Shonsey, but I can't be sure."

"I think I recognized Frank Canton," I said.

Ross timidly emerged from the cabin. "I believe the one you hit was Billy Lykins."

"You all right?" I asked Nate. The gunmen had been so close he had powder burns on his face.

"I'm fine. Glad I left my pistol under my pillow. Soon's they busted in pointing guns, I hauled it out and cut loose."

I shook my head. "I don't know how they managed to miss you in there. They almost hit me, and I was out here."

We reloaded and Nate dressed, and then we walked down to where they'd mounted. They'd been in such a hurry to leave they left their overcoats laying on the ground. Ross collected them while Nate stood watch and I cast about for sign, in case there was anything else to learn. There wasn't.

We returned to the cabin, and Ross got the coffee heating. We each drank a cup, and Nate and I mounted up. Ross declined to accompany us, saying, "I'm sorry boys, but I ain't no gunfighter. I'll stay here and keep an eye on the herd."

The assassin's trail started off to the south, then curved eastward until it headed north. We followed it a few miles until we cooled down and spent a moment reflecting on what outstanding country this was for an ambush. That dampened our ardour somewhat, and we returned to the cabin.

In the afternoon, I headed back to Buffalo, following the gunmen's trail. The trail swung around Buffalo and disappeared into the Bighorn Mountains. I peeled off and headed to town.

I'll say this for Red — he might not have as much experience as some lawmen, but he takes his job seriously. He got right to work, riding out to the scene. For my part, I rode north to check on Dave and Jack.

***

A couple days after the attack, Nate showed up with John A. Tisdale and Orley "Ranger" Jones. Nate had heard he should look for his enemies in Beaver Creek Canyon. "That's up here in your neck of the woods, and I figured you might want to ride along," Nate said. I was glad Nate had chosen such companions — Tisdale was very highly regarded and Ranger Jones was an affable but highly capable young cowhand. All three were deadly serious that day.

We rode up into the mountains, moving cautiously. Right at the mouth of the canyon were a lot of hoofprints, and about twice as many going in as came out. We dismounted, hobbled our horses, and proceeded on foot. About a mile into the canyon we found a camp with Mike Shonsey and six horses. Shonsey was a foreman for one of the big ranches, and the man Nate thought was the assassin's horse holder. He was answering nature's call with his back to us. A rifle and holstered revolver lay nearby.

I thumbed back the hammers on my shotgun. I said, "Don't move Mike, unless you want to meet your maker with your p----r in your hand."

He turned just enough to see me over his shoulder. "Nate? What's this all about?"

"Pretty sure you know, Mike. You're under arrest," I said. "Go ahead and put that thing away and turn around slow. I don't want to shoot you, but I don't want to not shoot you either."

He turned slowly, buttoning his pants. "I don't know what you're talking about, Nate."

John examined the horses. "These horses are worn down to a nub, and some've got Joe Elliot's brand on 'em."

Ranger went back for our horses. Champion found a tarp stained with blood.

"Where are the others?" I asked.

"What others?" Shonsey asked. "I don't know what you fellows are talking about."

Nate attacked Shonsey, knocking the larger man down, and pummeling him, shouting "You know! You were there! Who came after me?"

Tisdale dragged him back, and Shonsey, wide-eyed with fear, looked at me. "You gonna . . ." He stopped when Champion thumbed back the hammer of the Colt he suddenly held to Shonsey's head.

"Nate," I warned.

"This polecat tells me what I want to know, I'll let you take him in. He don't, I'll ventilate his skull, and you can take me in instead. This point, I don't much care which."

Nate was a hard man, but he was a good one, and not the type to commit cold-blooded murder, so I said

I was feeling the call, and excused myself. I found a place out of sight behind a rock, sat down, and got out my tobacco and papers. Being the sort to associate with bushwackers and assassins, Shonsey naturally assumed Nate guilty of the same failing, and I barely got a cigarette rolled before he broke, naming Joe Elliot, Frank Canton, Bill Lykens, and Fred Coates. Nate put his gun away.

John mopped his brow with a handkerchief. “I thought you were going to shoot him for sure.”

Nate shrugged. “Oh I would’ve, if he hadn’t talked.”

I documented everything in a little notebook I carried and rolled up the tarp, tying it to the back of my saddle. John and Ranger headed back south to their homes. I took charge of Shonsey while Nate drove the horses and we rode back to Buffalo, where I locked Shonsey up and filled Sheriff Angus in on the situation.

Red got Nate’s side of the story, and told him to go on home and be careful. Red continued his investigation diligently, but the felons had gone to ground and couldn’t be sniffed out.

The attack on Champion had people on edge. Some legal hocus-pocus got Shonsey transferred to Cheyenne. Around the end of November, John Tisdale came to town. He purchased supplies and Christmas gifts for his children, but nerves got the better of him when he thought about the long drive home and he couldn't bring himself to leave town.

It stormed like nobody's business the evening of Sunday, the 29th, and Frenchy and I were happy, snug, and warm at Charlie Chapin's saloon, listening to the rain bucket down. Frenchy liked to spend his free time "checking out *la compétition*" and we were enjoying drinks and cigars — or rather, I was enjoying them and Frenchy was happily verifying that Charlie's selection of smokes and potables was inferior to the Occidental's. With every drink he'd shudder, shake his head, and sadly say, "Ah, me." I noted however, that he didn't go through the drinks any slower. When I said something about it, he nodded patiently.

"What? I should insult my good friend *Monsieur* Chapin? It is not his fault he has not my refined palate." He flourished a wavering hand over the glasses littering the table. "I am many things, *mon ami*, but rude? Never!" Behind Frenchy, I could see Charlie laughing and doing a very creditable imitation of my friend. I just smiled and waved.

About that time, John Tisdale came in, very drunk, with his big mongrel dog, Ralph. Ralph was intimidating, but friendly and polite, and generally welcome wherever John went. John approached the bar and downed two or three shots of whisky in quick succession. Then he noticed us, and brought a bottle to our table. "Evenin' boys," he said as he sat heavily. He needed another drink like a river needs a glass of water.

We said hello and asked after his family. Ralph came around and sat between Frenchy and I so we could both pet his soaking fur. I had a great fondness for Ralph — he reminded me of Dob, the old dog from the ranch in California. Frenchy on the other hand, gave Ralph a cursory pat on the head, wiped his hand on a handkerchief and ignored him thereafter, despite Ralph applying all his charm. Finally, Ralph contented himself with my sole affections.

"Oh they're doon' good. Kids're lookin' forward to Christmas," John said.

"Are you alright, *mon ami*?" Frenchy asked him.

"I don' know," he slurred, "I jush don' know. You boys seen Champion? I bin lookin' all over for 'im."

Neither of us had. "What do you need him for?" Frenchy asked.

"Was hopin' I could pers — persh — talk him inta ridin 'long home wi' me tomorrow. 'S his doing that's got me in this fix." He shook his head bitterly. "Don' know what I's thinkin'. Shoulda known better than to get mished up in this b'iness."

"What business is that?" Frenchy asked.

"The wi'ness b'iness," John said, then looked at me, "You're inna same fish Nate."

"That business with Shonsey?" I asked. "The way the WSGA are passing out bribes, Nate'll be lucky if he doesn't end up arrested, and me with him."

John leaned forward. "Don'choo fool yershelf Nate. Fellas like Canton and Elliott don' like havin' their names drug inna dirt. They ain't gon' let this go unanshered." He took another unnecessary drink. "S'why I'm lookin' fer Champion. Issa long drive home an' I'm no kinda gunhand. Never fired a shot in anger in my life."

"John," I reasoned, "nobody wants to hurt you. You're one of the most liked and respected men in this part of the country."

"Don' matter none. The minute Shonshey said them names, he dug a grave fer all of us. Now lookit me. 'fraid to go home by m'self, like a d--ned schoolboy." Tears welled up in his eyes. "I'm 'shamed o' m'self. Whut kinda man leaves 'is wife 'n younguns alone at the house while he hidesh in town?"

Neither Frenchy nor I knew what to do. "Listen John," I said, "Why don't you get a good night's sleep." I gestured toward the rain sheeting the windows. "It'll be too wet for traveling tomorrow anyway. I've got business to attend to in the morning and then I'll help you look for Nate. If we still can't find him, I'll ride home with you."

"You'd do that Nate?"

I nodded.

"I too will ride along," Frenchy chimed in. "A trio as *féroce* as we will have nothing to fear."

Our offer reassured John, who took one last shot and stood up to leave. Weaving like a cottonwood in the wind, he doffed his hat to us. "You fellas're real gennelmen, G-d love you. I'll shee you tomorrow," he said, and lurched out the door.

In the morning, I attended to my affairs, had a bite of lunch with Esme, and then went looking for John. I couldn't find him anywhere, so I inquired after him at C. P. Organ's Mercantile.

"Yep," said C. P., "saw him just this morning. Poor fellow looked pale as death, and smelled like he'd been pickled. Didn't say much, just bought a real nice Colt shotgun and box of shells, and left."

I thanked him and hurried up Main street toward Billy Hunt's Livery. After I crossed the bridge that connected the two sides of town, I checked at the Occidental, but neither Tisdale nor Frenchy were there. I hurried across the street to the livery where I found the hulking Billy mucking out a stall.

"Yep, I seen John," Billy said in a high voice that never failed to surprise me, "He left outa here 'round — oh, I don't know — maybe nine-thirty or so?"

"Was anyone with him?"

"Not that I saw. I helped him get his horses harnessed up — he weren't too steady on his feet, to tell the truth — and he went on his way."

Back out on the street, I saw Frenchy enter the Occidental. I joined him and told him about Tisdale leaving alone. "What do you think got into him?" I asked.

Frenchy considered and then said, "Pride, *mon frere*, pride. No man likes to think he's made a fool of himself or shown the white feather[91] in front of men he respects."

"Do you think we should go after him?"

"*Non*. Your reasoning last night was sound — no one has any reason to hurt Monsieur Tisdale. He is liked and respected more than any other man in these parts. To follow him, now that he has screwed his courage to the sticking point, would be an insult. No man wants to be treated as a child, not even by his friends."

I conceded the point, and was also somewhat relieved, having awakened with a head like a brick, complete with a runny nose and sore throat. I was in no shape to be mucking about in the mud, so I went back to the tiny room I kept above Linn's Harness shop to nurse myself back to health. On my way, I bought a bottle of whisky, lemons, honey, and a tin of cinnamon to speed my recovery. I thought briefly about going to Esme's, but she was a terrible nurse, and I was a worse patient. For both our sakes I'd be better off on my own.

[91] To "show the white feather" is to show cowardice.

The next day, I slept late and woke up feeling on the mend. I fixed myself another hot toddy, and ventured out. I had breakfast at R.V. Stumbo's restaurant, then made my way uptown to the sheriff's office where Sheriff Angus was playing checkers with Deputy Johnny Donahue, a young fellow whose weedy appearance hid the appetite and constitution of a dray horse. Deputy Howie Roles, a tall, laconic, man with a shock of thick auburn hair had his chair leaned back against the wall, dozing with the latest edition of the *Buffalo Bulletin* in his hand.

"Nate, come over here and see if you can figure out how he's cheating," Johnny said. "He's beating me like a rented mule, and I can't figure out how he's doing it."

Red just rolled his eyes and made a move, chuckling at his adversary's groan. I sat down, put my feet up, and thumbed through an old copy of the Bulletin.

About 11:00, Red stood up, rubbed his belly and said, "I'm feeling a mite peckish. C'mon Johnny, I'll spot you to lunch, take your mind off what a lousy checker player you are." He winked at me. "Nate 'n Howie'll watch the office, won't you boys?" and they left without waiting for an answer. My full belly made it hard to sit still and stay awake, so I decided not to fight it. I moved into the sheriff's chair, propped my feet up on the desk, and managed to read about four words before my eyelids shut.

I couldn't have been asleep for more than a couple minutes when I was awakened by Elmer Freeman shaking my boot. "Nate! Nate! Where's Sheriff Angus?"

I sat up straight. "I don't know, Elmer. What's got you so riled up?"

"I think something's happened to John Tisdale." He explained that John had spent last night with Elmer at the Cross H and left this morning. "A couple hours later, I was riding south and come upon Charlie Basch riding north. He hadn't passed John, but he did see a fellow riding in and around that gulch the road goes through, and heard a couple shots from the gulch after he'd passed it. Well, that just didn't seem right to me, and I figured it might be something for the sheriff to handle."

I went out of there at a run, Elmer right behind me. I suspected Red and Johnny had gone to the Germania House, just south of Odile's — Red was partial to the German sausage they served there — and I was right.

Elmer told Red his story while Johnny and I fetched horses. We all met at the sheriff's office where we were joined by Tom Gardner. We rode as fast as the mud would allow and made it to the gulch about an hour later.

There was no sign of John or his wagon, but there was a blood trail, along with three sets of hoofprints including those of a horse that dragged its left front hoof. The trail led east down the gulch, and about 800 yards in, we found John. He'd been shot twice, one having glanced off his revolver, and a fatal shot through the body. He was lying sprawled on his back over the seat and into the bed of the wagon, where the toy drum he'd bought his son for Christmas lay in a puddle of blood. Tisdale's horses had been killed too — presumably those were the shots Basch had told Elmer about.

I went back up the gulch to the road and cast about for sign. Once I'd found all I could find, I rejoined the others and said, "Found a spot at the top of the gulch where two men spent some time hiding behind a bush. A ways back, two horses had been hobbled. Looks like when John's wagon started climbing out of the gulch they just stood up and shot him point blank. John would have been concentrating on his team and a sitting duck. There were two cartridge casings on the ground."

"So an ambush then."

"No doubt about that. When the deed was done, one man stood watch while the second fellow led John's team down the gulch and shot the horses."

"Why in h--l would they shoot the horses?" asked Johnny.

"Probably didn't want them pulling the wagon out where folks could find it," said Red.

"Couldn't they've just turned 'em loose instead?" Johnny was a good deputy, but soft-hearted, especially when it came to animals.

"No," said Red, a little exasperated, "valuable pair of horses like that, somebody's gonna notice 'em wandering around. They've got Tisdale's brand on 'em, and that'd raise an alarm almost as fast as if they'd drug the wagon and John along with them." To me he asked, "Can you trail them?"

"Yes. From the look of things, they weren't too concerned with hiding their tracks." I paused a moment, then said, "I know one of those horses belongs to a fellow calls himself George Wellman. His real name's Bill Morrow. He's working for the Hoe Ranch."

"What do you know about him?"

"I know he's a murderer and a coward and he changes names like mothers change diapers — whenever and wherever necessary. Called himself Ad Chapman for a while too. He's mean and disagreeable, and you cross him at your own peril. I learned that the hard way."

"So he's a gunfighter."

"Not that I know of, but bushwacking would be his style. He's a sneaky, slippery fellow, and he'll wait until you can't see him coming before he makes a move. But I make him as the second man, the one doing the cleanup work, which makes sense. The only thing he's better at than bullying those weaker than him is toadying those stronger."

That seemed to spark something in Red's mind. "What caliber were those cartridges you found?"

I showed them to him. "A .45-90 and a .44-40."

He nodded in agreement. "Frank Canton's got a Winchester chambered for .45-90s."

"That makes sense. I do know Morrow's pals with Canton."

"So what're we going to do here, Red?" asked Howie.

Red thought a moment, then turned to me. "Nate, I'd like you to take Johnny and track these fellows, but be careful. Don't get yourself in a fix. Howie, I want you to stay here with the body. Elmer, Tom, and I'll head back to town for a team of horses."

We all nodded in agreement.

"All right then boys," said Red, "let's get a move on. Howie, we'll be back just as quick as we can." Johnny and I mounted up and moved out. Behind us, Howie climbed the north wall of the gulch, Winchester in hand.

Johnny wanted to learn tracking, so I tried to show him what to look for, how to judge the size of a horse by its stride, how heavily loaded it was by the depth of the hoofprints and so on, but it was pretty clear he was more interested in the idea of tracking than actually learning how to track. After that we rode in silence. The trail led south along the road. Half a mile down the road, we found Tisdale's dog Ralph, shot dead. Poor old fellow must've been following the assassins. B-----ds.

We followed the trail until it crossed onto the TA Ranch, and then turned back. The TA was a WSGA outfit and even if we could find the assassins, there'd be no getting at them without shooting. It was no job for two men, so we returned to town, stopping to bury Ralph along the way. He deserved better than what he got. For that matter, so did Tisdale.

The next day, Johnny Jones rode into town to report Ranger missing.

Chapter Thirty-Six

Another murder; guilt; G-d has left Wyoming;
A pleasant night among friends; ambush; a frantic ride;
splinters; Doc Holbrook; Canton walks away clean;
bringing Joe Elliott in; looking for Morrow

Buffalo, Wyoming
December 1891 - February 1892

Two days after John Tisdale was ambushed, Jim Rinker rode into town and reported a murder. Sheriff Angus, Howie, Johnny, and I followed Rinker out to the bridge over Muddy Creek, where we found poor Ranger Jones dead in his wagon, shot twice in the back. The bed of the wagon was filled with lumber for the cabin he was building for his fiancée and himself. There was a third bullet hole through the back of the seat. I looked around and found where three men had hidden under the bridge. After Ranger crossed they came out, two on one side of the bridge and the third on the other, and fired. I scouted a little further out and found where three horses had been tethered, including one that drug its hoof. One more reason to put a bullet through Bill Morrow.

From the look of things, Ranger had been dead a few days — possibly even before John Tisdale. We all felt sick standing there. "Tisdale and Jones," Red said. "Why in h--l would anybody want them dead?"

"As soon as Shonsey said those names, he dug a grave for us all," I said quietly.

"What's that?" asked Red.

I repeated it. "John Tisdale told me that, the last time I saw him. I didn't think anything of it at the time, just put it down to nerves and drink. Some deputy I am."

Howie spoke up, a rarity for him, "Nate, that makes you or Champion next. Quit kicking yourself and let's get these b-----ds before they kill you or anyone else."

That put a little steel back in our spines, and I was grateful to Howie for it.

Ranger's team was nowhere to be seen, and I offered to sit with the body while Red and Rinker fetched horses to pull the wagon. Howard and John struck south to the Jones homestead to break the news to Johnny.

After we got Ranger taken care of, I checked in on Esme.

"You look like you've seen a ghost," she said.

"Worse." I told her about Ranger Jones.

"My G-d."

"I think G-d has left Wyoming."

She gave me coffee with whisky and sugar and rubbed my shoulders. "What will you do now?" she asked.

I took a sip. It was just what I needed — black as tar and sweet as sin. "I'm headed up to the ranch," I said. "I'm worried about Dave and Jack.

"I'll go with you."

"There's no need . . ."

She growled a bit in her throat. "Are we fighting," she asked, "or are we riding?"

"Get your horse, d-mmit."

***

We reached the ranch right after sundown, and in enough hurry that we forgot to call out. We were about fifty yards away when a shotgun blast split the night. "You best stop right there," Jack's voice shouted from the blackness of the porch.

"Jack, d--n you," shouted Esme, "it's me and Nate!"

"Alright then," he replied. "Come on in." We rode up and dismounted. "You two taken leave of your senses?" he asked. "Thought you knew better than to ride up 'thout hollerin' first."

Dave joined us on the porch. "What brings you out here so late?"

I told them about Tisdale and Jones.

"Heard about Mr. Tisdale," Dave said. "His poor wife and children." He shook his head sadly. "I'm sorry to hear about Mr. Ranger," he continued. "They was both good men."

Jack brought out a bottle and four tin cups and we talked half the night. We finally ran out of things to say and decided to call it a night. "You two stay in here," Dave said. "Jack and me'll sleep in the barn."

"Nonsense," said Esme. I'm not putting you out of your home. Besides, it's too cold to sleep in the barn. I can't have my business partner freezing to death. We'll all four bed down in here."

"Miz Esme," said Dave, "that just don't seem proper."

"Proper, schmopper," she said. "It's as cold and black out as Frank Canton's heart." That ended the conversation, and Dave and I bedded down on the floor near the stove, while Esme and Jack took the beds.

We put out the light, and settled in for the night. I was lying there sleepless, all those bodies swirling in my head when Dave spoke.

"Miz Esme?" he said. "Can I ask you a question?"

"Yes."

"I was just wonderin'— how's come you won't allow me to sleep in a warm, comfortable stack of hay for propriety's sake, but you're happy enough to take my bed and make me rest my old bones on this here hard floor?"

"'Cause I'm a lady, G-dd--mit, and ladies don't sleep on the f--kin' floor."

We all had a good laugh and it eased our minds a bit — enough that I could get to sleep. At some point in the night, I woke from a nightmare to find Esme lying beside me, clutching me tightly. She stroked my head and whispered, "Go back to sleep." When I woke again, the sky was light enough to see without a lamp. Esme was still lying beside me. She looked beautiful.

When I sat up, she opened her eyes. "You snore," she said.

"You fart."

We each knew what the other meant.

The door was open and Dave and Jack were outside smoking. "You two finally awake?" Jack asked. "All the moanin' and growlin' you was doin', I thought I was gonna have to dump a bucket of water on you."

"Should dump a bucket of water over yourself," Esme laughed, then sniffed. "Better make it two."

"At least two," Dave chimed in.

I rolled cigarettes for Esme and I, and Jack stood up. "While you lovebirds enjoy your smokes, I'll go get us some eggs and start breakfast." The sun was starting to peek over the ridge to the east, in front of the cabin.

Esme shaded her eyes. "Why don't you get the eggs, and I'll cook 'em."

Jack started for the steps. "That sounds like a good . . ." There was a shot, and he pitched forward off the porch. Immediately, there was another and Dave was flung against the wall. Esme jumped back inside and I dove off the side of the porch, and peeked around the corner. Jack was not moving. Dave was groaning on the porch, "Aw J---s, aw J---s." I could hear Esme cursing inside, and then she was firing back. I popped my head up to see her firing my pistol toward the rise where the shots were coming from with one hand as she dragged Dave inside with the other. Another shot hit the porch, and something stung my face like a hornet. I scooted back alongside the cabin wall, where I could stand.

Esme cried out in pain, and I moved back to the window. It shattered and she held out my Winchester. She had Dave's rifle in her other hand.

I took my rifle. "Are you okay?"

"I'm fine," she replied through gritted teeth, "but Dave's hurt bad!"

There was no way to fire from my position without stepping into the open. I asked her to give me some cover, and when she started shooting, I sprinted for the barn. I've never run faster than I did that day. Inside the barn, I threw open a shutter and started firing. The shooting from the ridge ceased soon after. A couple minutes later, I heard horses galloping away to the south. I ran back outside, eased up to the corner of the barn, and poked my head out. When nobody blew it off, I stepped out into the clear and, when that worked out alright, hurried to the cabin. As I stepped onto the porch, Jack rolled over and sat up.

"They gone?" he asked.

"Looks like it," I said. "You okay?"

"I'm fine," he said, holding his left arm to his chest. "Stupid b-----ds shot me in the wooden leg, but I think I broke my wrist when I landed."

I went inside to find Esme on her knees next to Dave, putting pressure on a chest wound. Her arms were soaked to the elbows with his blood, and her own ran down from a wound in her left bicep. Dave's breathing was shallow and bloody bubbles appeared on his lips. Esme looked up at me in desperation.

"He won't stop bleeding."

I slipped a hand under him. There was no exit wound. "The bullet's still in him." I ran to the bed, grabbed the sheet, and tore off a large strip. "Let me in there," I said. As soon as she moved aside, I pressed the bandage to the wound as hard as I could.

"Get him on his side!" barked Jack, hopping through the door. I rolled Dave onto his side.

"Help Esme!" I said. "She's hit too."

"I'm fine," Esme told Jack. "Help Dave."

She bandaged her own wound and Jack examined Dave, and then took over keeping pressure on the wound. "He needs a doctor," he said, a pleading, worried look in his eyes.

"Can we move him?"

"I don't think he'd make it to town. If we hurried, the bouncing'd kill him, and he don't have time for us to drive careful. You're going to have to fetch one."

I agreed, but hesitated, unwilling to leave them there defenseless. "Are you sure?"

"I'm fine," he said impatiently, and nodded at Esme. "Me and Miz Esme still have operatin' gun hands. 'Sides, them fellers is headed south. You're more likely to get shot than we are."

"G-dd--mit," Esme cried, "will you just go! We'll be fine."

I took one extra moment to kiss her and reload my Winchester before I ran to the barn, buckling on my gun belt as I ran. I didn't bother with a saddle, but put bridles on my horse, as well as Esme's and Dave's. With two extra mounts in tow, I set off at a gallop for town. When my mount began to flag I changed to Dave's horse and continued on. I made it to town on Esme's mare, the poor beast staggering down Main street. She was near collapse when I flung myself to the ground and ran to the sheriff's office.

Red, Howie, and Johnny all looked up in surprise when I burst through the door. "John," I gasped, nearly as exhausted as the horse, "find Doc Lott. Dave's been shot."

Johnnie just stared at me wide-eyed, his jaw hanging slack.

"Go d--mit! Now!" I roared, and he took off like he was shot from a gun.

"Nate," Red said, "what in h--l happened?"

"We were attacked out at the ranch," I said, accepting a glass of whisky from Howie. I downed it and held it out for more. While Howie poured, I continued. "They hit us right at sunup. Dave's hit bad in the chest. Es — I mean Ruth — was hit in the arm, and they blew Jack's leg off."

"Which one?" asked Howie.

Red and I looked at him in amazement. "Which one do you think?" Red asked. "If they'd blowed his good leg off, don't you think that would've gotten the first mention? Run and fetch Doc Holbrook," Red told him. Howie headed for the door and Red called after him, "Then get down to the livery and have some horses saddled!" He poured me another drink. "Sure you're okay?"

"I'm fine. Why?"

"'Cause you look like you've scrubbed your face with a porcupine."

I raised my hand to feel, but he caught my wrist. "Just sit still. Doc Holbrook'll fix you up."

That worthy dentist bustled through the door a few minutes later, every bit of eighty years old and as wide as he was tall, but with the energy of men half his age. "What's the emer . . ." He saw me and whistled. "Never mind." He sat down, selected a tool from his bag and went to work, plucking porch splinters from my face. "You're lucky," he said. "This could've been a lot worse."

Johnny came back in all out of breath. "Doc Lott's gone down to Cheyenne," he said, "and Doc Holland's gone fishing."

"John," Doc said calmly, "Run down to Pioneer Livery. Have them saddle my horse and bring it here. I'll go with them." John rushed back out.

While we waited, Red asked, "Did you get a look at them?"

"No," I said, "they had the sun at their backs and were shooting from cover. From the amount of lead they were throwing, there were two, maybe three of them."

He shook his head. "Just like Tisdale and Jones."

Howie and Johnny were soon back and we mounted up and rode out.

Without remounts, it took much longer to get back, but Dave was still breathing, barely. Red and I lifted him onto the table and Doc Holbrook went to work like a man who knew his business, with Esme assisting him.

Jack tottered outside on crutches and slumped onto a chair, his eyes frightened and forlorn. Red lay a hand on his shoulder. "Don't worry son. Doc was an Army doctor during the war, before he turned to dentistry. If anyone can help Dave, it's him."

Atop the ridge we found signs of three men and a lot of shells littering the ground. Back a ways, we found where their horses had been tied. Bill's horse was one of them. We walked back to their firing position.

"Anything you're seeing that I'm not?" Red asked.

"Not much," I said. "From the amount of grazing done by the horses and the way the grass here is still flattened, I'd say they got here in the night and waited."

"You can tell all that just from the grass?"

"Oh yeah," I said. "Of course all the cigar and cigarette butts help too." Neither of us laughed much.

***

The killings of Tisdale and Jones, and the attack on us had people frightened and angry. Just about every man in the county started carrying a rifle everywhere they went. A large faction was baying for Frank Canton's blood, Charlie Basch having identified Canton as the man he'd seen riding around the gulch that day. After that, most people held Canton responsible for all three attacks. At the end of the week, Canton strode into the sheriff's office and demanded to be arrested, jailed, and tried for Tisdale's murder. He claimed he was doing it to prove his innocence. I figured he'd gotten scared and decided he'd be safer in jail than out on the street or the plains.

The case was quickly brought to a preliminary hearing. It lasted one day. Canton had eight upstanding citizens including Dr.'s Lott and Holland swear that he was in Buffalo when Tisdale was murdered. The prosecution had Basch, who decided he wasn't sure the man he'd seen was Canton, but that it looked a lot like him, and was definitely riding Canton's horse, Fred. Justice Parmalee had no choice but to rule in Canton's favour and release him.

I stood with Esme and Red watching that smug, smiling s--theel walk away from the courthouse surrounded by laughing, back-slapping friends. "Y'know, Red," I said, "Tisdale was the only attack that had just two shooters."

"I was thinking the same thing," Red replied. "He's in this, up to his neck. Even if he didn't do Tisdale, he knows who did, and who put 'em up to it."

"Oh for the love of G-d," Esme said, "everyone knows who's behind all of this — including the lynchings. What you need to do is figure out how to prove it."

"What we need to do," Red said, "is find Joe Elliott and Fred Coates. We know they were involved in the attack on Nate Champion. If we can bring them in and make them talk, we might get somewhere."

"There's one more who I know was involved in these attacks," I said. "Bill Morrow. I've found his horse's tracks at all three ambushes. We need to drag him and the others out from under whatever rock they're hiding under, bring them in, and make them talk."

That was easier said than done. Before December was out, new charges had been filed against Canton, but he got wind of it and caught a train back east. Mike Shonsey had kept his mouth shut once he reached the safety of the Cheyenne jail, and was now out on bail and back to work as foreman of the Western Union Beef Company Ranch, another WSGA outfit. The trail had gone cold on the others. It was a big, wide-open country, and if a man didn't want to be found, he wasn't likely to be, short of stupidity or betrayal, but men of low character are seldom far from either. The only thing that could be done was wait.

We moved Dave into town as soon as Doc said we could. Esme gave her bed up for him, and had a cot just outside the door to sleep on. She and Miss Claudie took shifts, one sleeping on the cot, while the other nursed Dave. He was slowly improving, but had a long way to go. The bullet had nicked his lung, bounced off a rib, and traveled down his body to lodge against his right kneecap, where Doc Holbrook had finally located and removed it. I asked Esme why she was such a patient and attentive nurse to Dave when she'd been the exact opposite with me when I was injured.

She smiled sweetly and said, "Two reasons — first, he's always been easier to get along with than you.

Second, he makes me money. You only ever cost me money." The woman is incorrigible.

***

I spent every available minute searching for Bill Morrow, but it was like he'd dropped off the face of the earth. Oddly enough, it was he who found me.

Chapter Thirty-Seven

A warning; a stubborn woman; a fatalistic man; at the KC Ranch; captured!; Bill Morrow again; a siege; distraction and escape; eavesdropping on murderers; fire; death of a Champion

Buffalo, Wyoming
April 1892

March was a quiet time. It seemed like everyone in Johnson County was riled up and on the prod, going about in heavily armed groups, and primed for a fight — not the sort of unsuspecting, helpless, and outnumbered victims the WSGA's assassins liked. In addition, the WSGA's attention was taken up with legal manipulations and helping newspapers across the country paint Johnson County as a wild, lawless place where no decent, law-abiding citizen — such as the WSGA members — were safe from the murderous "rustlers" — essentially any settler or small rancher like Nate Champion, who stood up for their legal rights.

Along about the first week of April, I received a letter from Mischa, warning me to get out of Johnson County. It read in part:

> *. . . Something big is coming your way. I've seen a list of names with yours, Dave's, Ruth Good's, the sheriff and deputies, and somebody named Champion's on it, along with about sixty or seventy others. I don't know exactly what they're planning, but they're recruiting gunmen in Texas, and it's going to happen soon. If I learn more, I'll send word, but I hope you won't still be there to get it . . .*[92]

Poor Mischa! I felt terrible for him, and hoped that if Elliott or one of the others was brought to trial and induced to name their employers that Mischa wouldn't be implicated. I took his warning to heart, went to warn Red first, and then I tried to persuade Esme to leave town, at least for a while. She wasn't having any of it.

"I've never run from a fight in my life," she said, "and I'm not about to start now. Besides, if I leave, who's going to take care of David?" Dave was slowly recovering, but was still very weak and had had several

---

[92] There were seventy men on the WSGA "kill list" including the Johnson County Sheriff and Commissioners.

setbacks. Doc Holbrook was worried that some of his other organs had been damaged. He, assisted by Dr. Lott, had operated twice to stop him bleeding internally, and we all feared another setback would be the end of him.

Further argument was pointless, so I rode up to the ranch. Jack Flagg, another small rancher, had volunteered to put Dave and Esme's herd in with his own until Dave could come back, so there was nothing at the ranch to protect. I tried to convince Jack to move into town.

"You're too isolated out here," I said. "You'll be safe at Esme's."

"I like being isolated," he replied. "I hope those sons-of-b---hes hear I'm alone out here and decide to try something. I got nothing to do but sit here with a loaded rifle and look out the window over a clear field of fire. Any bushwacking b-----ds want to give me a try, I'll happily accommodate 'em! I don't doubt they'd get me, but I'll die happy knowin' I took some o' them with me."

"But what if Esme and Dave need your help? They're on this 'list' too, whatever it is."

"They're in town, and Nathan is there with 'em. I'd just be in their way."

"Nathan's a good boy, but I doubt he could hit the side of a barn if he was standing inside it. He's also got his own wife to worry about. If you won't go in for your own sake, or for mine, then do it for their sakes."

He shook his head sadly. "I can't do it Nate. I've had enough. I'm tired. I'm lonesome. You don't know what it's like, being how I am. I hate it, but I can't help it, and I'm tired of tryin'. I may not be willing to end it myself, but if someone wants to do it for me, I'd welcome it."

"Oh come on, Jack. You've never been one for self-pity, and you're as good a man as I've ever known."

He smiled wanly. "I 'preciate that Nate. I really do. And if I make it through whatever's coming, mebbe I'll feel diff'rent 'bout things." He laughed bitterly. "I been a coward all my life . . ."

"That's nonsense . . ." I started to reply.

"Just hear me out Nate," he said. "I've lived my whole G-dd--ned life in fear. Afraid of what I am, afraid them I love'll find out what I am 'n hate me for it. Afraid I wasn't man enough – didn't measure up. I've leaned on Dave all my life, and a few others for most of it 'cuz I didn't trust m'self. All the while bulls--ttin' them and m'self, pretendin' I was all man. Well, I ain't a-gonna do it no more. Time I stand on my own feet — well — foot, I guess. It's time I found out what I'm made of." He paused and stared into the distance, eyes glistening.

I didn't know what to say. I'd never heard him speak like that before.

Finally, he laughed again, and seemed to buck up. "Just don't think I'll make it easy for 'em though. I'm still man enough to put up a fight and don't think I won't. I may not be much of a man, but I'm no quitter. They want me dead, they'll have a h--luva bill to pay. But they'll have to pay it here. This has been the first half-way happy place I've been since the war. 'F'im gonna die, I'd just as soon do it here."

I spent the next day at the ranch helping Jack improve his fortifications, and the following day, the seventh of April, I struck out south for Nate Champion's, warning every ranch and farmhouse along the way. A big snowstorm rolled in that afternoon, and by the time I reached Nate's KC ranch, late on the afternoon of the eighth, I was near frozen, and glad of the warmth of his stove. He had a full house that night. In addition to Nate and me, there were Nick Ray, old Ben Jones and Billy Walker. Between the stove and the number of men packed into the cabin, it was a warm and cheerful night. Nick passed a bottle around, and we had quite a little party.

Around dawn, Ben went out to fetch water. Half an hour later, he still hadn't come back, so Billy and I went out to look for him in the barn. "He's probably got a bottle in there with him and don't want to share," said Billy.

Ben was in the barn, but he wasn't having a tipple, he was lying hog-tied with a pistol held at his head. Three other rough-looking customers were pointing guns our way and insisted we join them inside. "Anybody know these fellows?" one asked. None did, and he said to the man holding the gun on Ben, "George? You know these men?"

"George" was none other than Bill Morrow! His eyes opened wider than mine when he turned and saw me, and I thought sure I was a goner. He looked me right in the eye and said, "That little dark fellow, that's — um, hang on, I know 'im — oh yeah," he stammered, "that's Will Morrow. Not sure who the kid is." Fortunately Ben and Billy kept their mouths shut.

"Alright, get them tied up too," said the first man, a giant blonde fellow with a shaggy beard and a Texas accent, "and keep 'em quiet."

"I'll do it," said Bill. As he worked, he muttered, "Keep your mouth shut if you want to get out of this alive." Once we were securely trussed, the big fellow asked us, "Who else is in there?" nodding toward the cabin.

I said nothing, and Ben just growled deep in his throat, but Billy whined, "It's just Nate Champion and Nick Wray. Whatever you boys are after them for, it's nothin' to do with us."

I struggled, but it was no use — whatever his faults, Bill knew his way around a knot. I might as well have been paralyzed. Once Billy spilled his guts, they gagged us. To one of the gunman, a gray-haired old fellow about my age, the giant said, "Lefty, go tell the Major that Champion and Ray are inside."

Lefty slipped out the back door of the barn, and Bill joined the others at the barn door to watch the cabin, and they settled in, waiting for something. The graybeard came back in a few minutes later and nodded to the giant.

***

Hours passed, and I alternated between hoping Nate and Nick would come armed to find us, and fearing what would happen if they did. The four men in the barn were all I could see, but knew there must be others out there.

"What are we waiting for?" asked the fourth man finally. He was a twitchy, nervous-type in a bright red shirt and checked pants. "We gonna sit here all day?

"What do you reckon?" said the giant. "They're waiting for Champion to show hisself." Not too long after that, they all four ducked back.

The front door of the cabin opened and Nick stepped cautiously out a few paces, Winchester in hand, and stared suspiciously about the place. When he turned back to the cabin, a shot rang out. Blood exploded from Nick's head, and he went down hard, but began crawling for the door. Immediately a barrage of rifle fire opened up, blasting chunks from the cabin wall and digging up the dirt around him. He'd almost made it to the door when he collapsed.

The door opened and Nate stepped out firing rapidly. He grabbed Nick by the collar and dragged him inside. The gunfire continued like they were trying to shoot the place down. Nate returned their fire, moving from window to window. Soon I heard someone calling to "Cease fire!" and the shooting stopped, except for the occasional pot-shot.

Several hours later, a man came in and said, "Major Wolcott wants two of you to go find a ranch somewhere's close and buy some hay. We're going to burn these b-----ds out."

The giant looked around. "Wellman," he said to Bill Morrow, "take Lefty and get going." He and the nervy fellow turned back to watch the cabin.

As they passed us, Bill told graybeard, "Go on ahead. I want to check these fellas' ropes and I'll be right behind you." He bent to check our knots and I felt him press something into my hand. "Wait for your chance," he whispered, "and then high-tail it. Don't worry about Ben and Billy, they ain't on the list." Then he was gone, and I realized he'd given me a pen knife! I didn't know what he was up too, and at that moment I didn't care, I just started sawing at my ropes. The knife was small and dull, and the ropes thick and tough, but I went at it with a will. Other than sporadic firing both at and from the cabin, there was nothing to see. I got the rope sawed through, leaving just a few strands holding it all together. I began moving my arms and legs surreptitiously, restoring the circulation to my limbs. I wasn't interested so much in escape as I was in getting my hands on a gun. A surprise attack might give Nate a chance to get away too.

My chance finally came early in the afternoon. By that point, no one had fired for some time. I heard a wagon drive past behind the barn, headed for the bridge over the creek, and a horseman rode right up to the cabin. As he was about to dismount, I recognized Jack Flagg, the rancher who'd taken in Esme's herd. Less than a second later, someone yelled, "That's Jack Flagg! Shoot that sunovab---h!" Jack put the spurs to his mount and rode through frantic gunfire, out of my sight. The giant and the twitchy fellow joined in the firing, and I cut through the last strands of my rope. I gave the knife to Ben, rushed to the back of the barn, grabbed a scythe down from the wall, and turned back toward the door of the barn where the gunmen were still firing at Flagg.

Twitchy forgot himself so far as to step right out into the open for a shot at Flagg's back and got a bullet through the thigh from Nate for his trouble. The giant grabbed him and yanked him back inside. As he turned, he saw me, dropped Twitchy, and raised his rifle. I flung that scythe as viciously as I could. I missed, but it was close enough to spoil his aim. His shot buzzed past me and as he chambered another round, I scrambled out the back door.

The trees around the creek and bridge were full of gunmen yelling and firing at Flagg and the wagon[93]. The giant was lumbering along behind me, firing as fast as he could, but I made it away across the creek which, behind the barn, was blessedly empty of gunmen, and ran like my tail was on fire. I ran until I crossed a low ridge and flung myself on the ground gasping for air. I crawled back to the top of the ridge and peeked over. There was no one after me. As I caught my breath I wondered if Flagg and the wagon had gotten away. Based on the length of firing, and the fact that it tapered off, rather than stopping suddenly, I thought it possible that at least one had escaped.

I thought about going for help but if Jack or the driver had escaped, they would be mounted and able to raise help faster than I could on foot. If there was any chance I could help Nate, it was right here.

---

[93] The wagon was driven by Flagg's 17-year-old stepson Alonzo Taylor.

Once I was sure no one was coming to look for me I crept back to the creek. I lay in a depression in the ground watching and listening, until I located those in charge, and then worked my way into the brush, as close as I could get. I found a good vantage point near them where I was hidden but could see and hear pretty much everything. I learned that both Flagg and his companion had escaped and were last seen heading for Buffalo at speed. Pulling out my little notebook, I began writing down as much as I could, particularly the names. I recognized Frank Canton right off, and Wolcott and Irvine from our meeting at the Cheyenne Club. I was surprised to see Wolcott and Irvine. Usually men like them hired men like Canton to do the dirty work while they kept their hands clean. Going strictly by accents, at least half the men were from Texas.

A group pushed Flagg's wagon back across the creek and up to the barn. Wolcott and some other men headed for the barn, and Irvine told six men to prepare to direct their fire toward the only window that faced the barn. A few moments later, Wolcott and his men pushed the wagon, loaded with pitch pine and some hay, out of the barn. Irvine ordered his men to begin firing and Wolcott's group pushed the wagon right up to the wall of the cabin, lit it, and ran like h--l back to the barn.

In minutes, the wall of the cabin was ablaze, and the fire was spreading rapidly. No shots had been fired from the cabin for some time, and some began speculating that Champion must already be dead. By now, the cabin was completely engulfed in flame, and Nate burst through the door with a rifle in one hand and a revolver in the other, and fired at the men along the creek as he ran toward a shallow gully. He had reached the mouth of the gully unscathed when two men stepped out, blocking his path, and fired. Nate was hit in his left arm and dropped his rifle. He was raising his revolver to fire when he was hit in the chest. He was still on his feet when a volley of rifle fire blew him into the air to land flat on his back dead, gun still in hand.

The whole company of gunmen gathered around his body. Several removed their hats out of respect for a brave man who died game, including Wolcott who, accompanied by Irvine, Canton, and others pushed their way through to stand over the fruits of their labors.

They were too far away to hear what was said — and I was distracted by the sound of a hammer being pulled back directly behind my head.

"Turn around slow," said a vaguely familiar voice.

I turned and beheld Tom Horn holding a rifle on me.

"Howdy Mr. Luck," he said quietly. "You know your hide's worth $200?"

"I did not," I replied, "although I'd price it a great deal higher — especially if it were left unperforated."

"How much higher?"

"Does it matter? I don't have a penny on me, and there's only about twenty-three dollars in a jar back in my room."

He nodded. "Aw, to h--l with it. F'you ask me, that there Champion fella was worth a sight more than this whole crew combined."

"You sound like a man who's unhappy with his employment."

"The employment doesn't bother me," he said coldly. "But I don't care for their methods. A fella like that one there," he nodded to where the mob clustered around Nate's body, "deserves better than to be taken down by a pack o' coyotes." He lowered his rifle.

"Twenty-three dollars, huh?" He pointed at the deputy's badge on my chest. "That thing don't pay worth a d--n, does it?"

"No," I said, "but it's worth it."

He nodded again. "You've got sand," he said, "I'll give you that. I b'lieve I'm going back to Cheyenne, leave this sorry bunch to their business." He stalked away, pausing a few feet away to turn and say, "Don't forget, you owe me $200."

"Doubt I'll ever have it."

"Well," he drawled, "Maybe someday you can do me a good turn." Then he was gone[94]. I haven't seen him since.

I slipped from my hidey-hole, deciding there was nothing else to be done here, and retreated to a more secure place of concealment. The group broke up and

---

[94] While there is not a great deal of evidence to support the idea that Tom Horn was involved in the invasion of Johnson County, Charlie Siringo, in his book *Two Evil Isms: Pinkertonism and Anarchism* claims that Horn himself admitted his part in it to Siringo. Historian and Professor Larry Ball, in his book *Tom Horn in Life and Legend*, states that Billy Walker is the only first-hand source to place Horn at the KC Ranch that fateful day. Ball also states that it is possible that Horn was involved in recruiting gunmen for the invasion, and that he was present in Johnson County in the aftermath of the invasion as a Federal Marshal, operating under the name Tom Hale.

soon Ben and Billy staggered dead-limbed from the barn. Wolcott handed them something, and they mounted their horses and rode away in a hurry[95]. The gunmen busied themselves treating their wounded and about an hour later a couple wagons rolled up filled with supplies, and they set about preparing themselves a hot dinner. Once it got dark, I eased back up as close as I dared, close enough to hear the leaders arguing.

"D-mmit," Canton said, "we need to move on Buffalo now, before they can get organized or we've lost before we even get started!"

"It's too late, Frank," said Irvine. "We've wasted a whole d--ned day here trying to kill one man. By now, Flagg'll have the whole county roused. We've lost already. We need to get somewhere we can defend ourselves."

The argument went on until late in the night. I was near frozen to death when the army of killers finally rode out at a gallop toward Buffalo.

I sat in the warmth of the cabin's embers through the night, and at dawn walked down and sat beside Nate's

---

[95] According to John W. Davis in *Wyoming Range War: The Infamous Invasion of Johnson County*, the invaders paid Walker and Jones for the equipment they lost in the fire.

body. Someone had pinned a note saying "Thieves Beware" to his chest. The heat coming off the remains of the cabin cooled enough by afternoon that I was able to wrap Nick's charred remains in a horse blanket and drag it out to lay next to Nate[96].

[96] Champion was known to keep a diary, and wrote in it throughout the siege, right up to his break for freedom. It is poignant in its brief, but matter-of-fact telling of the tale. It can be quickly and easily found by simply Googling "Nate Champion's Diary".

Chapter Thirty-Eight

Rescue too late; back to Buffalo; sleep finally; a siege; the go-devil; military intervention; end of the invasion; A note; a meeting; ambush!; the end of Bill Morrow

Johnson County, Wyoming
April - May 1892

Sitting next to the bodies of my friends, I was conflicted — there was nothing I could do for Nate or Nick, but I didn't want to leave them for the scavengers. At the same time, I felt that I was needed elsewhere in the fight, but had no way of knowing where, or of getting anywhere. About noon, I'd got a shovel from the barn and started digging graves, but it was hard ground and my heart wasn't really in it. I hadn't made much progress when Sheriff Angus, six other men on horseback, and Frenchy and Jack driving a buckboard, arrived that evening.

Red took a look around. "C----t what a shame," was all he could bring himself to say.

I filled him in on what I had seen and heard. "So what do we do now?" I asked.

"First," he said, "we need to rest these horses." A couple of the men took the animals to the creek to water, and Red said, "To be honest Nate, I'm not sure. It's a h-lluva mess — no, it's a G-d d--ned invasion. They cut the telegraph lines a couple nights ago. Soon's I heard about this, I went to Captain Menardi, and he said the militia had received orders to stand down. We're on our own here Nate."

We spent two hours resting the horses, and headed back to Buffalo. "G-d only knows what kinda s--t these b-----ds'll get up to if they get there. It could be worse than this," Red said.

We wrapped the bodies in blankets and took them with us. We rode through the night, arriving in Buffalo about one a.m. The whole town was in an uproar, which reached a fever pitch when the heavily-armed crowd saw Nate and Nick's bodies. Howie Roles informed us that Dick Allen, one of the large ranchers, and a journalist named Clover — both of whom had been at the KC — had ridden into town yesterday unarmed, and that he was holding them in a cell. He also told us Jack Flagg and fifty or so men had ridden out last night to confront the invaders, and that more men were heading out to join them. Red thanked him, and told us all to get some rest, that we'd be riding out again that afternoon.

I hurried down to Esme's house, where Samson was sitting behind a window in the dark with a shotgun in his hand, a pistol in his belt, and a Winchester leaning against the wall next to him. Nathan was similarly situated behind an upstairs window at the back of the house. Esme, Odile, and Claudette were at Dave's bedside, armed with shotguns. Dave was conscious but weak, and a revolver lay next to his hand. Eleanor was crying in the cellar.

Esme leaned her shotgun against the wall, coming around the bed to embrace me fiercely, and I reciprocated with vigour. "Where the h--l have you been?" she whispered, her head pressed against my chest. "Are you all right?"

I held her tight, as her tears soaked my shirt. "I'm fine." We stood like that for not nearly long enough, then finally stepped back from each other. She sniffed and blew her nose, and I wiped my own tears away surreptitiously.

"You smell like a dead skunk," she said.

"I'm not surprised," I said.

She sent me upstairs to undress while she heated some water so I could wash. I told her it wasn't necessary, that I just wanted to lie down and sleep, but she insisted. "You're not laying down in any of my beds in that state," was how she put it.

While I washed, I told her about Nate and Nick. She didn't say anything, and when I'd finished cleaning up, she tucked me into bed, climbed in next to me fully dressed, and pulled me close to her. The last thing I remember was the clean scent of soap and lilac, and the feel of her hand stroking my head. As I slept, Coming Together came to me and spoke of beautiful things, and the two great loves of my life kept my nightmares at bay.

I woke about ten to the smell of cooking and realized I couldn't remember the last time I'd eaten. I ate hurriedly and Esme and I set off through a steady-falling snow for the Sheriff's office. Red told me that Jack Flagg, Arapahoe Brown, and others had the invaders surrounded at the TA Ranch, about fifteen miles south of Buffalo. "We're heading out there directly," he said. "If you need anything, Bob Foote's passing out guns and ammunition down at his store."

I was pretty well set, and headed for the livery for a mount. Esme followed along. "Where do you think you're going?" I asked.

"I'm going too," she said.

"I wish you wouldn't."

"Wish in one hand and s--t in the other, and see which fills up the fastest," she said. "Those no-accounts came up here to kill me too. I intend to see an end to this."

I saddled her gray gelding and she rode back up the street to arm herself. By the time I got my own mount saddled and joined the growing crowd — which included Frenchy and Jack — outside the Sheriff's office, she was back, riding astride in a pair of my old pants, a revolver on her hip and a Winchester in a saddle scabbard. Red finished making his preparations, and we set out at a gallop for the TA Ranch.

When we arrived, over two hundred small ranchers, settlers, and townsmen were attacking the ranch. The WSGA and their invading army had built a formidable breastwork, and the whole thing had settled into a siege. Any time one of the invaders was bold enough to show any part of himself, a volley taught them the error of their ways. There was near-continuous firing throughout the day, thanks to Bob Foote's generosity. In the evening, Red rode back to Buffalo. "You boys have things in hand here," he told Arapahoe Brown, who'd been elected Field Commander before our arrival. "Maybe I can get some help from Fort McKinney. I'll be back soon's I can."

Some of the boys had gathered a number of TA wagons, stripped them down, and used the running gears to begin constructing a go-devil[97]. They worked on that throughout the 12th, while the rest of us slowly tightened our circle, inching carefully forward. Our constant firing kept their heads down, and at least one old boy with a heavy Sharps buffalo gun worried the invaders by simply blowing random holes through their defenses. There was no place safe from that rifle. By the morning of the 13th, there were over four hundred of us surrounding the invaders, with more joining us every hour. Men were riding in from neighboring counties to help out. It was something to see — the small and the powerless coming out of the woodwork to take a crack at the mighty — this is what the best of America was to me, and I was proud to be

---

[97] A "go-devil" is a sort of breastwork on wheels, designed to allow fighters to approach an enemy's defenses safely.

a part of it. Many of us were veterans, so we knew our business. I didn't do much shooting personally, but Esme never missed a chance. The flutter of a sleeve or a glimpse of a hat was enough for her to send a round their way. She enjoyed herself enormously. Jack too seemed to be enjoying himself, sitting on a chair in the back of the wagon in plain sight, firing away, and daring the invaders to come get him. Occasionally, a shot would chip off a piece of the wagon, but he remained laughing and untouched.

That night, the go-devil was completed, and at dawn on the 13th, about fifteen of us began pushing the heavy beast toward the enemy. We were armed with rifles and a case of dynamite, planning to get as close as we could and drive them into the open with the explosives. Without their log defenses, they would be sitting ducks. We were almost within throwing range, when trumpets sounded. I imagine the besieged thought it must be Judgment Day.

***

It wasn't the Lord, it was the U.S. Cavalry, and Red was with them. He called for us to cease fire, an order we complied with reluctantly. The soldiers took custody of the invaders and held them at the fort, where at least one of them died from his wounds, and that was pretty much the end of the shooting part of the war.

Most of the remainder is being fought in the courts and newspapers. The good folks of Johnson county were enraged to learn that Governor Barber had likely known about the invasion since its inception, and had ordered the militia to refuse aid to the sheriff. In addition, he had appealed to President Harrison to have the army intervene in order to spare his powerful friends.

Except for Nate Champion and Nick Ray the invasion had been a complete and embarrassing bust. It would have been funny were it not so tragic. But there was one last unforeseen development to come.

***

After the army took custody of Wolcott, Irvine, Canton, and the rest, things settled down a bit, although most men still went armed. The legal machinations of the WSGA and their allies made it clear fairly early that the invaders would likely never pay for their crimes, but many of us were heartened by the fact that we had handed them a thrashing which they barely survived and would not soon forget.

About a week after the siege, I asked Esme to take a ride with me, and once well away from any witnesses, I unburdened myself.

"You know," I said, "It's probably not good for a man to be alone too long."

"Mm-hmm."

"I'd forgotten what it felt like to feel happy, to feel . . ."

"Oh, for the love of G-d, Nate," she said, "will you just ask already?"

"What?"

"All right, I'll ask you — do you want to marry me?"

"Well would you want to marry me?"

"Lord love you Nate, you're either the dumbest smart man or smartest dumb man I've ever known, but you're also the only one I've ever loved. I don't care if we get married or not. As far as I'm concerned, we're as good as married now, but if you want to make it official, then I do too." We dismounted and held hands while we walked in silence for a while.

"I do." I said.

"Well then, it's settled. When and where?"

"I hadn't gotten that far in my thinking," I said. "I didn't dare."

"You are an idiot," she said, and kissed my cheek, "but you're my idiot."

She and Odile, aided by Eleanor got to work planning the wedding. I decided that discretion was the better part of valour, and stayed well out of their way.

Dave's recovery continued slowly, but the herd was plenty safe with Jack Flagg, so I spent most of my time close to Esme's house — the invasion may have failed, but that list was still out there. One morning there was a note left for me at the sheriff's office. It read:

Nate,

I have information you'll want to hear. Meet me where we met when you first came here, at noon tomorrow.

George Wellman

After he'd saved my life at the KC Ranch, I decided I owed him at least that much. The next day was a fine May day and I left early, scouting for an ambush. Once satisfied that there wasn't, I lit a fire and got some coffee boiling. I was about to pour a cup when I saw two riders approaching, Bill, and another man. I stood up and jacked a cartridge into the chamber of my rifle.

Bill left the other man out of earshot and rode up alone. He was wearing a Federal Marshal's star.

I nodded past him at the other man. "Who's that?"

"Aw, that's just Tom Hathaway. He's alright," Bill said. "I just want to talk, Nate."

"I don't know that I've got anything to say to you other than you're under arrest."

"What for?"

"Murder and attempted murder."

"I haven't killed or tried to kill anybody."

"The h--l you say. I saw you at the KC Ranch, remember?"

"And if you'll remember, it was me gave you the knife so you could escape. If I wanted you dead, all I had to do was tell 'em your name, but I didn't."

"That's the only reason we're talking now."

"I'm looking for a way out, Nate. These people scare the h--l out of me. I can give you names . . ."

"I've got names," I said. "I wrote down everything I saw at the KC."

"I was there when they were planning this whole thing. I've got information on the lynchings, the killings, on everything. I've got stuff on all those fellows, including the ones that didn't come along on their little hunting trip."

"Let's talk about Tisdale, Jones, and the attack at Dave's," I said. "I know you were there."

"Yes I was there," he admitted desperately, "But I didn't shoot anybody. I swear to G-d, Nate, I did what I could. I fired first, trying to warn 'em. I was the one who shot Jack's wooden leg. I shot Ranger Jones' wagon seat. I shot to miss Tisdale too. If I'd done anything more, Canton would've left me dead on the ground with them. It was Canton and Elliot did the killing."

"Why were you even there?"

"Canton doesn't trust me, wanted to make sure if he hung, I'd hang too."

"So why are you coming to me with this? Why not go straight to Sheriff Angus?"

"I want you to vouch for me with the sheriff. I think they're planning to put Tisdale and Jones on me, to lower the heat on them a bit. I don't plan to let 'em do it," he said. "I might've been there, but I never hurt anybody."

I didn't like any of this. What he said made sense, but this was Bill Morrow.

"So what do you say?" he asked.

"I'm thinking."

"G-dd-mmit Nate! You've always been so high and mighty — Mr. Always-Gotta-Do-The-Right-Thing — and here the right thing is, staring you right in the face, but you've gotta think about it? You're a G-d d--ned hypocrite! If you want the b-----ds behind all this to pay, I'm your best bet, and you know it."

I hated to admit it, but he was right. The right thing to do was to do the right thing, regardless of my feelings. "Fine," I said, disgusted. "I'll take you in to the sheriff. But you'd better hold up your end."

He nodded, relieved. "I will. I give you my word — I'll tell everything I've seen and heard. And I'll tell you something else . . ."

There was a shot, and his horse bolted from underneath him. He hit the ground and barely moved.

I snapped three shots in the direction the shot had come from, and dragged Bill to a lower place that might be a little safer. I led my horse to over to Bill, but before I could lift him onto it, a shot tore my horse's throat out and punched through my left shoulder, knocking me flat. I dragged Bill behind its body, lay my rifle across the saddle and fired two more shots. I couldn't see what I was shooting at, but wanted to let whoever it was know they'd failed. Hathaway had high-tailed it north, and I hoped help would soon be on the way.

Bill looked terrible. The shot had gone in his left side and out his right, and there was foamy blood on his lips — at least one, if not both of his lungs had been hit. "Oh J---s," he gurgled and coughed up blood. "I don't want to die."

"Shut up Bill. Nobody's dying." A shot thumped into my horse's body, and a second buzzed over my head. The shots were all coming from the same place, so I hoped it was one shooter. With any luck, I could hold out until help came. I wasn't optimistic about Bill though. He was bleeding badly and, now that the shock was wearing off, practically howling with pain, or would have been if he could breathe properly. I stanched the bleeding as best I could and tried to make him comfortable.

"Don't lie to me Nate," he gasped. "I'm done for."

I wiped the sweat and tears from his terrified face. "Just be still Bill. Save your breath."

"This is what I get for trying to do the right thing."

"Just be still. You'll do it yet." I poked my head up for a look. There was a ridge about a hundred yards off that had to be where the bushwacker was hiding. It was the only place with a vantage point high enough to fire into this depression. Sure enough, I saw a muzzle flash and I fired back, glad to finally have something to aim at. I fired another round and ducked back down. "How you doing Bill?"

He grasped my arm with a trembling hand. "Nate," he said, "you reckon I'm bound for hell?"

"I don't know Bill," I said. "If you're relying on God's grace, I reckon you've got at least as much chance as most folks." It felt odd to be comforting someone I'd once been so determined to kill.

We lay like that for some time, sporadically firing and being fired upon. I wished for Bill's sake he'd pass out, but he lay there suffering like nothing I'd ever seen. Finally, it was too much for him. "Please Nate," he gasped. "If you got any mercy, help me."

"Bill, you know there's nothing I can do for you."

He looked at me with imploring eyes. "There's one thing." I felt his hand fumble for my Colt.

I didn't know what else to do. I nodded. "Alright Bill."

"Wait!" He fumbled inside his coat, and came out with a blood-stained notebook. Pressing it into my chest, he said, "Here. It's all in here." Then he lay his head back and closed his eyes. "Okay," he groaned, "do . . ."

I fired.

***

No more shots came from the ridge, and as I lay there behind my dead horse next to the body of the man I'd counted as an enemy for most of my life, I couldn't help but reflect. I began to see that I was wrong, at least about him and me, and I lay there and shed a tear while I prayed for the soul of the man I had thought my enemy.

Chapter Thirty-Nine

Evidence; planning a wedding; newspaper lies; power and injustice; my arrest; frustrating my attorney; my legal strategy; A surprise; an unpalatable deal; fantasy and reality; resolution

Johnson County, Wyoming
May - December 1892

Not long after I fired that last shot, the bushwacker must have slipped away, for no more shots were fired. I sat next to Bill's cooling body and couldn't help but be angry — not so much at Bill, but at the world we lived in that put the two of us on opposite sides of so many terrible events.

While I sat there, I thumbed through Bill's blood-stained notebook. He must have had misgivings for some time, and had extensive notes on everything he'd seen and heard regarding the WSGA's intentions. Maybe he'd hoped having all this written down might save him. I think it got him killed. I tucked the book into my pocket when I heard Red and his posse approaching — I didn't know what use I could make of it, but I didn't want anybody knowing I had it either.

I told Red how Bill had turned himself in to me, and about the ambush and we took the body to Buffalo.

***

Esme continued planning our wedding — for someone who prided herself on unconventionality, she flung herself into organizing our nuptials with an enthusiasm I found confusing and intimidating. Walks Through and Natasha came to town to help out. I admit I was concerned about how Tasha might feel about Esme, but they were united by their love of bullying me, and got along like a house afire. I was bulldogged through wedding suit fittings and other unspeakable horrors, so I spent as much time as I could working — or hiding, as the ladies put it — at the ranch with Jack and Dave, who had finally recovered enough to escape from under Esme and Claudette's attentive thumbs.

Bill's murder attracted a lot of attention in the papers. His status as a Federal Marshall — an appointment arranged by the WSGA — made it easy for the Cheyenne and eastern papers to paint it as the sort of lawlessness that justified the invasion. After all, someone had to enforce the rule of law, and if the legally elected officials wouldn't do it, then — according to those papers — it clearly fell to the law-abiding citizens of the WSGA to do so, especially since they were the party suffering from all the injustice.

I didn't want to end up like Bill, but I thought his notebook and mine could, and should, be used against the WSGA. I hid them in Dave's barn, wrapped in oilskin, while I considered how best to use them.

Around the end of May, I rode into town — Esme had set the date for the wedding as June 10th, and even Twisted Hair was coming in. I knew she'd have things for me to do, so I decided to face my fate like a man. I was looking forward to being married much more than I was the wedding.

I met Red, looking very somber, on the road to town.

"Howdy Nate," he said. "I was just riding out to find you."

"Well, I'm glad I saved you most of the trip anyway. What can I do for you?"

He handed me a paper. "That's a warrant for your arrest for the murder of George Wellman. I hate to do it Nate, but I've got to take you in."

"Aw, Red, what kind of bulls--t is this? I've told you what happened, and so did Tom Hathaway."

He took his hat off and wiped his forehead. "I know it Nate, but Hathaway's disappeared, and they've got a judge to sign this warrant. I've got no choice. I'm d--ned sorry."

I shrugged. "Not your fault. I can't even say I'm surprised. You want my gun and badge?"

"Keep 'em. I want folks to see you coming in willingly, armed, badged, and without restraints. Show 'em all we both know this is nonsense, but that the law still applies in Johnson County."

And that's how I ended up in jail.

Esme was beside herself about it, and I felt bad for Red after the lambasting she gave him, but once she calmed down, she saw he'd had no choice. Nathan agreed to act as my attorney and the legal maneuvering began. The state tried to move me to Cheyenne but Nathan did a fine job of fighting that, and I remained in the Johnson County lockup.

Nathan was not sanguine about my chances at trial though, especially since I refused to speak in my own defense, beyond pleading not guilty. "D-mmit man," he said after a preliminary hearing, "you've got to help me out, or there's nothing I can do for you."

"Don't worry, I'll have plenty to say when the time comes." I didn't want to tip my hand too soon.

"Well don't wait too long. Their case is hogwash, but it's pretty hogwash, and I don't have anything to work with."

Days turned into weeks, turned into months, and things looked progressively worse. Once the trial date was finally set, it was time to tell Esme and Nathan my plan.

"I want a trial," I told them. "I want as much attention and newspaper coverage as we can manage." I told them about the notebooks and where to find them.

They both looked at me in shock. Nate was the first to recover. "That's the dumbest thing I've ever heard. Do you want to hang?" he asked. "You, of all people, should know how powerful these men are. They write the laws. They buy the judges. Those notebooks will never see the light of day — they'll see to that.

Esme was just as aghast. "What the h--l is wrong with you?" Esme asked. "What possible difference do you think that will make?"

"Nathan, I believe in you," I said. "If any lawyer can get those books in, it's you."

"My G-d, you really have taken leave of your senses," Nathan said. "I've never tried a case like this! They've got more lawyers than they have gunmen . . ."

"I don't care about winning. I care about exposing them. I've spent my entire life fighting men like these, and those notebooks are the best weapons I've ever had. I've only ever managed to fight the men who did their bidding. Those books are a shot directly at the men behind all this."

"And what good do you think that's going to do?" asked Esme. "What good is it if firing that shot puts your neck in a noose?" She was near tears, although whether from sadness, frustration, or anger, I couldn't say.

I hated being the source of her pain, but my mind was made up. Finally, Nathan said, "Alright. Fine. You win. At least tell me where they are so I can make sure they'll do what you believe they will."

That made sense, so I told him, and they left.

***

A few weeks later, three days before the trial was due to begin, Red strode in and flung open the cell door. "Nate, you're free to go."

"What?"

"They've arrested some scut down in Cheyenne for Wellman's murder."

I was stunned. I was also half convinced that I'd be shot dead as soon as I left the courthouse. In a daze, I wandered out onto the street and up to Esme's. She and Nathan were waiting for me, along with Dave, Jack, Natasha, Walks Through, Twisted Hair, Samson, Odile, and Claudette, all smiling congratulations.

Nathan led Esme and me into a separate room where we found Mischa and that head b-----d of the WSGA, Major Wolcott. Mischa embraced me, beaming happily, and Wolcott looked like his wedding tackle was in a vice.

"Tolya," Mischa said, "you are a lucky man."

"I am?" I was waiting for the other shoe to drop.

"You're especially lucky to have an attorney like Nathan here, who is a much better legal strategist than you."

I looked at Nathan. "What did you do?"

Mischa answered. "He's kept your neck out of the noose, and made a deal that keeps you safe . . ."

"So long as he keeps to the agreement," interrupted Wolcott, with all the spite and bile he had.

"What deal?"

"One moment," Mischa said, and asked Nathan to leave us. Once he was gone, Mischa said, "He worked out the deal, but there are caveats that he is better off not knowing — for everyone's sake." He lit a cigar, sat down, and said, "The Major here, and the rest of the WSGA, were dismayed to learn of those notebooks."

"They prove nothing," said Wolcott.

Mischa stared him down. "If they were to come out at trial, and make no mistake, you and the others will stand trial for your actions, those notebooks could tip the scales against you. However, what they do or don't prove will remain unknown."

"But . . ." I started from my seat, but Esme pulled me back down.

Mischa held up his hand for me to be quiet and looked at Wolcott. "Major, you have the floor."

Wolcott was red-faced and seething as he pointed at me. "You need to understand, Mr. Luck. The WSGA has long arms, and never forgets an injury. If those notebooks ever come to light, you will die. Your fiancée will die. Your friends and family will all die. That is as sure as the sunrise, I promise you." He sat down and stared out the window.

"Tolya," Mischa said, "these men can carry out that threat, even from a prison cell. There's no way of knowing how their trial will go . . ."

"Oh come on Mischa, we all know . . ." Esme pinched the back of my hand. Hard. I shut up.

"Regardless, Tolya, your only concern now is keeping yourself and those you love safe. Think of those books as life insurance. They are safe in the hands of someone who will happily use them to maximum effect should anything suspicious befall any of us. Yes, I include myself. I have made my own sworn statement regarding every shady deal I saw them make, and secured it with the notebooks. This is the last dealing I will ever have with them. So, you see, my own life and those of my family are tied to your decision."

"Well Nate," Esme said softly, "what do you say?"

I stood and looked at Wolcott. "I say if I had a gun right now, you'd be a dead man Major," I said, sneering at the title. He bristled at that, springing to his feet.

Mischa interposed himself between us, telling him to sit down. To me he said, "Tolya. I know this is a lot to take in, but please, I beg you — for all our sakes — Go get some air. Think."

I stormed from the room and out the back door, out onto the prairie. My first thought was to get a gun, shoot Wolcott, and then go to Cheyenne and kill as many WSGAers as I could. I slowly cooled down, and turned back toward the house. Through the window I could see almost everyone I loved chatting pleasantly, celebrating my freedom. I realized my murderous fantasy was just that — I had killed, yes, but I was no mad dog.

Still, it felt like a surrender when victory — however Pyrrhic — seemed within my grasp. Surely even the WSGA would balk when it came to killing innocents? And then I thought of all they'd already done and knew that men like these would always carry out their threats. To them, we were not even human beings, just obstacles to be overcome.

But someone, sometime, had to stand up and say, "No more," didn't they? If not me, then who?

I might have gone on for hours arguing with myself when I heard Coming Together's quiet voice, clear and crisp as a distant eagle's cry on a still winter morning, "My love, your fight is not finished, and you cannot fight if you are dead."

She always was smarter than I.

I returned to the room and Esme held my hand as I spoke to Wolcott. "If it were only me, I would happily swing if I could put your heads in the noose too, but I won't risk the lives of those I love. I've lost too much to the likes of you already."

Mischa sighed with relief. "So we are agreed?"

"We are," I said. Wolcott nodded.

"Major?" Mischa said forcefully, "you need to say it."

"Very well," said the self-important little toad. "Agreed." He rose to leave.

"Major," Esme said sweetly, "I suggest you leave the back way."

And that was the end of the war for me[98].

***

I find it hard now to place too much blame on Bill Morrow. At the beginning of this writing, I cursed his

---

[98] A man named Henry Smith was tried in Cheyenne for conspiracy to deprive a citizen of rights in the murder of George Wellman. He was acquitted. The last man killed in the Johnson County War was Nate Champion's brother, Dudley. He was killed by Mike Shonsey.

black heart, but I know now that I was wrong. He was just a man trying to get ahead in the world as he understood it. Hating him is like hating the ink on the page of an unjust law — he was only the pen, not the hand that wielded it.

For now, I intend to make the most of what life remains to me: marrying Esme, caring for my family, working to build a better future for my children, my friends, and my country. I will keep fighting. I look around me at my family and friends and know that I do not fight alone. It is a fight that I know they, and millions of others like them, like Ollokot and Joseph, Black Kettle, One Eye, and Buffalo Calf Woman, Nate Champion, Ella Watson, and John Tisdale will carry on long after I am gone, with courage, determination, and a devotion to the ideals of peace and liberty that brought me to these shores so many years ago. Some day — I believe — we will win. I have to believe that.

Author's Notes:

On characters:

Nate, Esme, Jack, Dave, Frenchy, and Nate's children are all fictional characters. Coming Together, although fictional, is named in honor of a Nez Perce warrior woman who was killed in the war. The manner of my Coming Together's death actually happened to an unknown Nez Perce woman. Bill Morrow, Ad Chapman, and George Wellman were all three real men who actually did all the things their composite character does in this book (with the exception of Part One: Cowboy).

Chief Joseph, Ollokot, their wives, Wahlitits, his wife, Yellow Wolf, Rainbow, Five Wounds, Black Kettle, One Eye, Ned Wynkoop, John Chivington, Silas Soule, Uncle John Smith, Red Angus and his deputies, Nate Champion, Ranger Jones, John Tisdale, Ella Watson, and Jim Averell, and almost all of the other soldiers, settlers, lawmen, Nez Perce, and Cheyenne men and women were real people. I've done my best to represent their cultures, struggles, and humanity honestly and authentically.

Any errors are strictly my fault.

On sources:

While *A Rare and Dangerous Beast* is a novel, I have done everything in my ability to remain as close to the facts of the events portrayed as possible, using first-hand accounts when available. A more complete list of sources is included as a bibliography, but for anyone wanting to know more about these events, I recommend these books as a starting point:

The primary resources for "Part Two: Soldier", were Ovando Hollister's *Boldly They Rode: A History of the First Colorado Regiment*, Tom Bensing's *Silas Soule: A Short Eventful Life of Moral Courage*, Louis Kraft's *Ned Wynkoop and the Lonely Road from Sand Creek*, George Bird Grinnell's two-volume *The Cheyenne Indians*, and George E. Hyde's *Life of George Bent: Written from His Letters.*

The primary resources for "Part Three: Indian", were *Yellow Wolf, His Own Story*, and *Hear Me My Chiefs! Nez Perce Legends and History*, by Lucullus V. McWhorter, Daniel J. Sharfstein's *Thunder in the Mountains: Chief Joseph, Oliver Otis Howard, and the Nez Perce War*, Kent Nerburn's *Chief Joseph & the Flight of the Nez Perce*, and Alvin M. Josephy Jr.'s *The Nez Perce Indians and the Opening of the Northwest.*

John W. Davis' *Wyoming Range War; The Infamous Invasion of Johnson County*, was the primary resource for "Part Four: Lawman".

Acknowledgements

I would like to thank Miami University for the opportunity, and especially Brian Roley, Margaret Luongo, TaraShea Nesbit, and Jody Bates, and all the fantastic writers from workshop for their invaluable support, criticisms, and advice.

Thanks are also due to Dave McCoy, the best and most long-suffering friend and accidental research assistant ever, Nakia Williamson-Cloud, Nez Perce Tribal Cultural Resources Program Director for taking time out of his busy day to speak to an astonishingly unprepared aspiring writer and steer me toward a wealth of fantastic sources, and Nancy Tabb, Local History Librarian at the Johnson County Library in Buffalo, Wyoming.

I also need to thank the wonderfully helpful young lady at the Nez Perce Wallowa Homeland in Wallowa, and the equally helpful young ladies at the Jim Gatchell Memorial Museum in Buffalo, Wyoming – I apologize for forgetting to write down your names, but I am very grateful for your fantastic help. Once again, any errors in this book are solely my fault.

I am also eternally grateful to George Macdonald Fraser, Thomas Berger, Larry McMurtry, Elmer

Kelton and too many others to list for showing me how this should be done.

Thanks as well to all those who were gracious enough to read various incarnations of this thing, and continued to offer much-needed encouragement throughout.

Thanks also to all those who I should have thanked, but missed, and thanks to you, dear reader for taking the time. I hope you enjoyed the ride.

Finally, special thanks to my wife Jess. You are the best, baby.

Bibliography

Ball, Larry D. *Tom Horn in Life and Legend.* Google Books ed. University of Oklahoma Press, 2014.

Bensing, Tom. *Silas Soule: A Short Eventful Life of Moral Courage*. Kindle ed., Dog Ear Publishing, 2012.

Curtin, Jeremiah. *A Journey in Southern Siberia.* Kindle ed., Evinity Publishing Inc, 2009.

Hyde, *George E. Life of George Bent: Written from His Letters.* Edited by Savoie Lottinville. Kindle ed., University of Oklahoma Press, 2015.

Davis, John W. *Wyoming Range War: The Infamous Invasion of Johnson County.* Nook ed. University of Oklahoma Press, 2011.

Greene, Jerome A. *Beyond Bear's Paw: The Nez Perce Indians in Canada.* University of Oklahoma Press, 2018.

Grinnell, George Bird. *The Cheyenne Indians, Volume 1: History and Society*. Nook ed., UNP – Bison Books, 2014.

---. *The Cheyenne Indians, Volume 2: War, Ceremonies, and Religion.* Nook ed., UNP – Bison Books, 2014.

Hollister, Ovando, J. *Boldly They Rode: A History of The First Colorado Regiment.* Kindle ed., Pickle Partners Publishing, 2015.

Josephy, Alvin M. Jr. *Nez Perce Country*. University of Nebraska Press, 2007.

---. *The Nez Perce Indians and the Opening of the Northwest*. Mariner Books, 1997.

Kanzanjian, Howard, and Chris Ness. *Mochi's War: The Tragedy of Sand Creek*. Nook ed., TwoDot, 2015.

Kelman, Ari. *A Misplaced Massacre: Struggling over the Memory of Sand Creek*. Nook ed., Harvard University Press, 2013.

Kraft, Louis. *Ned Wynkoop and the Lonely Road from Sand Creek*. Kindle ed., University of Oklahoma Press, 2011.

Locke, John. *The John Locke Collection*. Nook ed., Charles River Editors, 2018.

McWhorter, Lucullus V. *Hear Me My Chiefs! Nez Perce Legends and History*. Caxton Press, 1992.

---. *Yellow Wolf: His Own Story*. Caxton Press, 2008.

Mendoza, Patrick M, et al. *Four Great Rivers to Cross: Cheyenne History, Culture, and Traditions*. Teacher Ideas Press, 1998.

Mill, John Stuart. *The John Stuart Mill Collection*. Nook ed. Charles River Editors, 2018.

---. *On Liberty*. Nook ed., MobileReference, 2010.

Nerburn, Kent. *Chief Joseph & the Flight of the Nez Perce.* Nook ed., HarperCollins Publishers. 2009.

Primary Accounts: *The Sand Creek Massacre.* Nook ed., Charles River Editors, 2011.

Rousseau, Jean-Jacques. *The Social Contract.* Nook ed., Philosophical Library/Open Road, 2016.

Sand Creek Papers: Documents of a Massacre. Nook ed., Big Byte Books, 2016.

Sharfstein, Daniel J. *Thunder in the Mountains: Chief Joseph, Oliver Otis Howard, and the Nez Perce War.* Nook ed., W.W. Norton & Company, Inc, 2017.

Siringo, Charles A. *Two Evil Isms: Pinkertonism and Anarchism.* Kindle ed., Steck-Vaughn Company, 1967.

Smith, Helena Huntington. *The War on Powder River: The History of an Insurrection.* University of Nebraska Press, 1966.

Milton Keynes UK
Ingram Content Group UK Ltd.
UKHW020939201123
432909UK00012B/278